The Pagan Wall

THE PAGAN WALL

David Arnason

Talonbooks   •   Vancouver   •   1992

Copyright © 1992 David Arnason

Published with the assistance of the Canada Council

Talonbooks
201/1019 East Cordova Street
Vancouver, British Columbia
Canada V6A 1M8

Typeset in Weiss by Pièce de Résistance Ltée, and printed and
bound in Canada by Hignell Printing.

First printing June 1992

Canadian Cataloguing in Publication Data

Arnason, David, 1940—
  The pagan wall

      ISBN 0-88922-312-2

    I. Title.
PS8551.R765P3 1992   C813'.54   C92-091268-0
PR9199.3.A76P3 1992   76289

for Karl

Richard was still light-headed when they surfaced from the underpass that led from the Frankfurt station onto the Kaiserstrasse. It was a grey day, the clouds high and undefined and the wind bitter cold. The first thing Richard noticed was that the light was different, a cool light full of blues and greys that made the sign Sex Shop and a series of incomprehensible German invitations seem especially obscene. The naked women portrayed on the sign looked as if they'd had premonitions of the cold their images would face. They appeared to resent their nakedness.

From the air, coming out of the Atlantic night into a German dawn, they saw the sunlight above the thin clouds, golden and warm. The thick blue mist in the distance, Lois had insisted, was pollution. She'd been reading about the Rhine Valley. Richard had been surprised. He'd assumed that the mist was fog. They'd been married for only a couple of years, but Richard was still unprepared when Lois had more information than he had. His first wife had not been like that at all. She would never have prepared for a trip by reading. She would have had less information than Richard.

They stepped into the doorway of a camera shop, just to be out of the bitter wind for a minute. Richard converted the cost of a Minolta into Canadian dollars. It seemed very expensive.

"I thought it was going to be warm," Lois said. "Not tropical, but certainly not like this. This is colder than Winnipeg."

"You told me not to bring my leather jacket," Richard answered, then, realizing what he had said sounded like an accusation rather than the simple statement of fact he had intended, he added, "It's my fault. After forty Winnipeg winters, I imagine every other place in the world as warm."

"No," Lois told Richard, taking him by the arm and leading him back out into the street. "You're guilty of a lot of things, but I won't hold you responsible for the European weather."

Richard had wanted to stay in the warmth of the coffee shop at the station, until the train to Strasbourg left, another three hours, but Lois had insisted on exploring. Lois spoke some German. Her first husband had been German and had insisted that she take courses at the university. She had offered to go exploring by herself, but Richard was terrified that if she walked alone into the streets of Frankfurt, she would never return. He hated the idea of being alone.

"The light here is different," Richard said to himself, deliberately moving his lips so that he wouldn't forget this first impression. He thought that things looked the way they do through Polaroid sunglasses, only not dark. The light seemed to be coming to him at angles. He decided not to share his perception with Lois.

"Das Gute Essen," Lois read from the sign on a store across the street. "Good things to eat. Let's go take a look." There was almost no traffic, though the Kaiserstrasse looked like a street that ought to be busy, and so they crossed without going to the light on the corner.

"It's Sunday," Lois said, as if she had read his mind.

"Right," Richard said. "Of course."

Inside, the store was blazingly bright. The floor was white, the counters were white, and the people serving the few customers who moved down the aisles were dressed in white. The place seemed filled with glass, and mirrors gave the impression that the aisles stretched to infinity. Along the right, a bewildering array of patés and cheeses seemed to overflow from the white metal shelves. To the left, oranges and lemons and grapefruits were piled up, each shining as if it had been individually polished. Behind a circular island in the centre, two butchers bobbed and nodded.

Richard was amazed at the meat. Each piece had been carefully cut and presented as if it were part of an exhibit in an art gallery. Even what was apparently a dish of brains looked exquisite and healthy. Behind the butchers, Richard could see sweeping rows of wine bottles, sparkling water and bright blue and green fluids whose names he did not know. Richard felt that what he was seeing ought to be sterile and cold, but instead it was warm and appetizing. His mouth watered even though he was looking at raw meat. The butchers were apparently aware that Richard and Lois could not speak German, and it was clear the butchers could not speak English. Still, the good will was palpable. You could feel it in the air. The butchers beamed and nodded their heads, making soft cooing sounds. Richard and Lois smiled back, pointing at things that the butchers pulled from the shelves to show them. Lois said something in German, and the butchers exploded into volubility, apparently delighted that communication had been achieved.

"What did they say?" Richard asked, but Lois had turned a bright pink. She said something that set the butchers off on another round. Lois stuttered and hummed. She said *danke* and slipped away to the rear of the shop. Richard followed and she told him with deep humiliation, "I didn't understand a word they said."

They were standing in an area filled with chocolates and candies. The air smelled sweet and perfumed. A beautiful older woman in a blue flowered dress said something soft and lilting to Lois, but she didn't understand that either. Quite suddenly, Richard felt deeply inferior. He knew that there was no store so beautiful, so filled with the objects of desire in all of Canada. He remembered the Safeway store down the street from their house as dismal and dirty. The little butcher shops of the north end of his city seemed dark and diseased in comparison to this place of airy light and soft perfume.

"Come on," he told, Lois, feeling now the threat of the place, "let's get out of here."

"No," Lois said. "I want to stay."

"Come," he insisted, and he took her hand and led her from the store. Outside, a piece of torn newspaper blew out of an alley and wrapped itself around Richard's ankles. He kicked it free. Down a side street he could read a sign that said 24-Hour Sex Shows.

Like the other signs, most of the words were in English. Richard wondered what the German for *sex* was, and why the signs were in English.

"That was such a beautiful store," Lois said. There were tears in her eyes. Richard looked around him. Everything was blue or grey. Even the signs, which should have been brightly coloured, red and yellow, were tinted with shades of blue and grey. They had come to a square with a memorial to Goethe, and blue and grey pigeons hovered and circled in the air. Goethe gazed upward and outward, as if he were a prince. Suddenly, Richard felt how much he loved his wife and how little he could do to console her.

"It's Europe," he said to her. "There are lots of places like that." Lois had never been to Europe. Richard had been five times, but he had always gone as a tourist for only a few weeks, and now they were going to live in France for a whole year. In two hours they would catch the train for Strasbourg. They were going to live in Strasbourg because Richard had described the cathedral and the canals to Lois during the painful time when both their marriages had ended and they were deciding whether they would dare to try again. They had made a pact that they would go and live in Strasbourg and walk down and look at the cathedral every night. They would go to concerts and plays, and they would learn to speak French.

That was five years ago, and now they were in Frankfurt, under a grey sky, on their way to Strasbourg, where they didn't know anybody and had no place to live. Richard was going to write his book. Lois's fantasy was that she would study the *nouvelle cuisine*. She would receive a diploma, and when they returned to Winnipeg she might open a small restaurant in St. Adolphe, just south of the city. Customers would have to make reservations a week in advance and Lois would cook for them. They would only have four tables. Richard knew the fantasy could never work, but Lois was so happy and so vulnerable when she talked about it that Richard did not have the heart to explain to her that she must surely fail. And even though she did not open a restaurant she would learn valuable information about cooking and presenting food.

She would also draw. Lois did lovely water-colour sketches of children at play. She had even illustrated two children's books for a local publisher. Richard preferred this vision of her, the *artiste* exploring a new world. And it did not include him, as the restaurant must, both as financier and worker.

Lois had stopped weeping by the time they got back to the station. The streets had been empty, but the station was bustling and full of people. The platform was open to the air where the trains came in and pigeons walked right into the little restaurants around the central foyer. Lois had put on what Richard had come to think of as her brave face. She talked cheerfully, but with a slow deliberation that seemed to be covering something close to hysteria.

"It was beautiful," she said. "Nothing I can ever do will be like that. I will always break things and smudge glasses and leave burns and the smell of smoke." They had found a table and Lois was looking through the wallet that contained extra European money from one of Richard's holidays. She found a ten-mark note and some coins, and when the waiter came she ordered coffee in what sounded to Richard like fluent German.

"And I cannot speak German," she added, "and I will never learn French."

Richard thought about the book he was going to write in Strasbourg. It was supposed to be about Heidegger, who was his specialty. He had even taught a graduate course devoted entirely to him. In the blue-grey Frankfurt station under the angular light, Richard decided that he knew nothing of Heidegger. It had not seemed important back home that he did not speak German, that he read in translation, but here, in the heart of Europe, it seemed a monstrous presumption. The book was already impossible.

He thought of Winnipeg with its low buildings and its thick yellow prairie sun, and it seemed to him an ancient city, settled and fixed forever on the banks of its rivers. Here, everything seemed new, even the ancient buildings. It was as if the Europe he had always imagined had been abandoned and taken over by some alien race. He thought again of Winnipeg, but could only imagine it as a spot on a globe.

He took Lois's hand. "It will be better," he told her. "It will be much better when we get to Strasbourg." He looked into her eyes, but they were blue and grey, and he couldn't tell whether she believed him or not.

***

The studio they had rented overlooked the rue Schweighaeuser, and from their third-floor window Lois could watch the Jews walk by, the men in their dark-blue suits, the women in peasant dresses and polka-dotted head scarves. Even the tiniest boys, toddlers really, wore yarmulkes. Whole families walked by, looking reserved and ceremonial. Compared to them, the other passers-by seemed rushed and furtive. Lois wondered whether they had somehow survived the war, or whether they had originally lived somewhere else and come here after the war was over.

Richard had gone out for his morning run, and Lois was grateful for his absence. Since they had arrived, the only time she was out of his presence was when he jogged or when he made his brief trips to the university. When he came back from the university, he was always upset. He had arranged to work with a colleague whose expertise was also in the field of Heidegger studies. The man, however, had disappeared, leaving no explanation. The secretaries at the university had told Richard that Monsieur Delacroix had gone to his father's funeral, that he would be back in two months, three months at the latest. In the three weeks they had been in Strasbourg, Richard had met no one else.

"They run this goddamn university by remote control," he told Lois. "There is never anybody there. Even if I go to rooms where classes are scheduled or to meetings, nobody shows up, not even the students. It turns out that half the faculty lives in Paris and only comes out for a few hours a week to teach a class or two. I can't see why the students aren't rioting in the streets."

The students, as Lois pointed out to him, were doing precisely that, but in Paris, not in Strasbourg. One of them had just been shot, and slogans were spray-painted on buildings everywhere.

"In every city in Europe," Richard went on, "there's a North-American professor like me, on sabbatical, working on a book that will almost certainly never see the light of day, spending half his time trying to track down some elusive European academic who only agreed to work with him so that he could get his own turn to come to North America to write some equally obscure and needless book. I'll bet there's a dozen in Strasbourg alone. Whenever I see a guy who looks middle-aged and inadequate, peering into some window as if he didn't want people to know he was lost, I feel like going over to him and asking him what university he's from."

"He'll turn up. Just be patient."

"I guess."

Lois turned back to her grammar text and began to write out the list of reflexive verbs. She copied them neatly into the graph-paper notebook she had bought in a *papeterie* the second day they had been here. She had been surprised to discover that she could not buy ordinary lined paper, but now she preferred the delicate boxes of the graph paper, and had already decided she would take several notebooks home with her.

On the street below, a man cycled by with an armload of baguettes. He looked like Peter Sellers, and Lois tucked away this impression to tell Richard later. *Je me lave*, she wrote, *tu te laves*. Richard seemed increasingly intense since they had arrived in Europe. It was his intensity that had drawn her to him in the first place. He seemed to care about everything. He listened carefully to her and argued with her about ideas. All the men she had known before had explained things to her. Richard would sometimes brood for days about something she had said, then bring the matter up again. He would not accept her insistence that it didn't matter.

"Things matter," he would say. "You can't go around not meaning things." It was even worse when she convinced him of some idea. She felt the enormous responsibility of having made him change his mind. He wasn't talking much these days though. Strasbourg seemed to amaze him, and he had started taking detailed notes about odd things like the kinds of bricks and the shapes of roofs. Richard looked at the parts of buildings, which always surprised Lois, who preferred to see them as a whole.

He was also drinking too much, and Lois decided she was going to have to find some way of telling him this without angering him. She was worried about her own drinking. Every night they had a whole bottle of wine with supper and then drank Spanish rum and Coke until they went to bed. Other people never noticed when Richard was drunk, but she could tell by the restrained, slow formality of his speech. He was drinking nearly half a bottle of rum every night.

Lois put down her list of verbs and started composing in her head the sentence she would say to the receptionist at the language school. She was certain the receptionist would speak English, but she wanted to start out right. She was going to register for the intermediate level but was worried that if she made too many mistakes they would put her in beginner's. The director's name was André Le Maître. Andy the master, she thought. She might have to talk to him. She imagined that he would be tall and handsome, speaking English with a slight accent as he flourished long, elegant hands.

The buzzer rang with a sudden sharp insistence. Richard back from his run. Lois walked over to the buzzer and pressed the button for the gate. Then she counted to ten and pushed it again for the front door. She left the door of the studio open. Everything in France was double- and triple-locked, and Lois wondered whether there was really more danger of intruders here or whether the French were by nature more concerned about security. She had never thought of the French as a group before. In fact, she had always insisted that people were merely people everywhere, and thought that referring to groups as "the French" or "the Germans" was racist. Richard called her a wishy-washy liberal, but she didn't mind. Better to be wishy-washy than to be trapped in some system that had nothing to do with reality.

Richard clumped up the stairs, no doubt disturbing the second-floor Lecontes. Monsieur and Madame Leconte were both physicists at the university. They seemed particularly furtive. They had a sixteen-year-old daughter, a mousey thing who practised scales incessantly on her piano. She seemed to have little talent but enormous drive, or else the Lecontes, unable to hear her wooden touch, were forcing her on to some hopeless dream of the concert stage.

Richard arrived, his sweatsuit soaked. She could smell him before he loomed in the doorway, his face still strained from effort. "Dogshit," he said, in what was already becoming a ritual. "When I get back, the only thing I will be able to remember about this place will be the dogshit. Every time I pass a pile of turds I'll get nostalgic."

Richard dropped to the rug and began to do push-ups. In the tiny studio, he seemed enormous. Lois's first husband had been a small man, lighter than she. They had been able to wear the same jackets and shirts. Richard was a foot taller than her and a hundred pounds heavier. He exercised a full hour every day to control his weight. He had been unable to bring his weights with him, and was talking about buying a set here. Lois was usually prepared to humour him, but the weights, she thought, were too much. They could hardly pass each other in the studio as it was. Last week Richard had arrived home with a twenty-eight-inch television he had rented. It took up as much space as an armchair. It was a bargain, he had told her, no more expensive than a fourteen-inch set, which might have fit.

Richard turned on the television as he rolled over to do his sit-ups. Everything on French television looked to Lois as if it were an amateur performance. A bunch of adults were badly dressed as animals and were singing a song that couldn't possibly appeal to children, a sort of Maurice Chevalier ballad. The song descended into chaos, an argument between the kangaroo and the wolf. Richard laughed from the rug where he was counting out his sit-ups and had got to a hundred and sixty.

"Do you want to know what's funny?" he asked her, knowing already that she would refuse.

"No," Lois told him. "It would lose something in the translation."

"Have it your way."

"Thank you." Somewhere, Richard had apparently learned to speak French. He had never lived in France, had studied only a little more than Lois at school, but he seemed to understand it. He read Le Monde every day, rarely having to look up a word in the dictionary. He could translate from the television if Lois would let him, and he spoke it with great confidence wherever they went. At first Lois was embarrassed, because his accent sounded so bad

15

to her ear, but nobody else seemed to mind, and she had begun to count on him to speak for both of them. The French spoke too fast. Even when she knew all the words, she couldn't understand them. The one person she could understand completely in French was Richard. He wanted to speak it to her at home, but she refused. She didn't want to end up speaking it with his accent.

Richard slipped off his sweatsuit, leaving it in the middle of the floor, and walked into the bathroom. Naked, he looked even larger than when he was clothed. Lois gathered up her coat and her umbrella, and when she looked into the bathroom he was sitting on the edge of the tub, glumly watching the meagre flow of water.

"It takes twenty minutes," he told her, "for this stupid tub to gather enough water to cover a human body."

"It's just that your body is over-sized," Lois said. "I'm gone."

"Where are you going?"

"I told you. I'm going to register for a French course."

"You don't know where it is. You'll get lost. Wait for a few minutes and I'll come along."

"I don't want you to come along. I can find it by myself. I have a map, and I can follow a map. I can read the street names. I don't have to know what they mean."

"Well, don't make it an evening course," Richard said, climbing into the tub. "I don't want all our evenings screwed up."

"I'll take it when it's offered," Lois replied. "If it interferes with something you want to do, I simply won't go." And she stepped out the door, closing it with a soft click to remind Richard that there was no need to slam it.

On the sidewalk, Lois was less confident. The streets of Strasbourg were bewildering. They seemed to form concentric circles around the cathedral, interspersed with endless canals and a river. She followed rue Schweighaeuser to Robertsau where a tangle of streets met with the rue de la Forêt Noire. There, in front of a flower stand, she consulted her map. It appeared that if she continued straight down the rue de la Forêt Noire to the Palais de Justice, she could follow a canal to the language school, which appeared to be in the middle of a shopping centre. A pretty girl came out of the flower kiosk and asked her something in French, Lois hesitated for a second, then realized that the girl had offered to help her.

16

"Non, merci," she replied, then smiled, uncertain of whether her answer was sufficiently polite. The girl turned to her flowers and began arranging a bouquet. Lois continued, over the pont John F. Kennedy, past the American consulate and the Mobil gas station. It was several blocks before she realized that she may have turned in the wrong direction, in which case the road would soon lead her to Germany.

The Palais de Justice loomed on Lois's left, apparently on the wrong street, but she could see the canal beyond it. She crossed the traffic circle, scampering out of the way of a Citroën, which, in spite of the fact that there were no other cars in the entire circle, did not feel it was necessary to change lanes to avoid her. There was no traffic at all on the road along the canal, and Lois began to feel she must have lost her way. She seemed to be in a manufacturing district. Instead of store fronts, there were blank brick walls on both sides of the canal. The sidewalk was under repair in many places, and Lois had to step into the street to avoid the piles of brick and clay. She passed a tavern sandwiched between two heavy buildings. Inside, men stood crushed tightly together like people at a successful cocktail party. They had glasses of red, green and amber liquids, which they held high so that they would not spill if jostled. She remembered the bottles in that first store in Germany, and wondered if this was the liquor that had come in those beautiful bottles. The atmosphere seemed festive, though it was not yet ten o'clock in the morning.

Farther on, she passed a store that sold Icelandic woollens, and she wondered who would go so far out of the way to find such exotic merchandise. Then she rounded a bend and was in an area that she recognized as part of the shopping area near the cathedral. The street number of the language school led her to a large, shiny tower complex with chrome letters on it that read Centre des Halles. Richard had told her that this was City Hall.

Inside was an enormous shopping centre, and Lois promised herself that she would come back when she could go slowly and thoroughly through the stores. She had put together a list of clothes she wanted to buy in France. Most of them she had seen in *Elle*, to which she had subscribed ever since they had decided to take the trip. She had not yet been able to find anything she wanted.

A sort of dark leaf-green colour seemed to be in vogue, and, though Lois had not yet seen anyone wearing it, all the clothes in the windows of the shop were green, a colour she could not wear.

The language school, when she found it up on the fifth floor, looked like a bank. The secretaries were behind heavy plate-glass windows. They could speak through a chrome grill, and there was a tray where papers could be passed back and forth. It looked as if they were prepared for armed robbery, which seemed impossible here, at the top of a concrete building with no means of escape. The glass seemed designed to prevent communication, but Lois recited her carefully rehearsed phrase. "Pardonnez-moi, je veux parler avec monsieur le directeur." The secretary answered with a volley of French. Lois shook her head and asked again, "Monsieur le directeur." The secretary answered much more slowly now, explaining that the director was not in, that she would have to speak to his assistant, Monsieur Leforge. Lois nodded, and the secretary motioned her to a door that seemed miraculously to have manifested itself in the plate-glass wall. The secretary led her down a short hallway to an open-doored office. She said something to whoever was inside, then motioned to Lois, "Entrez."

Monsieur Leforge was precisely what Lois had expected the director to be. He was tall and slender, dressed in a perfectly tailored dark-blue suit with a red tie. He was destroying a paper clip with his elegant hands. He motioned to Lois to sit down, and when she had, he spoke to her slowly and clearly. She did not understand a word he said. She tried to remember the phrases she had memorized, but nothing came to her mind but the list of reflexive verbs and an image of Richard butting out a cigarette. It struck her as odd that she should think of Richard smoking, since he had quit nearly three years ago. She tried to concentrate on what she had to say, but she could think of nothing except that tears were running down her cheek. I am going to faint, she thought, and leaned forward in her chair so that when she fell she would not hit her head on the desk.

She had no memory later of having fainted, but Monsieur Leforge was around the desk in a moment. He caught Lois and picked her up as if she were a feather. He is as strong as Richard, she thought, though he is much smaller. Carefully, he sat her back in the chair. She was intensely aware of his hands on her body, of the smell of a cologne she had caught several times in the streets of Strasbourg.

"Are you okay?" he asked her in a clipped and fluent English. "Is there something the matter?" Then, seeing that she did not lose her balance, he moved to the door and called for a glass of water.

Lois felt her face flush.

"No, no," she said. "It's fine. I'm all right. I was just dizzy for a moment." The secretary she had first spoken to entered the room with a paper cup. Monsieur Leforge took it from her and offered it to Lois. He placed a burning hand on her shoulder as he did so. Lois drank the water, which was warm, but not salty as she had expected. Monsieur Leforge took his hand, reluctantly it seemed, from her shoulder and sat down on the edge of his desk. The secretary hesitated a moment, then left the room. The room seemed intensely intimate, and Lois felt a pang of guilt.

"I wish to take the intermediate course in French," she told the assistant director. "I don't speak it very well, but I am quite good at the grammar." She bit her lower lip, because she could feel tears forming again.

"Of course, of course," he murmured. "The intermediate course. Perhaps even the advanced if you desire. Are you sure you are all right?"

"I'm fine," she said. "You see, it's just that I don't want to do the verbs again. I always seem to get into courses where we never speak, but only do verbs."

"No, no," he replied. "To speak is important. It is the most important thing."

Lois felt herself recovering. "It's just that everyone speaks so fast," she said, "but I guess you catch on to it after a while." Monsieur Leforge became suddenly efficient. He brought out forms, filled them out for her, explained that because enrollment was so low, it always was during the spring term, there would be one section of intermediate. It would run six o'clock to eight o'clock every Tuesday and Thursday. There was no other possibility. It was too late now for the present course, but she could begin on the fifteenth of April.

Lois walked back by way of the cathedral. She could follow the steeple until she came to the central square, and from there she knew the way home. She remembered Monsieur Leforge's hands on her, and she felt her face flush. Richard would be angry because the course was in the evenings, even though it was almost the afternoon and she would be back by eight thirty. There would still be time to do things.

She stopped at a little kiosk and bought herself a tiny strawberry ice cream cone. Classes didn't start for another month. She would convince Richard that they should go south. They had bought three-week Eurail passes. They had been going to wait until summer, and then go either to Spain or to Greece. She rehearsed the conversation she would have with Richard. She would point out how tired he was, how he couldn't do anything until his colleague came back anyway. They would go to Paris and get on a train and see where it would take them. If they went south, almost anything could happen.

***

The road south from Strasbourg to Colmar was flat and smooth, the flood plain of the Rhine. Richard thought he could remember something about Roman outposts in the area, but the memory wouldn't focus. The traffic was very fast, and the green Fiat van Richard had rented for the day shuddered as he tried to keep it at a hundred and ten kilometres. Whenever he drove slower, the traffic piled up behind him, and kamikaze drivers, anxious to pass, squeezed in, scant inches in front of him, to avoid imminent collision with oncoming traffic.

Lois thought the van was cute and she had insisted on taking a picture of Richard sitting on the fender in front of the Palais de l'Europe. The picture-taking had set them back a half-hour, and Richard was annoyed by that and by the traffic. For the last couple of weeks, he had done almost nothing but watch television.

The French Open was being televised, and Richard had watched Jannick Noah serving and volleying as the sunlight and the breeze ruffled the hair of the crowd at Nice. In Strasbourg, the grey skies settled lower and the incessant rain beat down day after day. The leaves had slipped onto the trees almost unnoticed, and the vulgar beauty of the magnolia blossoms was diminished by the dismal light that filtered through the clouds. Today was the first day of sunlight in weeks, and Richard did not want to miss a second.

Lois reached into the wicker picnic basket she had bought specifically for this occasion and offered Richard a can of orange juice. He shook his head, and she opened it and drank from it herself.

"This time next week," she said, "we'll be in Spain. Or maybe Italy. It will be warm and sunny and the orange trees will be in blossom."

"Will they?" Richard asked. Travelling south was Lois's plan, and Richard realized that he had not given it much thought. He had no idea what vegetation they would encounter. "Will there be palm trees?" he added.

"Hordes of them," Lois answered. "And towers and minarets. Things like that. Don't you pay attention at the movies?"

Richard realized that Lois was teasing him, but that she was also correct. He had not paid attention at the movies. Since their arrival in Europe, he had become aware that he had never looked carefully at his surroundings before. Everything here was somehow strange and different, but he wasn't sure whether he had simply failed to see the same things at home. The blackbirds, for instance, looked like the blackbirds at home, but they whistled a clear sound that made him think of robins. Did robins whistle?

"No," Richard answered, honestly, he thought. "I never paid attention to anything but epistemology. Only words are real."

"Meaning?" Lois asked.

"Nothing." And again Richard was struck by the accidental honesty of his answer. He was pleased, and added, "Just an essay topic for Philosophy 101."

"Well, you're off duty now," Lois said. "And I assure you the palm trees will be lush."

The fields on either side were an indeterminate green, and Richard couldn't figure out what was growing in any of them. He had learned to identify barley by its beard, wheat by its stalk, oats by its delicate wavering, and flax by its pale-blue sheen. None of these crops showed anything he could identify.

"What does that sign mean?" Lois asked.

Richard had only caught a glimpse of it, a black shape on a green background. He reached into the webbed pocket of the door and passed a map and a card explaining the road signs to Lois.

"Here," he said. "I'm the driver and you're the navigator. What does the sign mean, and how many miles to Colmar?"

Lois studied the card with pictures of signs.

"It's not here. I think it must mean 'cows crossing.' The black thing looked like a cow."

"It did not." Richard replied, though he could not remember what it did look like. They drove in silence for a moment as Lois studied the map. They were going to Colmar, because Lois wanted to see the Issenheim altarpiece in the museum there. She had studied art history at the university, and had written a paper about it. At first, she had wanted to go alone on the train and spend the day at the museum. Richard had reluctantly agreed, but when on impulse he had rented the little van they had decided that they would both go.

"Turn here," Lois told him. They were approaching an interchange, and a large green sign with an arrow clearly indicated Colmar was dead ahead.

"Are you sure?" Richard asked, already turning because he had no other choice. "I don't think this is the way to Colmar." The sign as they entered the smaller highway read Obernai and Mont Ste. Odile. Ahead of them rose a smooth, enormous hill with no others surrounding it, a giant pimple on the otherwise flat landscape.

"No. Ste. Odile. Remember, I read you a piece about it the other day. It's a monastery on the top of a mountain. You can see all the way to the Black Forest. It's not much out of the way."

Richard was uncertain how to respond. The unfocussed annoyance he had felt from the beginning of the trip came back with greater force. The road had begun to undulate in small rises and dips, and it curved through vineyards that had just come into pale-green leaf.

"What's the matter?" Lois responded to his silence. "Don't you want to go? If you don't want to go we can turn around and go on to Colmar."

"It's fine," Richard said, "only a little unexpected. I was expecting an art gallery, not a monastery."

"No," Lois said. "Turn around. It was a mistake. I shouldn't have decided without asking you."

Richard made no move to turn, but after a moment he said, "I'm sorry. I'm just cranky this morning. Let's just make it an adventure and see what we see." They skirted Obernai and began a steep, winding climb up the mountain, past a few low buildings and a spectacular pink hotel. The trees were tall. Their upper branches formed a canopy that blocked the sunlight. There was little undergrowth, and the path they could see winding below them looked foreign and threatening.

They broke suddenly into sunlight and grass. A sign indicated parking was available in a shallow dip to the left. Richard pulled in and parked close to the only other vehicle there, a silver Mercedes with German license plates. It blocked a path that led down into the darkness of the forest below.

Richard and Lois followed another path, which led upwards to a long, narrow meadow. At the far end, they could see the dark shapes of buildings.

"This is a strange place for a parking lot," Richard said. "It's about a half a mile from the monastery." The path through the meadow wound around an ancient willow, and they came on a couple lying on a blanket near a large, black motorcycle. They were both blond, the girl's hair long and flowing, the man's short and evenly cropped. They might have been brother and sister. Both were dressed in tight, form-fitting nylon suits in a harlequin pattern of red and black diamonds. Their helmets on the grass beside the motorcycle gleamed malignantly black. Richard nodded a hello as he passed, but they made no response. The girl fiddled with the settings on a small, black radio, and settled for what seemed to Richard to be marching music.

"I wonder what planet they're from," Lois said as soon as they were out of earshot.

"I suppose that's what everyone will be wearing when we get home," Richard replied. They climbed up a set of steps into another parking lot. Here there were a half-dozen cars and a tour bus.

"We must have been in the overflow lot," Lois said.

"How was I supposed to know. It said parking," Richard answered, as if he had been accused of incompetence for not finding the right lot.

Lois did not reply. They had reached the gate to the monastery, and she was trying to read a sign that was densely lettered but had blurred from the effects of sun and rain. Richard had learned by now not to translate for her. The sign said that an ancient wall ran ten kilometres around the top of the hill. It had been constructed about four thousand years ago. A map indicated that the circuit began where they stood and ended in the lower parking lot where the Mercedes was parked.

"What does *paien* mean?" Lois asked. She had consulted her little pocket dictionary, apparently without success.

"Pagan," Richard told her. "The Pagan Wall. It's apparently one of the wonders of the universe. It's ten kilometres long and fifteen feet high in places. Parts of it are still perfectly preserved."

Lois put away her dictionary. "Thank you," she said, and Richard realized he had translated too much. They passed through a long, narrow archway, a sort of tunnel, and emerged in the grounds of the monastery. Richard paid the commissionaire, a short, balding man, with a fifty-franc note, and took his change without even noticing how much he had paid.

Except for a busload of tourists, the place was deserted. The tourists moved like a single organism, broadening and narrowing in shape to fit the architecture until they flowed into a small chapel. By the time Richard and Lois walked across the central square to the chapel, a service was in progress. They sat for a few moments in the back, and listened until two of the tourists stood and sang in German. Richard wanted to leave, but Lois, whispering, insisted they stay until the song was over. The voices seemed raw and lonesome to Richard. The service was Catholic, but the denial in the songs seemed Protestant. Lois thought the music was beautiful, and after they had left and gone to explore the ramparts she accused Richard of reading his own mood into the music.

The day was perfectly clear, sunny with no clouds, but the blue haze of pollution that hung over the Rhine meant that they could not see the Black Forest.

"Conditions are perfect," Richard said. "If you can't see the Black Forest today, you're never going to see it." He pointed to the sign that indicated the direction of the German border. They must be thinking of the last century. Nobody's seen the Black Forest from here since the Industrial Revolution."

"Maybe some days are better," Lois told him. "Sundays, when the factories aren't working."

"I don't think it's factories," he answered. "Somebody told me it was potash mines, like in Saskatchewan."

Richard fed a two-franc coin into something that looked like a parking meter and turned the dial to English. A syrupy British voice began to tell them the history of the place. Richard realized that he had to pay close attention to understand. The female voice wasn't quite right, the vowels too fruity, the sibilants slightly too heavy. He realized that he was listening to a German voice speaking what sounded like a slightly contemptuous parody of Queen Elizabeth.

Lois disappeared into a building, leaving Richard alone with the voice. He abandoned it to to its description of the fourteenth century, and descended a set of stairs. He met Lois at the foot of them, coming down a narrow hallway. They followed a set of arrows that led them to the sarcophagus of the saint herself. Her stone coffin was scarcely four feet long, a sandstone box in a room lit by candles.

"She must be the patron saint of dwarves," Richard whispered to Lois, unsure why he was whispering because they were the only people in the room. Lois laughed, and Richard was suddenly pleased. The echo of her laughter was bright in the hollow room. They turned to go, and in the hallway passed an old couple and a beautiful, blonde young woman. The girl looked confused until the man touched her back and indicated with his hand that she should enter the crypt.

"She's frightened," Lois told Richard. "Did you see her eyes?"

"I think she's probably mentally retarded," Richard replied. "Her eyes just seemed blank."

"No. She's too beautiful to be retarded. She could never take care of herself like that."

"Maybe somebody else takes care of her, washes her, puts on her make-up."

"Not like that they don't." Lois seemed suddenly aware of her own image, and she brushed her hair back.

"I'm hungry," she said. "There's a little dining hall off the main square. Let's get lunch."

"It's only eleven o'clock."

"We were up early."

Richard realized that this was true, that he was hungry himself. They made their way to the central square, past the ramparts and the stunning view of the blue, polluted Rhine. The tourists had occupied all the benches in the central square and were eating identical lunches, a large sandwich and a can of Kronenberg beer. In the dining hall, workers on break were eating plates of assorted meats and cheeses and drinking beer. Their fare didn't seem available at the counter. Richard had a small bottle of red wine and a sausage, which to his surprise turned out to be hot. Lois took a salad and a plastic glass so she could share Richard's wine.

They sat at the end of a long, wooden table where they could look at the other tourists. At the far end of their table, a short, heavy man, immaculate in a blue, three-piece suit, nursed a beer. Across from him sat a dark-haired young woman in a plain, black dress. They gave no indication that they knew each other. The man had silver hair and gleaming silver glasses.

"You always see people like that," Lois said.

"Like what?"

"You know, in Europe. You get tourists who come dressed to work in the office. They don't seem to realize they are on holiday, and they sit on the beach with polished black oxfords."

"Like Antonio," Richard laughed. Tony Verni was a lecturer in economics at the university. Richard had invited him to their cottage, and he had arrived in full formal dress and sat stiffly in a lawn chair on the sand for the whole afternoon. When Lois asked after his wife, he had told them that he hadn't realized she had been included in the invitation.

"Yes," Lois said. "Like Antonio." The older couple with the beautiful girl came into the dining hall. They each took a salad, and joined the grey-haired man and the dark lady. Or at least, they sat next to them. It was hard to say whether they were together or not. The older man talked intensely to the girl in what sounded at a distance like German.

"Time to move," Richard said. It was already nearly noon, and he wasn't sure how far it was going to be to Colmar. Out in the courtyard, Lois discovered the washrooms down a narrow staircase, and apparently under the walls of the monastery. Richard waited for a moment, then decided to go himself. His mother had always insisted he go before he got into the car. Under such pressure, he had always found himself unable. Now, he was frustrated because he did not have the franc necessary to make the turnstile revolve. Annoyed, he jumped over it. Seconds later, the little commissionaire who had taken their money appeared, whistling softly. Richard brazened it out, marching out the un-guarded exit.

He waited outside the women's washroom for what seemed to him a long time. Just at the moment when he decided that he should do something, Lois appeared across the courtyard out of a door-way. She waved a book and a roll of film at him, and motioned to him to join her. Richard realized that there was nothing he could say that would not sound petty, so he swallowed his annoyance and waved back.

"Can we go look at the Pagan Wall?" she asked. She seemed excited. "I met this guy who speaks English in there," and she indicated the door she had come out of, "and he said it's terrific. He said it's better than the pyramids. There's an old castle, and a Druid altar and it's apparently a great walk."

Richard felt his annoyance return and was angry with himself. "Right," he said. "The Pagan Wall it is. But that means no Colmar today." Lois seemed disappointed. "It's not far to Colmar," she said. "We could still go."

"Not in time to see anything," Richard told her. "I've got to get this car back by six, or we pay extra."

"We can go to Colmar another time," she said. "Or if you don't want to come, I could go myself on the train."

27

"I want to come," Richard reminded her. "I want to see this famous altar."

"Altarpiece," she corrected. "Maybe next week?"

"Next week we'll be in Italy and Greece.

"Or maybe Spain. We'll go to Colmar when we come back." They had reached the gate and an arrow pointed down a flight of stairs to the Pagan Wall. Richard helped Lois load her camera, and she took a picture of him coming down the stairs towards her. The grey-haired man and the dark woman stopped behind him, but not far enough to be out of the picture.

The path led downwards steeply. The high wall that surrounded the abbey blended into the ancient pagan wall. The wall was in remarkably good shape, but it was soon clear that the section near the abbey had been restored. After less than a kilometre, the wall existed only in sections, odd piles of rocks on their right, and down the hill to their left, individual rocks that had rolled down the hillside. Richard examined the wall carefully. Some of the rocks seemed to have been made from concrete, and he wondered whether cement had existed four thousand years ago. Some of the rocks had odd shapes chiselled out of them, but Richard had no idea what the shapes might be for or what they might mean.

Lois had continued walking when Richard stopped to examine the wall more closely. Now, she was out of sight, ahead where the path turned. Richard had wanted to warn her that forest paths can lead anywhere, that sometimes they just petered out into nothingness. He called out her name, but she didn't answer. He felt a momentary panic, a sense that she was somehow vulnerable. He started to run after her on the uneven path, but found after a few steps that he was going faster than he wanted to. He slowed as he reached the corner, feeling the pressure on his knee, and suddenly slipped off the path and into the bushes on his left. He came to a stop about twenty feet below, his slide stopped by an enormous rock.

When Richard got to his feet, he was surprised to discover that he was unhurt. His pants and his shirt were smeared with grass and mud, but they were not torn. His knees and ankles did not seem sprained, and, though he was sure he would be stiff later on, he was keenly aware that he had been lucky. He looked up at the mass of greenery above. If he had been badly hurt, Lois would not have found him.

Richard had just begun his climb back to the trail when he heard the low roar of a motor. Through a clearing, he could see another path that wound below. At first he saw nothing, but then a heavy, black motorcycle appeared, driven by someone in a red and black nylon suit with a shiny helmet. He couldn't tell whether it was a man or a woman. Something bulky was tied to the passenger's seat behind the driver. The motorcycle disappeared on the other side of the opening, but a moment later, another figure, identical to the first, loped across the clearing in a gentle jog, shiny black helmet and all. Richard identified the figures as the couple he and Lois had seen near the parking lot.

Lois was still nowhere to be seen when Richard pulled himself over the little lip of the slope down which he had fallen. He called her name, then listened for her reply. Nothing. He called again, louder now and with a note of urgency. Lois's voice came faintly from the wrong direction, back where they had come from. Richard called again, then sat down on the path to wait.

In a moment, Lois appeared. When she saw Richard, she broke into a run, and Richard called to her, "Careful. I nearly broke my neck that way." She slowed, and Richard pointed to the bushes where he had fallen.

"Right here is the site of the swan dive of the century," he said, pulling the branches aside to show her where he had fallen.

"What's this?" Lois asked, bending to examine something. Richard, too, bent to see. There, stretched tightly across the path about four inches above the ground was a thin strand of wire.

"That's what tripped me," Richard said. "Who'd do a stupid trick like that?"

"I walked right by here twice," Lois told him. "How come it didn't trip me?" Richard unwound the wire from the tree and began to coil it up.

"I don't know," he answered.

"What happened?" Lois asked. "Did you get hurt?"

"No," Richard said, "I don't think so. You disappeared when I was examining the wall. I called, but you didn't answer. I was worried. I ran to see if something was wrong. And I tripped."

"I answered," Lois replied defensively. "I don't have as loud a voice as you. And when you didn't come, I came back to look for you."

"And I was there," Richard said, pointing to the rock below. I slid all the way down to that rock."

"But you're all right?"

"I'm all right."

"What are you going to do with the wire?"

"I'm going to give it to the commissionaire and report this. If this is somebody's idea of a joke, it's a really dangerous one."

"Well, come on," Lois said. "There's an incredible view ahead. A ruined castle." They rounded another bend, and a set of steps led up to a platform on a high part of the wall. From the platform they could see across a broad valley to an old castle, which from where they stood seemed complete and undamaged. Castle Mensheim, the sign said. Constructed about 1155. Destroyed in 1430. Tiny figures scurried around the base of the castle, and the sun gleamed off an automobile.

A telescope on the platform offered a view of the castle for two francs. Lois asked Richard for a coin, and he reached into his pocket and found one. She put the coin in the slot and aimed the telescope at the castle. Richard took the coil of wire out of his pocket and examined it carefully. The wire was copper-coloured and flexible. It looked exactly like the snare wire he had used as a kid to trap rabbits.

"That's strange," Lois said.

"What's strange?"

"It's the people from the abbey, the old couple and the beautiful girl."

"What about them?"

"They've got the trunk of a car open. I think it's a Mercedes, and they're putting something in the trunk."

"What sort of thing?"

"I don't know. It was on the back of a motorcycle, but it's certainly heavy."

"Let me see," Richard said. Lois stepped back and Richard peered into the telescope. At first he saw nothing but the wall of the castle, but he adjusted the telescope and caught sight of the open trunk of a silver Mercedes and two figures in red and black harlequin costume. The telescope clicked and went black, but not before Richard had noticed that they were both blond. He checked his pockets, but he had no more coins, and Lois had left her purse behind, locked in the little green Fiat van.

"It's odd," Richard said a little later, when they paused to rest by a sign that indicated they were a half-kilometre from a Druid altar. "We haven't seen anybody else on the trail. You'd think somebody else would have taken the walk." A path led off to the right, and another sign indicated that they could return to the abbey now, but if they went on it would be another five kilometres.

"I met somebody," Lois said. "I met a couple of joggers. They had handkerchiefs tied around their heads. Besides, it's not really odd. Everybody's going in the same direction, except those joggers. There could be hundreds of people on the trail, and you'd never see anyone unless they were going either faster or slower than you."

"Right," Richard answered. Then, indicating the new path, "Do you want to go back?"

"No. I'd like to see the Druid altar. If you're okay, I mean."

"I'm fine."

The path had run level for a long way, but now it started a gentle climb. Richard was beginning to feel stiff from his fall. His shoulder ached and he could feel a tightness in his chest. The sausage he had eaten for lunch was beginning to give him indigestion. After a few minutes he could feel a stitch in his side, as if he had run too far. Lois, anxious to see the Druid altar, had moved ahead of him on the path, but she turned around now and came back.

"You're sure you're all right?"

"I'm fine," Richard said. "I'm just having a minor heart attack."

"Can you feel pain in your arms?" Lois asked. She had taken a course in cardiopulmonary resuscitation and had memorized the signs of a heart attack. Because of Richard's size, she was certain this would happen to him one day. It had become a half-serious joke between them.

"No," Richard said. "It's just indigestion from the sausage." He managed a tiny belch and said, "There. All better."

"Don't be disgusting."

Richard sat down on a stone outcropping of the wall. "Go ahead. I'm just going to catch my breath here. I'll be along in a minute."

"You're sure you won't fall off any more cliffs?"

"Certain."

Richard wasn't sure he wanted Lois to go ahead without him, but she was visibly eager, and he wanted to salvage a day that seemed certain to go wrong. As Lois disappeared around another corner, he thought about how few arguments they'd had in their marriage. At first he had thought that Lois was the most agreeable person he had ever met. It was a couple of years before he realized that she would agree to anything he suggested, but if she did not like it she would sulk later, sometimes for days. He had confronted her with this discovery, but she had denied it vehemently. Still, he found himself second-guessing her, trying to figure out what he could do that would make her happy.

She did seem concerned about his heart, and Richard found himself sharing her concern. Before they had left, he had gone to his doctor without telling Lois and had a complete check-up. He had even insisted on a stress test. The doctor told him he was in excellent shape. His heart was perfect, his blood pressure in the normal range, his cholesterol levels low. The doctor, himself overweight, and to Richard's eye a perfect candidate for a heart attack, said that, whatever killed Richard, it would not be his heart. The doctor's remarks had left Richard somewhat reassured but considerably less confident in medical science.

He had told Lois nothing about the visit. Increasingly, he thought about his own death, what shape it might take. The one thing he was sure of was that he would not be ready. Against the average ordinariness of everyday life, the question itself seemed presumptuous, something for people who were not engaged in the process of living.

Richard had taken a few steps and found the tightness gone when he heard Lois scream, a short, sharp scream of pure terror, followed by his name. He burst into a run that he realized after a few seconds he could not keep up, but he did not slow down. His mind was devoid of everything but a few images: Lois, an assailant, a struggle. Lois called again, much closer now, and through the thinning trees ahead he could see her ahead. She stumbled, caught her balance and continued. When she saw Richard, she slowed to a walk, and as he came up to her she said, heaving and panting, "Richard, there's a body, a man, I think he's dead."

"Where?"

"On the altar. He's lying there, stretched out. I thought he was sleeping. I didn't want to come too close, but then I saw the blood on the rock."

"I'll check," Richard said, starting down the path.

"No, don't. Let's go back. We can report it." Lois's voice was almost hysterical. "We can just tell them. Richard, I'm scared."

"He might be alive," Richard said. "We can't just leave him there."

"I'm not going," Lois said. "I don't want to see him again."

"Well, wait here. I'll be back in a minute."

"No. I'll come. I don't want to be alone."

Lois followed a couple of steps behind as Richard moved up the path. Richard's senses were intensely aware as he chose his steps precisely, trying to make no sound. This is exactly like deer hunting, he thought. What had been flat land to the left began to take on a gentle slope, and the underbrush disappeared. A path led off to the left. The wall itself became more defined, taller.

The Druid altar was an enormous slab of rock balanced on two other rocks, a primitive table. It was a few steps to the left of the path and lower down the slope. Without the sign, anyone would have passed it by. A man lay spread-eagled on the rock. He was dark, with short-cropped hair, dressed in dark-blue slacks and a paler blue, short-sleeved shirt. A pool of blood had started to congeal on his left side, and it was instantly clear to Richard that he was dead.

Richard clambered down and made the short jump that put him on a slab of rock just above the body. Streaks of blood on the rocks nearby indicated that the body had been dragged there. Richard climbed down to the ground and began to follow the scuff marks where the man had been dragged.

"Don't," Lois called to him. "Let's just get the police. Whoever killed him might still be there."

Richard stared at the trees, but he saw nothing. The body had been dragged uphill, but it was impossible to tell how far. Below, the undergrowth closed in, a tangle of green and black.

"I'd better find out who he is," Richard said, climbing back to the slab of the altar.

"Don't touch him. There might be fingerprints." Lois remained unmoving on the path above. Richard leaned over the body but not too closely. A pin on the man's collar read Canadian Armed Forces, Lahr. Suddenly, the dead man seemed more real, and Richard recoiled.

"He's a Canadian," Richard told Lois. "The badge says Canadian Armed Forces, Lahr. He must be a serviceman from the base in Germany." Richard clambered up the rocks and joined Lois on the path.

"Let's go," she said.

"Just a minute." Richard reached around Lois's neck and took the camera from her. He snapped a picture from where they stood, then hesitated a moment and snapped another. "Okay," he said. "Let's go."

***

Lois remembered the trip back to the abbey as a nightmare. The path through the forest was dark and treacherous. Richard led at a fast walk and she had trouble keeping up, though at the same time she wanted to run. Richard was reassuring, but after his fall, he, too, seemed vulnerable. He appeared larger somehow, as if he had grown physically to confront this challenge. She remembered how secure she had felt to be able to walk down dark streets with Richard, who was larger than almost anyone they met, and who seemed completely unaware of the danger of dark streets. Now, for all his apparent confidence, he seemed shaken. Branches reached out to whip against them as they passed.

At the abbey, the commissionaire seemed bewildered. He kept asking Richard to repeat what he had said, and Lois wondered whether excitement had made Richard's French, always heavily accented, now incomprehensible, or whether the little commissionaire didn't want to believe the story. Perhaps he felt that if he kept asking, Richard would have to deliver a more acceptable version. She, at least, understood. Finally, the commissionaire consented to call the police, muttering all the time at the impossibility of the situation. "C'est pas possible," he repeated, as if he could solve the situation by denying it.

The wait for the police seemed interminable. When at last they arrived, two gendarmes in an unmarked car, they were as incredulous as the commissionaire. Richard repeated his story several times. He tried English, but the taller of the two gendarmes dismissed the language with a wave of his hand as if it were some annoyance that had got in the way. Finally, the smaller, heavier officer went off down the path with a young gardener in overalls whom he summoned from a bed of roses to show him the way.

The other officer attempted to interview Lois. She couldn't understand any of his questions, so in desperation she simply repeated that, yes, she had found a man dead on a stone. She didn't know whether to say *roche* or *pierre* and she tried them both. After a few moments, the gendarme gave up on her and went into the commissionaire's office and made a phone call. Then he left them on a bench and went out into the nearer parking lot, apparently to copy down the license numbers of the cars. He spent several minutes in deep discussion with the tour bus driver, who had all his charges loaded in the bus, but was apparently waiting for something.

The mystery was solved when a young couple appeared. The gendarme questioned them for a minute, then allowed them to board the bus. The driver closed the door, and the bus disappeared from Lois's view. It reappeared briefly at the crest of the hill, which Lois could see over the abbey wall, and then it was gone.

When the second gendarme returned with the gardener in tow, he was red in the face from exertion, and angry. He confronted Richard with a great deal of arm-waving. Richard was angry himself, and she could hear what she had come to call his classroom voice, slow, deep and firm. He used a few curses in English, which the officers appeared to understand and resent. Lois felt her stomach tighten. She hated confrontations. Richard always said that he, too, hated them, but he never avoided them. Finally, he left the officers and came over to the bench where Lois was sitting.

"They can't find the body," he told her. "They say there is nothing there. Either they've gone to the wrong place, or somebody has removed it. Anyway, I've got to go and show them where it is. Will you be okay here?"

Lois felt a sudden chill. If the body was gone, then the murderers had probably been watching them all along. She remembered her sense of violation when, years ago, a thief had broken into her house and stolen her rings. The rings had been in her drawer, hidden under panties and brassieres. For weeks she had not wanted to wear them, the vision of some dark and slimy creature among her private things always in the back of her mind.

"Can I come?" she asked. "I don't want to stay here by myself."

"I don't think so." Richard said. "But I'll see." He went over to the gate where the gendarmes were waiting.

Lois could tell from the negative head-shaking of the officers that she was not going to be allowed to go. In fact, her presence seemed a problem they had not considered, and they conferred earnestly, pointing towards the dining room.

Richard came back and told her, "You'll have to stay. In fact they were horrified that I would even suggest your coming. The commissionaire will wait with you in the dining hall." The little man came over and asked her slowly and clearly whether she would like a glass of wine. She told him yes, and he motioned her gallantly in the direction of the dining hall.

Lois could hear the sound of sirens quite close, not the rising and falling wail of North American police cars, but the insistent bell-ringing they heard every night from their studio in Strasbourg. They had ascended the steps to the dining hall by the time the cars arrived, about a half-dozen, it appeared. Men in trench coats got out and joined Richard and the gendarmes at the gate. Lois wanted to go back, but the commissionaire gently touched her waist and motioned her into the building.

The dozen or so working men seated at the long, wooden tables in the dining hall stared at her, and a couple of women came out of the kitchen to see the source of so much commotion. They seemed less curious than actively hostile. The commissionaire was now full of self-importance at his role in the affair. He scurried over to the counter and brought them each a half-bottle of white wine and a glass. He did not bother to pay, and the owl-eyed woman guarding the till did not challenge him.

The commissionaire opened the bottles and poured the wine with such ceremony that Lois half-expected him to want to clink glasses. Instead, he asked her questions with slow solemnity, as if he were being patient with a difficult child. Lois found she could understand him perfectly when he spoke so slowly. She was anxious to tell what she knew before she forgot it. The incident was beginning to take on the quality of a dream, and Lois was afraid she might forget it all. She could never remember dreams. Richard remembered dreams so clearly that Lois sometimes thought he was inventing them, elaborating on the sketchy details. All she could ever recall were fragments and impressions.

The commissionaire seemed to have no difficulty understanding her either. He paid attention, and after a few minutes Lois realized that she had just spoken more French than ever before in her life. She found she was unreasonably happy. She was speaking French at last. If everybody spoke to her as slowly as this man and paid attention to her replies, she would have no difficulty. As she gained confidence, her sentences became longer, and it seemed easy to find the word she wanted. Her feeling that she was somehow swamped and drowning in the language had vanished.

Lois poured herself a second glass of wine. She could feel the alcohol relaxing her. She explained to the commissionaire that she was Canadian. The commissionaire seemed pleased. He saw many Canadians. Every day there were Canadians visiting the abbey. They wore little flags, he told her, indicating his lapel. They were a patriotic people, the Canadians. They seemed to love their flag. He had thought that she and Richard were Americans because they were not wearing flags.

The commissionaire filled Lois's glass again. He was refilling his own when a large man in a rumpled green sweater joined them. He slumped into a chair next to the commissionaire and spoke to him in French. The commissionaire responded, and the language turned opaque to Lois. She couldn't understand what was said, but she recognized the obsequiousness in the commissionaire's voice and the easy authority in the other man's. The commissionaire got up, and, bowing and demanding pardon, rushed from the room. Lois was filled with a sudden resentment. She had enjoyed talking with the little man. He had just begun telling her about his cousin in Rivière du Loup when the burly man had appeared from nowhere. He had curly, steel-grey hair and a moustache that looked as if it had been painted on with a burnt match.

"Pardon me, Madame Angantyr," he said, reaching into his pocket for a pipe, which he lit with an oddly shaped silver lighter. "A difficult business, this, uncomfortable for all concerned. Accidental intrusions into our everyday life." His English was heavily accented, but elegant. He looked as if he might once have been an actor but had now given up the discipline of the body needed to keep in shape. He puffed a blue cloud of smoke and it hung above the table between them. "Inspector Kessler," he informed her almost as an afterthought.

"Lois," she replied. "Lois Jensen," stressing the surname so that he would notice the difference between her name and Richard's.

"Yes," he said. "You are North American," as if that were sufficient explanation. "André Kessler. An Alsatian mixture of French and German. And your name is Danish," he announced as a fact.

"My grandparents came from Denmark." Nobody had ever before identified her name as Danish. The inspector examined his nails, which were stubby, as if he chewed them.

"And you are here for a year. A sabbatical for your husband. And for you?"

"I am here to learn French. And to draw," she added. "I illustrate children's books." She wondered if this were too monstrous a claim, but having a profession to announce made her feel more secure.

"And you know of course of Hansi?"

Lois nodded.

"Yes," he said. "Of course. The Alsace of the spirit. Storks and spires and happy children." Lois thought of the placemats with the Hansi drawings she had been given as a wedding present. They were exactly that. But then much of Alsace did look like Hansi drawings, the houses she thought of as Tudor, the mountain villages.

"And Urquhart," he added. "You know the work of Tobi Urquhart?" He took Lois's hesitation as an answer in the negative and went on. "There is an exhibition right now," he glanced at his watch, "until the twenty-seventh at the *Bagatelle*. You know it?"

The *Bagatelle* was an old Rhine barge converted to an art gallery. It was anchored on the Lille River, and Lois and Richard passed it every day when they walked to the cathedral. She had seen the posters for the exhibit. "Beautiful paintings," the inspector said. "Illustrations for fairy tales filled with the cruelty that the tales themselves contain. Look especially at *Capon Rouge* and the wolf. It is elegantly erotic, as decadent as a Beardsley or a Klimt and thoroughly suitable for children."

"The body," Lois prompted. Somehow she hoped he might have information.

"Ah yes, the body," the inspector sighed as if he found the subject distasteful. "Always the question of the body." He paused. "Was it very horrible?" His voice was gentle and concerned.

"Yes," Lois replied, feeling tears well up at the unexpected sympathy. "It was grotesque. It was dark along the forest path, but then at the Druid shrine the sun shone through the trees, and he was just there, in the light. He was stretched out on the rock like a sacrifice."

"The crucified Canadian," the inspector muttered as if to himself. "You know, in the First War, it was the great myth. All the soldiers in the line told the story of a Canadian officer who had been crucified by the Germans within sight of his own lines. Nobody had actually seen it, but everyone knew someone who had. It happened at Béthune, it happened at Passchendaele, it happened at Vimy. An apocryphal story, of course, to illustrate the barbarism of the Germans, but why a Canadian?" He looked at Lois as if he expected her to answer.

"Was he a Canadian?" Lois asked.

"The body?" The inspector hesitated a moment, as if the information were confidential. "We don't know. We've phoned to the Canadian base at Lahr to see if there are any soldiers missing. But there are always soldiers missing and that may not help." The inspector looked sad.

"Perhaps they'll find the body," Lois said, to cheer him up.

"No, they won't find the body. There will be no trace of the body."

"But the blood. There will be blood."

"Yes. The blood of a chicken perhaps. They may find that."

"But what has happened?" The inspector seemed so dismally unhappy now that Lois wished she could change the subject.

"There is much speculation. My men believe it is a hoax perpetrated by your husband to gain publicity in the North American press. The workers believe it is a *crime passionelle*. You have been unfaithful to your husband. He has brought you here to witness the murder of your lover. They think you must be very hard because you do not weep."

Lois found this version almost comical, but was pleased at her celebrity. "And what do you think?" she asked.

"I think it is all very strange," he said. "A murder with no body, no motive and no suspects. Does it not strike you also as strange?"

"Yes," Lois said. "It is strange." And as she said this, it struck her as odd that the inspector did not seem particularly interested in her version of events. After all, she was the one who had discovered the body. She tried to think of details that might help an investigation.

"I didn't realize that he was dead until I came quite near to him," she told the inspector. "And even then, I wasn't sure until Richard went over to investigate."

"Your husband tells me he is a philosopher," the inspector said.

"He teaches philosophy at the university," Lois answered. "It's been disappointing for him here. He's writing a book about Heidegger. The fellow he was supposed to work with has disappeared, and nobody seems to know how to get in touch with him."

The inspector looked intensely interested.

"Monsieur Delacroix," Lois added.

"A pity," the inspector said, "about his father. A brilliant painter. Hervé was devastated by his suicide."

"Was it a suicide? Nobody said it was a suicide." Lois was pleased that she had this information for Richard.

"A messy business. At the family chalet in Provence." The inspector pointed a finger at his temple and pulled an imaginary trigger. "Hervé has, of course, taken the year off." Then in explanation the inspector added, "We fish together, Hervé and I. Every year in Norway."

"He's not coming back?"

"Only to fish."

"Why didn't they tell Richard that at the university?" Lois thought of Richard walking all the way to the university every day for no reason.

"It is the university," the inspector said. "One makes allowances. They believe it is possible that Hervé might return, though he has said he will not. They cannot discount the possibility of his return."

Lois wondered what this information might mean to Richard, whether he would want to stay in Strasbourg after all. She thought of her course and decided she would do everything in her power to convince him to stay. The sunlight which had been shining through the window onto the table disappeared and the room grew darker.

"What does he do, your husband?" the inspector asked. "How does he spend his time?"

Lois pondered the question. Richard watched television. He jogged. He walked to the university, and lately he had brought home a bunch of books about war, which he had found in the library of the Canadian Studies department. They had both been amazed that such a program should exist in France. It was difficult enough to find one at home. At the same time, it struck Lois that the question was odd.

"You don't suspect us, do you?" she asked.

"Oh no, of course not," the inspector protested. "It is a question of drugs, or spies, or organized crime. We are bit players. Your job is to discover the victim. Mine is to present as many details as I can to the officers of Interpol, who will fit this into some much larger puzzle. Perhaps years later in the back pages of a newspaper we will read that someone has been arrested for a murder at the Pagan Wall. Most likely, we will never hear of this again."

The inspector's pipe had gone out, and he lit it again. For a moment, Lois thought he looked comical, as if he hadn't quite dressed for his role. He leaned towards her and said in a confidential tone, "My job is to investigate the teller of the tale so that I can assess the information I am given, determine how much weight to give each detail. You see, the event is over. It has disappeared into time. I am left with a story. I wish that story to be as complete as possible. I wish to have the biography of the storyteller, to know

41

the other stories he has told. A murder has occurred. All the necessary details for its solution were present here today. You and your husband noticed a million details today, but you remember only a select few. If you had come prepared for a murder, you would have noticed others. I will not solve this murder, but if I can discover the correct details and put them in the right order, then someone who has more details than I have will discover the murderer."

"I'm not sure I understand," Lois said.

"Think of this as a novel," the inspector answered. "And imagine that this is chapter ten. Imagine a reader who has read the first nine chapters. Would not that reader, who knows the names of the characters, who has seen the pattern of events, be more able to predict the ending than we who have read only this tenth chapter? And is it not important that the events of chapter ten, after all the most interesting and important chapter, be conveyed to him clearly?"

Lois nodded. "Richard takes notes," she said. "Since he found out that Delacroix wasn't there, he has been taking detailed notes and reading books about war." She thought that Richard's habit of note-taking might make him a better witness.

"What does he take notes about?" the inspector asked.

"Everything," Lois said. "About bricks and their shapes and textures. About roofs and canals. About clothing. Mostly just about ordinary things." Telling these intimate details about Richard made Lois feel she was betraying him. He was even shy about telling her about his notes. He would not be pleased that she had told a stranger. Still, she went on. "The other day, he stopped at a clothing store and spent an hour describing everything in the window."

"He is curious about things," the inspector said, apparently pleased. "He is a writer."

"No," Lois said. "Though I think he should be. He'd be better at it than philosophy. Actually, he hates philosophy." Lois's sense of betrayal was even stronger now. Shortly after her first marriage she had had a brief affair with a co-worker in an office where she had once worked, an older man. She remembered that he had told her intimate details about his wife, and she had been appalled. She had not wanted to know this other person so intimately, and she sensed that his violation of his secret life with his wife made him untrustworthy. She had said nothing about her husband and was proud of her fidelity. He had been bewildered when she broke off the affair after a couple of meetings. Now, she felt she was betraying Richard more profoundly than she had betrayed her first husband.

"He is a romantic?" the inspector probed.

"He is a good man," she answered defensively. "He succeeds at everything he does."

The inspector saw that he had pushed too far, and changed the subject. "Ah," he said, "perhaps I have engaged in too much idle talk. You are not planning on leaving soon?"

"Just for a holiday. We are going south for three weeks."

"You are rich. You can holiday in the south."

"No, not really. Actually, Richard is on a reduced salary during his sabbatical. And I'm not working at all. We're certainly not rich. But we have saved for this."

"Good. Then I will see you on your return." He paused. "They have come back." He indicated the window, and Lois could see one of the gendarmes, though she could not see Richard. The window was to the inspector's back, and Lois wondered how he could have known of their return. The inspector got up just as the little commissionaire entered the room.

"I'm sorry," he said, "but I must . . . ," and he shrugged his shoulders, as if that were all the explanation necessary. As the inspector left, the little commissionaire touched her arm and said, "Je vous en prie?" indicating the door the inspector had left open.

***

Richard had to stop jogging and wait for the traffic light to change at the pont John F. Kennedy. A light rain had been falling for weeks. A woman on the other side of the street had stopped so that her dog could shit in the middle of the sidewalk. The dog was a

Doberman pinscher, and even though it seemed embarrassed in its odd posture, it still looked vicious. *Méchant chien,* Richard thought, starting to jog again now that the light had changed.

Richard had decided that if he were ever going to be fluent in French, he would have to learn to think in the language. At first he had been excited to discover that he could function in the language, ask directions, buy things in stores, hold brief conversations about the weather. Now he was becoming more frustrated. He could understand when people spoke directly to him, but on the street, he would catch brief snatches of conversation which would drift into incoherence. He would watch television, confident that he could understand everything, until someone from a rural area was interviewed and then he would not understand a word. Lois was going to take classes when they got back from their trip south. Maybe he would too. Each morning as he jogged, he held a sub-vocal conversation with himself in French.

Just before he reached the rowing club, Richard took the three steps down from the sidewalk to the path that ran along the canal. The dogshit was heavier here, and he had to keep his eyes on the ground. A sight-seeing boat filled with tourists churned past, and several of them waved. Richard waved back. He crossed the canal at the footbridge, speeding up so the turnstile spun as he slipped through. A couple of cyclists moved into single file so he could pass. At each end of the footbridge was a sign forbidding cyclists, yet in the six weeks Richard had jogged this route, he had never encountered a pedestrian on the bridge. It seemed to be used exclusively by cyclists.

By the time Richard passed the Palais de l'Europe the rain had started to fall heavily. Buses parked near the sidewalk were filled with tourists waiting for a break in the rain. The pain in his chest that had flared up a few moments before, as he passed the Foire de Printemps, seemed to have vanished, and Richard picked up speed tentatively, conscious of the rhythms of his body. Indigestion, he decided. The pain seemed to have nothing to do with effort. It was as likely to come when he was lying still as when he was running hard. Lois wanted him to go to a doctor, but Richard resisted. He'd had indigestion all his life. It ran in the family, some failure in the balance of acids in the stomach. He tried to think of the French word for *antacid*. *Antacide?* Words like *soulagement* and *dérangement* flitted somewhere in his mind, but he couldn't frame a sentence.

Richard remembered that he had to phone the inspector. He had promised that he would let him know when they were leaving. Two young men in raincoats gave Richard a thumbs-up sign as he met them. Richard felt his body moving faster as he passed and had to make a conscious effort to slow down. He couldn't tell whether the water that dripped from his forehead was sweat or rain.

The inspector had been interested in Richard's note-taking, though not in the notes themselves. He had asked Richard dozens of trivial questions about how he selected the details he chose to include in his notes. At first Richard had told him that the details were random and arbitrary, what happened to be in his way when he felt like making notes, but even as he said that, he realized there would be some principle of selection operating. The same evening they had returned from Mont Ste. Odile he had re-read his notebook, a green children's notebook that Lois had bought, intending to keep her own journal, but had given to him when she found she didn't want to use it. All its details, he discovered, were architectural. He had no notes about people and almost none about the natural world. The construction of roads and bridges, the items in stores, the pictures on advertisements and posters, these made up the bulk of his observations. He had sat down and written for two hours, trying to recall every detail of the walk, the body, the conversation with the inspector.

The interview with Kessler had lasted much longer than Richard had expected, and it hadn't been anything like what he expected of a police interview. The inspector had rambled, told anecdotes and asked questions that seemed to have nothing to do with the body. At one point Richard had asked him why all the signs for sex shops in Frankfurt were in English. Kessler had told him that there was no word for *sex* in German, and so they had to borrow it from the English. Or yes, there was a verb, *geschlechtsverkehr*, which meant something like "gender-traffic" or "gender-trading," but it was not the same as in English, where sex seemed to be an object rather than a relationship. A commodity. The sex shops, he had explained, were the residue of the war. They had come into being to serve the occupying forces, and they remained to serve the tourist trade. The pornography districts were always near foreign bases.

The allée de la Robertsau was unusually quiet. Most days, Richard had to wait for a break in the traffic before he crossed the street and rounded the corner to what he had begun to think of as the home stretch. Now, he crossed at the little boulangerie where each morning he bought the day's baguettes. A shiny black motorcycle was parked right on the sidewalk, and as he slowed to avoid it, Richard looked into the window of the boulangerie. Inside, he could see a young couple, both blond and dressed in identical black leather suits. They were poring over a map, and the old woman who ran the place was helping them. For a moment Richard thought they might be the couple he had seen in the parking lot at the abbey, but the image was too fleeting for him to be sure. He looked for a silver Mercedes and counted three parked between him and his turnoff at the rue Schweighaeuser.

Back at the studio, Richard stripped. His tracksuit was soaked from a combination of rain and sweat. It would take two days to dry, Richard knew. He was beginning to resent wearing clothes that were always damp and smelling vaguely of mildew. Very unusual weather, everybody told him. The worst spring in living memory. It's normally dry and warm in the spring. Except for that day at the Pagan Wall, it had been three weeks since Richard had seen the sun. He worked his way through his exercise program with slow deliberation, curls, sit-ups, push-ups, stretches. He thought of himself as chaotic and disorganized, but he loved the absolute rigidity of his program, repeated identically every day.

He had just settled into the bathtub when the bell rang. It would be Lois back from the library. He stepped from the tub, pressed the button, counted to ten, then pressed it again. He settled back in the tub and watched the water make its slow progress in immersing him. Lois, annoyed by the water system, talked frequently with the landlord, a Lebanese physicist who seemed to believe the problem was sand in the lines. He had come over a couple of times, a short, heavy-set man, who spoke of bleeding the lines as if it were a medical procedure. Nothing he did changed anything, and Richard was sure the problem was insoluble, a legacy of the past century, when the house had been built.

Richard lay in the bath until the water became uncomfortable. There was no way of warming it without keeping a steady flow from the hot water tap. Still, it was the first bathtub he had ever found that fit him. He could stretch out full-length. In the cramped studio, this was the only luxury. He dried himself with a towel that was still soggy from the dampness of the room.

He dressed in the hallway that also served as a closet. They were going to Paris on the afternoon train and Richard wanted to be comfortable. He chose a pair of grey corduroy pants and a white shirt. He couldn't find his blue sweater and he called for Lois. She didn't answer. Richard walked into the main room of the studio, repeating her name, and saw the inspector seated in the armchair, reading from the green notebook.

Kessler looked up when Richard entered. "You write well," he said. "I like your descriptions. It is important not to forget to be astonished."

The inspector's decision to read his journal struck Richard as so deep a violation of his privacy that he didn't know how to respond. Kessler was still wearing his khaki raincoat, and in spite of his jaunty moustache he looked as shabby as the old green armchair in which he sat.

"Thank you." Richard was uncertain whether the sarcasm in his voice would be evident to the inspector. At any rate, Kessler appeared to take no notice. "It's interesting, isn't it, how a diary lies, how you always miss the most important things. Of course, yours is a journal, not a diary, and so you are free from having to make personal declarations. I prefer that sort. Give me the objective journal where the writer's disguises reveal him most fully."

"It's a private journal," Richard said. "What is in there is none of your business."

"Oh, but it is," the inspector told him, holding the journal in the air as if he intended to hand it to Richard, but then drawing it back. "I am attempting to solve a crime to which you are a witness. I might have seized that journal as evidence and taken it home to read at my leisure. May I have the picture?"

"What picture?" Richard asked.

"The picture of the body on the altar. You neglected to mention it. Since we do not have a good solid material body to work with, we will have to make do with an image. Don't worry. The image will be almost as good as the body for our purposes, though it will be difficult to do an autopsy. There's not much we can do with mere nothingness."

"I forgot," Richard said. "I absolutely clean forgot about the photo when I was talking with you."

"But you did not forget to remark on it in your journal?"

"I didn't make the connection."

The inspector seemed skeptical.

"Honestly, I simply failed to think about it." This was a half-truth. Richard had not made the connection as he wrote in the diary, but the next day, as he was jogging, he had realized with a shock that he had the picture. He had intended to give it to the inspector as soon as it was developed, but he wanted to see it first, and he was not certain whether the inspector would show him the picture if he surrendered the film. "Actually," Richard confessed, "I did think of it later, but I had already sent in the film to get it developed. I was going to give it to you when it came back."

"Good," the inspector said. "Then may I have it?"

"I haven't picked it up yet. It wasn't ready. Lois might have it when she comes back from the library. She walks right by the photo shop."

"What is the name of the shop? I can get it myself."

"I don't know," Richard said. "I can't remember the name. But it's just a half-block away. Something *Papeterie.*"

"Will your wife be long?"

"No. I don't think so. She should have been home by now." Richard looked at his watch. It was twelve thirty.

"You took other pictures I presume. The abbey, the crypt, the people in the parking lot."

"I don't know. Lois took the pictures. All but the body." It struck him then that whoever had done the murder might be in the background of one of the photographs. "Do you know who it was?" he asked. "Was it a Canadian soldier?"

"We don't know," the inspector said. "The Canadian army is loath to admit that any of its soldiers are missing. Your photo is a lucky break. Now we will be able to identify the body. We may even be able to determine whether it was in fact dead."

Richard looked at the inspector.

"It was dead all right," he said.

"Well, it might have been a joke played on you. An actor feigning death. When you leave, he simply walks away."

"The blood. There was blood," Richard reminded the inspector.

"It might have been tomato juice."

"Was it?"

"No," the inspector said. "It was blood. Type A. RH positive." Richard went to the window and looked out over the flags of the European nations at the entry to the allée de la Robertsau. He half expected to see Lois rounding the corner, but she did not appear.

"Won't you take off your coat?" Richard asked the inspector.

"Thank you." The inspector took off his coat and draped it over the back of a chair. "You know of Lacan?" he asked.

Richard nodded. "A psychoanalyst."

"Yes," the inspector said, "but also much more. He is popular also on your side of the Atlantic?"

"Mostly among the literary types. I don't think he's taken seriously by psychologists."

"I worked with Lacan. I was his patient." The inspector looked at Richard to see if there would be a reaction to this confession.

"Isn't that unusual?" Richard asked. "Back home the police are not very keen on psychoanalysis. They leave that to the criminals."

"It was not because I was mad," the inspector informed Richard. "I wanted to be an actor. I had auditioned twice for the Ecole Nationale here in Strasbourg, but they had turned me down. A question of self-knowledge they told me. And so I went to Lacan to find that knowledge."

"And did you find it?"

"I found a story. The story of my life. A brutal father, a gentle mother, a monstrous self. Everybody's story."

"Not mine," Richard said. "I was the oldest of nine children. Both my parents were gentle. We lived in the country where we couldn't get into trouble and everybody was allowed to do anything he wanted. There was no brutality. There wasn't even any discipline. When I got older I went off to the university. The first time I came back, I discovered that my bed had been given to a younger brother, and I had to sleep on the chesterfield. I was treated as a guest. Everybody was polite to me, but it was clear that I no longer belonged. Since then I haven't been back, except as a guest."

"It was not a close family?"

Richard thought about that. "Yes, it was a close family. I don't know why I'm telling you this. But my parents had only so much to go around. There wasn't enough for nine children, so they simply set me adrift."

"And you are drifting still?"

Richard ignored the question. "Kessler," he said. "That's German isn't it? How does a German come to be a French police inspector?"

"It's Alsatian," Kessler replied. "Neither quite French nor quite German. And so I find in myself the old *Erbfeindschaft*, the inherited animosity between the French and the Germans. The part of me that is German does not like the French part, and vice versa."

"That must be fun," Richard said. "Carrying around a thousand-year-old conflict in your head."

"Interesting, yes," Kessler said. "Fun, no."

The bell rang and Richard got up. "That will be Lois," he said.

Richard stepped out of the studio into the staircase, leaving the inspector alone in the room. He could hear Lois below, opening the mailbox which, though locked in the house behind a locked gate, was itself locked and could be opened only with an enormous key. In a moment she appeared around the landing, her books over her shoulder in the enormous purple combination purse and briefcase she had bought for the trip and already regretted.

"Another letter from Mom," she called, "and something from the university for you." Lois's mother lived near them at home, but Richard had always thought of her relationship to Lois as distant. They phoned each other every week, but sometimes months went by without their meeting. Now, she sent a letter every day. Sometimes the mail would get bunched up and they would receive four or five letters at a time. Lois explained that her mother loved writing letters, that she liked people more in the abstract than in the flesh. Nobody else wrote them any letters, and Richard had already begun to look forward to the daily touch with home.

"Did you get the pictures?" he called.

"Yes," she answered. "And the picture you took of the body turned out. Now they're going to have to believe us." Her look of triumph turned to surprise, and Richard sensed rather than saw that Kessler was behind him.

"That's wonderful," the inspector said. "I can hardly wait to see it." Richard had the sudden feeling that this was a moment he was going to remember, himself and Kessler looking over the bannister at Lois poised awkwardly on the steps, standing in the light and looking up at them.

In a moment they were settled in the studio. Lois offered to make coffee, and, though Kessler refused, Richard accepted, and Kessler, seeing that coffee was going to be made anyway, agreed to have a cup. Richard and the inspector both tried to explain to Lois the occasion of their being in the apartment together, as if they were small boys who had been caught doing something they shouldn't. Lois extracted the photographs from her bag and handed them, a bit defiantly, to Richard. Richard expected the inspector to leap to his feet and look at the photos, but the inspector remained in his chair and chatted with Lois. He asked Lois whether she had had a chance to see the Urquhart exhibition, and to Richard's surprise, she answered that she had.

The two photos of the body were on top, and Richard realized that Lois must have already looked at them. The photos were identical, as if they had been made from a single negative. Richard stared at the top photo, knowing the inspector would take them away and wanting to memorize the details. The body did not look dead. It looked like a man resting on a slab of rock, having, as a joke, adopted the posture of a sacrificial victim, his hands outstretched to either side. The photo wasn't in perfect focus. The man had tightly cropped hair, and his face, though it looked peaceful, was bland and undistinguished. Light seemed to have obliterated his features. The dark-blue slacks Richard remembered were black, and the pale-blue shirt came out as white. It was impossible to tell what kind of shoes he was wearing but his socks appeared to be white. There was no sign of blood on the rock, and, when Richard reconstructed the angle of the shot in his mind, that made sense. The blood had been pooled close to the body on the left side and would be hidden in a picture taken from the right.

Richard leafed through the rest of the pictures. Himself on the steps at the beginning of the walk, a man and a woman just above him, a long panoramic shot that faded into the blue of pollution and was almost featureless, the central square of the abbey with dozens of tourists from the bus eating their sandwiches and drinking Kronenberg beer. He looked more closely and noticed that the couple with the motorcycle and the space-ship outfit were just coming in and paying their admission at the gate.

The rest of the photographs had been taken elsewhere. Richard lounged in front of the Palais de l'Europe. He stood in a crowd at the zoo, watching the storks, he looked in a window at an assortment of meats, though the glare on the glass mirrored the passers-by and you could not see what was in the window. A number of pictures had been taken of the back garden in bloom. The *Bagatelle* was moored on the Lille River not far from the cathedral. Lois was seated at a sidewalk cafe, raising a glass of Poire William. Richard had taken that photo himself. Lois looked beautiful in the picture, and he glanced up to see if she would confirm the image. She was standing in the doorway, telling the inspector about a drawing of little children that made the children look like evil dwarves.

Richard handed the photographs to the inspector. He leafed through them, spending no more time on the pictures of the body than any other. The espresso maker had started to bubble, and Lois took out three small cups from the shelf in the kitchen. She poured them each a cup. Richard and Lois both took their coffee black, and Richard was surprised to discover that the inspector wanted both cream and sugar. Lois had filled his cup too full to add either, and she had to pour his coffee into a larger cup.

"This is wonderful," the inspector said, and at first it wasn't clear whether he meant the coffee or the photographs. "We should have no difficulty making an identification now." He sipped his coffee and shuffled through the photographs again. "Do you recognize anybody?" he asked Lois. She walked over to the chair and sat on the arm by the inspector.

"Do you mean people I remember seeing at the abbey or people I knew before?"

"Either."

"Well, I saw almost all these people. In fact, I guess, since I took their picture, I did see them all." She took a photo from the inspector and scanned it carefully. "These people," she said, indicating with her finger, "had lunch at the same table with us. They didn't look as if they were dressed for hiking in the woods, but see, they're coming down the steps to the path around the Pagan Wall. I saw the woman later on the path, when I was looking for Richard after he fell, but the man wasn't with her anymore."

"By the way," Richard asked, "did you ever figure out what that business about the wire was?"

"It probably wasn't meant for you," the inspector replied. "I think you just walked into the middle of a drama that didn't have any parts for you, and you stumbled over one of the props."

"It was snare wire," Richard told him. "Just exactly the kind of snare wire I used to use myself for rabbits when I was a kid on the farm."

"The people at the gate, they were the couple with the motorcycle," Lois went on.

"And they were the couple I saw on the trail when I fell. Then we saw them at the castle putting something into the trunk of a car."

"I don't think so, Richard," Lois said. "I think those people were dressed in black. The people we saw with the motorcycle were much more colourful."

Richard remembered the couple with the motorcycle at the boulangerie. He was at the point of mentioning it to the inspector when Lois stood up and took one of the photos over to the window. She pored over it for a moment, and when the inspector stood up to join her she said, excited now, "Look, isn't that the guy who was killed, see, in the corner there, talking to the blonde girl?"

Richard looked over her shoulder. The face was indistinct, and didn't look to him like the face of the body. The woman beside him, though, was unmistakeable. She was the beautiful girl Richard had thought was retarded. In the photo, her face was animated.

"I don't know," the inspector said. "We'll be able to tell better once we get these things blown up. It's amazing what the lab can do these days. Computers will make these look like close-ups." He stood and picked up his coat in indication that he intended to leave. "If you wouldn't mind loaning me the negatives for a few days?" he said, a question that needed no answer.

"Don't you want the photos?" Lois asked him.

"No, you look at them carefully and see if you notice anything else. I'll drop by and talk to you soon."

"We're going on a holiday tomorrow," Richard reminded him. "I told you about that before. We're going south."

"Right," the inspector said. "Italy and Greece?"

"We're not sure," Lois said.

"Well, as soon as you get back, give me a call," the inspector answered. He handed Richard a card. It had his name and a phone number embossed over the raised design of a castle. "My private number," he explained. "If you phone the police department they will never have heard of me." Richard must have registered his surprise, because Kessler went on, "It's nothing mysterious. This is France, and we do things our way."

After the inspector left, Richard and Lois didn't say much. Richard spread out some crackers and pâté on the red and white dishes that had come with the suite, making sure he took the cracked plate for himself. He poured them each a glass of Pineau de Charente. The sweet taste was sharply refreshing.

"Well, here's to Europe," Lois said. "Not precisely what I had expected."

* * *

Lois pulled the blankets around her head but she could still hear the noise of the television set. Richard was watching a documentary about Turkey. It had been prepared by the Turkish government, Richard had told her, to show how European they were so that they could get into the Common Market. It seemed to be a variety show, and Lois had watched the first hour with fascination. The women were all blonde and blue-eyed. They didn't look like any Turks she had ever seen. The men were dark and stocky. They looked like Turks all right, but their routines looked like bad imitations of fifties American television. One of the guys seemed like a darker version of Red Skelton. Almost all the songs were in English, and the comic skits had been badly dubbed into French. Lois couldn't understand what they were saying, but every so often Richard groaned.

The other night they had watched the Eurovision song contest. Turkey was the only country that got no votes. The Turks had voted heavily for the Spaniards, perhaps, as Richard had suggested, because they had established stronger trading ties with them, but if the voting had been political, the Turks had made a serious miscalculation. The Spaniards cast their vote for the Swedes. The dark girl who had sung for the Turks, and danced a sort of belly dance as she did, had seemed profoundly earthy and sensual to Lois, though apparently she had offended the rest of Europe. The winner was an Irishman named Johnny, who had a flat, AM-radio sort of voice, and sang a song that had about three notes in it. This was his second win. He didn't seem to have any surname.

Lois gave up the effort of clinging to her side of the hide-a-bed and allowed herself to roll into the middle. Richard grunted and moved to accommodate her. He had been reading a book called *The Road Past Vimy* while he watched the frantic Turks. Now he put the book on the arm of the hide-a-bed and rolled over, pressing himself against her and reaching around to stroke her breast.

"No," she told him. "Tomorrow."

"Tomorrow we're going to Paris," he said, as if that were an insurmountable obstacle to lovemaking.

"They have beds in Paris" she said. "In fact, Paris is famous for its romance. You don't want to wear yourself out before you get there."

"I think I could handle two nights in a row," Richard said. "I did it once before in the late sixties."

"No sarcasm after midnight," Lois replied, getting out of bed and stumbling towards the kitchen. The studio was so small that when the bed was pulled out there was no way to move around without climbing over things. She poured herself a glass of brandy and perched on a chair. Richard clicked the remote control and the television faded, easing the room into darkness. A moment later Richard flicked on the lamp by the bed. Lois took a large sip of the brandy and felt her body warm. She had drunk two cups of espresso at supper, and she knew she was not going to sleep for a long time. Richard would be asleep in minutes, and she would listen to him breathe. Since he had started to worry about his heart she had paid attention to his breathing. It seemed that every so often he stopped breathing for a few seconds, then caught himself with a sudden deep intake of breath. She hadn't told him this, because she did not want to worry him.

"I'm going to go for a little walk," she told him. "You can go to sleep. I'll only be gone for a few minutes."

"Are you insane?" he asked, getting up and with some reluctance slipping on his grey corduroy jeans. "This is the main pick-up area for prostitutes in the city. The rue de la Forêt Noire."

"How do you know this?" she asked him. Lois had walked down the street several times on her way down to the little shop to buy magazines and newspapers. It carried the English version of *Time.* Richard read only French magazines, and he disapproved of Lois's choice. Even in English, he had told her, it was a right-wing rag. Lois didn't care. It seemed an oasis in the sea of language in which she felt herself drowning.

"I walk there every day on my way to the university," Richard went on. "The street is littered with condoms." Lois remembered seeing condoms on the edge of the road, but had assumed these were simply signs of the difference between French and Canadian customs.

"Actually," Richard continued, "the guy who runs the Xerox room at the English department told me. He doesn't like Germans, and blames the immorality of the area on them."

"I want to see the prostitutes." Lois said, and she realized that she was not being perverse, though sometimes she did act perversely and was sorry for it later. She really did want to see them. She wanted to see a transaction occur, a car stop, some negotiations, the woman enter the car. "I'm serious," she said, finding her sweater folded over the chair. "I really do want to see them."

"It's raining," Richard said, peering through the window into the third-storey darkness. "You'll need a raincoat and an umbrella, and the prostitutes will probably have closed up for the night."

The prostitutes had not given up, they discovered, soon after they had crossed the street and turned left. In a pool of light under a lamppost, the dark figure of a woman leaned into the passenger's window of a car. The rain was a light haze, and the slick streets reflected light sharply, though the night seemed even darker where there was no light. Apparently the negotiations were unsuccessful, because, just as Richard and Lois approached the woman, she stepped back from the car, and it roared away into the darkness, the wheels squealing in contempt.

Richard, embarrassed at their nearness to this encounter, moved closer to the hedge at the edge of the sidewalk. The woman leaned back against the pole. She wore a leather miniskirt and vest over a white blouse. Her high boots flared at the top, just above her knees, and it struck Lois that, though the woman was perfectly dressed for her craft, she would not have been out of place at a sophisticated cocktail party. Lois would have liked to talk to her, to discover what had brought her to this place on this rainy night, but she knew that was impossible. As they passed, Lois had a clear view of the woman's profile. She was pretty, almost beautiful. Her blonde hair was cut short and curled under. Her nose was finely shaped, her chin small but clearly defined. She had seemed like a large woman when she leaned into the car, but up close she seemed tiny. Lois guessed that she would not weigh more than a hundred pounds.

The next corner was empty, but, at the third, a dark woman, tall and slightly overweight, huddled under an umbrella. A silver Mercedes pulled up as Richard and Lois approached, a few words were spoken, and the woman climbed into the car. The car turned the corner and pulled over to the curb at the end of a short block that led to a little park.

"Want to walk by and see what they're doing?" Richard asked.

"Sure," Lois said, and turned the corner.

"Hold it." Richard caught her arm. "That's an easy way to get yourself killed. Come on." He led her down the street. Lois was disappointed. She was not sure what she wanted to see, but she was certain that some small drama was being enacted in that car. Richard's reluctance surprised her. He was so large that she had never imagined that he might be frightened. At home, he had always seemed unaware that places were dangerous, but here he seemed cautious.

"Have you ever gone to a prostitute?" Lois asked Richard as they turned around at the boulevard de la Marne, and crossed the street so that on the return trip they would be across the street from the women. Lois had counted nine.

"Of course not." Richard told her. "You've asked me that before and the answer is still no."

"I thought you might have lied because you didn't want me to know."

"Would you have minded?"

"No," Lois answered, and realized this was true. If Richard had been to a prostitute, he would have been able to tell her more.

"Would you like to try it?" Richard asked. "Stand on a street corner and sell yourself to whoever came by? Would you find that exciting?"

"Don't be stupid," she answered. "I just think it's fascinating that people do it."

"It's grim and sordid that they have to," Richard said.

On the way back, they saw two more transactions successfully concluded. The cars were both gleaming and expensive, and, in spite of the prejudice of the man who ran the Xerox machine, they both had French licence plates. The rain had started to fall more heavily now, and there wasn't room for both of them under the umbrella. Lois left the umbrella to Richard, and let herself get wet. When they reached the first lamppost, the blonde woman was gone. The pool of light was empty.

"Look," Richard joked. "There's a vacancy. You could start your career over there."

"That's not funny," Lois said, and Richard said he was sorry. They had left the gate open, but someone had closed it, and in the darkness Richard had trouble finding his key. They tiptoed up the stairs so as not to wake the sleeping landlord on the first floor and the sleeping professors on the second.

After they climbed into bed Lois ran her hands along her body. It felt cold and clammy to her, like touching someone else's flesh. Richard reached over and stroked her, and his hand seemed hot and dry.

"You want to make love now?" he asked her.

"Sure," she said. "Why not?"

* * *

The next morning, when they were walking to the railway station, Lois pointed out the window of the library where she sat. Every morning when Richard did his exercise program, Lois packed up her books and went there to study French. When Richard pointed out that she might as well study in the studio since he wasn't there anyway, she said it gave structure to her day. It was like going to work. An old man with heavy glasses looked out Lois's window. Lois explained that he was there every day, writing something into children's notebooks in an elegant hand. Sometimes he spoke to her in what she guessed was Alsatian, a strange mixture of German and French. She never understood what he said, but she always answered *oui*, and he seemed satisfied with that answer.

They were passing the cathedral now, the square in front dotted with tourists as usual. It had stopped raining, but the sky was still low and grey. Black men with armloads of belts and bangles and leather hats confronted the tourists. They had stopped approaching Richard about a month ago. He had decided that this was not because they recognized him but because he no longer looked like a tourist. He counted it a breakthrough, like the night Lois had wakened him to tell him he was talking in his sleep in French. A mime in top hat and tails pretended to be a wooden statue in front of a little bar. German tourists poured the water out of the plastic chairs, wiped the seats with napkins and sat down. A beautiful girl with long, dark hair and dressed in leather appeared for a moment in the doorway of a souvenir shop, then disappeared inside again.

Lois craned her head to look at the spire of the cathedral. "It's incredible, isn't it?" she said. The square in front of the cathedral was deliberately too small. There was no place from which you could see the entire cathedral. Inside or out, you had to look upwards. Richard assumed this was the intent of the builders. Everything made you look upwards and feel dwarfed.

"Just what I was about to say," Richard told her, and laughed. It was a secret ritual they had developed. Every time they passed the cathedral, one of them would say, "It's incredible, isn't it?" and the other would reply, "Just what I was about to say." They had become almost superstitious about it, afraid that if they broke the pattern, something awful would happen. Richard was aware that in France he had become superstitious. He sensed imminent catastrophe and his own helplessness. He guessed that his floundering in the sea of a new language was the cause of his anxiety, but that didn't help to release it. He had to concentrate as hard as he could in order to understand, and he carried that concentration into the minute details of everyday life.

"I like the idea of its being there," Lois said. "Even though we go away, it will still be right there until we come back."

Richard looked up at the spire a final time. He wondered whether their return would seem like a homecoming.

The Strasbourg station was as cold and uncomfortable as ever. The glass and chrome magazine store and the discreet lighting could not hide the fact that the station was slipping into decadence. Near the door, a couple of *clochards* sprawled on the floor beside dirty hats with a few francs spilled in them as bait. Awaiting their inheritance. Richard had noticed that Catholic countries gave money to beggars and Protestant countries did not. He regarded himself as an atheist, but decided that he was a Protestant atheist. He felt guilty if he did not give money, but even guiltier if he did. Still, in France he would pay his dues. He reached his hand into his pocket and found a ten-franc coin. He dropped it into the hat of the older *clochard*, who woke from his trance when he heard the heavy sound of the dropping coin. "Merci, merci, merci, merci, merci," he chanted. "Merci, m'sieur." The other *clochard* gave Richard a poisoned glare.

Richard spent twenty minutes in a line listening to an elderly woman argue with the ticket seller that the train stopped in a village called something like Armien or Ormien. She claimed her mother lived there and said that she made the trip every month. The ticket seller kept repeating, "C'est pas possible," and insisted there was no station in the village. He showed the woman his schedule. Richard was uneasy. The train for Paris left in ten minutes and there seemed no solution to the problem. In the end, the ticket seller gave her a ticket to someplace, and she left grumbling. Richard bought two tickets, stamped them as they entered the tunnel, and made his way to the stairs up to gate six.

He was already to the top of the stairs before he even looked for Lois. For a moment he didn't see her, then she appeared around the corner. She'd picked up a copy of *Elle* magazine and was reading it as she walked. She saw Richard and hurried. "Don't worry," she told him, "they're not going to leave early."

"I don't know," Richard answered. "French trains wait for nobody." He asked a woman in a vaguely official uniform if this was the train to Paris. The woman told him that it was the right train but that he would have to pay a supplement. She led him to a kiosk where another woman wrote out a special ticket and charged him two hundred francs. It was, she told him, a special fast train, its first trip out of Strasbourg, and there would be free champagne. Richard calculated the exchange in his head. For forty-four dollars there would have to be a lot of champagne.

Richard had not spoken to the inspector before they left, or rather, he had tried but failed to speak to him. He was tempted to phone the police, but remembered the inspector's instructions and called the private number. The telephone had been answered by a woman whose voice sounded terribly old and frail. No, she had told him, André was not there, he was not expected, who could know when to expect him, Richard should call Hervé, perhaps they were fishing.

"It seems an awfully long time ago," Lois said, when Richard wondered aloud whether he should make one more try to contact the inspector. "And besides," she added, "it's not your problem. You don't have to find the murderer."

"You're right," Richard told her, and he tried to relax. In the last few days before they left he had thought increasingly of the murder. The missing soldier. He wondered how the authorities would report the murder to the next of kin. Missing in action? Maybe the soldier had been from Winnipeg, had lived near them. Richard wondered whether he might have seen him, shopping in Safeway or having a beer at the Montcalm Hotel.

The first-class carriage looked as if it had been designed to travel in outer space. Shining chrome gleamed everywhere, and the seats were individual, large armchairs with plenty of foot room. The train started to move so smoothly that Richard was startled to discover they were leaving the station. A hostess came by and informed them there would be free wine or champagne in the bar car in ten minutes. She left them menus in case they would like to order lunch.

Richard wondered whether he should go to Freiburg. Heidegger had lived there for most of his life, had made the famous rector's address, which had destroyed his reputation there. Richard had seen pictures of Heidegger, a glum-looking man who also looked arrogant. He imagined Heidegger living in a little hut in the Black Forest, old and bent over like a troll or some sort of spirit of the woods. He would talk to the roots and branches. Would seeing the places where Heidegger had been matter at all? Richard doubted it.

The pain came again, a swift, sharp stab in the left side of his chest that startled him and made him freeze in the act of putting the menu in the leather side pocket of the seat. It faded, leaving Richard feeling empty, the reverberation of the pain still there though the pain itself had gone.

"What's the matter?" Lois asked, more curious than concerned.

"Nothing. Minor heart attack. I'll be okay in a second."

"Richard!" Lois seemed concerned now.

"It's nothing. Indigestion. It happens all the time. I was going to get some antacid, but I couldn't think of the word."

"It's the same word, only with an *e* on the end. I think. Just a minute." Lois scrambled in her purse for her *Petit Larousse*. The

Christmas after their wedding, she had given Richard a dieter's gourmet cookbook, which turned out to be designed for people who had recently suffered coronaries. The introduction, an upbeat story by the author about how she had fed her ailing husband salt-free, cholesterol-free foods until his damaged heart stopped beating in an automobile accident had so depressed Richard that he gave the book away.

"I am not going to have a heart attack," Richard told Lois. "I come from a large family and no one has ever suffered a heart attack." He told her this as much to reassure himself as to console her. Lois believed that all men were in continual danger of heart attacks, and the number of men she could name who had suffered early and crippling attacks was impressive. Richard had not feared for his heart before, but since he had married Lois it remained a nagging worry.

"No numbness in the arms?"

"No," Richard said. "Simple indigestion. Anyway, a man should at least have the freedom to contemplate his own death."

They decided against having lunch after deciphering the cost. In the bar car they drank their free champagne and listened to a young woman play piano and sing songs by Fauré, accompanied by a Spanish-looking man who played a mournful cello. They passed a moving stream of farms and towns and open fields. From time to time a canal would join the railway for a few miles, then wind off on its own way across the country. They got back to their seats just as the train pulled into the suburbs of Paris.

***

"There it is, Maubert Mutualité," Richard said, hoisting their bags off the seat beside him and pushing through the crowd to the door of the bus. Lois followed, pressing tightly against his back so that she would not be separated from him by the crowd. An old woman slipped between them and stood there triumphantly, blocking Lois's way to the door. Lois pushed around her, ignoring her protests, and burst out onto the pavement just as the bus began to move. Richard had already pulled the map from his pocket and was turning it in his hands, trying to make the streets on the map match the real streets of the city. He seemed oblivious to the chaos that surrounded them.

They were in some sort of market. Open stalls on the street were piled high with vegetables, green mounds of cabbages and lettuce, red and green and yellow peppers, orange carrots and bright-red tomatoes. The pavement was bright with water, as if it had just rained, and the colours of the vegetables were reflected in the pools. The noise of the street was loud and distracting. Hawkers shouted out their prices, and buyers disputed hotly with sellers. It was hard to tell who was a customer, who was staff. Lois caught a sharp whiff of fish and turned to see that she was standing right next to a stall where shrimp and scallops and oysters were displayed in beds of ice.

She realized with surprise that Richard was talking to her. "Just past that Vietnamese restaurant," he said, picking up the bags and walking past a table piled high with fruit, then winding his way through the maze of stalls, past baskets full of bottles of wine, across a plaza in front of a red and yellow ornately decorated building. They turned the corner onto a street heavy with traffic, and seemed suddenly in a different city. The brilliant colours of the market vanished, the street became grey, and the sound of traffic obliterated the calls of the vendors. Lois felt cheated, as if something rich and important had been taken from her.

"This is Monge," Richard said. "We'll be up a couple of blocks, then down a side street. Richard was carrying everything, including Lois's purse, and he looked a little ridiculous and out of place among the hurrying Parisians.

"Here, let me take some of that." Lois said, pulling the two travelling bags and her purse from his shoulder, leaving him with the big, red and blue backpack and his leather case.

"I'm fine," Richard said, but he seemed relieved that she had shouldered some of the burden. "That was terrific," he went on, "that market. Let's just get checked in and come back."

Lois was surprised at his response. She thought he hadn't even noticed where they were. They passed a store with wicker furniture displayed along the sidewalk and another with gleaming black Japanese pianos. They turned a corner down a narrow street that dropped sharply, and found themselves looking into the lobby of the Hotel Savoy. The glass doors threw them back their own reflection so that they seemed to be already standing inside at the desk.

They registered and explored their room. Richard was amazed by a shower that doubled as a steam bath. Then they went out to discover the city. Lois sensed an excitement in the air that she had never encountered anywhere else. The people on the sidewalks seemed filled with intent. A young man on roller skates hurtled down the street, keeping pace with the traffic. An old man with a long, yellow-stained beard walked a cat on a leash in front of a church. Lovers lurked in corners everywhere, nuzzling each other with an eagerness that Lois felt as a tightening in her own body. They stopped at a little pastry shop, and Richard bought them each an éclair. The street led downwards toward the river, and they could see the towers of Notre Dame.

Just as they reached the bottom of the street, Lois cried out in surprise. An old woman had slipped through the gates into the yard of an old grey church. As she moved into the courtyard, thousands of birds descended, fluttering around her, squawking and crying. She tossed handfuls of seed from an old brown bag she carried, flinging it high in the air as though to defend herself from the birds. She called to the birds in high, bird-like cries herself. Lois felt she had been touched by some moment of special grace.

"Look, Richard," she said. "That old woman. Look how the birds surround her." Richard put his arm around her, and Lois knew that he sensed her excitement. She wanted him to share the experience, to understand how special it was to be in Paris at this spot at this moment. She knew she would remember it forever, exactly as it was happening now.

"Maybe she's a witch," Richard said. "Maybe those are the spirits of people she's enchanted." Lois pressed herself against Richard, wanting him to hold her.

"Souls," she said. "They're the souls of her victims. She's feeding them manna and they're weeping because she won't let them go back to their graves." It was evening now. The sun had set, and even though the sky was still clear, the brilliance of Paris had faded into greys and browns. A slight breeze had begun to stir, and there was a chill in it.

It was dark in Notre Dame Cathedral when they entered. Hundreds of candles glimmered in trays, and Lois caught the sweet odour of the smoke. A priest was conducting a service, and about fifty people were sitting in the pews, taking part. Lois felt she was an intruder here, that these people deserved their privacy. The light from the candles and the sing-song voice of the priest made the space intimate and enclosed.

"Let's go," she whispered to Richard, and even her whisper sounded loud and intrusive.

"Okay," he answered. "You're the one who likes cathedrals."

They wound their way back through streets filled with little Greek and Italian restaurants, where men stood in doorways and shouted at them, inviting them in, offering special bargains, just for them. Richard bought them each a sandwich of meat carved from an enormous barbecued roast that turned on a spit in a brightly lit window. At night, the colours seemed as intense as they had during the day. Through windows, Lois could see red and white, and blue and white checked tablecloths with coloured candles. The sandwich had tasted wonderful at first, but after a few mouthfuls it tasted flat and fatty. Lois threw it into a trash can, and a man who had been lingering near a parked car dashed up and grabbed it. He brushed it off, and when Lois stared at him, he glared back fiercely and began to eat.

The next morning, Richard was glum. He had sat up reading about the war until late in the night. He had been drinking dark rum mixed with funny sweet Coke that he'd found in the little refrigerator by their bed, and now he had a hangover. He complained that the Coke was ridiculously expensive. Lois had woken up fitfully during the night, and, every time she opened her eyes, she had seen Richard sipping his rum, and brooding. He hadn't seemed to be reading, and she didn't know if he'd slept at all.

In the hotel restaurant, they were brought a pot of coffee and a half a baguette each by one of the tall, beautiful black women who apparently worked in the kitchen. The women shouted at each other and seemed genuinely angry. Lois asked Richard what they were saying. He told her that they had such strong accents he couldn't understand a word they said. Every so often, the *madame* of the hotel, a squat, ugly white woman, would enter the fray, shouting at each of the black women in turn. Lois was reminded of *Alice in Wonderland*.

"I suppose one of them will turn into a pig," she said to Richard.

"It will be the owner," Richard replied. "She's halfway there already."

They had decided to spend the day in museums, first the Pompidou in the morning to see modern art, then the Louvre in the afternoon. Lois wanted to see the *Mona Lisa*. She knew it would be a disappointment, but she wanted to see it anyway. Richard argued that trying to see the Louvre and the Pompidou in one day was insane.

"It will be a blur, " he said. "People take months just to see one of them properly."

"We are only reconnoitring," she reminded him. Back in Strasbourg, they had agreed that they would see as many things as they could this time. Later, they would make another trip when they could spend a lot of time looking at the things they really wanted to see. Richard had a way of becoming compulsively interested, and when that happened Lois knew it would be impossible to get him to do anything else. He was already absorbed in his books about the wars. She did not want him to get started on anything new here.

"Right," Richard said, "the entire history of the world's art in eight hours."

And it had seemed like that. Lois didn't like the Pompidou gallery, an odd blue building with its stairways and halls wrapped around the outside in tubes like exposed plumbing. Richard had explained that this was postmodern architecture, and claimed to like it himself. The main exhibit had been actual parts of airplanes that had crashed. Twisted pieces of metal had been welded to shiny pedestals and given long titles in French. Lois translated one of the titles as *Blue Madonna of the Waking Dawn*. She didn't bother asking Richard to help her. Whatever it actually was would be equally incomprehensible. She liked best the bread and camembert they had with a glass of beer in the upstairs gallery.

The Louvre was under renovation, and they had to enter from a door at the back of the building. By the time they reached the *Mona Lisa*, Lois was exhausted by the images that stretched to the very ceilings of the rooms. An area had been roped off, and a bunch of tourists strained at the ropes as a guide explained something to them in Japanese. The Japanese were short, and Lois could easily see over them. The *Mona Lisa* was under glass, but it looked exactly as it did in all the reproductions. She found she was pleased that it was so ordinary. It would have been disturbing to discover that it had some special meaning that you could only uncover by seeing the original. She thought about the bird woman. That was special. All day she had been haunted by the image of the old woman and her birds. Richard had been excited by a painting by Botticelli, but it had seemed stylized and dead compared to her own memory.

Then Lois was struck quite suddenly by what she would do. She would write a children's book about the bird woman, and call it "The Bird Lady of Paris." That would be its name. "The Bird Lady of Paris." She would do the illustrations first, then write a story to explain them. She was filled with an exhilarating energy. Richard had wandered off to another room. She could see him looking at a horse that was rearing thirty feet into the air. She felt herself quite alone in the room with the *Mona Lisa*. The Japanese tourists had vanished, and Lois was alone at the rope. She leaned over and whispered to the Mona Lisa, "Thanks."

Then, feeling vulnerable and alone, she looked for Richard, but he was gone. Lois hurried into the next room, where she had seen him staring up at the lunging horse. A few people sat around on the benches in the centre of the room, but there seemed to be a crowd in the next gallery. She hurried into the room, but she didn't see Richard anywhere. She pushed through the confused crowd. People were moving away from some centre to which she was drawn. Suddenly, she found herself looking down at an elderly woman who lay on the floor motionless. One of the guards had rolled up his jacket and put it under her head. The woman was dressed in a grey suit, which was hitched up towards her waist, showing her thighs. Her glasses still hung crookedly on her face, but her mouth was open and her eyes had rolled back into her head so that Lois could only see the yellowing whites. She looked very dead.

Something about the woman looked familiar, and Lois realized with a start that she had seen her before. She was the old German woman who had been with the beautiful girl at Mont Ste. Odile. Lois drew in her breath sharply, and the crowd turned to her. She could feel the pressure of hostile eyes on her. Mont Ste. Odile, the body, the inspector, everything that had seemed interesting before, a kind of puzzle, now seemed close and dangerous. She turned and started to run away from the woman on the floor. Somebody caught her arm and she spun around. A voice asked, "What's wrong? Do you know who she is?"

"No," Lois said. "I've never seen her before in my life." A sandy-haired man with an open face and freckles still held her arm. She pulled herself free, looking around for Richard, who was still nowhere to be seen.

"Look," the man said, "if you get in any trouble give me a call." He pulled a card out from his pocket and thrust it at Lois.

"Thanks," she said, and she slipped it into the pocket of her coat without looking at it. She hurried back the way she had come, not glancing back at all. Richard would be searching for her by now, and he would go to the *Mona Lisa*. They had agreed that if they ever got separated they would go back to the last place they had seen each other.

The *Mona Lisa* was not where Lois had remembered it. She wandered through rooms, all of which looked the same, and she had the sense that people were watching her. Finally, she asked a guard for help. He turned up his hands in confusion at her breathless English. Lois told herself to calm down, and she took a slow, deliberate breath. Then, as clearly as she could, she asked for directions in French. The guard listened, and answered something incomprehensible. Then, signalling for her to follow, he led her around a corner into the next room.

Richard was standing by the rope that fenced off the painting. He was talking to a girl with long, blonde hair. As Lois approached, the girl noticed Richard's glance of recognition and turned. Lois saw immediately that she was the beautiful girl from Mont Ste. Odile.

"Lois," Richard said, "I want you to meet Alexandra. She's just come to Paris to work as a *jeune fille au pair.*" Richard seemed flushed and embarrassed, uncomfortable to be making this introduction. "Remember," he said, "we saw her at Mont Ste. Odile?"

"Hello," Lois said, and the girl answered, "Hello."

"She's German," Richard explained. "She isn't really comfortable in English. She prefers French." The girl nodded as if to say this were true.

"Where did you find her?" Lois asked, realizing as she did that her voice sounded cold and mean.

"Right here," Richard said. "She was just standing here looking at the Mona Lisa, and I was waiting for you, and I realized I'd seen her before so I said hello."

Lois thought of the woman lying on the floor. "Her mother," Lois said. "Something's happened. I saw her collapsed on the floor in another room." She swept her arm to indicate the direction.

"Are you sure?" Richard asked, suddenly tense.

"I think so. A grey-haired woman about my size?" she asked the girl. The girl shook her head in incomprehension. Richard explained in French and the girl reacted in panic."

"Wo?" she asked. "Wo ist sie?"

"Hier." Lois answered. She felt pleased that she could understand the question and could answer. The German felt more comfortable to her than French did, more like her own language. She led Richard and the girl to the room where the woman had been, but she was gone. A few people stood around looking at paintings, and in the far corner the Japanese were listening to their tour guide as he pointed at a painting too small to make out at that distance. The guard by the door was not the one who had been there with the woman.

"It was right here," she said. "She had collapsed," and fearing to frighten the girl further, she added, "she probably fainted. It's so tiring walking around this place."

Richard asked the girl some questions in French, then talked to the guard. The guard didn't seem to know much. He had just come on duty. Yes, he had heard that a woman had collapsed. She had been taken away, he did not know where. Richard explained all this. They would have to go to the main office to get information.

There didn't seem to be any main office, other than the place that checked coats, but a few enquiries led them to an unobtrusive door and an extremely thin man who told them that they would have to consult the police. Richard argued with him, and after a few moments of head-shaking, he led them to an office and left them standing in the doorway while he telephoned.

"She is dead," he told them, as if that settled everything. "They believe that she is dead." He spoke to them in English in a light accent that did not sound French.

"Where is she?" Richard asked.

"You will have to go to the police station," the thin man replied, then shifted to French as if directions could be better given in that language.

"Right," Richard said. "Thanks." Lois had not understood a word of the directions, and the girl had not understood anything at all. Perhaps she did not even know that her mother was dead. She stood close to Richard, and did not ask any questions, as if that could keep her safe.

"We'll go back to the hotel," Richard told Lois, "and we'll talk there." Richard led the way towards the exit, but the girl held back, whispering something to Lois that she couldn't quite understand. Lois stopped Richard, and the girl pulled a black tag out of her pocket and pointed to the cloakroom. Richard took the tag and retrieved two bags and two nearly identical trenchcoats.

On the way back to the hotel, they passed what looked to Lois like the police station. At least, a couple of gendarmes armed with machine guns paraded back and forth in front of the building. She asked Richard, who said he thought it was an embassy. The girl said nothing, and seemed much younger now than she had before. She had apparently given herself into their keeping, and was without volition of her own.

When they were settled in the little cafe attached to the hotel and had ordered coffee, Richard took the girl's hand and spoke quietly. Lois felt as if she didn't belong there, as if she were spying on something personal that had nothing to do with her. The girl listened without emotion. She took out a little notebook from her handbag and wrote down some numbers for Richard. The coffee arrived, and Richard paid for it. Then he asked Lois to take care of the girl, and said that he would have to make some phone calls.

After he had gone, Lois tried to speak to the girl, but she didn't understand Lois's French. When Lois spoke to her in German, she answered in a volley that Lois failed to comprehend. Then they sat there silently. The girl began to weep, and Lois reached into her pocket for a Kleenex to offer her. She found instead the card that the American had slipped her. It said Robert Ferguson, Imports and Exports. It gave phone numbers in Paris, Toronto and Dallas. She realized then that the man was a Canadian, and she tried to remember what he had looked like. She found she couldn't remember him at all, except that his voice had sounded kind. Richard came through the door, and Lois slipped the card back into her pocket. There was no point in telling Richard about it. He would be angry if she told him, and it certainly wasn't her fault that the man had passed her the card.

Richard was intense when he came back. He switched between English and French. The girl was to be taken to the *au pair* service headquarters. They were expecting her. Everything would be taken care of. The *au pair* service was quite a distance by Metro. They would have to leave immediately. The girl stood up from her chair, and Richard helped her on with her coat.

At that moment, Lois had the premonition that he would leave her. The beautiful blonde girl standing beside him on the other side of the table seemed right for him. Richard's whole body seemed tense and alive.

"You go with her," Lois told him. "I'm terribly tired. I just want to go to bed."

"Are you sure you're all right?" Richard asked.

"I'll be fine," she answered. "I'd just slow you down. I really want to go to bed."

"Okay," he said. "I'll be back as soon as I can." Lois watched as they left the cafe. Richard took the girl's arm to steer her through the door in a way she remembered he had used to touch her. After they were gone, she went up to the room and got into bed. She wept for a few moments, then she remembered the old woman and the birds. In a few minutes she felt calm. If Richard was gone, he was gone. She would feed the birds.

She fell into a dream in which she was flying over the tiled roofs of Paris.

***

By the time Richard and the girl had reached the boulevard Ste. Germaine, a light snow had begun to fall, and through the blur the lights that were just coming on were large and round. The colours were all soft pastels against the uniform dark grey of the city. It seemed odd that snow should be falling, but everyone told him that this was the coldest winter in history. The girl clung to Richard's arm and leaned against him so that he had to walk more slowly than he had expected. They passed through the darkened market past the Maubert Mutualité entrance to the subway. Richard had checked with the hotelkeeper, who had shown him a map. The coloured lines had confused Richard, and he had decided that he could get the train he wanted by walking over to the rue St. Michel and catching the Metro there. The girl smelled faintly of perfume, and Richard wondered whether they looked like lovers to the people they met in the street.

The girl seemed to have given herself over entirely to Richard's care, and he found it difficult to talk with her. She answered every question with a brief phrase, switching now to a light but exotically accented English. She remembered Mont Ste. Odile, it had been her uncle's idea to go there. She had another uncle in Philadelphia. Perhaps some year she would go to the United States. She did not know anyone else there, though her uncle had known several people. Richard asked her about the couple on the motorcycle. She knew many people who had motorcycles. It was impossible to know.

They found their way through the staircases of the Luxembourg Metro and settled onto the train. The girl seemed more willing to talk now. Her uncle owned a trucking company. His trucks carried things around Europe. He lived in Kehl, but he did most of his business in Strasbourg.

Something in the train, perhaps the light or the blurred faces on the platforms as they passed, brought the girl back to her grief, and she leaned her head against Richard and began to weep. She spoke softly in German, and Richard stroked her hair and whispered back to her in English, "It's okay, it's okay, it's okay." The only other passengers on the train were black, three very tall, very thin men who spoke to each other in some language full of clicking sounds. They got off at Denfert Rocherau, and Richard barely realized in time that it was also his stop. He and the girl leaped from the train just as the whistle sounded and the doors began to close.

He had lost all sense of direction when they emerged from the Metro. During the trip, it had become dark, and the snow had become heavier. It made a carpet about a half-inch thick on the streets, and his feet were wet before they had gone a block. Richard wasn't sure where they were going. He was hoping to find someone he could ask directions from, but the streets seemed oddly deserted. It was only seven o'clock. There should have been people everywhere. The girl seemed to recognize where they were. She led him around a corner, and suddenly they were at a door with a sign that read Bureau des Visites Etrangères.

They were greeted by a tall, hefty woman with a fluty voice. The girl, Alexandra, spoke to her in German, and the woman answered. For several moments they spoke, then Alexandra thanked Richard for everything, and shook his hand. The woman motioned for her to follow her through a door into the interior of the building. For a moment, Richard felt panic. The girl was going to disappear, and that would be the last he would see of her. He didn't even know her last name. He called to the woman, who had already disappeared, and she came back. Richard explained that he was a friend of the family, that he would have to speak to the uncle. He asked for the name of the family where she would stay. The woman seemed suspicious, but she wrote down a name and address on a piece of paper. Before she gave it to Richard, she spoke in German to the girl. The girl looked surprised, but she nodded, and answered something Richard did not understand. The woman passed him the paper, and she and the girl disappeared through the door, leaving him alone in the anteroom. Richard glanced at the paper. The address he had been given was in Kehl,

Germany. He put the paper away in his wallet, then walked out into the snow.

The streets, which had seemed empty moments before, now were filled with people. The Metro was jammed, and Richard had to stand all the way back to the Luxembourg station. He didn't think about Lois at all until he was nearly back at the hotel. He wanted to talk to the inspector. He was certain the girl was somehow the key to what had happened at the Pagan Wall. He remembered the scent of her perfume and her soft weeping.

Richard did not want to go back into the hotel. He would have to explain things to Lois, and yet there was nothing he could explain. He stopped at a bar and ordered a beer. The bar was full of men in groups of three or four, talking intensely. A couple of them were drinking beer, but most had a green liquid that turned cloudy when they mixed it with water. Richard found himself unable to think in the bar. All that filled his mind were vague impressions, the texture of the seats on the Metro, the softness of the girl's hair, the fuzziness of the early evening light. For a long time he sipped at his beer, looking out the window at the cars that barely crawled down the snow-covered street.

When he walked out of the bar, he was struck with the melodramatic nature of his position. Here he was in Paris, where he had never been before, brooding on a murder and still entranced by his brief encounter with a beautiful girl. His response to the girl, he decided, was adolescent. It was a situation with no possibilities, and if he thought about it rationally for a moment, he did not wish it to have any possibilities. He remembered the pain of those months when his marriage had broken up and the difficulty that he had felt in committing himself to Lois. He felt a great weariness. He could not go through that again. Lois, back in their bed in the hotel, was less threatening now. He was eager to get back.

When he got back to the room, she was asleep. Richard entered as quietly as he could. Lois was a light sleeper and he expected she would wake up. He was quiet more as a gesture than in any real attempt to keep her from waking. He turned on the lamp by the bed. Lois had rolled over to the far edge and wrapped herself in the covers. Her breathing was deep and regular. Richard took the key from the dresser where he had placed it, and unlocked the refrigerator. He took out a bottle of Coke, found the bottle of rum in his suitcase and mixed himself a drink. It struck him that he had not had supper, and he was hungry. He thought about asking Lois if she wanted to go out for something, but she was sleeping more deeply than he had ever seen and he did not want to wake her.

He went back to the suitcase and took out the three books he had found in his office at the university. The office doubled as the library for the Canadian Studies Centre. He'd read *Generals Die in Bed* in Strasbourg, a novel about the Canadian army in the Great War, and he was beginning to conceive of a trip up to the area of the Somme. He'd always planned to read something by Margaret Atwood, and he'd brought a copy of *Dancing Girls* with him. The third book was by a writer he'd never heard of, Robert Kroetsch. The book was called *What the Crow Said,* and Richard had taken it because he'd skimmed the first chapter and it was about a girl who was seduced by a hive of bees.

It seemed too much to start a new book, so Richard opened *Generals Die in Bed* again and began to re-read the section where the narrator stuck his bayonet into the German soldier. The language was raw and plain, almost clumsy. The sentences were short and simple. Richard read slowly through a scene where the Canadian and German soldiers were trapped together in a shell crater during a bombardment. They spoke to each other as tenderly as brothers. When he reached the end of the section, he could feel that his eyes were full of tears. He flipped through the book to the section near the end where the Canadian army mutinied in Arras. He had never heard of this mutiny. The description of the stores full of rich goods and the starving soldiers looting the place filled him with a desire to go there. He decided that he would suggest it to Lois in the morning.

Richard mixed himself another drink of the thick, dark African rum. He opened the Atwood book and selected a story called "Rape Fantasies," but the narrator of the story had such a relentless perky optimism that he put it down and turned on the television set. The first channel he tried had a game show, the second had a group of people sitting around a table talking furiously. Every one of them was smoking, and the cigarette smoke hung as a diseased haze. On the third channel, sepia-toned horses pulled an artillery gun through a sea of mud. Then soldiers plodded through trenches half-filled with water, and ran out into a formless no-man's-land where they died in awkward poses. The announcer, in the sombre tones reserved for documentaries about war, explained that these were the Canadian forces at Vimy Ridge. Thirty-six hundred men had died in order to gain three miles of territory. The camera focussed on broken shells and old rifles, photos obviously taken much later than the footage of the men and horses, but still old enough to share the grey-brown quality of old film.

Richard watched the film intensely. It appeared to be a Canadian film. Several old men were interviewed in an old-folks' home. One described how his hand had been severed by machine-gun fire at Passchendaele. Then the footage showed more men dying and horses exploding in a place that didn't look any different from Vimy Ridge. Richard found that he had finished his rum, and mixed another one, using the last ice cube. He was beginning to feel dizzy, but he also felt comfortable and warm. The film seemed to have been presented especially for him, and he was disturbed when the television burst into colour, and a news announcer promised a sight of Helmut Kohl immediately after the ads that followed. He turned off the set as an elegant couple, both smoking, sat down to an elegant meal. He turned out the light and undressed in darkness.

Richard tugged gently at the blankets in which Lois had rolled herself. For a moment she resisted, then she rolled over into his arms. He was startled to discover that she was weeping. "I thought you weren't coming back," she wept. And Richard, not knowing what to say, whispered, "It's okay, it's okay, it's okay."

* * *

Lois woke up in the morning to the door clicking shut. She opened her eyes to see Richard, his face flushed by cold, standing at the foot of the bed. He was wearing his leather jacket and a plaid scarf.

"Where did you get that scarf?" she asked.

"I bought it at a little sidewalk stand over on St. Michel," he told her. "Are you over your craziness?"

"I think so," Lois said. "I was just in a really strange mood. What time is it?"

It was eight o'clock. She had slept for most of fourteen hours, and she had wakened out of a dream of terrifying loss when Richard had come to bed. She remembered weeping and Richard comforting her. She could see on his face that he was still bewildered by her reaction. At the same time, she felt that something important and reassuring had happened during the night. She thought of the bird woman and her birds and the strange, old, long-bearded man with his cat on a leash. She imagined them to be friends, huddled together in some alleyway during the cold winter nights. Their images were so clear to her that she wanted to start drawing them right away.

Richard was intense and nervous. He stared through the window down into the courtyard below their room, and he kept looking at his watch and saying that if they did not hurry they would miss breakfast. Lois wanted to take a shower. She told Richard to go down and order. She would follow in a couple of minutes.

The shower was in what had obviously at one time been a closet. It was narrow, dark with royal-blue ceramic tiles, but the water was hot, and the shower head sprayed the water like hard, sharp needles. Lois felt exhilarated after her long sleep. She scrubbed herself hard, washed her hair, then stepped out into the cold room. She towelled thoroughly, until she felt her body warm and red. A pretty good body, she thought to herself, catching a glimpse in the mirror. Breasts a little too large and calves a little too thin, but otherwise pretty good. She had noticed, working out in the gymnasium and at the swimming pool, that other women of her age had started to sag and lose their shape. That hadn't happened to her yet. She remembered one of Richard's friends saying at a party that after forty a woman loses either her face or her body, and she wondered which would go first. She put on her make-up, naked in front of the mirror, then dressed and went down to join Richard.

Richard was just finishing his baguette when Lois joined him. The tall black woman came over immediately and poured her a café au lait, and handed her a baguette and a pot of strawberry jam. Lois was hungry and only then remembered that she had not eaten the night before. "I could eat a horse," she told Richard.

"Around here you have to read the menus carefully or you might end up doing just that," Richard replied. A truck was parked in front of the window of the cafe, blocking off all traffic in the street. Several of the cars behind the truck honked their horns from time to time, and one of the drivers got out of his car and went over to argue with the driver of the truck. Nothing seemed to make any difference, and the driver sat impassively in his seat, pretending not to hear the man who shouted and shook a fist at him.

"She says it was a goat," Richard said.

"What was a goat?"

"What they loaded off the motorcycle into the trunk of the car at Mont Ste. Odile. She says her uncle bought it from a farmer for meat. The Martians on the motorcycle are the farmer's children."

"She's lying," Lois told him.

"No, I don't think so," Richard said. "She didn't seem like she was lying. I think she simply didn't understand what was going on."

"Just because she's beautiful doesn't mean that she can't tell a lie," Lois said. "All the beautiful girls in your classes are brilliant. I don't think you have a lot of objectivity when it comes to beautiful women."

"That's not true," Richard said. There was a tone of resentment in his voice. "Or not entirely true, at any rate. Anyway, this is a girl, not a woman, and she was pretty broken up."

"She was hardly broken up at all," Lois answered. "I don't believe that woman was her mother. If her mother was dead, she would have been a lot more upset than she was."

"She was in shock."

"Well, I think she's due for more shock. You'd better phone the inspector. This might be all he needs."

"No, I don't think so." Richard looked embarrassed. He hesitated a moment then said, "Look, I'll talk to him when we get back. If I call him now, he'll insist we stay in Paris until he comes here, then we'll have to wait for days, and our Eurail passes will be all used up. We won't be able to go anywhere."

Lois did not want to stay in Paris. The bird woman and the cat man were all she wanted of Paris for a while. "All right," she said. "But I think you're just trying to protect the girl, who is probably a mass murderess. And I think she's a lot older than she looks." Lois wasn't sure why she had said this, but it struck her at that moment that it was probably true. The girl had looked older when they had first seen her.

Lois discovered that she had already eaten her entire baguette, and she looked around to see if anyone had seen her. There was no one else in the cafe except the black woman waiting to clean the table.

"Don't be stupid," Richard said. "She's not a murderess."

"I don't care about the stupid murder anyway," Lois said. "I want to go south and get warm."

"Gare d'Austerlitz." Richard told her. "That's where we go to catch trains going south. I checked with the hotelkeeper this morning."

"Well, let's go then," said Lois. "Let's head south." She got up from her chair, and Richard followed her up the stairs to their room. The moment they entered, Lois sensed that something was wrong. "Wait," she told Richard, pushing him back to the door.

"What is it?" he asked.

"I don't know. I think somebody has been in here."

"Chambermaids," Richard told her, pushing past. "Strange people sometimes go into your room in a hotel. They're called chambermaids." Nevertheless, he moved a bit cautiously, flinging open the bathroom door and looking into the closet. The bed had been made, but everything that had been on it had been put back exactly as it had been, Richard's sweater, Lois's make-up bag, even a single sock, its mate lying on a chair. Richard seemed relieved to find that there was no one there, and his exuberance seemed to Lois a little contrived.

"Come on," he said. "Let's just pack up and go. We won't leave a forwarding address, and they won't be able to find us."

Lois checked her suitcase. Nothing seemed to have been touched. "All right," she answered. "But we won't decide where we're going until we get to the station. Then it's either Spain or Italy."

"Maybe straight through to Greece."

"Maybe."

It took only a moment to pack their bags, and as they left the room Richard leaned over and kissed Lois on the cheek. "Southward, ho," he said. They discovered an elevator directly across from their door. They saw it only because its doors were open. Closed, the doors formed a full-length mirror. Richard got in, taking both bags, and Lois saw that there would be almost no room for her.

"I'll see you downstairs," she told Richard, backing out just as the doors closed. She skipped down the three flights of stairs, arriving at the bottom before the elevator. When, a moment later, the elevator arrived with their bags, Richard was not in it. Confused, she turned to see him sprinting down the stairs.

"The stupid elevator stopped halfway down," he told her. "Then as soon as I got out of it, it left." He seemed more annoyed than the event called for. The door of the elevator began to close again, threatening to take away their bags once more. Lois put her shoulder into the opening, forcing the doors apart. They seemed much more reluctant to open than she had expected.

Richard had a brief argument with the hotelkeeper's wife as he paid his bill. It seemed to him that the room was ten francs more expensive than he had been quoted by the hotelkeeper. The woman insisted that Richard must have misunderstood, that the price he spoke of was for another room. Richard insisted that she call her husband. She replied with a torrent of French that seemed to Lois abusive, though she did not understand it. She could feel her own face becoming flushed. She walked out to the door and into the street to wait for Richard. She hated confrontations, especially when Richard entered them. They filled her with a kind of hopeless anger.

A big, black motorcycle was parked across the street, behind the spot where the truck had blocked traffic. The truck, at least, was gone. When Richard arrived, Lois steered him by the motorcycle without comment. He didn't seem to notice it, and she was glad. He had taken to looking at all couples on motorcycles as potentially the couple from Mont Ste. Odile.

"What did you do?" she asked Richard.

"I paid her," he answered. "What else is there to do? But I sure do hate being cheated."

"Maybe it was a misunderstanding," Lois said.

"There was no misunderstanding. I was simply cheated."

Lois calculated a moment. "Ten francs. That comes to two dollars and change."

"That's not the point," Richard said, but he seemed to cheer up nevertheless. They found their way to the rue Monge, and started down towards the river. The sun had come out, and most of the snow had melted. The street steamed, and along the sidewalks merchants had pushed stalls out into the flow of traffic. At the store that sold wicker things, an old woman was piling baskets along the sidewalk.

Richard had to change some traveller's cheques, so they stopped at a little bank. He rang the doorbell, and the clerk buzzed him inside. Lois remained outside. On the other side of the street, the old man with the cat had taken it off the leash, and it was sitting on his shoulder. He had put his hat down on the sidewalk. An old woman on her way into the church dropped a coin in it. Lois found a note pad and a pen in her handbag, and on impulse she took them out and started to sketch. It was the wrong material, a letterpad and a ballpoint pen, but she worked intently, hoping to get the main details before Richard came back.

The church was made from red brick, dirtied by soot, but not nearly as old as she had remembered. It was set back from the corner, so that it had its own square in front of it. The narrow facade and the large buildings that surrounded it made it seem smaller than it really was. Lois caught the arch of the doors, the curving lines of the windows that struggled with the severe angularity of the buildings on either side. She caught the old man with his cat, only a few lines, but the fierce pride behind the beggar's humility seemed all there. An old woman sat off to the side on a bench, guarding a large, brown wicker basket. The bird woman, Lois decided, and she surrounded her with birds. The sketch seemed vibrant and full of life to Lois. She stopped sketching, afraid that one more line might ruin it.

When Richard came out, she realized that he had been gone

a long time. He glanced at her sketch and said, "Very nice," but he really didn't look at it. She felt disappointed, but at the same time glad. The experience was hers alone, and if he had pointed out some flaw in the sketch he might have ruined it for her.

"I don't think my spirit can take much more of this," Richard said. "First, I had to wait while some thug exchanged two hundred American dollars that he probably got by rolling some poor American. All this with elaborate paperwork, but no need to prove his identity. Then I can't find my passport. And six credit cards, a driver's license, enough identification to choke a horse is not enough."

"Have you lost your passport?"

"No, it was in my back pocket, the stupidest place you can carry a passport. I did get the money."

When they reached the corner of rue Ste. Germaine, the market was in full progress. The noise was nearly deafening. Men hawked their wares in loud voices, calling customers over, importuning them to buy. Lois would have liked to stay longer, but the suitcases made them out of place, hampered their movements. They went down the stairs to the cool artificial light of the subway. A man tried to hawk a book of tickets to them, but Richard refused. When they got out to the tracks, there was only them and a man sleeping on a bench, covered with newspaper. A moment later, a train came by, and in a second they were swept off to the Gare d'Austerlitz.

Most of the people at the station were dark, Mediterranean. Whole huge families seemed to have gathered, either to meet someone or see someone off. They shouted to each other in sing-song Italian, and Spanish, and wide-eyed infants stared at Richard and Lois as they passed. Lois had expected that there would be a train leaving soon for some destination they might like to go to, but there didn't seem to be. They settled for the night train to Barcelona, leaving at ten that evening. Richard went over to another wicket and paid a special fee for the sleeping car. It was noon. They had ten hours to wait until the train left.

They decided to go to the d'Orsay gallery and look at Impressionist paintings. Richard wasn't sure where it was. He thought it overlooked the Seine, across from the Louvre. They thought they would take the Metro to the Odeon station, then walk back. Lois was hungry, so they looked for a restaurant down a side street called rue Princess, but what had seemed a restaurant turned out to be an English-language bookstore called The Village Voice.

They went in because they saw a poster announcing a reading by a Canadian writer. A poet named Fred Wah would read there that night at eight o'clock. There was a collection of his books, one of which appeared to be hand-made, in the window. A fellow who looked vaguely Chinese and a tall woman were speaking to the owner. Lois wondered whether they might be Canadians, but she didn't want to go close enough to hear what they were saying. The people left, and the woman came over and asked Lois if she could be of help. She spoke English well, with the kind of accent that actresses put on when they want to be seductive. Lois said no, she was just looking. Richard asked for a book on Druids, and the woman found one for him. He also bought a book called *Vimy*, by Pierre Berton. Lois was surprised because she didn't think Richard liked Pierre Berton. He always turned him off whenever he appeared on television.

When they left the store, Richard said, "That was him, that was Fred Wah."

"How do you know?"

"I saw his picture on the back of his book. He won the Governor-General's Award. There was a little gold seal that said so."

"Have you ever heard of him?" Lois asked.

"No, but that doesn't mean anything. I don't know many writers. He's probably famous."

They found a small restaurant just around the corner. It served hamburgers, and on a whim Lois ordered one. When it came, she couldn't eat it. She had expected something quite different. Richard ate it for her, and she ordered a large chocolate sundae instead. They shared a beer, though it didn't go well with the ice cream, and so Lois only had a couple of sips. Later, they found the d'Orsay, but most of the famous paintings Lois had expected to see were out on loan to exhibitions in other places. She found the painting by Rousseau of the lion on the desert, and she looked at it for a long time. Then they walked all the way to the Champs Elysée. It was nine o'clock when they got back to the Gare d'Austerlitz, and Lois was exhausted. She had no idea what the sleeping coach would be like. She hoped the bed would be comfortable.

They found a no-smoking car about halfway down the length of the train on track six. The *couchettes* were already made up, the seats configured to make two bunks on either side of the compartment. Richard and Lois chose one near the centre of the car, on the theory that other passengers would take the first open space and they might escape having anybody share their compartment. They stashed their bags under the lower bunks, and Richard went off to find some food. Apparently there would be no food car on the train.

Lois watched through the window into the car on the next track, the train to Nice. A family had taken over the roomette, and pulled the blinds open. The car appeared to have three bunks on each side, and the mother was tucking in children on the upper bunks. Two men, one of them presumably the father, had opened the window and were leaning out, looking down the length of the train. Each had a beer, and they laughed as they chatted to each other.

Richard came back in a few minutes. He had bought a couple of sandwiches, three bottles of beer, a bottle of wine, a Toblerone chocolate bar and two oranges. The train was not going to leave until midnight, he told Lois. They would arrive in Barcelona at noon tomorrow. They might as well make themselves comfortable.

"So we're committed to Spain?" Lois asked.

"Not necessarily. We might circle back along the Mediterranean to Italy."

Richard opened a beer and settled down to read his book about the Druids. Lois had a copy of *Paris Match* she had brought all the way from Strasbourg. She had tried reading sections from it, but she was about ready to give up. She and Richard had each turned on the little night light by the head of the bed, leaving the rest of the compartment in darkness. Richard wanted to pull the blinds as well, but she wouldn't let him. The people on the other train seemed so happy and so contented with what they were doing that she would sooner watch them than read.

She had almost fallen asleep when the slight tug of the train told her they were moving. She was glad nobody else had come to share their compartment. She had barely thought this, however, when the door opened, and a man entered. He was dark and good-looking, like the models for clothing that appeared in European magazines. He apologized for disturbing them, and explained that the train was crowded. He had no place else to go.

Richard invited him in in French, but as soon as he was seated the man asked if they would mind speaking to him in English. He was on his way to Perpignan, he said, to take an advanced course in English. He would be spending two weeks in an immersion course run by an Irish couple. It was said to be effective. He was an engineer, he said, a senior engineer for the telephone company. In three months he would be sent to America to try to sell Minitel to Americans. Richard explained that he and Lois were Canadians. The engineer seemed pleased to hear this, and told them he might go to Quebec while he was there.

The car was dim and comfortable. It seemed to Lois that the engineer was someone they had known for a long time. The lights of Paris flashed by as the train picked up speed, but they didn't seem to have any purpose or to be attached to anything. They were simply lights, random points of illumination. Lois looked at the engineer, his cheek line sharpened by the horizontal line of shadow, and tried to think who he was like. He reminded her of someone, but she couldn't say who.

It had been the coldest winter in history, the young engineer said. Snow in Paris at this late date was unheard of. In Perpignan it would be summer. It was where he had been born, and he would also visit with his parents. Yes, it would be summer in Barcelona too.

Lois noticed that the windows of the train were streaked with rain. She asked the engineer whether he had a family. Yes. A wife, two daughters. His wife was from Normandy. He shrugged his shoulders as if there were some common joke about people from Normandy that only needed to be hinted at. His English was stiffly formal, with little trace of a French accent. Lois suggested that he was wasting his money taking a course in English. He laughed. It was the company's money. She was very kind, but often, if people spoke too fast, he did not understand. If he was going to negotiate contracts, he would have to understand everything.

Abruptly, he stood and said, "It is possible to sleep." He clambered to the upper bunk above Lois, and was silent. Richard opened another beer, a perverse gesture, Lois thought. He started reading his book about Druids again. Lois fell into a fitful sleep and woke to see Richard still reading. Later, it was dark in the compartment, but she could hear him shifting and moaning. He was too big for the *couchette*, his legs were too long. After a while, he began to snore lightly.

Lois, confused, woke to the stirring above her. The engineer was packing things into his bag. His jeans appeared over the side of the bunk, held by one hand. Then his legs, sliding into his jeans. As he touched the floor, he pulled the pants over his hips. Lois, for just a second, caught sight of his red bikini shorts, the bulge of his penis. It seemed deliberately offered, no accidental occurrence. Richard had rolled into a sitting position, and looked as if he were about to ask the engineer some question, but before he could form any words, the man said, "Perpignan," and slipped out the door.

Lois reached over and opened the blinds so that light flooded into the room. Outside was another world. Some time during the night, they had crossed the northward-seeking line of spring. The grass was green, leaves were everywhere, and pink and white blossoms seemed to explode from the trees. The yellow sunlight was full of warmth, and the houses were painted bright colours. Richard reached into his bag and passed Lois an orange. She held it in her hand in the direct sunlight, and it seemed solid and palpable. She peeled it slowly, and when she bit into it, her mouth was filled with a fresh sweetness. The sound of the train seemed full of joy.

***

Lois hated Barcelona. She didn't say much at first, but Richard sensed a deep discomfort in her. They'd both started the day full of excitement, tense with discovery. Lois had spotted the first palm tree, Richard had got the first glimpse of the sea, sparkling in the tense Mediterranean light. The train had ducked underground as they entered Barcelona, and when they had come up the escalator into the brilliant sunlight and the bustle of the city, they were disoriented, as if they had spent the winter underground. They were accosted by a little man who had lived in Philadelphia, he said in perfect English, and offered them a lift downtown. The price he asked seemed ridiculously low to Richard. Lois was reluctant, but Richard didn't want to go back down into the darkness to find another taxi. The little man led them to his Mercedes, which he had parked on the sidewalk. It had no meter and no markings, and didn't seem to be a taxi at all.

He took them to the most expensive hotel in Barcelona, and when Richard did not want to stay there, he drove them around the corner to a dingy, smaller building. He asked for twice the money he had originally bargained for and Richard paid him, happy to get settled somewhere. Lois had read an article about false taxis, she told Richard later. They were dangerous. Tourists would be taken to the outskirts of the city, robbed at gunpoint, sometimes murdered. The hotel room seemed ordinary but adequate to Richard. It had a balcony with glass doors that actually opened. Lois thought the place was filthy. She wouldn't take off her shoes, and she wouldn't unpack her bags.

They spent three days in Barcelona. Richard loved the narrow streets, so full of life and excitement at night. Lois thought the people hard and aggressive, the narrow streets dirty and dangerous. They visited the cathedral, walked for miles along the seashore, though even there Lois found danger. After the first day, the temperature dropped, and though the days remained brilliant, the wind was sharp. Only a couple of other people, an old woman with a shopping bag, and an old, white-bearded man sat on the benches and watched the gulls. They drank beer and ate scallops and shrimps in the little snack bars, throwing the paper plates on the floor like everybody else. Lois complained that the food was bland and tasteless. The only time she was happy was when she sat in bed, sipping the warm dark rum and Coke that Richard mixed for them, and reading the Margaret Atwood stories. Even then, she wouldn't get up to go to the bathroom without putting on her shoes.

Richard read the book on the Druids and found himself increasingly fascinated by them. The book did not mention the Pagan Wall, but it talked about other hill forts and a sophisticated culture of priests who regarded the invading Romans as barbarians. The book had originally been written in German and was translated into English. Richard had always thought of the Druids as British, but the book scarcely mentioned England, giving only a couple of pages and a small illustration to Stonehenge. The Druids it spoke of comprised a vast empire over northern Europe. What fascinated Richard in particular was their method of sacrifice. The sacrificial victim was always given a full meal, then had his throat slit as he lay, spread-eagled on an altar. The body he and Lois had discovered had been laid out, he realized with a small shock, in precisely the correct position for a sacrifice.

The Druids, he also discovered, did not sacrifice their victims to propitiate gods. The sacrifices were meant as a form of divination, a reading of future events. Apparently the evidence of bodies discovered in bogs suggested that the victims went happily to their deaths. Richard wondered whether the inspector knew about Druid practices. The third morning, he bought some wrapping paper from a department store around the corner from the hotel, and sent the book to the inspector. He had underlined some passages in red, and he wondered how the inspector would respond.

They were both happy when the train pulled out of Barcelona on its way to Madrid. Without actually discussing it, they had decided, or at least Richard had decided, because it was he who made the reservations for the train, that they would go one further step into the heart of Spain. In Madrid, they would decide where to go next. The train swept along the Mediterranean shore, past beautiful but empty stretches of beach with only the odd romantic walker, and through the backyards of polluted industrial towns. Then it turned inward, into the country, climbing through green highlands until it came to a high rocky plateau. Here, everything was red. They saw no vegetation, no water, only an enormous sweeping desert of red stones. Every so often they would pass a hut made of red stone and a fence of red rock, a poor farm that blended so well with the desert that it was gone before you were certain it had been there at all. In the distance, whole cities seemed carved into the sides of cliffs, but it was impossible to tell if these were actually habitations or only strange geological formations.

Richard had never seen anything like this, or even imagined that it could exist. It was not what he had expected of Spain. He kept thinking of Hemingway's title "Hills like White Elephants," but these hills were nothing like white elephants. They were like somebody's imagination of what life on Mars might be. Lois was not nearly as impressed. She had bought a sketch pad in Barcelona, and was doing a series of sketches, she said. It didn't look like a series to Richard. She had only two images, a woman in a churchyard surrounded by birds, and an old man in front of a church with a cat on his shoulder. She made dozens of sketches, each varying in only a few details from the other.

Gradually, the landscape flattened, became green. Rivers appeared, cultivated fields and farmhouses. The train made more frequent stops, and other people got on. Then, just as they reached the outskirts of a city, the train stopped. For about a half-hour it did not move. Then came an announcement in Spanish. Richard asked people what was wrong, but no one seemed to speak English. Finally he tried French, and an old woman explained that the train had broken down, that in a few moments another train would come along, and they could take it. They were not far from the central station in Madrid.

In a little while the new train came along, and all the passengers climbed on. The new train had half the number of cars as the old one, so people stood up and crowded onto each others' laps. They passed through a shanty town of houses made from boxes and bits of sheet metal. The word *barrios* came into Richard's mind, but he didn't know whether the term referred only to Latin America, or whether it had come from Spain.

A couple of hours later, they had found a little cafe bar that seemed an odd combination of a saloon and a high-class restaurant. At one end of the room, waiters dressed in tuxedos served patrons at tables draped with white linen tablecloths. At the other, people clustered around a bar, laughing and talking. Lois was not much happier with their new hotel, the Hotel Sur, directly across the street from the railway station. It seemed to Richard a step up from the one in Barcelona, certainly cleaner, with a broad balcony you could sit on.

Richard had ordered fish, red snapper he suspected, though he wasn't sure. Lois had ordered beefsteak because the name appeared in quotation marks on the menu, and she didn't feel like taking chances. It was already dark, but the darkness seemed suffused with a red light, the source of which was not apparent. The bar end of the room in which they sat was bathed in thick yellow light, the far end dark, lit by sparse red candles. They were in the exact centre, not quite with either the remote diners or the laughing drinkers.

"Well," Lois said, "what next?"

"What do you mean?"

"Where are we going from here?"

Richard thought for a minute. He knew that Lois had talked about the Costa Del Sol, but he didn't want to go there. Italy now seemed too distant, and Richard had already decided that they would drift down to Portugal.

"A couple of days here, then Lisbon?"

"No Costa Del Sol?"

"There are beautiful beaches in the south of Portugal. Then maybe Seville."

Lois didn't answer, and Richard took that as a form of assent. "We can go to the Prado while we're here," he told her. "It's got Bosch's *Garden of Delights.*" Richard knew it was one of Lois's favourite paintings, but he didn't know whether she knew it was in Madrid.

Lois was suddenly animated. She wanted to know where the Prado was, and so they consulted the map Richard had picked up at the hotel. It was only a couple of blocks from where they were. Lois wanted to reconnoitre it before they went back to the hotel. The waiter arrived bringing their food, and they put the map away. Richard's fish was not anything he had ever eaten before and he found the taste mild but offensive. Lois's beefsteak arrived smothered in onions, and cooked a uniform black.

She didn't seem bothered by the food, hardly touched it. At a table near the bar, a local melodrama was being played out. A young woman, darkly Spanish like a player in a silent film, pointedly ignored an older man who stood a few feet away from her, staring at her but saying nothing. The young woman hugged a boy of about eight, who sat at the table doing his homework. The older man went to the bar and bought a beer, which he brought over and gave to the young woman. She took the beer, shouted at him, a flood of curses, and went back to hugging and whispering to the boy, who seemed to want no more to do with her than she did with the older man. Lois was fascinated.

"Do you think they're a family?" she asked Richard.

"No. I think she's a prostitute and that's her kid. The old guy is trying to make a deal."

Lois watched for a while as Richard finished his meal.

"No," she said. "There's something between them."

"Well, we'll never know," Richard told her, calling for the bill.

Lois brooded about the strange couple as they walked by the darkened Prado a little later. When they woke up the next day, the first thing she said was, "I think they were probably married and had had a falling out."

"He's much too old for her," Richard said. "He's actually probably her father trying to make her give up her evil ways and come home."

Lois fell in love with the *Garden of Delights*. Richard left her with it while he toured through the rest of the museum and found a room with eight Boticellis, none of which he had ever seen reproduced. He came to fetch her, but she wouldn't leave. They went for lunch in the cafeteria, then Lois went back to look at the Bosch again. Finally, Richard convinced her to leave so that they could go look at Picasso's *Guernica*, which was stored by itself in another museum. Lois had spent five hours looking at one painting, and when they found the Picasso museum around the corner she was too tired to do more than glance at it. Instead, they went out and sat in the Luxembourg Gardens, and Lois fell asleep on a bench with her head in Richard's lap.

She awoke refreshed and hungry, and insisted that they go back to the cafe bar. Richard wanted to try something different, but Lois was determined. When they got back, the same drama was enfolding. It was as if they had never left, except that the eight-year-old was missing, and even he arrived a little later. The young woman cursed the older man. He bought her beer and stood near her to be abused. At another table, an older couple, in their sixties Richard guessed, talked in low and passionate tones, a lover's quarrel. The Spaniards seemed aggressive, passionate, filled with subdued violence. Lois was fascinated. Again, Richard could not get her to leave. He and Lois always treated each other with elaborate politeness. They had even talked about it, made an agreement. They remembered the endings of their own first marriages as filled with anger and accusation, and had promised each other peace. Now Richard had begun to wonder whether something was missing.

The first thing Lois said when they left the cafe bar was, "Can you imagine living your life at that kind of intensity?" She put her arm around Richard and pulled him to her.

Richard kissed her softly on the cheek and said, "Let's go back to the hotel and make love." She murmured assent. They had to wait to cross the street because a group of striking workers was marching by. They marched in ordered ranks, carrying hand-painted banners. It was already ten o'clock in the evening. The street they had come down was narrow and dark. They sang a sort of marching song and disappeared into the railway station.

"This is a surreal country," Richard told Lois. "No wonder Dali could make those strange paintings. He's actually a realist."

Back at the Hotel Sur, the clerk stopped them just before they climbed the stairs to their room. He handed Richard a message. It was from the inspector. It said, "Stay at the Hotel Britannica in Lisbon." It was signed André K.

They stayed nearly a week in Madrid, partly out of a desire not to be under the control of anyone else. "How did he find out where we are?" Lois asked Richard, "And how does he know we're going to Lisbon?"

"Interpol," Richard told her, though he actually didn't know himself. "They probably have every hotel register in Europe on a computer."

"We didn't sign anything," she reminded him. "They didn't even ask our names. They just gave us the key. They don't know who we are."

"Yes they do," Richard told her. "I showed him my passport when I tried to cash a traveller's cheque." Only the clerk had refused to cash the cheque, had merely glanced at the passport out of politeness. Nobody but the manager could cash cheques, and the manager was never there. The message was furtive and melodramatic, like something out of a cheap movie.

"Maybe we won't go to Lisbon after all," Richard said, and he held to that until they were actually on the train. Lois wanted to spend all her time in the Prado. After a couple of days, she even stopped complaining about the hotel. Richard began to read about Vimy Ridge. He thought that he might suggest a trip up from Paris on the way back, but he hadn't told Lois yet.

He had begun to formulate a plan to write a novel about the Canadian army. It would take place during both wars, a father and a son, each killed in battle. The story would be told by the grandson, who would return to visit the battlefields where his father and grandfather had died. One would die at Vimy, the other at Dieppe during the raid in 1942. He would also have to find some excuse for visiting Dieppe.

Richard didn't dare tell Lois about the novel. It seemed to him a huge arrogance, a kind of presumptuousness that might make her laugh. Yet he was convinced that he could do it. He had the discipline. He'd sat down and written a Ph.D. dissertation, and that had taken writing nearly every day for three years. What he'd do, he thought, is write a novel that was totally honest. He didn't think it had been done before. His characters would think all the horrible, selfish thoughts that people think. They would be brave and cowardly at the same time. They would think a lot about sex, they might even masturbate to entertain themselves in the filthy trenches. Their deaths would be as painful and horrible as real deaths, and as unexpected. He had never read a novel in which the hero dies before the end. His characters would die in mid-sentence, and then they would be gone completely, and the novel would start up again from another point of view. He wasn't sure that people would want to read that kind of novel, but the important thing seemed to Richard that he write the novel, not that other people read it.

Madrid seemed to be filled with strikes. Wherever they went, they encountered small groups of people walking in orderly fashion, carrying banners. Nobody seemed to pay any attention to them. One day they came to the central square of the city, and it was filled with young people. Richard thought they might be university students, but they seemed too young to be university students. Somebody had wrapped a statue in toilet paper. A middle-aged man had climbed up and was tearing the the toilet paper from the statue. He shouted at the crowd, and they jeered him. When he was finished, he stomped into a shoe store on the corner. As soon as he was gone, two young men, children really, climbed up and began to wrap the statue again.

Richard and Lois had supper in a little restaurant overlooking the square. Dozens of police cars arrived, their blue lights flashing, and large policemen formed phalanxes with their leather-covered sticks held vertically. The crowd of children, high-school students Richard decided, paid no attention to the police. They milled about and chanted slogans, and seemed in no hurry to leave. From the quiet of the restaurant, up on the second floor so they could see the entire square, the event seemed carefully choreographed.

"We might be witnessing something important," Richard told Lois, "some event that will go down in Spanish history as a turning point."

"I hope not," Lois answered. She had ordered a *paella* and Richard had ordered squid. Of the dishes the waiter brought just at that moment, Lois's seemed far the more appetizing. When the waiter was gone she continued. "I hope there isn't any violence. I don't want to see anyone get hurt." She paused a moment, aware that she sounded pretentious. "I mean," she explained, "I personally do not wish to witness a murder. Or be the victim of one." When they got back down to the street, the atmosphere had changed considerably. The voices of the crowd were now angry, full of threats. More and more police were coming from every direction. Richard and Lois hurried away, back towards their hotel. The streets were filled with people also trying to get away from the square. Some of them were running, but Richard resisted the impulse to join them. At every moment he expected to hear shots in the distance, but after a few minutes the crowds thinned and they were back near their hotel.

Lois wanted to check the cafe bar again, but there was no drama there. They each had a beer and watched while a group of about a dozen people dressed in tuxedos and evening gowns came in, ordered cocktails and stood around as if they were at a cocktail party in somebody's house. They chatted and laughed for about a half an hour and then they left.

"What do you think that was all about?" Lois asked.

"It's a strange country," Richard said. "What do you think about going to Lisbon tonight?"

"Right now?"

"Yes. We'll grab our bags and catch the night train."

"I thought you didn't want to see the inspector."

"After a week in this place, the inspector seems normal and reasonable. Actually, I'm looking forward to seeing him again."

"Do you think he'll have read your book on the Druids?"

"I don't know how he could have got it before he sent the message. Unless the European mails are a lot better than the Canadian mails. Anyway, he may have some information about the murder."

"He may not be there, you know," Lois said. "It's been a whole week."

"If he could find us here, then he'll find us in Lisbon."

They sat for a moment in silence, and then Richard said, "Maybe I'll write a novel. What do you think?"

"That would be nice," Lois said, "as long as it isn't about bullfights."

* * *

Lois woke with a start from a dream about her mother. She and her mother were skiing down a mountainside. Lois had never actually seen her mother ski, but in the dream she moved with a surprising elegance and grace. Lois complimented her mother, telling her how beautifully she skied. Her mother turned to her in sudden anger and accused Lois of being selfish and never paying attention to other people. Her mother's face was contorted with rage.

She could hear Richard's voice, but she couldn't figure out where he was. Then the clicking of the rails reminded her that they were on the train to Lisbon. She checked her watch. It was eight o'clock, morning, and all the blinds in the car were drawn, so that she was in total darkness. She turned on the light, slipped into her clothes, and opened the door into the aisleway. Richard was leaning against the window, talking to a beautiful girl with long, dark hair. She was tall, dressed in a white dressing gown, and she leaned over so that her face was very close to Richard's. Her eyes were pale blue, and they were peculiarly unfocussed. She appeared to be looking right through Richard. The two of them were sharing a cinnamon bun, obviously the girl's contribution, and drinking an orange drink, Richard's, from a single straw. Richard was talking about Bobby Orr and the Boston Bruins.

Lois felt a surge of anger. Her mother's unfair accusation rang in her ears, and Richard's betrayal seemed an unbearable addition. He grinned at her, a half-smile that was a mixture of guilt and pride. He seemed pleased with himself, having discovered this Amazon, and seduced her into a clandestine breakfast.

Richard introduced them formally. "Lois, this is Sandy. She's an American living in Madrid. She's a singer."

"A back-up singer only," the girl explained, and she gave the name of someone that she apparently expected Lois to recognize, but whose name was so Spanish that Lois could not remember it a second after she had heard it. "I dance and do the da da da's in the background." She looked exactly like the kind of person who did things like that.

Memory drifted back to Lois. The Spanish railways were on strike, and they had sat in the train for hours, waiting for it to leave and watching the strikers march up and down the platform with their placards. At some point a couple of girls had knocked on the door and asked if they could borrow her husband. They had needed somebody to open a bottle of wine, and Richard had gone over to help them. Lois, half-asleep when they knocked, had no memory of Richard's return, but she recognized the voice. It was a deliberate little-girl voice, so filled with artifice that it stirred her anger again.

"Can I borrow your toothbrush?" Lois asked Richard. "I seem to have left mine in Madrid."

"Toothpaste," he corrected her.

"No," she said, "I've got my toothpaste. It's the brush I'm missing."

"Right," he said. "Toothbrush," and he vanished into the compartment. Lois knew she was going to have to explain this later, but she didn't care. The only real arguments they had ever had were over Lois's suspicion that Richard sometimes used her toothbrush out of absent-mindedness.

The girl smiled sweetly and told Lois, "You must come from a big family like me. There were eight of us kids, and we had two toothbrushes among us. I was fifteen years old before I even knew that people were supposed to have their own toothbrushes." This confession, of a kind of impoverished innocence that Richard would admire, made the girl even more intolerable.

"I'm sorry," Lois said. "I've been travelling for too long, and I'm starting to get cranky. I think I'd better get some breakfast." From the window, now that she looked, she could see a spectacular landscape, though it was blurred by a heavy mist. It was what she had always imagined Ireland would be like. The fields and the trees were a brilliant green. Stone fences snaked in every direction, and low cottages built of the same grey stone as the fences dotted the landscape. Cattle and goats grazed peacefully, and though the area did not seem mountainous or even hilly, from time to time the train squeezed through a rock cut. Then unexpectedly they flashed by a garden with green trees covered with brilliant oranges.

Richard appeared out of the compartment. "One toothbrush," he said, holding up his grubby green brush with the little rubber pick on the end.

"Maybe I'll settle for an orange," Lois said. "I don't think I trust the water on this train." She turned to the girl and asked, "How about you? Would you like an orange?"

"That would be terrific," the girl answered. "I don't trust the water either." Richard sighed, returned to the compartment and emerged with two oranges.

"Aren't you going to have one?" the girl asked.

"No," Richard said. "I trust the water." And holding his toothbrush in front of him like a banner, he walked off to the washroom at the end of the car.

"I wonder if you can eat those oranges, " Lois said. They were passing another farm with trees covered with oranges.

"No," Sandy said. "They're terribly sour. I've tried them and you can't take more than one bite."

"Why do they grow them then?"

"I don't know. Marmalade probably." They stood a few moments in silence, and as they followed a turn in the river, an old stone castle appeared out of the mist. It covered almost the whole of a tiny island, turning a bulge in the river into a moat.

"Are you a hockey fan?" Lois asked.

"No," the girl said. "I'm from Boston. My dad once took me to a game and I saw Bobby Orr."

Lois found herself liking Sandy. She had come over to Europe with her boyfriend, who was studying for his Ph.D. in Spanish and Portuguese. She had worked as a model for a while, until she got the job with the singer. She had broken up with her boyfriend over that, and now she had to decide whether she would accompany the singer on a trip to Brazil. She was meeting her boyfriend in Lisbon, to see whether they could patch things up. She doubted it would work. It was a great opportunity, going to Brazil, and the pay was good.

Richard returned and told them that he'd met a man waiting for the washroom who had told him that Spanish and Portuguese were much alike, only Portuguese was Spanish without the bones.

"That's Cervantes," the girl said. "It's my boyfriend's favourite quotation." She announced that she was going to catch a bit more sleep. The train wouldn't get to Lisbon until noon. She'd made the trip several times.

After she had disappeared into her own compartment, Lois said, "She's quite nice."

"I think she's a congenital liar," Richard said.

"Why?"

"I don't know. I just think so. There's something weird about her."

"She's certainly beautiful," Lois said.

"She's that all right. Did you notice her eyes?"

"What about them."

"They sparkle. I've read the phrase a thousand times, but I've never seen eyes that actually sparkled before. Hers sparkled."

"Do you think she's in trouble?" Lois asked.

"No," Richard answered, "girls like that are never in trouble.

They only have to stand around for a few moments and some man will come by and protect them."

He seemed depressed, and they stood for a few moments in silence. At last, just to break the silence, Lois spoke. "What about this novel. When are you going to write it?"

"I don't know." Richard sighed. "I'll probably never write it."

"What about Heidegger?" Lois asked. "What happened to him?"

"The old Nazi? I don't know what to do about him. He seemed perfectly safe in Canada, but the wars took place in Europe."

"Was he really a Nazi?" Lois asked. She had heard Richard make the accusation before, but he had always done it almost affectionately, like calling the head of the department a fascist.

"Yep," Richard said. "Or at least he was a member of the party. Only for a while, about a year, but how long do you have to be a Nazi? Maybe even Hitler recanted at the end. Heidegger didn't. He lived for a long time, but he never spoke about that time. He never said he was sorry. The worst thing is, I don't know whether it was some personal aberration or the direct consequence of what he thought. Maybe if I keep on studying Heidegger I'll turn into a Nazi."

Lois didn't know how to answer this. "What about your colleagues?" she asked. "What do they think about Heidegger?"

"They don't think about him. They don't talk about him. He's a 'continental' philosopher, and so beyond the pale. I think I might be the only philosophy professor in Canada who has ever even read him. That's how you get to be an expert in this business."

"Well, write a novel then."

"Yes," Richard said. "A novel about wars. And about the Nazis on both sides."

Richard seemed to Lois increasingly brooding. The trip had been her idea, an attempt to get him to relax. Now he brooded about train schedules and exchange rates and the cost of the trip. He had a book in which he wrote down everything he spent, and converted the costs into Canadian currency. They were not short of money, and he never seemed to keep track of it at home. He was always afraid that she was going to get lost, and his continual concern had begun to oppress her. She remembered her anger at discovering him talking to the beautiful Sandy. Still, it was better than having him brooding in the compartment.

Richard had opened the door and was in the process of converting the beds back into seats again. He wanted his English-Portuguese phrase book.

"You're going to learn Portuguese before we get to Lisbon?"

"I'm going to learn the numbers, and how to ask for the bill, and the names of seafood and how to ask whether the tip is included or not." For the next four hours he struggled with the language, muttering to himself in a low whisper, and then the train pulled into the outskirts of Lisbon. Lois tested him as he counted to a hundred and ordered a plateful of squid and a beer from her.

Lois's first impression of Lisbon was that it was a city of taxis. They came out of the station to a sea of green taxicabs, all waiting in perfect order. It didn't seem possible that the train could have carried enough people to fill all the cars. The driver they got spoke neither English nor French, but Richard passed him a sheet that had the name and address of the Hotel Britannica on it. The driver took them along the Avenida Infante Dom Henrique, a wide road that curved by a sparkling blue bay with very little traffic until he made a sudden turn that brought them to the centre of the city, the Avenida da Liberdade. Lois thought she had never seen a street quite so expansive. Several lanes of traffic moved down either side of a broad boulevard, so wide that it supported outdoor cafes, small forests of palm trees and elaborate fountains.

The driver pulled onto a side street and drove right past the Hotel Britannica. Richard didn't notice, but Lois did, and they were nearly a block past before the driver understood what Lois had said. He shrugged his shoulders and continued around the block, apologizing profusely, but failing to turn off his meter. He got caught in a traffic jam caused by a truck apparently unloading beer and in no hurry to move, despite the dozen cars blowing their horns. They could see the Hotel Britannica about a half-block away. Richard , over the driver's protests, insisted that they leave the car and walk. He paid the driver the fare on the meter, but offered him no tip. On the way to the hotel he fumed in a silent rage, and Lois wondered whether some small frustration would someday lead him to that heart attack. She thought of mentioning it to him, but realized that would only give him one more reason for anger.

There was no message from the inspector when they registered. Richard was disappointed, but Lois was glad. The visit from the inspector loomed like some sort of test, and she didn't want to face it. Instead, they went to their room, a large, old room with high ceilings and what the proprietors thought of as proper British decoration, an umbrella stand, a roll-top writing desk and a four-poster bed.

Richard wanted to write, and he sat at the desk, hunched over, for a long time. At first, he just sat, but after a while he started to write intently. Lois fell asleep and dreamt again of her mother, swimming now with elegant strokes. She and her father followed in a boat. When she awoke, she remembered that her mother had swum Christina Lake one summer, a distance of nearly a mile, though Lois had not been in the boat. She had watched from the cottage on the side of the mountain until her mother had disappeared in the distance.

There was still no message when they went out for supper. The clerk, in what was intended as an upper-class English accent, gave them directions to the old city. A couple of prostitutes stood at the entrance to the hotel. Two more stood at the corner, and each doorway on the short side street to the Avenida da Liberdade harboured at least one. Lois counted eleven in a space of about a hundred yards. On the main street itself there were fewer, though Lois could see them down every side street they passed.

"Why do you think there are so many prostitutes?" she asked Richard.

"Where?"

"Everywhere." Lois was amazed that Richard hadn't noticed. "Look," she said, and pointed to a group of women leaning against the wall beside the entrance to another hotel.

"Maybe they're just waiting for a bus."

"They're prostitutes all right," she said, and Richard laughed.

"This is no place to bring a wife."

Richard wanted to tease, but she wasn't in the mood for it. She said nothing, and a moment later the broad avenue ended in a square, and narrow side streets wound steeply uphill. They chose one, rounded a corner, and found themselves in an unexpected festive atmosphere. The shops were brightly lit against the dusk.

Most of the shops were shoe stores or places that sold leather. The prices were low. The stores seemed to have a large number of employees, and when Lois went into a leather store to look at purses, she was surrounded by clerks. After that, she stuck to looking in the windows. Richard kept pointing out shoes and suggesting she buy them. It was how he shopped. He never had any idea in advance of what he wanted to buy, and he never had any idea of how the things he bought would work with the rest of his wardrobe. He kept buying things he refused to wear even once, but he never took them back. After about a year he would ask her to give them away.

Before they knew it, they were in darkness, and the bright lights of the shops cast strange, elongated shadows in the narrow streets. Lois stepped from a curb and watched three shadows step with her, then circle around as another shadow joined. From around the corner, she could hear a voice rising and falling in an eerie melody that for some reason made her think of Africa. They rounded the corner to a square with a bench in the centre. Over to one side, a tiny, round blind woman sat on a stool at the door to a grocery store. Many of the people who passed stopped and dropped coins into a pail beside her. She nodded and beamed at the sound of the coins, but she did not stop singing. Lois thought it was the most beautiful voice she had ever heard.

Richard was already past when Lois caught his arm. "Wait," she said, "I want to hear some more." She took him over to the bench and they sat and listened. The old woman was almost grotesque. Her eyes seemed to have no pupils. They flashed white in the harsh light. Her grey dress was shapeless, and her body hung in rolls of fat. All her teeth were rotten and black, but the voice that poured out of her was strong and clear, and filled with a terrible sadness.

"Aren't you going to draw her?" Richard asked.

"No," Lois said. "It wouldn't be fair." She wasn't sure why she said this, but it seemed right. She imagined how she might sketch the woman for a children's book, but she knew in advance that it wouldn't work. The old woman would come out cute, and there was nothing cute about her. Her voice hinted at some immense tragedy, some wrenching loss, and, though the woman was old and seemed full of decay, the voice was of a woman who was young and powerful. Her life seemed authentic in a way Lois's could never be. Anything she had to say seemed like idle talk in comparison to the depth of anxiety in the voice of this old woman who sat there in the light and sang.

After they'd listened for about a half-hour, Richard walked over and gave the old woman a handful of coins. She could tell by the rattle in her pail that she had been given a considerable amount, and she nodded and smiled, half standing into a grotesque curtsey. She completed a few more phrases, then huddled to her feet, picked up her stool and scurried around a corner into the dark, which seemed to stretch all the way to nothingness.

"I guess that put her over the top for a bottle of port," Richard said.

Lois could feel tears forming hot in her eyes. "I don't think I've ever heard anything more beautiful," she said. And later, over supper in a little seafood place back near the hotel, she could think and talk about nothing else. Even when the inspector sat down next to Richard and murmured his hello, her mind would not give up the haunting rhythms of grief and loss.

***

"Well," the inspector said as the waiter passed them brandy, "this is indeed a pleasure." He wore a neat, three-piece suit in a style that Richard thought of as Italian, and his tie looked expensive. He must have ordered the brandy in advance and waited for the correct moment to join them, because the brandy arrived at almost the same second as the inspector himself. He proposed a toast with a slight tilt of his glass, and Lois and Richard responded.

"First things first," the inspector said. "David Mann, aged thirty-three, corporal in the Canadian Armed Forces, stationed at Lahr, but missing almost from the moment of his arrival. Canadian of German extraction. Born in Kitchener, Ontario. Does the name mean anything to you?"

"No," Richard answered. "I've never heard of him. Should I have?"

"No," the inspector answered. "Nobody seems to have heard of him. He reported at Lahr, but nobody remembers having seen him, though apparently he signed documents. Reports from Canada say only that he was a hard worker, but unsociable. He has no relatives, his parents are dead, and he had no friends. He has left about as small a trace of himself in the world as it is possible to leave."

"But you've identified him positively?"

"We've identified him from the photograph. It is a close match, but of course not positive."

"So, no body," Lois said.

"A nobody with no body," the inspector agreed. He swirled the brandy in his glass and held it up to the light. "They make wonderful brandy in Portugal," he said. "Some of it is as good as the finest cognac, and it is hardly more expensive than wine."

"But this man was very real and very dead."

"David Mann," the inspector said, and for a moment he seemed profoundly tired. "Even the most ordinary die," he said. "As soon as you are born you are old enough to die." He swallowed his brandy and signalled to the waiter, who hurried over with a bottle and refilled the glass. "Canadians have a reputation, you know, for being faceless, for being able to disappear in a crowd. I'm sure it's unfair, but there it is. Who was this man? Who did he think he was? What adventure was he on? Because it is almost certain that he was on an adventure, that his anonymity is some sort of lie."

"Maybe he was just in the wrong place at the wrong time," Richard suggested. "Maybe he was just an ordinary guy passing by."

"The thing about ordinary people," the inspector said, "is that they are no different from us. We take pleasure and enjoy ourselves in the same way they do. They read books, go to art galleries just as we do, and they make the same sort of judgements. They are just as offended by the 'great masses' as we are, and they, too, shrink back. We are shocked by the same things. That indefinable 'they' is also us. We are all made from the minute events that add up to *la vie quotidienne.*"

"And since you mentioned art galleries," Richard said, "what happened to the woman who collapsed in the Louvre?"

The inspector looked up. He had been staring into his brandy glass. "The woman at the Louvre?" he said.

"Yes," Lois said. "The mother of the girl. The one at Mont Ste. Odile. Alexandra."

"Perhaps," the inspector said, "you would explain further?"

Richard told the inspector about the events of that day, about the girl's explanation and about the place he had taken her. He thought of the piece of paper in his wallet with the German address, but decided against giving it to him. If the inspector could find them in Lisbon, he could find the girl.

The inspector nodded throughout the story. When Richard was finished he thanked him.

"We will of course investigate. We are investigating," he corrected himself. "Still, it will probably lead to nothing. The girl has most likely told you the simple truth. Things that happen at the same time and place often seem linked through their nearness, though there need be no connection."

"Metonymy," Richard said.

"Yes," the inspector answered. "But a murder is not quite a poem, and the figures are not the same." Lois had ceased to pay attention to the conversation. Her eyes had taken on a dreamy, distant quality, and she was watching another table where the guests had just been served a seafood platter so piled with food as to go beyond any dream of hunger. She looked frail and vulnerable at that moment, and Richard felt that he must somehow protect her.

"Are we in any danger?" he asked the inspector. "I mean, you've played the super policeman and tracked us down in the middle of nowhere. It's impressive. But do you mind telling me how you do it and why."

The inspector sighed. "Interpol," he said. "A marvellous institution, but it is all more mundane than it looks. They traced you to Barcelona. I guessed that you would go to Madrid and had the hotels checked. I am not here to meet you. I am on holiday. I left a message for you to go to the Hotel Britannica simply because it is where I stay when I am in Lisbon. I saw that you were registered. And this," he indicated the restaurant with a sweep of his hand, "is simply the nearest decent restaurant. I saw you sitting here. Otherwise I should have rung your room tomorrow or perhaps met you at breakfast."

It was a little too simple an explanation for Richard, but he didn't say so.

"And so there is no danger?"

"I didn't say that. Oh, and thank you for the book on the Druids. I've read it and I'll leave it at the desk for you. You will want to talk to Delacroix about this subject. It is one of his specialties." He waved to the waiter, who again came over and refilled the glasses.

"I'd like to talk to Delacroix about a number of things," Richard said. "Assuming of course that his existence is more verifiable than Mann's."

"Oh, I'm sure you'll meet him soon. Have you ever heard of the Hallstatt group?"

"No." Richard said. "Doesn't the term refer to one of the early periods of Celtic settlement? It was in the Druid book."

"Yes, but there is also an organization by that name."

"In Alsace?"

"In Germany and France. They don't make the distinction as carefully as modern geographers."

"Is this a neo-Nazi organization?" Lois asked.

"No," the inspector said. "They are more complex than that. It started as a philosophical movement among some of the students at the University of Freiburg a few years ago. It is very much concerned with language and history. They argue that the German language, because it is so deeply rooted in place, is able to express philosophical ideas much better than other languages. You can think more deeply in German. And they are interested in the history of the area."

"It sounds a lot like Heidegger," Richard said.

"Exactly," the inspector said. "The movement began in 1976, shortly after Heidegger's death. Heidegger's work is important for them, though they don't connect it with Nazis, with the war and all that. And they're interested in the Druids, too, or rather, the

Celts. The Druid thing is only part of it, part of the concern about the importance of history."

"And your speech about 'ordinary people,' that was disguised Heidegger, a sort of little test for me?"

"I knew you would recognize it. Don't think of it as a test, but rather as a compliment, like serving a guest a wine you know he is fond of. And after all, Heidegger did make some good points."

"That's what I thought," Richard said. "Though I'm less and less certain about it. I don't suppose you've heard from your friend, Delacroix, the reason I'm on this continent?"

"I'm meeting Hervé in Genoa next week. We will plan our fishing trip in Norway. The most wonderful salmon in the whole world. I don't suppose you'd be free to join us?"

Richard was uncertain how to respond, or even whether the invitation was more than a sort of politeness that he was honour-bound to refuse. "I'd certainly like to meet Mr. Delacroix," he said. "But as to the fishing, I'd have to think about that."

"Take your time," the inspector said, as if the invitation were made out of deep friendship. "I'll check with you back in Strasbourg. I have spoken of you to Hervé, and he is also anxious to meet you."

Richard saw that Lois was still not paying any attention to the conversation. She seemed deeply interested in something that was going on in the kitchen, where white-suited workers could be glimpsed as the swinging doors opened and closed. Kessler reached for the bill, but Richard refused to let him pay for more than the brandy. Kessler seemed fluent in Portuguese, and he joked with the waiter as they left.

Lois stepped out into the street before the men. Just before they stepped through the door, the inspector whispered to Richard, "And of course I'll need the girl's address in Paris. You can leave it with the desk clerk, and I'll pick it up in the morning."

For a moment Richard was tempted to tell the inspector he did not know her address, but he just said, "Okay, only don't frighten her."

"Of course not," the inspector answered. "That's not part of our procedure."

On the way back to the hotel, the inspector chatted about the glories of Lisbon. He recommended the market especially, calling it the best in all of Europe. A prostitute, bolder than the others, spoke to them out of the darkness of a hidden doorway, and the inspector answered her cheerfully. He seemed full of good humour this evening, so magnanimous that he dropped a few coins into a sleeping beggar's hat without waking him.

That night Richard did not sleep well. He dreamed about fishing in Norway, and woke to see that Lois was sitting at the low desk in the room, sketching. Later he felt her body against his, cold, so she must just have come to bed. As the room lightened with dawn, he got up to go the bathroom. His mouth felt thick and foul from the brandy, so he brushed his teeth and washed, spraying cold water onto his face.

On his way back to bed he stopped to look at Lois's sketches. The light in the room made them strangely distorted, so he carried them to window. He understood then that what he had seen was not a trick of the light. The sketches of the old woman were like nothing that Lois had ever done before. They were certainly not meant for children. The old woman whose singing they had listened to squatted in these poses like some evil toad. The passers-by were wispy figures, frail spectres passing before their tormentor. Richard was struck that he had never thought before that the Devil might be a woman.

***

The train rattled down from Lisbon, swaying and creaking as it bent around curves too tight to have been designed for trains. Richard looked down into the back gardens behind shanties, a few cabbages, an orange tree, green and loaded with oranges, though it was early in the season.

Lois was trying to sleep. She seemed to need more sleep these days. They had got up early to go to the market In Lisbon, and Richard's mind was still lush with the mounds of gigantic fish, the piles of vegetables, the trucks and carts, the sing-song bargaining.

The swaying African women selling nuts and spices in the street, baskets balanced on their heads, had been singing a song whose rhythm had planted itself somewhere just behind his waking.

Lois moaned, a soft nasal sound in the noisy compartment, and Richard decided she was probably dreaming about the rat. After the market, they had sat on the rocky beach watching the fishermen casting for tiny silver fish that Lois had guessed were destined to be sardines. A big, grey rat had slipped from behind a rock just at Lois's feet, then scampered to safety a metre away. Its claws made a metallic noise as it ran. He had heard the noise of the scraping feet, but he did not see the rat.

Richard was looking for cork trees. He was supposed to wake Lois when he found them. Along the way there were huge trees with numbers on them, but they did not look like cork trees to Richard, and he didn't want to awaken Lois. They had been travelling for three weeks now, and Lois was beginning to feel cramped by small hotel rooms and even smaller compartments on trains. Richard had been trying to compensate by creating minor diversions so that they could be apart for a few minutes each day. This was hard for him, because he was still terrified that she would come to harm in one of the cities they passed through. He thought of the narrow winding streets of Barcelona and the dark, furtive figures in alleyways. Lois looks exactly like what she is, he thought, a frail blonde figure, lost in a strange country.

They rounded a high hill, and on the highway below, along the curve of a river, a convoy of Japanese jeep-style vehicles followed each other in tight formation. Suzukis, they looked like to Richard, but he couldn't read the insignia at this distance.

Richard was worried about his eyes. Lately, it seemed to him that they were beginning to fail. He couldn't read a book without holding it at an awkward distance, and he couldn't make out road signs that he ought to be able to read with ease. It seemed perverse to him that his eyes should be failing in two directions. His knees were stiff every morning, and he had begun to listen to the sounds his body made. He wondered whether the sounds were new or whether he had just started to pay attention to them.

Richard listened for his heartbeat, soft and regular inside him. He felt as if he could actually hear it. For several months now, he had found himself waking in bed feeling that his heart had stopped, and that he was falling. He would have to lunge forwards into consciousness, and that would sometimes wake Lois. He tried to remember whether he had ever contemplated his own death back in Canada. He must have, but he couldn't remember death taking on the urgency it seemed to have taken since they had landed in Frankfurt. It was there, somewhere beyond his gaze, something like a horizon, moving in time.

The train rounded another curve and Richard watched a peasant on a motorcycle so laden with produce that the driver was barely visible. He rolled the word *peasant* on his tongue, whispered it aloud. He wondered why he didn't think of the man as a farmer. Lois was certainly asleep now, her mouth slightly open, and he was grateful when the door slid open and a woman with a young boy entered, waking her. Richard had never liked to see anyone asleep. The vulnerability of the sleeper frightened him and made him think of death.

For the next hour Richard and Lois were silent. The woman who had intruded was pretty in a dark and heavy-set way, but her child was badly behaved. He chattered to his mother in Portuguese, climbed on the seats, ate chocolate with loud sucking sounds. The mother was doting, catching quick glances at Richard and Lois to see if they'd noticed how beautiful and clever the child was. When the train stopped at Portimão, the mother and child left. They were picked up in a silver limousine, but two other cars had also arrived, and the welcoming committee consisted of about fifteen people.

"Must be somebody important," Lois said. "The young heir to the family fortunes, allowed to do precisely as he wishes."

"You don't know," Richard replied. "Maybe he's suffering from an incurable disease and they're trying to make his last moments as happy as can be."

Lois had lost interest. She searched through her bag for an orange. "I'm going to suffer from an incurable disease if I have to sleep on another bed as bad as that one in the Hotel Sur."

They had been staying in two-star hotels. Most of the rooms would have been condemned in Canada, but Richard was determined not to make judgements. They were only in the hotels for a few hours. What difference did it make?

"It will be better in Faro," he told her. "It's a tourist place, right on the ocean. In the off-season there'll be lots of good cheap places."

He imagined a cabin on the beach, surf rolling in. He realized that he was thinking of Hawaii. Richard had chosen Faro because one of the secretaries at work had been there. She had loved the place and talked about it for weeks. In Lisbon, it had seemed like the natural next place.

The train started with a jolt, and Richard was aware that he was now riding backwards. A conductor wearing an official jacket, but old, faded jeans, poked his head into the compartment. Richard passed him their tickets and asked, "How long is it until we get to Faro, à quelle heure arriverons-nous à Faro?"

The conductor ignored both Richard's languages and replied with a volley of Portuguese. Richard turned up both his palms and opened his eyes wide in a gesture of incomprehension. The conductor hesitated a second, then replied in a heavily accented English.

"No Faro. This train Lagos."

"Faro," Richard informed him, pointing to the ticket he had just cancelled.

"No Faro," the conductor repeated. "This train Lagos." He clasped his hands together and said, "Portimão." Then he unclasped his hands and said, "Zoop, Faro," indicating that his left hand had gone on to Faro. Then he said, "Zoop, Lagos," indicating that they were now on the train to Lagos. Before Richard could ask him anything more, he sprinted from the compartment and swung down onto the platform of a station where the train slowed but did not stop. The sign on a bar at the station said Snack Bar.

Richard felt slow panic rising in him. "What does he mean, Lagos?" he asked Lois, though he didn't expect a reply. "They've broken the train into two parts, and we're on the wrong part. Let me see the map."

He took the map from the side compartment of his leather travelling bag, and studied it intently. The names of the towns were tiny and blurred. There was no stop before Lagos. They would have to wait for hours to catch the next train back. Richard hated waiting for trains, hated the impossible-to-comprehend schedules that were never correct anyway, and the station clerks, who apparently spoke no language at all.

Lois had curled her feet up on the seat, even though you were not allowed to do that, and she was happier than she had been in days.

"Good," she said. "We're going to Lagos."

"What do you mean, 'good,'" Richard said, trying not to sound cranky. "We're going to have to sit for hours at the station, and by the time we get to Faro it will be midnight."

"We're not going to Faro. We're going to Lagos. It's out of your hands."

Richard took a deep breath and looked out the window. They were passing another orchard heavy with bright oranges on dark-green trees. In the distance he could see low purple mountains. He thought about the drawings of the old woman, her features contorted in a horrible grimace and wondered whether he should ask Lois about them, but decided to wait.

"What's in Lagos?" he asked.

"It doesn't matter," Lois said. "We're going to spend a week there."

"Don't be stupid."

"A week. At least."

Richard stared out the window the rest of the way. They passed through the purple mountains, which were covered with what looked like white roses, and where rain fell in a delicate mist. He felt something heavy in his chest, like the constrictions he used to get when he smoked. Lois read an article about China from the *International Herald Tribune,* and her chin jutted forward. Richard could tell that the next few days were going to be difficult. As the train dropped from the mountains down to the coast, they moved into sunlight, but Richard felt the heaviness in his chest increase, and it seemed to him that he could scarcely breathe.

At the station a dozen older women carried cardboard signs advertising in English, Beachside Room For Two, 2,000 Escudos, and Good Clean Room, All Conv. 2,100 Escudos. Richard converted the numbers to Canadian dollars.

"Hey," he told Lois. "These are great deals."

"Forget it. You're no longer in charge."

Outside the station there were no taxis. Even the importunate renters of beachside rooms were on foot. They followed Richard and Lois all the way to the bridge before veering off. The canal Richard and Lois crossed was filled with brilliantly painted boats, red and blue and green. All the buildings in Lagos were snow-white. They followed the winding road down to what they believed must be the centre of the town. The road was cobbled, and sidewalk cafes announced their menus on blackboards mounted along the street, Fish and Chips, 200 Pesetas, Steak and Kidney Pie, 350 pesetas, Bangers and Eggs 250 Pesetas. The soft lilt of British voices was everywhere.

"This is bizarre," Richard told Lois. "This is a tourist trap for the English."

"I like it." Lois had never been to England. Richard had been there twice before and hated it. Back in Strasbourg, they had discussed the possibility of going to England while they were in Europe, but Richard had refused to go back.

The street turned into a driveway heavy with flowers. They arrived at the front door of the Hotel Lagos, a huge, snow-white structure of terraces and balconies and glass. Richard had a sense of *déjà vu*, but he realized that what he remembered was a scene out of some Hollywood movie.

"This is it," Lois told him. "We're staying here." The big, glass doors had five stars on them.

"Don't be stupid. This place will be incredibly expensive. We can get a two-star place for a third the cost."

When Lois turned towards him, Richard could see that her eyes were glassy. He couldn't tell if she were weeping or only angry.

"I'm staying here," she said. "What are we doing travelling through Europe like paupers? We have enough money to stay here. This is the first time we've taken a holiday together. I am not going to stay in another rat-hole."

Richard felt the pain in his chest tightening, but just as suddenly it left him exhausted and limp.

"Right," he said. "Lead on."

They entered into a cavernous opening. A red carpet swirled up a curving staircase to the reception desk on a mezzanine balcony. Huge crystal chandeliers fragmented the light and distributed it in shimmering flakes on the white wall. Lois registered, and told Richard that the cost would be forty-nine dollars a day, cheaper than the Hotel Sur. She led him down a wide corridor flanked with white leather chairs and sofas, to their room.

The room was also white, huge with a white rug and white curtains. From their balcony they could see the blue shimmer of the ocean. Richard took the bottle from his suitcase and poured them each a rum and Coke. Lois took a bath in the huge white bathtub while Richard explored the room. It had white built-in closets and drawers and a safe with a strangely shaped key. Richard put all his money in the safe and locked it with the key. Out on the balcony, under a chair, he discovered a pair of glasses left by a previous guest. They were thin, wire-rimmed glasses, and when Richard put them on he discovered he could read the room-service menu without difficulty. When Lois entered the room, naked after her bath, he realized that he could see her more clearly than he had been able to for years.

The evening passed in a haze. They walked down to the ocean. They ate squid in a cafe filled with English people. They got drunk on brandy in the hotel bar. They made love. When Richard woke up the next morning, sunlight was streaming into the room from the balcony. He took a deep breath.

His wife was perched on the back of a white armchair, and he could see her perfectly clearly with his naked eyes.

* * *

The first day in Lagos, they explored the town, walking along the cobbled streets and poking into the little shops. Richard bought a leather cap that looked ridiculous on him, and together they bought a gigantic beach towel. The place was full of English tourists, their fluted accents piping above the soft purr of Portuguese, and most of the restaurants seemed aimed at serving them. The few restaurants that served Portuguese food had the same menu, a limited offering that specialized in squid.

The second day, they rented a car, an Austin Mini. Richard chose it over a larger Renault because he said it reminded him of the car he had driven when he was in graduate school. They decided they would drive into the countryside and see what they could find.

From the town, there was no indication of mountains, but the road climbed steeply, and before long they were looking over a deep valley. A sign by the side of the road said Barragen de Bravura. The palm trees and orange orchards of the coast gave way to wild, tangled shrubs and a sort of wild-rose tree with white blossoms. Richard stopped the car and clambered down the bank at the side of the road to a small grove. He picked one of the white roses and brought it to the car.

"Here," he said, "a flower for a beautiful lady." The flower was firm and waxy, Lois discovered, but it had no scent.

The Austin Mini swung around a hairpin bend to a parking space where the road ended. Below them, they could catch a flash of steel-grey water. It had been cloudy when they left Lagos, and they had driven through mist as they climbed the mountain. Now the mist had thickened into rain. Richard wanted to wait in the car until the rain stopped, but Lois convinced him to walk down to the lake. She felt strong here. The continual moving from place to place, never stopping for long enough to get at all comfortable where you were, had begun to bother her. Since their airplane had settled in under the blue fog at the Frankfurt airport, she had felt increasingly vulnerable, but something here made her feel at home.

They wound down a narrow trail that led by a house almost hidden in the bushes. A car was parked beside it, and a road led down to the lake. When they got there, the lake was a dark, shiny grey, and the trees and clouds reflected in it were also grey and black. All colour seemed to have drained from the landscape, leaving only shapes and contrasts. Even the leaves of the shrubs, wet with the gentle rain, were silvery green. Richard dipped his fingers in the water and said it was cold. Lois felt for herself. The water was cold, crystal-clear and pure. Being in the mountains excited her. It reminded her of picnics with her parents in the Kootenays back home, and of waiting for the ferry across the Columbia River where she had watched an osprey diving for fish.

On an impulse, she got down on her knees to wash her face in the water. She was momentarily aware of herself bent over the water like a woman leaning out of a window. The shock of the cold water on her skin was more than she had expected, and she gasped. She splashed her face again and again. She could see her reflection in the water blurring and coming into focus as she dipped her hands in the lake. The face she saw was pretty but distant, someone she had once known but forgotten.

Richard teased her on the way back. Her mascara had run, he said, and she looked childlike and sad, like a circus clown modelling herself on Charlie Chaplin. In the car, she took a towel and wiped off the make-up, but she did not replace it for the rest of the day.

The third day, they went looking for a castle. The map took them over the mountain and back down to another part of the coast. On the way, they saw in the distance huge, white villas, remote and inaccessible. The clerk at the hotel had told them that these belonged to wealthy northerners, Scandinavians and Germans. She thought about the women imprisoned in these places, but when she told Richard of her thoughts he laughed and said they had servants and swimming pools.

Along the road they passed signs with pictures of the castle, but they could not find it. When they realized they were lost, they stopped at a garage in a village called Aljezur to ask directions. The clerk there seemed embarrassed. He explained that it was a very poor castle, hardly anything at all, not worth visiting. It would only be a waste of time. Finally, he pointed out the trail, back across the bridge they had just crossed, and through the narrow streets of the village.

The road was steep and it curved through the yards of the inhabitants. They drove through a muddy stretch between a house and barn and emerged at the top of a hill that they hadn't noticed before. The town wound around the base of a hill that seemed from the bottom to be no more than a gentle rise, but which from the top commanded a clear view in every direction. The guidebook explained that these were the ruins of a Moorish castle. There was nothing left but rock foundations and a pit, which might have been a dungeon or a cellar. The grass and flowers were knee-deep and there were no paths. They might have been the only visitors in years. They took pictures of each other lying in the red and yellow flowers, and peering up out of the darkness of what might have been a dungeon.

On the way back, they followed the coast to Sagres, a winding road that led past cactuses with tulip flowers. The air was heavy with the smell of Eucalyptus trees. They stopped at a roadside cafe and ordered rabbit. Richard said it was too early in the day to drink, but Lois ordered a glass of red wine anyway. She found she couldn't eat the rabbit, even though, as Richard said, it tasted like over-cooked chicken. Richard ate most of hers as well.

Later that evening they went to a bar in Lagos, where they sat drinking beer until a young couple arrived, their backpacks decorated with large Canadian flags. Lois started to talk to the girl, and in a few minutes the couple had joined them. They had been travelling for six months, hitch-hiking around Greece, and hadn't seen any English-language newspapers. Canada might be as far away as the moon, they said. They had met a lot of Americans, but hardly any Canadians. Lois told them about the car and invited them out for a ride in the countryside. They said they would like to, but they weren't sure. If they were coming, they would arrive at the hotel at nine o'clock the next morning. The girl suggested Cape St. Vincent. The guidebook said it was the most western part of Europe, she told them, further west even than Ireland.

The next day the young couple were not there, and so, Lois driving, they made their way to Faro, getting lost in a detour through the intricate maze of streets in Portimão. It was another day of grey rain. The traffic was heavy, and she felt tense and restrained. Richard kept his window open and the camera in his lap. He was trying to take pictures of old Portuguese women dressed in black. "Kitchen witches," he called them. The sun came out briefly in Faro, just long enough for them to have lunch at a sidewalk restaurant and watch the waiter chase away a little beggar boy who returned as soon as the waiter left. Richard tossed the boy a coin, and he disappeared.

The following morning they decided to drive out to Cape St. Vincent. The day was brilliant and already hot by the time the sparrows in the tree outside the room awakened them. They picked up the little Mini in the underground parking lot, and as they came up from the darkness into the syrupy golden light, they saw the young Canadian couple waving and grinning.

Their names were Catherine and Roy. Richard had forgotten, and Lois had to remind him. Catherine was dark and small. Roy was as tall as Richard, so blond that his hair was almost a shock of white. They crawled into the inadequate back seat of the Mini, giggling and happy, glad that Richard and Lois were going to Cape St. Vincent. They would pass a youth hostel that was famous all over Europe, a fort that had turned into a prison before becoming a hostel. You still had to sleep in cells. It was just outside a town called Sagres.

Richard drove very fast along the narrow road that followed the coastline. Every so often Lois caught a flash of blue, but there never seemed any place where you could get to the water. After a while the lush farmlands gave way to rough scrub trees and reddish rock. The couple in the back seat chatted about their weeks in Greece, their plans to separate and visit relatives in Scotland and in Germany. Roy explained that the lighthouse at Cape St. Vincent was the third brightest in the world. Or else that was some other lighthouse, but he thought it must be this one.

They drove past Sagres, a corner with a flashing light, past the prison-hostel, grey and forbidding on the edge of a cliff, past the succession of barren rocks, until they arrived at the lighthouse. In all that emptiness, the rocky point of land was crowded. A swarm of German tourists entering the gates merged momentarily with the Japanese coming out, a swirling mass that a moment later had congealed again into separate groups. From the cliff wall of the lighthouse, Lois looked down into water that crashed and swirled, a visible maelstrom from that angle, something she had only seen in pictures before. Richard would not stay and watch. He hated heights, said they made him dizzy. He went back to sit in the car. Lois didn't want to leave. The place and moment seemed significant, loaded with some meaning she could not unravel. In the distance, she could see ships passing by. If I were a mermaid, she thought, I would sing to them.

The young couple took romantic pictures of each other. After they left, Lois waited another five minutes, checking the time on her watch. Then she headed back to the car. Now she felt guilty that she had acted selfishly, kept the others waiting.

Richard was sitting on the hood of the car, eating some giant deep-fried pastry dusted with fine, white sugar. He seemed happy, explaining to Catherine and Roy about the body they had found, its disappearance, and the inspector. He imitated the inspector's accent and bearing with a sharp authenticity that reminded Lois suddenly of the inspector's presence. Richard wasn't really good at imitating people, though he liked to do it, but in some turn of the head, some rhythm and inflection he had caught the inspector exactly.

"Find any more bodies?" Roy called out to Lois as she approached.

"Just a couple," she answered, "back there in the courtyard," and she gestured toward the lighthouse. "They'll probably be gone before you can find them. That's what usually happens." She saw that in the far end of the parking lot the people from the buses were milling around a couple of stands.

"What are they selling?" she asked Richard.

"Tablecloths," he said. "Beautiful white tablecloths and smaller blue and white ones covered with roosters."

Lois was tempted, but she had the vision of herself hauling a snow-white tablecloth around Europe, worrying about it wherever she went. She decided against even looking. Richard offered her a bite of his pastry and offered to get one for her. Lois refused. She felt she was hovering on an edge. She didn't think she had gained weight since her arrival, but she felt at the same time that one wrong choice might tumble her over into fatness.

When they got into the car, Lois slid the seat as far forward as it would go so that there would be room for Roy's legs. She felt cramped and confined, her face too close to the windshield. The rear-view mirror was so close that she could see only her eyes reflected. Grey eyes, she thought. Eyes without colour.

"There has to be a beach somewhere," Richard said, as he retraced the route along the flat and treeless cliffs.

"Surely there'd be a sign," Catherine suggested.

"No," Roy answered. "There are never signs. You have to happen on them. Or else somebody tells you."

Without warning, Richard pulled the car off the road onto the red flats that led to the cliff. They climbed out of the car, Roy, who had been cramped in the back seat, stretching luxuriously. Lois walked down a little rocky path that led to the edge of the cliff but turned before it got there. She climbed over a couple of low rocks, eager to be the first to see the shoreline.

What she saw took her breath away. The slow, breaking waves of the surf surged up a broad stretch of golden sand. It was the scene from every travel brochure. Strange fairy-tale rock formations rose on either side, and where the rocks on the far point obscured a farther bay, caves tunnelled into the cliff face. She realized she must have cried out, because the others were beside her almost at once. They gave little whoops of joy and started to scramble back down the path, which soon gave way to a set of steep concrete stairs.

By the time Lois reached the beach, the others had already removed their shoes and socks, and were dancing in the chilly water. The beach stretched for less than a quarter of a mile, and, although there were no other vehicles near, it was dotted with figures. Most of them, she realized with a start, were naked. Two young men played a sweeping game of tennis with balls and rackets, but without a net. Little groups sat sunning themselves along the edge of the cliff, and a few people splashed and swam in the water, which was shallow for a long way out. The cliffs protected them from three sides, and in that enclosed space it was very hot.

"It must be ninety above," Catherine said, slipping out of the light jacket she had been wearing. Richard had brought along the camera, and was trying to get the others to pose for a picture. Roy was anxious but Catherine resisted. "Pictures never look like me," she complained.

"If it doesn't turn out good, I promise to destroy it, okay?" Richard said, and with some reluctance, Catherine agreed. Just a few feet away, Lois realized, a family was picnicking behind a rock. The father was a short, fat man wearing only a Greek fisherman's hat. The mother, also naked, was pregnant, and they had three children, all of whom, however, were wearing bathing suits. They watched the Canadians with interest but without defiance. Lois felt herself an intruder, threatening the vulnerability of these naked people, though they themselves seemed unaware of their nakedness.

They found a spot to sit down on the far side of the bay. Roy ran back to the car to pick up a blanket and the picnic lunch he and Catherine had brought, a couple of loaves of bread, a chunk of cheese and two bottles of red wine. They sat in the sun and ate the food. Roy and Catherine found a little tidal pool full of tiny fish a few feet away, and they sat on the edge with their feet in the water, which they said was almost hot. Richard went to explore the caves. Lois took off as many clothes as she dared, put on her sunglasses and watched the people.

The two tennis players had made their way down the beach until they were quite near. They ran back and forth, their penises swinging comically as they jumped and dived to get difficult shots. They would be good players under different conditions. A reddish dog, some version of an Irish setter, ran with them, chasing the ball and refusing to give it back whenever he managed to get it.

There were more women than men on the beach, and, except for the couple with children, they all looked young. A couple came around the cliff, past the caves where Richard was exploring, and set a blanket down close to Lois. The man was dark and looked bad-tempered. The girl was blonde and tanned. She looked Swedish. She seemed a little overweight in the long hippie-style dress she was wearing. They both took off all their clothes immediately, and Lois realized that she was mistaken. The girl's body was as close to perfect as anything she had ever seen. The man was good-looking, but his penis was shrivelled, hardly more than a pink bud in the dark hair that surrounded it.

The tennis players stopped their game to welcome a black man. They ran up to him, and he put his arms around their shoulders, and the three of them marched up the beach, a tall black man in a red and white striped shirt, and two naked white men. She realized they were probably gay. For some reason she could not explain to herself, she was disappointed. She felt a cold hand on her back, and realized that Richard had returned.

"Don't," she said.

"Look," he answered. "Wet."

Lois looked. Richard was wearing only his jeans, their cuffs rolled up. His hair was wet, and his chest was covered with beads of water.

"You went swimming? Naked?"

"Just through the cave. It opens into another bay. I just took off my clothes and went in for a swim."

"Why there? Why not here?"

Richard shrugged to indicate Roy and Catherine, who seemed to be asleep, their arms around each other on the edge of the tidal pool. "The kids," he said. "Canadians never take off their clothes in front of each other."

"What's the water like?" Lois asked. "Is it cold?"

"Beautiful. Refreshing. A little cool but, really, no problem."

"Let's go," she said. She got up from the blanket and headed for the caves, Richard following. The caves were dark and gloomy, vaulted like miniature cathedrals, and the walls were covered with crustaceans. Richard indicated a cave that led off to the left and they emerged into blinding sunshine and another bay. A half-dozen people sunned themselves at a distance, but nobody was near.

Richard slipped out of his jeans and shorts and put them on top of a rock near the cave entrance. He turned and ran out into the water. Lois slipped out of her clothes and followed. The water struck her as bitterly cold, but she ran out until it was deep enough that she could plunge under. She rose, the salt taste in her mouth, and began a slow, strong crawl. All her senses were intensely alive. She tasted and smelled the water. The drops that splashed in front of her were crystal, shading to green. "I am alive," she thought, speaking the words to herself as she thought them. "I am alive in the cold Atlantic."

On the way back, Richard and Roy argued about travelling. Roy said he wanted to travel out of pure curiosity. "I want to see things just for the sake of having seen them," he said. "I don't need any reason. I mean, things like cathedrals or wrecked castles don't have some large meaning. It's nice to speculate about history, but these things don't signify anything in my life. I travel because I'm curious. Period."

Lois could see Richard becoming professorial. "Curiosity isn't enough," he told Roy. "You're alive and, because you're alive, you have a responsibility to make sense of your life." It struck her that he missed his classes and his colleagues, though he never mentioned them. She had heard him in arguments with students and other professors, but his arguments had nothing to do with their lives, and he never made them at home. Lois remembered the clarity of the water and her own sense that her swim had some sort of meaning greater than the details of her ordinary life. She had always hesitated to enter things, but she had begun to wonder whether it took some total immersion to get at the heart of things.

But what exactly had she learned? That she was alive and could feel things? Surely that was the most obvious fact there was. And yet she felt she had never been so aware of herself and her sensations. She could feel the roughness of the towel she had put over the seat, the cold smoothness of the door handle where her leg touched it. She could smell the coconut of Catherine's suntan lotion. She licked her upper lip. She could still taste the ocean salt. She felt sad. Her own death seemed somewhere vastly distant, but Richard's seemed much nearer on the horizon of events. She reached over and stroked his knee.

They let Roy and Catherine out at the hostel. Some of the women selling tablecloths from the lighthouse had moved here, and Lois bought an elegant white tablecloth because it was round and would fit on the round table at home. Richard bought more of the deep-fried pastries from the van that sold them, and gave one each to Roy and Catherine. By the time Lois got back to the car, they had exchanged addresses and promised to write. They embraced awkwardly, Roy planting a whisper of a kiss on Lois's cheek. For a long time she could feel it there, as if it kept a real existence after they had driven all the way back to the hotel and taken the elevator up to their room.

The next day they went back to the beach. The same people were there, but without the other Canadians to keep them hesitant, Richard and Lois took off their clothes and sunned themselves naked on the sand. Lois was struck that she was not embarrassed, that nobody paid any attention to them. They stayed until late in the afternoon, when the sun dipped down behind the cliff and it got suddenly cold.

They decided to stay on in Lagos, drawn by the lure and the freedom of the beach. Richard had a sunburn, because he wouldn't wear suntan lotion, and because he had fallen asleep on the blanket and Lois had forgotten to tell him to roll over. Like an omelette, she thought, I should turn him like an omelette. The morning had been cloudy, so they had waited until noon to head out. Now there was sporadic sunshine.

When they got to the bottom of the concrete stairs, they saw that they were the only people on the beach. The stretch of golden sand glistened before them, but they had taken only a few steps before they realized that what was glistening was oil. Perfectly circular patches, from the size of a coin to the size of a pancake, were everywhere. It was difficult to walk without stepping on one. Richard bent down to pick one up, deceived by the hard, shiny surface into thinking that it was solid. His hand turned black from the oil, and he could not clean it off, neither with water nor with the towel he used to rub it. They found a clean spot large enough for the blanket high on the far side of the beach, but after a few minutes the sun went behind a cloud, and a cold wind swept in from the sea. They drank a bottle of wine and ate the cheese and bread they had brought, but the beach was damaged now. Nothing good could happen there.

They got into the car and headed back under the low Atlantic clouds. She thought they were going back to the hotel, but Richard turned off the road onto what seemed no more than a trail through a field. A hand-painted sign read Castelejo Aguia. The road wound for several miles through land too rough for anything but scattered bushes to grow. Then it stopped abruptly at the edge of the ocean. A wall of rock loomed high above them to the left, and Lois saw that they were at the base of the cliff on which the lighthouse stood. The beach was composed of smooth large stones. The waves, enormous and grey, smashed on the rocks with a rage that sent spray high into the air and wet them as they walked.

Richard wanted to take a picture of Lois sitting on a boulder, against the fury of the ocean. She climbed up to the top of the rock and composed herself as Richard fumbled with the camera, trying to keep the lens from getting wet. The wind blew the spume of a wave, and water hit Lois, soaking her. Her hair fell in strings, and she realized that she was as wet as if she had been swimming in all her clothes. At that moment, Lois was exultant. Richard was aiming the camera now, trying to get her into focus. Lois suddenly saw herself from his perspective, herself wind-blown and wet against the fury of the waves, herself watching.

***

They arrived in Seville just as the light failed. Richard had been amazed at the long, green rolling hills of southern Spain. They looked exactly like southern Alberta in the spring. The train seemed not to follow roads, but to have headed out on its own through green wheat fields, far from any houses. Every so often, snow-white cities appeared in the distance like mirages. They shimmered on the horizon for a minute and then were gone. Richard had begun to make notes for his novel. He would write about three generations of fathers and sons, and war would be the centre of the work. He had tried a couple of times to begin writing a part of the text, but realized that he was not going to be able to write it until after he had visited the battlefields. He could imagine what his men might do or say, but he could not imagine where they might be. He tried to imagine the Somme as no different from country fields in Canada, but he knew that was wrong. He was anxious to leave Spain, to go to the north of France. He felt certain that the battlefields themselves would give him signs.

The smell of orange blossoms hung heavy on the warm night air. There were no taxis anywhere, but a man who claimed to be from Vancouver gave them directions to the hotel Inglaterra on the Plaza Nueva. The clerk who led them to their room cautioned them about carrying leather bags. Men with knives, he said, would cut the straps and run away with them. He advised them to put everything of value in the hotel safe, and they did. It was nearly midnight before they decided to walk out into the streets to find something to eat.

The streets were filled with excitement. The narrow winding lanes of the old city were brilliantly lit. A few stores were still open, selling expensive clothes, and small sidewalk cafes merged so that it was hard to say where one ended and the other began. Everywhere, Richard saw beautiful women dressed in elegant clothes, and thin, narrow men, who looked like the models in clothing ads. He had never seen so many beautiful people. They heard no English anywhere, only the soft, fluent lilt of Spanish.

They ordered shrimp, and the waiter brought them a giant plate. Most of the tables were full, and the laughter and joking of people made the air tense. It was midnight, but it seemed like early evening. Two pretty little girls in dirty dresses were going from table to table, begging. They looked to be about six years old. They laughed and giggled, and showed something to people. Nobody paid much attention to them. After a while, they arrived at Richard and Lois's table, and unfolded their treasure from a dirty, red rag they placed on the table. It was a dead sparrow. They offered it to Lois, who refused it with a nod of the head. They said something Richard didn't understand, and, when he told them, in English, that he did not speak Spanish, the nearer one shouted something, then spat at him. They grabbed up the sparrow and ran between the tables, still shouting until they disappeared around a corner.

"They're going to die of disease," Richard said.

"They'll die of something," Lois answered. "I can't imagine them surviving to grow up."

"Look at the wealth," Richard said. "Have you ever seen so many incredibly well-dressed people in one place?" As if to prove his point, a long, black limousine pulled up at the corner of the street, out of an alleyway Richard had not noticed. Two couples, the men in tuxedos, the women in evening gowns, appeared from inside the restaurant. A chauffeur opened the doors for them and they got in the car. It pulled away soundlessly.

Later, back at the hotel, Lois sketched the children. In her picture they stood on their tiptoes, holding up the sparrow as an offering.

There was nothing innocent in their faces at all. Although they had the soft round bodies of children, they looked old and profoundly evil.

"Christ," Richard told her, "You must have spent too much time looking at Bosch. Those little girls look like killers."

"I was just imagining what they might become," she answered.

"What happened to all those sweet little kids and the twittering birds?" he asked.

"I can still do them. You want a twittering bird?" With a few deft strokes she drew in an angelic bird hovering just over one of the girl's shoulders.

"Terrific. Now it looks like a combined effort of Walt Disney and Heironymous Bosch. You'll have no trouble selling these."

"No," Lois answered. "I don't suppose."

That night Richard dreamed about the couple on the motorcycle. In the dream, he was driving down a dark street, and they followed him. The motorcycle was huge, much bigger than Richard's car, and Richard felt a panicked need to escape. He woke up unsure where he was, his chest tight with pain, and he didn't go back to sleep until dawn flooded the room with light. Then he slept fitfully until Lois woke him, showered and dressed, ready to go.

They were in the enormous cathedral, looking at a huge, golden altar, when Richard was suddenly overcome with a feeling of profound weakness. He felt himself slipping, and realized that he was going to faint. He remembered that you should put your head between your knees if you are going to faint, and so he allowed himself to slip to the ground, curling his head between his knees as he did so. He could hear a man talking with an American accent, telling someone that Christopher Columbus was buried in this very church, only they weren't sure where.

Lois knelt beside him, and he could hear her voice, distant and, it seemed to him, addressed to someone else, asking what was wrong. For a moment, Richard felt that it would be easy to slip away to sleep, and that seemed inviting. Then, the world rushed back in on him. He felt the cool air of the cathedral, and could see a maze of legs surrounding him.

"I'm all right," he said, rising to his feet. About a half-dozen people who had surrounded him murmured sympathetically. "It's okay," he said. "I'm fine," and he headed out towards the bright light from the door. Lois caught his arm.

"What happened?"

"Nothing. I just got a little woozy, that's all. I couldn't sleep last night, and I guess I'm just over-tired."

"Let's go back to Strasbourg," Lois said. "Let's just put an end to all this moving around and stay in one place for a while."

"We'll go back to Paris," Richard said. "Then we'll decide." He was already certain that he wanted to go to Dieppe, but it was the wrong time to mention it. He imagined Dieppe as cool and peaceful. They had arrived at a little sidewalk cafe, and Lois insisted they wait a minute while Richard recovered from his dizzy spell. They each ordered a beer, though Lois thought it was probably not wise for Richard to drink.

"It's okay," Richard told her. "It was just a momentary thing. These things happen to everyone."

Lois pulled out some photographs from her little backpack. She had left her purse at the hotel, in the safe, but she had transferred most of its contents to the blue and red backpack. Richard did not want to look at the pictures again. The shop in Lagos that had developed them had distorted all the colours, and the photos annoyed Richard, showing him in places he could not remember.

Richard leaned back in the shade, under the soft Seville sun, and looked at the line of rooftops. Everything was scrolled and etched, and the leaves of the trees were the dark green of midsummer. Lois was seated directly in the sun, and she seemed to glow, as if she herself were giving off light.

Then, soundlessly and without warning, he found himself witness to a strange tableau. A man on a small motorcycle was leaning over the table and picking up Lois's backpack. Lois had obviously seen him, and had grabbed one of the shoulder straps. Richard sat paralyzed, unable to move. In slow motion the motorcyclist tugged on the backpack, pulling Lois over a chair and down onto the street. She would not let go, and the motorcyclist reluctantly released his hold to steady his machine.

Then, with a sudden rush, Richard's reflexes began to work. He hurtled into the street and ran after the motorcycle. The cyclist slowed, and turned to look over his shoulder, and at that moment Richard nearly caught him. His hand grazed the seat of the cycle as he lunged to try and overturn it. The driver put on a burst of speed that shot him into the heavy traffic of a cross street, and he was nearly hit by a car. Richard shouted, "Thief," at the retreating figure, then remembering his phrase book, called out, "Ladron," but by then the figure had already merged into the traffic.

When he got back to Lois, a crowd had gathered, expressing sympathy. The thief had been hiding near a church across the street, they indicated. They shook their heads, and the waiter, who spoke a few words of English, kept repeating, "Terrible." Nobody volunteered to call the police, however. Lois was bruised, and she had scraped her knee when she had been dragged into the street, but she insisted she was all right. The waiter brought them each a free beer from the bar, and they sat down, trying to piece together every detail of what had happened.

"I saw him out of the corner of my eye," Lois said. "Somehow, I knew what he was going to do, so I grabbed for my bag." She was flushed but pleased with herself.

"I nearly got him," Richard said. "I was inches away."

"And what would you have done with him if you had got him?"

"I don't know. Hold him for the police."

"I'm glad you didn't catch him." Lois said. "If you had caught him it would have been much worse."

They had just finished their beer when Lois pointed to a motorcycle driving slowly toward them. "That's him," she said. The motorcyclist drove steadily along the street until he was directly across from them. He glared at Richard, and Richard felt he had never seen such hatred. Then the man pulled a small pistol from his pocket, pointed it at Richard and fired. It made a sharp pinging sound, and the cyclist roared away. Richard felt nothing. He ran his hand over his chest, expecting to feel blood, but there was nothing. There was nobody else in the street, no witnesses, no sign that anything had happened.

"Quick," Richard said to Lois. He led her by the hand across the street, back towards the cathedral. A line of taxis was parked across from the main entrance. Richard pushed Lois into the first taxi and told the man, "Hotel Inglaterra." The driver pointed down the street to indicate that the trip was too short to be worthwhile, but Richard pulled a handful of bills out of his pocket and gave them to him. The driver smiled, and pulled out into the traffic. He turned the wrong way and made an elaborate detour around the cathedral and an ancient castle that brought them to the hotel from the opposite direction.

Lois had said nothing during the entire trip, but now back at the hotel she was full of questions.

"What happened?" she asked. "What is this all about?"

"He shot at me," Richard said. "He had a pistol and he fired at me. For a while I thought he had hit me, but I seem to be okay."

"I thought he just shook his fist at you. I didn't see any pistol."

"I saw the pistol. It was tiny and silver, and I heard the bullet go ping as it hit something."

"We'd better call the police." Lois said. She had begun to tremble. "I hate this city. I want to get out of here."

"It would do no good to call the police," Richard said. "They'd never catch that guy, and we'd spend days sitting around filling out forms." They were standing in the centre of the large, open reception area. The clerk behind the desk was in low-toned argument with someone over the telephone.

"Well, let's just go," Lois said. "Let's get our stuff and catch the first train out of here."

It was early afternoon when they got to the station. The train to Madrid did not leave until ten o'clock. Richard checked their bags, leaving them in the care of a man with a toothless grin. Then they went out into the city again. Lois wanted to stay in the station, but Richard assured her that there would be no danger.

"It was an isolated incident" he told her. "That guy was just a common thief, trying to pick off your bag. The problem was that you were tougher than he was. Then I chased him. I called him a thief, and that wrecked his dignity. The shot was probably just aimed to frighten me. He couldn't have missed at that distance if he wanted to hit."

Lois agreed, with some misgivings, and they found their way to a market where people were selling leather belts and purses.

Lois bought a little change purse, and Richard debated over a wallet before deciding it was too big to fit into his pocket without inviting pickpockets. Since the morning's incident, everything seemed insecure and dangerous. Lois was glad when Richard suggested that they find a restaurant where they could have a beer and a meal. The little place they found was dark and quiet, and by the time they left for the train they were both feeling the effects of the sharp Spanish beer.

They arrived in Madrid in early morning, and found they would have to go to another station to catch the train to Paris. The second station was huge, clean and modern. It looked like an airport. They had barely enough time to buy some bread and cheese and a couple of bottles of wine before the train hauled them out of the lush south and into an area of high sierras and cool distances. The sky was a soft grey, and the landscape had changed from hot greens and yellows to earth tones, brown and black and burnt umber.

It was just dark when they hit the border. They had to switch to a French train that would take them through Bordeaux and on to Paris. In the first-class section of the train, they had seen almost no other travellers. Now, as they lined up to go through customs, they realized that the train was filled with swarthy travellers, whole Spanish families, and Arabs with headdresses that reminded Richard of the pictures of Yasser Arafat he had seen in magazines. The customs officials seemed aggressive and angry. They shouted at people and hauled them out of line. When their turn came, Richard was prepared to make his case, but the official just waved them through as if he didn't see them.

Richard felt immensely tired when he got on the French train. There were no sleeping compartments, and he hoped that no one would join them, so that they might stretch out on the seats. Just as they were pulling out, a fat British boy joined them. He dropped his bag in the compartment, and left. Richard stretched out, hoping he could get some sleep before the boy returned. When he woke up to the grey light of dawn in the outskirts of Paris, the bag was gone. Lois was sitting up, reading the Margaret Atwood novel, and the passage-way was crowded with people.

"Paris?" Richard asked, rubbing his neck, which was stiff from the night's cramped ride.

"Paris," she answered.

***

"If you want to go to Dieppe," Lois said, "why don't we just get on a train and go to Dieppe?" They were walking down the rue Ste. Germaine, and Richard had stopped for a moment to rest. He was carrying the two large suitcases, and had been for some time. They had tried several hotels but they were all full.

"I don't know," Richard said. "Does it sound like some sort of monstrous arrogance to you? What do I know about writing a novel?"

"You'll never know unless you try." Lois answered. She realized that she sounded like an encouraging mother, but Richard seemed to brighten when she spoke, so she went on. "Look, we've got this year when we can do whatever we want. We might never get another one. So what if you don't get it written? At least you'll have had the experience of trying. And you don't seem too keen on Heidegger."

Richard laughed. "Rotten old Heidegger. The source of all my problems. Why didn't I choose somebody like Sartre? At least his politics were acceptable."

"Why didn't you?"

"I don't think you choose philosophers. They choose you. It's like catching a virus or something. You wake up one morning and you don't feel right, and suddenly you realize you've been infected by Bertrand Russell. Actually it was because we had to teach a course in twentieth-century European philosophy. The English department needed it. Nobody else wanted to teach it and I got it because I was the junior man."

"But you're not any more."

"No, but now it's too late. I've been infected."

Richard picked up the bags and they moved on. Lois spotted a little hotel down a side street just as they arrived at the Opera. It was called the Hotel Maricourt, and it had one room left. They registered. Lois had half-expected a note from the inspector. She wanted to talk to him about the motorcyclist in Seville, and she wanted to talk to someone about Richard's health, which seemed to her to be in danger. He had stopped complaining about the pain in his chest, but she could sometimes see that he was suffering even when he denied it.

The room was small, but, like the room in the Savoy, it had a convertible bathroom. This one could also serve as a sauna. Richard was pleased. He wanted to take a sauna and go to sleep. He hadn't been able to sleep on the train, he said. Lying in bed, a few minutes later, Lois realized that she was not at all tired herself. She didn't want to be here in this darkened room lying awake and listening to Richard breathe.

"I'm going out for a walk," she told Richard. He didn't answer, so she got up and dressed herself. She wasn't sure he had heard her. He would probably have insisted on getting up and coming with her if he had. She contemplated shaking him awake, then decided to write him a note instead. She wrote in large letters on a page she tore out of her notebook, and only at that moment realized that none of the hotels they had stayed in had notepaper and pens for customers.

She knew that Richard would be upset when he woke up and discovered that she was not there and for a moment she decided that she would stay. Then it struck her that Richard would sleep for hours. He would probably not even wake up before she returned. She put the note on the table beside him, under his watch where he would be sure to see it.

Outside, the morning sky was grey. The light seemed to have no specific source, but to emanate from the buildings and sidewalks themselves. She followed a street that led vaguely downhill until she found herself at the river. She turned right and realized that she was going in the direction of the Louvre. It was colder than she had expected, and the thought of going into a warm place was attractive. An hour, she thought. She would go into the Louvre and look at the *Mona Lisa* again, and be back before Richard woke up.

Lois pictured the *Mona Lisa* on its wall. It was too early for tourists, she decided. With any luck, there might not be anyone else there at all. Then it struck her that the Louvre might not yet be open. She remembered the old woman lying without dignity on the floor of the museum, and the bewildered daughter. She wondered whether the woman had died, and how long it had taken before the girl found out, one way or the other.

And at that moment she remembered the card that the man had given her. She had put it in her purse, she was sure of that. She looked through her bag but didn't find it in a quick search. Finally, she located it behind her MasterCard, and it struck her that during the time in Portugal and Spain she had not used her card. Richard had paid for everything.

Lois looked at the card. Robert Ferguson, Imports and Exports. It had a Paris telephone number. He might know what had happened to the old woman. She could phone him and he might be able to tell her. The audaciousness of the idea sent a thrill through her. She could feel her face flush, and she turned down a side street without even realizing she had done so.

There was no danger, she decided. He did not know who she was. She would simply remind him of the woman and ask if he knew what had happened to her. She could hang up any time she wanted. Lois rehearsed the sentences she would use. She wondered what Richard would say when she told him. Probably, there would be nothing to tell. And even if there was, perhaps she would not tell him.

The street Lois was walking along was narrow and dirty. It didn't seem to have any shops or businesses. The doors were numbered but otherwise blank. Through a soapy window she could see what looked like antiques, but they were piled without order, so she assumed it must be a warehouse. At last, she reached a broad street and realized that she was back on the rue Ste. Germaine.

She turned left, away from the hotel. None of the cafes she passed had pay telephones. Finally, she stopped at a place where the smell of coffee and croissants reminded her that she was hungry. She ordered a café au lait and a croissant from a waiter who did not seem surprised at her French. When he brought the order, she asked him where she could find a phone. He motioned toward the back of the cafe, and she followed him. He led her to an office next to the washrooms, and indicated that she should use the telephone there.

Lois dialed the number with some anxiety. A woman answered, and when she asked for Mr. Ferguson, she was told to wait. A moment later his English-accented voice spoke to her in French. Lois answered in English, explained that she was the person he had given his card to at the Louvre. She was careful not to give her name, and the voice said nothing until after she had asked about the old woman. Then it said with a sharp authority, "Where are you now?"

"I'm in a cafe on the rue Ste. Germaine."

"What's the name of the cafe?"

Lois glanced at a letter on the desk. It was addressed to the Cafe Lecteur. For a moment she hesitated, then she gave the name.

"Stay there," the voice told her. "I'll see you in fifteen minutes." The click at the other end of the line seemed sharply final.

Lois stood in the little office for a moment holding the receiver in her hand as if she were waiting for someone to return. After a moment she made her way back into the cafe. There was nothing holding her there. She didn't have to wait. She could go back to the hotel and pretend that this had never happened.

Instead she picked up her café au lait and croissant, and moved to a seat in the corner so that she would see him as soon as he arrived. She wished she had something to read so that she would not look as if she were waiting. She remembered the little sketch pad in her purse and took it out and began to sketch the interior of the cafe in thin, wavery lines. The figures looked Giacometti-like, but Lois was pleased. It was a style she had never attempted before. Something about the lines themselves suggested Paris, though the interior might have been anywhere.

When the voice above her said "Lois?" she was startled. The man before her was tall and athletic. His hair was short and sandy, and his broad face was heavily freckled. He wore a short-sleeved shirt, and Lois noticed that his arms were also heavily freckled and covered with long blond hair that looked as if it had been bleached by the sun. He shouldn't be attractive, Lois thought, but he is.

"May I please sit down?"

"Yes, of course," Lois answered. "Mr. Ferguson?"

"Robert." He sat down, and without asking permission picked up Lois's sketch pad. "That's very good," he said. "You're an artist." He said it not as a question but as a fact, and Lois, whose first impulse was to apologize, simply said, "Yes."

"I better begin with an explanation," he began. "I'm with the CSIS." When Lois showed no sign of recognition he went on. "The Canadian Security Intelligence Service. Remember? We were created a few years ago because the Mounties kept burning down barns and getting their names in the papers." He smiled, and it struck Lois that he looked like an ex-surfer.

"You're a spy," she answered. There had been something teasing in his voice that made her want to respond in kind.

"Not exactly," he answered. "I'm here at the invitation of the French government. We're missing a Canadian soldier. Apparently you might have seen him."

"How did you know who I was?" Lois asked. "That day in the Louvre."

"I recognized you from your photograph." He drew a picture from his pocket and showed it to her. It was the one Richard had taken of her at the Palais de l'Europe the day they had gone to Mont Ste. Odile. Lois didn't often like pictures of herself, but this one was flattering. Often her head looked too small, but this picture showed her leaning toward the camera, caught laughing.

"Kessler?"

Robert nodded.

"Is he for real?" Lois asked. "I mean, he doesn't seem like a policeman. You can't get him through the regular police. You have to leave messages with his mother. And then he keeps dropping out of thin air in places where you don't expect him. He joined us for dinner in Lisbon and even we didn't know where we were. What kind of policeman is that?"

"He's with a special detachment of the French Intelligence. I don't know much about him either, other than that he's supposed to be brilliant. A little slow and philosophical for my taste, but apparently he gets results. And, in this business, that's what counts. Where's your husband?"

Lois was unsettled for a moment by the sudden shift in topic. "Richard?" she asked.

"That's the one."

"He's back at the hotel. Sleeping. He was tired from the night train from Madrid. He doesn't fit on the seats. He didn't get much sleep. What happened to the old lady in the Louvre?" Changing the topic was a game that two could play.

"She died. It was a heart attack. She was probably dead before she hit the floor."

"And the girl?"

"She's working as an *au pair*."

"What's going on?" Lois asked. "Can't you give us any real answers? I'm starting to get paranoid. What was that woman doing in the Louvre? What were you doing there? What is this all about, anyway?"

The waiter hovered nearby but Robert dismissed him with a shake of his head. "Too much coffee already," he said. "My nerves are jangled by noon from too much coffee." He placed both his hands on the table and opened them slowly, as if to show by that gesture that the topic was not easily explained.

"Look," he said. "I'm not sure where to begin or what you already know. You are involved in something that may be quite large or may be nothing at all. First your questions. The old lady was in the Louvre looking at pictures. She'd brought her daughter in to work as an *au pair* girl. I was following them because they appear in your pictures from the Pagan Wall and because the daughter may have been involved with Mann, the missing soldier. On the other hand, maybe they are just ordinary people who made the mistake of being in the same place as you and getting photographed. It doesn't matter. Even spies and criminals lead ordinary lives. They go to art galleries and movies. They have jobs. They die of heart attacks when they least expect it."

"So nobody was following us. It was just a coincidence that we were all at the same place in the Louvre at the same time."

"I didn't say nobody was following you. But I wasn't following you, and the girl and her mother weren't following you." Robert stroked his chin as if he were accustomed to wearing a beard and had only recently shaved it off. "As much as I can say is that there is a very real right-wing movement operating in the Black Forest and in Alsace. Or maybe it isn't right-wing. Maybe it's just what it says it is, an historical society. Anyway, I'm here in case there is some connection with our armed forces in Lahr and Baden. The group has some connection with Heidegger, and some connection with Druidism. Now, you are the only witnesses to what might be a connection. You found a body on a Druid shrine. And your husband is an expert on Heidegger."

"He's not really an expert," Lois said. "He just teaches a class on him. Or to be fair, he's as close to an expert as you'll find in Canada, but he doesn't really think of himself that way."

"He's here to write a book on Heidegger?"

"That's what he said when he got his sabbatical. But I don't think he's going to write about Heidegger." She decided not to tell Robert about Richard's novel. She half-expected Richard to walk in the door. He would have woken up, found her note, and gone out looking for her. She put the sketch pad back in her purse and took out enough money to pay for her breakfast and what she hoped was an adequate tip.

"I have to go," Lois said. "I left Richard sleeping. If he wakes up and I'm not there he'll be worried."

Robert said nothing, but he got up from his chair and moved hers to help her get out from behind the table. At the door, a family of American tourists was pushing its way in, and she felt Robert's hand softly on the small of her back, guiding her out.

Lois turned towards Robert once they were out in the street, intending to say good-bye, wondering whether she would be expected to shake his hand. Instead, with a motion of his chin, he indicated the direction of the hotel, and said, "I'll walk a ways with you. I need the fresh air."

Lois didn't know what to say, so she said nothing. After a while Robert asked her, "Are you going to tell your husband about this meeting?"

"Of course," she said. "Why wouldn't I?"

"I just wondered. You never know what other people will do." He walked along in silence for a minute, then he asked her to wait a moment while he picked up a newspaper at a small shop. Back on the sidewalk, he seemed to have shifted into a different mood.

He chatted about Canadians in Paris, and how you could tell them from Americans. When Lois asked him about the import-export business and the Texas address on his card, he laughed. He said he'd been in Texas on a golf scholarship, and it was the only accent he could do with any flair.

"It's my cover," he said, demonstrating his skill. "Not a very romantic one, but it gets me special rates in some hotels."

When they reached the Opera, Lois thanked him and turned to go down the side street to the Hotel Maricourt. To her surprise, he took both her hands in his. "If you're back in Paris, either with your husband or alone, give me a call," he said. "I'll buy supper and we can get up-to-date on the mystery." His hands were dry and surprisingly warm. He left Lois no chance to answer, but turned and hurried back down the street the way they had come. She stood and watched him for a while, but he did not look back.

Even as she climbed the stairs to the room, Lois was unsure what she would tell Richard. Not to tell him would seem like betrayal, or at least she was sure that Richard would regard it as betrayal if he ever found out. And if she told him, he would be upset that she had chosen to arrange a meeting without telling him. Not that she had arranged the meeting. Lois felt both guilty and justified at the same time.

When she unlocked the room and entered, she found Richard was gone. Her note was exactly as she had left it, and it was impossible to know whether Richard had read it or not. The empty room seemed darkly oppressive, and Lois didn't want to stay in it. She checked the bathroom, though she knew Richard would not be there, then she went down into the lobby.

The woman at the desk, who acted as if she were the owner and not an employee, chatted to her in French. Lois caught only the general drift of her conversation, but understood her to be recommending a trip to Montmarte. Lois smiled and nodded as if she understood perfectly and took a chair by the window where she could watch the street. She felt alone and wished Richard would come back. She composed a question in French in her mind, and asked the woman at the desk whether she had seen Richard. Yes, the woman agreed, she certainly had. He had gone out.

There were several magazines in a rack in the corner. Lois chose one and leafed through it slowly. The language was abstruse, and she couldn't concentrate on the pictures. There was not much traffic on the street. From time to time, working men in dark clothes or elegantly dressed women passed by. There did not seem to be any other class of walkers in the area.

The time passed slowly, and still Richard did not come. She went back to the room and tried to sleep, but she was not sleepy. After a while she decided the waiting was easier in the hotel foyer. An old woman had taken her place and Lois had to sit so that she looked down the street in a direction from which she knew Richard would not arrive. She felt anxious and angry at the same time. Richard should have left a note.

She took out her sketch pad, but after a few strokes she put it back. The old woman glared at her, and all the lines she had drawn seemed wrong. When Richard appeared around the corner, she felt a sudden surge of relief.

"Guess what?" he said, leaning down to kiss her on the cheek.

"What?"

"I've been playing detective. I found out that the old woman in the Louvre died from a heart attack."

"Oh," Lois said. "How did you find that out?"

"Remember the German girl, the daughter?"

Lois nodded.

"I walked down to that reception place for *au pair* girls and got her address. At first they didn't want to give it to me, but I said that I was her cousin from Canada and in the end they told me. I phoned her, and she said that her mother really had died. Apparently it was horrible for her. Nobody told her anything for a week. Finally her uncle came and told her. By that time the body had been taken back to Kehl and the funeral was over. They hadn't been able to find her, and nobody knew where she was." Richard's eyes were bright, and he seemed animated.

"You didn't see her in person?"

"No, I phoned her. Why?"

"Nothing," Lois said. "It's just that you took so long."

"A couple of hours. I didn't know when you'd be back."

"Were you angry because I went out?"

"No, of course not. When you spend as much time together as we do, you've got to get out for a few minutes on your own or else you'll go mad. I wish you'd woken me up first though."

Suddenly Lois felt a deep despair. Everything secure seemed threatened. "Let's go home, Richard," she said. "Let's just get a plane and go back to Canada."

"Why?"

"I'm afraid something terrible is going to happen."

"Don't worry," Richard told her. "Nothing terrible is going to happen." He extended his hand and she stood up from the chair. He gave her a hug and said, "I'll take care of you. Now let's go get something to eat."

***

The taxi driver seemed bewildered when Richard asked him whether he could get them to the Gare St. Lazare in fifteen minutes.

"Ah, non," he answered. "C'est pas possible."

But he did. He got them all the way from the Gare du Nord in thirteen minutes. Richard told him that they had bought their tickets but no one had explained to them that they were in the wrong station. On the head-long trip, as the driver sped down sidewalks and careened the wrong way down one-way streets, he murmured a running condemnation of French bureaucracy, and when Richard tipped him fifty francs, he shrugged and said, "C'est la France."

There were two seats left on the train, in a second-class smoking car, and the air was already blue with smoke when they entered. The seats were at opposite ends of the car, and no provision had been made for luggage. Richard saw Lois into the first seat, beside a woman in an expensive business suit, then made his way with both suitcases to the far end of the car. He left the suitcases in the aisle and settled in beside an androgynous figure who was studying a book full of technical documents and graphs, making meticulous notes in the margin. Everybody in that section of the car seemed to be smoking perfumed cigarettes.

The train slipped out of Paris and into the countryside before Richard had settled in with any comfort. He wanted to read his copy of *Le Monde,* but had forgotten to have their tickets stamped before they got on the train, so he would have to convince the conductor he could not speak French. Otherwise, the conductor, he had been told, could fine him a hundred francs on the spot.

And so Richard studied the other passengers as he waited. There seemed an odd mix of travellers. Three men and a woman across the aisle looked like commuters on a North-American train, but the woman across from him, gap-toothed and dressed in black, might have slipped onto the train from another century. Her wicker basket was loaded with vegetables, and Richard sensed rather than smelled garlic on her breath. She seemed perfectly comfortable, perfectly in control. The androgynous student, the flirtatious business people, one of the men reading aloud now from a magazine on skiing, all seemed innocent. The old woman was vaguely threatening.

The conductor arrived, pushing through a door in the end of the car that Richard had assumed led to the engine. Richard showed him both tickets, and pointed to Lois at the far end of the car. When the conductor pointed out that they were not stamped, Richard pretended confusion and asked whether the conductor spoke English. The conductor did not, but he explained to Richard in slow meticulous French that he must have his ticket stamped, and told him that he would have to pay. Richard, abandoning his defense, reached for his wallet, but the conductor waved it away, and Richard wondered whether he had understood after all.

At the first stop, a third of the passengers left. Richard had guessed that the woman across the aisle and the man who read from the skiing magazine were lovers, they had spoken to each other in low whispers, but the man got off the train before the woman. Through the window, Richard could see him welcomed by a wife and two daughters standing beside a little Renault 5. He imagined that domestic scene unravelling, the pretty wife in tears, the children wide-eyed and bewildered, and he thought back seven years to the break-up of his own marriage. Richard did not like to think about that time, and he had devised methods for obliterating those memories when they arrived. He began to sing to himself, "Swing low, sweet chariot," and he only realized when the student in the next seat turned to him that he was singing aloud.

After the second stop, the old woman and the student, who Richard had concluded was a girl, both left. Lois came to join him, hoisting their luggage onto the seat across from them. The seat across the aisle was empty, but the skiing magazine had been left behind. Richard reached over and took it. It smelled strongly perfumed, and Richard wondered whether the smell was from the woman or the man.

"It's beautiful, isn't it?" Lois said, looking out the window at the brilliant green Normandy hills and the sharp, white farmhouses. Richard agreed that it was beautiful, and wondered how he had failed to notice the transition in the landscape. Everywhere there were dairy cattle, sway-backed, black and white Holsteins, standing in open meadows or penned behind barns. In one field, a couple of goats grazed with the cattle.

When Lois had first suggested the trip in Paris, Richard had resisted. It seemed to him that going to Dieppe might commit him more deeply to the novel than he was prepared for. Now, watching the farms pass slowly by, he became increasingly convinced that he would find something that mattered here, where so many young Canadians had died. At the same time, he knew that he wouldn't have taken the trip without Lois's insistence. He reflected that even though they had been together for five years, he didn't know her very well. Since Portugal, something had changed. He wondered whether he had discovered something new about her that he should have noticed before, or whether she had made some decision of which this was the consequence.

By the time they got to Dieppe, the only other passengers on the car were two young boys with huge Canadian flags sewn to their backpacks. They seemed friendly, and Lois chatted with them. Richard hung back. He did not want the acquaintance to go any farther. Whatever was going to happen, he did not want to share it with these boys, younger even than his own students, but the same age, he reflected, as the men who died in the raid on Dieppe.

The station was empty, cavernous. Everything was closed. The few travellers who had disembarked with them were picked up by waiting cars. Even the young Canadians had somehow disappeared. The air was damp, familiar, the sharp, musty smell of the ocean.

"It's wonderful," Lois said. "I love it already." Seagulls whirled over the harbour, which was filled with boats of every kind from merchant-marine freighters with swinging cranes down to tiny, wooden sailboats. Heavy clouds hung overhead, and the streets were wet with rain. From low in the west, golden sunshine brightened everything, defining sharply the buildings, the trees and the boats.

"We'd better try to find a taxi," Richard said.

"No, let's not." Lois was clearly excited by the scene. "Let's just follow the harbour down to the shore. There have to be hotels along the beach."

Richard was unsure. He didn't want to discover things suddenly. He wanted to check out the lay of the land, make plans, but her enthusiasm swept him along. Their progress was easy, downhill all the way through the liquid yellow light to the sudden and surprising stretch of beach. It was simply there, before they had expected it. Facing them was the ocean. To their right was the Hotel Aguado. The hotel was full of windows, bright and airy, and the clerk behind the desk was smiling and friendly. He welcomed them in before they had even decided whether this was the hotel they wanted, and they submitted to his open invitation.

Their room was enormous, surprisingly finished in Spanish style, whites, with a deep, leather chesterfield and chair, like the room in the Hotel Lagos. The window looked over the bay. They were on the fourth floor, and Richard could see the whole sweep of beach as far as the cliffs on each side. He imagined a machine gun in the window, a machine gun in every window, and himself watching the landing boats in the swell at the shore, the men running up the beach, the crumpled bodies falling. The movies, exactly.

When they walked down to the beach, they found they were the only people there. The beach was black. The stones were smooth and oval, from an inch to about three inches in diameter. There was no sand, only the smooth black stones. Many of the stones had holes in them. Richard started collecting smaller ones. He decided he would take them home and fill a pottery bowl with them. The stones of Dieppe.

Just then, the sun sank below the horizon, and a chilly wind blew in off the bay. Lois was also collecting stones. She laughed and showed one to Richard. It was smooth and regular, exactly the shape of the head of a penis. She put it into her pocket.

What are you going to do with that?" Richard asked.

"You never know. I might need it some day."

"Not for a little while yet," Richard informed her, and they held hands and walked up the beach. They decided to follow the sweeping concrete walkway down to the cliffs, but the distance was farther than it appeared. They passed a glassed-in bar right on the edge of the beach. Two men and a woman, all of them dressed completely in white, were drinking beer. A little farther on was a broad wading pool, and the walkway ended at a closed restaurant. From the top of the cliff, some large, grey structure, a castle or a fortress, loomed. They decided to go back to the hotel, and discovered that the beach was lined with hotels. Every building was a hotel.

That night, Richard dreamed of war, not the Raid on Dieppe, but some far more sinister war where helicopters hovered like dragonflies, and jets whined overhead. As he explained the dream to Lois at breakfast, he realized that the images were from television news reports of the Vietnam war. The couple at the next table were fat and English. Richard spoke to Lois in French so that the English couple would not open conversation. They were not fooled.

"You Americans?" the man asked.

"Canadians," Lois told him. Richard started to speak to Lois in French once more, but the man was undeterred.

"What part of Canada?" he asked.

Lois told him, "Winnipeg."

"Oh, thought it might be Montreal, you speaking French and all. I was in Montreal in 1956. Saw Elvis Presley on the t.v. in a hotel."

"It's a small world," Richard said. Lois gently kicked him under the table and in reply he raised his eyes as if in prayer, a sign he would be good. It turned out that the couple had honeymooned here, but not together. Each had been married to someone else, but it was here that they met and they were back to celebrate.

"What are you doing in Dieppe?" they asked Richard and Lois.

"There were some Canadians here in forty-two," Richard told them. "I just wanted to see if anyone remembered them."

"They remember them alright," the man said. "The whole town's full of Canadian flags."

And it was. It had rained hard during the night and the streets were bright with water. The main street of Dieppe was decorated with the flags of dozens of countries, as if some celebration were about to take place. Canadian flags hung everywhere. Richard felt some stir of national pride and wondered whether this was a legitimate emotion. It felt foreign to him, something that happens to people in American novels.

The street swarmed with people. Richard was surprised. It was still early spring, not yet the tourist season. Other towns in France looked like this on a market Saturday, yet here was Dieppe, on a Monday morning, with a bustling crowd and a sense of festive excitement. Street vendors pushed carts loaded with hot chestnuts. Bins of fruit and vegetables had been stuck out into the centre of the street. An ice table loaded with dozens of different kinds of fresh fish jutted out of the wide-open doorway of a fish store. The smell of bread from a boulangerie made Richard sharply hungry, though he had just finished breakfast.

"It's wonderful," Lois said. "This is what I've been looking for all over Europe. Let's stay here for a few days."

"We've got to get back to Strasbourg," Richard told her.

"Why?" she asked. "Monsieur Delacroix will still be at his father's endless funeral. And I thought you'd given up on Heidegger."

"Maybe," Richard said. "We'll see." He wasn't sure himself whether he was speaking of Heidegger or of staying in Dieppe.

The girl at the *Tourisme* gave them a mimeographed history of the Raid on Dieppe. It seemed amateurish, written on a typewriter with a faulty *e* and filled with grammar and spelling mistakes. She also gave them a hand-drawn map showing where the various

Canadian units had landed. Richard wanted to see the beach at Pourville and the war museum on the way. The map marked Pourville as the place where the South Saskatchewan regiment had attacked, and Richard suddenly felt a strong sense of the prairies. There was one bus a day, the girl informed them, and it had already gone. They would have to walk. Yes, quite a few Canadians came by, but they wanted to see the beach at Dieppe. Nobody wanted to go to Pourville.

The road to Pourville wound five kilometres along the coast, and at first there were elegant houses along the way. Past the new high school, things began to thin out. The big houses gave way to fields and barns, to house trailers and shanties. Just as they crested a hill, they found themselves at the museum, a low German bunker, with old tanks and rusting artillery surrounded by a high, metal fence. They were about to enter the compound when a woman leaped into her car and careened out to meet them.

"Non, non." she told them. "C'est pas possible." It was, it seemed, ten minutes until lunch. The museum must close for three hours.

The road from the museum to Pourville was all downhill. Here, the shell holes had not been filled in, and the shattered remains of concrete bunkers littered the fields and the higher ground at the edge of the cliffs. From a hairpin turn they were given a sudden view of the bay. Richard was amazed at how narrow the beach was, not a quarter of a mile from where the cliffs ended to where they began again.

The cliffs gleamed brilliantly white and ochre in the bright sunlight, but in the few minutes it took Richard and Lois to make their way down to the beach, the sun had disappeared and it had begun to rain, a cold, slanting rain driven by a breeze from the channel. They lunched at the Hotel Normandie, waiting for the rain to stop. They ate shrimp and mussels and listened to the strange sibilant language of a blond and elegant family who looked like the kind of people who appear in ads for Volvos. Lois guessed that they were Finnish.

It was still raining when they left the restaurant. Richard had left his umbrella and his raincoat back at the hotel. Lois had a yellow plastic slicker that rolled up in a package she could carry in her purse. Across the street, at a grocery store, Richard was offered an orange garbage bag to put over his head. The woman who offered this remembered the day of the raid. August 19, 1942. She had been ten years old. The Germans put machine guns in the upstairs windows. She and her parents were taken about ten kilometres behind the lines and kept there for a week. The Germans, she told him, were very polite. They explained that the Canadians would be attacking, but the attack would not take long. The Germans were well-prepared. She liked Canadians, she said, because they died to save her country. She would not take any payment for the garbage bag.

The rain was even heavier when they got to the beach. The garbage bag was awkward. Richard tore a hole for his face and wore it like a hood. He pulled it down to cover his shoulders and this restricted his arms. The pilings from some long-vanished pier marched in from the ocean like soldiers slugging their way through the low tide to land. Seagulls whirled and cried, almost invisible behind the rain from the grey sky.

At the top of the cliff, impossibly high, a concrete pillbox brooded over the beach. A couple of crows circled it. Richard tried to imagine men on the beach fighting their way through barbed wire, climbing ropes to get to the top of the cliff. He remembered a movie with John Wayne, the mortars firing the hooks high over the cliffs. From where Richard stood, he could see that the enterprise was absolutely impossible. How could a single man have survived? He suddenly felt vulnerable and exposed.

Richard tried to imagine farm boys from Saskatchewan. He tried to force himself to think like a farm boy from Saskatchewan but found it impossible, a maudlin exercise. This was what he had come for, and he was disappointed. He felt nothing. He wanted to weep, to feel some sense of awe or danger, but what he felt was wet and uncomfortable. The beach was littered with debris, old styrofoam cups, plastic detergent containers and shredded fragments of bright blue polyethylene. He tried to imagine blood on the beach, and was aware for the first time that the attack took place in daylight. For some reason, he had always imagined the attack at night, and he realized then that all the movies about the Second World War were in black and white. And they were all American.

Richard was suddenly aware of how strange he must look in his orange garbage bag. He tore it off and threw it on the beach.

"If I'm going to get wet," he told Lois, "then I'm going to get wet. But I am not going to look ridiculous."

Lois laughed, and her laugh sounded happy. "It doesn't matter if you look ridiculous," she said. "There's nobody to see you."

And of course there wasn't. The beach was empty except for the seagulls. Ahead of them was a low concrete bunker. The walls were three feet thick and a couple of windows faced the ocean. Richard crawled through a window and looked out. He supposed that this must have been part of the German defence system, but it seemed odd. It was no more than four feet high, and there was no floor, only the stones of the beach. At high tide, it would be completely under water. But what else could it be?

Lois took out her little Nikon, and she snapped a picture of Richard leaning out the window.

"Look fierce," she told him. "Pretend you're an enemy soldier." Richard made a face, and she moved closer to snap another picture. Richard could see himself, distorted in the camera lens, a hole like a bullethole in the centre of the image.

"It's too bad I didn't get one of you in your garbage bag," she said. "When we get home, I'm going to start a special album called "Richard in Funny Costume." Lois was exhilarated. She smiled a teasing smile, inviting him to banter.

Richard wanted to enter Lois's happiness, but he felt that something was missing, something had failed to happen. The stones of the beach and the white cliffs streaked with ochre were unreadable. The rain had fuzzed the horizon so there was no difference between water and sky.

"Let's go back to Dieppe," he said. "I'm cold and I'm soaked."

"Okay. Lead on."

The trip back was easier than Richard had expected. The rain let up as soon as they started, and by the time they had climbed the hill to the road above Pourville Richard was warm from the effort. The museum was open now, a school bus parked by the main bunker. He wasn't sure he wanted to go in, the effort seemed too great, but it had begun to rain again, and Lois said that at least it would be somewhere to stay until it stopped.

They arrived at the bunker just as the French school children were leaving. They were as chaotic and unruly as children every- where, but they were dressed like adults. The girls all wore long coats, and the boys wore little suits. An old man collected the tickets from Richard and pointed down a staircase towards a room filled with guns and bayonets. Faceless mannequins were dressed in a variety of uniforms: French, German, English, American, Canadian, even Italian, as if these nations had solved their differences and had united to face some common enemy. As of course they had, Richard thought.

The bunker turned out to be a real German *blockhaus*, and each of the rooms was identified as kitchen, dining room, barracks, according to its ancient function. Now they housed a collection of military junk, broken artillery, parts of machines. Everything looked filthy, covered with a thick layer of dust. Framed pages from newspapers on the wall revealed that the raid was expected for days before it came. Copies of leaflets, distributed by the Canadians themselves, informed the French that this was simply a raid and not the invasion. The French were encouraged to cooperate with the Germans and do nothing to put themselves in danger.

Richard was amazed. The Canadian army had chosen an almost impossible place to attack, and had made as certain as it could that the enemy would be properly prepared. It was suicide, he told Lois. Or better still, murder. Mountbatten had ordered the attack, Richard remembered, and so was responsible for the deaths. In this case, the deaths of young men from Saskatchewan. Richard was beginning to feel the anger that failed him on the beach, but his anger was turned towards the English, not the Germans. He thought of the English couple at breakfast, but they were too distant for him to hate.

Lois stayed, deciphering a local newspaper, but Richard, restless, moved on, following the footsteps painted on the floor. He walked through a room filled with pictures of the beach after the raid. The bodies had been cleaned up, but broken and abandoned vehicles and material were everywhere.

Then, startlingly, Richard was in a large room filled with motor- cycles. They were so beautiful Richard was stunned. He had never liked motorcycles, ridden them rarely, and then with fear, but these, all a uniform, camouflage grey, seemed to him perfect. They were much smaller than the Japanese motorcycles that he saw everywhere, but they were spare and exquisitely crafted. When Lois found him a half-hour later, he was gently stroking the body of a motorcycle with an Italian name, a kind of motorcycle he had never heard of before.

Lois had phoned for a taxi from Dieppe, and it had already arrived. She had been looking for Richard, had passed through the room three times without seeing him. What was he doing? Hiding underneath the motorcycles? Richard didn't know. He had been unaware of the passing of time. He tried to explain to Lois.

"Look," he said. "They are the most beautiful machines I have ever seen."

Lois tried to understand.

"The motorcycles?"

"They're perfect," Richard said. "They are absolutely perfect." It seemed to him they contained everything that was missing on the beach.

He hardly noticed the trip back to the hotel. He had forgotten that he was wet and cold, and did not notice it until he became aware of his teeth chattering as he showered. For dinner he ordered a fish whose French name he could not decipher, a thin triangular fish. Richard stripped the flesh from the elegant bones of the wings, and later he drank more Calvados than he should. Lois drank mineral water, but she stayed up with him until it was very late. Richard counted the stones he had picked up on the beach. He thought he should make love to Lois, but he drifted into sleep before he could act.

Richard woke up suddenly. Somebody was shaking him, and he didn't know where he was. The space seemed cavernous and dark.

"Richard, what's the matter?" Lois asked him. "You must have had a nightmare. You were thrashing around and trying to scream."

"I was dreaming," he answered. "I was dreaming about the motorcycles."

And the next morning when the train to Paris pulled out of Dieppe station ten minutes early, it still seemed to him the right answer.

**

For a month, it rained every day in Strasbourg. Sometimes the sun would come out for an hour or so late in the day, but by dark it would be raining again. The light was a silver-grey that brightened in the morning and settled to a deep blue by evening. It was the same light Lois and Richard had noticed when they had arrived in Frankfurt. The studio was damp and crammed, and Lois took to spending more and more time in the library.

She memorized verbs. She wrote out long lists of definitions and said them over and over to herself. Two evenings a week, from six o'clock to eight o'clock, she attended classes in a building whose name she translated as the Chamber of Commerce Hall. While she'd been away, they had changed the system. Now she had two teachers, a highly dramatic man with a thin moustache who was named Jules and who reminded her of Charlie Chaplin, and a matronly woman named Avril who apparently took in boarders. Two of the students in the class lived with her, Chaim, a young Israeli, and Fatima, who was Turkish.

At first Lois was embarrassed because everybody seemed to speak better French than she did. Hans, a German contractor from across the border who wanted to learn the language so he could deal with his French suppliers; Leah, the Indian wife of a German diplomat; Lydia, a Scottish *au pair* girl; and an Iranian woman with an unpronounceable name, who each week invited the group to address her by a different name. She had been Greta, Georgia, and Ginny. This week she was Jean. Lois soon discovered, however, that, though they were all adept at introducing themselves and making small talk, she was in fact the best student in the class. She knew more words than anyone else, and she could tell the difference between the past and present tense.

During the classes, she could understand the teacher perfectly, whichever teacher it was. She hardly ever missed a word. Outside, it was as if she had never studied French. Everything slipped by her in a maddening mélange that seemed familiar, but which she could not understand.

Richard continued to jog. He was starting to run further and further. He was up to five miles now, by his estimate, and he seemed to be losing weight. Their refrigerator could make fourteen ice cubes a day, and Richard hoarded them for the evening. When Lois got home at eight thirty in the evening, Richard would have supper prepared, and a rum and Coke with ice cubes for each of them. They would drink an entire bottle of wine, and when they walked out to look at the cathedral, they would both be a little drunk.

Richard had started to write his novel. He went to the university every day and wrote for four hours. Lois was amazed at the stack of papers he carried with him, and its growing bulk. He wouldn't let her read it, but liked to talk about what might happen in it, and she enjoyed the game of speculating about what the characters should do. She didn't know whether he ever took her suggestions, and he wouldn't tell her.

Lately he had decided that he had to go to Vimy Ridge. His novel, he said, was pushing backward. Dieppe was not enough. He was going to have to go to the north of France where Canadian troops had fought in the First World War. He was going to talk to the man from whom they had rented the little green van. The cost would be high, but there didn't seem much choice. They could take a train, but the battlefields weren't in the towns, and he would have to rent a car anyway. Lois didn't want to miss her classes, but she knew she would have to go. His entire vision of the trip included her.

He had also got out his Heidegger books and began to read them again. He said that only Heidegger could explain what had happened between the wars. He'd finally bought an umbrella, and each night as they walked to the cathedral in the rain, he tried to explain phenomenology to her. It all seemed perfectly clear and logical when he talked about it, but the next day she couldn't remember a word.

They hardly made love any more, but it didn't matter. Richard was obsessed by his work, but he was also happy. He talked to her intently, but he didn't seem really to know that she was there. He never asked her where she had been or what she was doing. He listened when she told him about her class, but he never asked for more information than she volunteered.

Then one day, late in the afternoon, the telephone rang. Lois hesitated before she answered it. She didn't want to stumble through a confusing attempt to comprehend someone and end up bewildered. When she decided to answer on the sixth ring, it was Richard. He had finally met Monsieur Delacroix. He would be bringing him home for supper. Could Lois pick up something at the Galeries Gourmands?

"But it's my class tonight," she objected.

"Lois, could you do it as a favour? This is really important to me. And could you pick up a couple of bottles of good wine?"

He had left her no room for argument.

"Okay," she said. "Anything in particular you want?" She felt her muscles grow tense. She licked her lips and found that they were dry.

"No," Richard answered. "Just be the perfect hostess. And don't be angry," he added. "I'll make it up to you. The class can get along without you for one night."

"What time?"

"About eight o'clock."

"Right," she answered, with a little more military precision than she had intended. Richard's good-bye registered his disappointment.

Lois looked around the studio and tried to imagine three people in it. She looked at the list of verbs she had been preparing for the class and felt her disappointment as a physical thing. Her arms seemed heavy. At the same time she told herself she was being unreasonable. Richard would do the same for her without hesitation.

She set the table slowly, then decided she would do everything that could be done immediately. On her way to the grocery store, she noticed a little shop that sold take-out gourmet meals. She had passed that way many times before without seeing it, and it was really little more than a doorway. The shop itself was less than six feet wide.

She went in. A young man with a handkerchief tied around his head so that he looked as if he were pretending to be an Arab asked if he could help her. There seemed to be only four choices. Lois chose salmon with truffles in a white sauce. The man spooned it carefully into a plastic container, weighed it, and announced the price. Four hundred francs.

Lois calculated. Eighty-eight dollars. For a moment she waited, saying nothing but determined to apologize and refuse the order. Then in a moment of decision she took out her credit card and asked the man if he could accept it. The man smiled and nodded.

Good, Lois thought. Richard will not know what this cost. Then, as if it were a natural consequence of her purchase, she decided that she would go to class after all. She picked up some cheese at a little store next door and hurried home. She put the food in the refrigerator, piled her books on the table where Richard would see them if he returned early, and, taking only a pen and a piece of paper, set off for class.

The class was a disappointment from the start. Only two other people showed up, and neither of them were prepared for the class. The instructor had brought a videotape of a story in which a young man apparently searched for his lover at a railway station. Afterwards, he asked them questions, and it seemed that the young man had been an employee of the railway who had stolen money and was trying to avoid being caught.

When Lois announced that she would have to leave early, the entire class dispersed. The young Israeli boy decided to walk part of the way home with her. He had family in Montreal, he told her, and he wanted to emigrate to Canada. As soon as they were outside the building, he switched from his broken French into surprisingly good English. Lois had never heard him speak English before, and she was irrationally disappointed that he was so good at it.

She bought a couple of bottles of wine on the way. The young man extolled the virtues of Israeli wine, and wanted her to try a bottle he had found on the shelf. Lois was sure that Richard would not much like the idea, but she didn't see how she could refuse to buy it without hurting Chaim's feelings. In the end she bought three bottles of wine, and after saying good-bye to Chaim at the corner, she slipped into the house and hid the Israeli wine under the staircase.

She checked her watch. It was exactly eight 'o clock. She realized that the guilt she felt was exactly the kind of guilt she remembered from her childhood. She took a deep breath. Richard is not my father, she told herself. I can do what I want.

When she opened the door, she saw that Richard was already home. Sitting across from him in the armchair was an elegant man in a dark, three-piece suit. His hair was a steel-grey, and he wore thin, round, wire-rimmed glasses.

"Sorry," Lois said. "I had to run out to get wine. Been waiting long?"

"Not very," Richard said. "Lois, this is Hervé Delacroix. Hervé, my wife, Lois."

"Charmed," Hervé answered, making a slight bow, but not offering a hand. He half-stood from the chair, then settled back into it.

"Hervé knew Heidegger personally," Richard informed Lois. "He has a new book that's just about to come out. It's about Druids."

"Celts, actually."

"Is it in German?" Lois asked.

"No," Hervé answered. "It is in French. But already the translator is working on an English version. The two will be nearly simultaneously published." Lois noticed that his accent was softer than the accent of Paris. It sounded almost German to her, and she guessed that he was a native Alsatian. Richard had opened a bottle of Pineau de Charente, and he and Hervé each had a glass of the clear liquor. Richard offered Lois some, which she refused. Instead, she got four ice cubes out of the refrigerator and mixed herself a rum and Coke. Then she put the salmon into the oven to warm it, and joined the men once more.

"Hervé and the inspector have invited me to join them on a fishing expedition," Richard announced. "They're going salmon fishing in Iceland."

"I thought it was Norway you went to," Lois said.

"Usually, it is," Hervé answered. "But this time we are making a special expedition. André has been to Iceland many times, but I have never been myself. It will be," he paused and shrugged his shoulders, "an adventure."

"Are you going?" Lois asked Richard.

"I don't know. What do you think?"

"I think you should go."

"It would only be a week."

"Go."

"I'll let you know in a couple of days," Richard told Hervé. "I'm going to have to check the finances."

Lois had been dreading the supper, but it passed smoothly. Richard was astonished by the salmon. He pronounced it one of the finest meals he had ever eaten, and asked Lois where she had got it. Lois was as vague as she dared be. She said she thought she could find the shop again but she wasn't sure. It was in the Petite France area, and she always got lost in the winding streets and canals. She did not say what it had cost, and Richard didn't ask.

Richard and Hervé spoke only English, and Lois was grateful. Tonight the conversation was clear, and it included her. They talked about the difference between French and Canadian universities, and Lois decided that she liked the Canadian system much better. By the time they were through, she was sure that she would never have gotten a degree in France.

Hervé refused brandy and left early. He had many things to do at the university, he said. After the fishing trip he would have to go back to Provence again to settle his father's affairs. In the meantime, he had students to meet and colleagues to consult with. Richard could find him at the university any afternoon after two o'clock.

Richard walked him down the stairs and out to the gate. Through the open window, Lois could hear their voices, but she could not make out what they were saying. It had started to rain again, a soft, fine mist that drifted into the room with a light breeze. Lois wrapped up the cheeses and put them away. When Richard returned, he poured them each a large snifter of brandy.

"That's way too much," Lois said. "If I drink all that, I'll have a terrible hangover tomorrow."

"We'll stay in bed until the hangovers are all gone," Richard answered, and he proposed a toast. "To us and the future and happiness." They clinked glasses, and Richard drank down his entire brandy in one swallow, then poured himself another.

"Everything is working," he said. "I'll probably never finish the novel, but it's great fun working at it. The elusive Monsieur Delacroix has resurfaced, and I'm interested in Heidegger again. We were talking about the late Heidegger. Heidegger as poet. 'What is spoken is never, and in no language, what is said.' That's one of his best lines."

"What does it mean?"

"Just what it says. Whatever you say has more meaning than the words themselves. Nothing is what it seems."

"Are we going to walk to the cathedral?" Lois asked.

"No we're not," Richard said. "Tonight we're going to resume our intermittent love life." He bent over and kissed her gently on her eyes.

Lois drained her brandy and said, "Well, let's get at it. Unless you actually mean something else." When she stood up she found she was so dizzy that she nearly fell. Richard cleared away the dishes while she transformed the couch into a bed. When she curled up in it, she could hear him whistling to himself as he washed the dishes. She fell asleep almost instantly, but woke to find he was rubbing her back. For a long time he rubbed her body and she lay in a half-sleep she hoped might go on forever. When they made love, it was rough and almost painful, but her body responded immediately. She felt herself relax, and she was asleep before she could say what she had wanted to say. In the very last moment she couldn't remember what it was.

* * *

The plane circled mountains that dropped straight cliffs to the sea, then settled in to Keflavik airbase. Customs seemed the merest formality. The officer, behind a cage like a teller in a bank, glanced at their passports and waved them through. He appeared to know most of the travellers by name.

They were met by a large young man, blond with blue eyes. He was as tall as Richard but much heavier. Muscles bulged under his shirt, and he looked as if he spent a lot of his time lifting weights. He spoke to the inspector in what sounded to Richard like impeccable French. Kessler answered in English, and the young man switched smoothly to a slightly sibilant and sing-song English.

"I will be taking you to the Saga Guesthouse," he said. "From there we will go to the interior. But we will be a day late. There have been floods from heavy rain." His language was almost excessively formal. "My name is Helgi," he added, and he shook their hands firmly in turn.

When they left the airport, Richard was amazed by the air. It was cool and damp, but it seemed the clearest air he had ever breathed. The sun was not shining, but the light had an almost hallucinatory clarity. Distant objects were sharp and distinct. The Icelander escorted them to a large, black, four-wheel-drive Ford, with over-sized tires.

"It is necessary," he said, pointing to the tires, "in order to travel in the interior. It is also necessary in order to travel anywhere at all, as you shall see." Richard assumed that this was intended as humour, and Kessler confirmed this.

"The roads of Iceland are terrible," he said. "Almost none of them are paved, and the drivers are worse than the French."

As if to prove the point, the driver travelled at break-neck speed. The road, however, was paved and smooth. The driver explained that this was courtesy of the Americans, who owned the airbase, and who in case of war would have to get to Rekjavik in order to take over the country. He seemed to find the idea funny, and laughed to himself.

The country was like nothing Richard had ever imagined. Low, rolling, black hills stretched into the distance without trees or grass. A faint, green moss covered the gravel, but everywhere there were the tracks of bulldozers, as if the road had just been made and the equipment hidden away.

"Some of those tracks are fifty years old," Kessler explained. "The ecosystem is so fragile that it takes a hundred years to grow back the lichen scraped off by the tractors. Wait till we get to the interior. The Americans sent their astronauts to train here, because it is so much like the surface of the moon." A bus lurched by them just as they crested a hill. Richard expected the passengers, their companions from the flight, to be terrified, but those he could see through the window appeared to be either asleep or reading. None of the faces looked out the window.

Richard had informed his companions that he intended to learn German, and they were debating the wisdom of this course.

"It is pointless to learn German except as a first language," Delacroix insisted. "All Germans can speak English, and so you do not need it in order to travel. And the subtleties of the language are so complex that you cannot hope to master them unless you begin with the first breath you draw in this world. If you learn German in order to read the philosophers all you will guarantee is that you will misunderstand them."

"Nonsense, my dear Hervé," the inspector replied. "Sheer mystification. Like any other language, German is a set of signs around which meanings cluster like flies around garbage. It is always in transition, now this meaning to the fore, now that one. Often it is the foreigner who is most sensitive to this shifting in the language, this life of the language. The native speaker is trapped by the meanings of his childhood. And they are different from the meanings of his children's life."

"He argues for the sake of argument," Hervé told Richard, as if Kessler were not in the car. "You are a sophist, André. You do not believe a word you say."

"Ah, but I do, I do," Kessler replied. "Helgi," he said, touching the shoulder of the driver, who appeared not to have been paying any attention to the conversation, "how many languages do you speak?"

"Nine," the driver answered, listing them. "Icelandic, Danish, Norwegian, Swedish, English, German, French, Russian and Greek."

"And which do you prefer?"

"Greek. Because it is my newest language, and I am a little in love with it. It still holds mysteries."

"But if you could speak one language for the rest of your days, what would it be?" Hervé interrupted.

"Icelandic. Though my life would be much poorer."

"You see?" said Hervé, triumphant.

"I see nothing," the inspector returned. "Only that we cling to what is most familiar. There are only a couple of hundred thousand Icelanders," he explained to Richard. "And nobody else speaks their language, so they must speak all others."

"It is the language of the sagas," the driver said, as if that put the question to rest. By now they were approaching the outskirts of Rekjavik. The houses were low, suburban, but made from black concrete, and without decoration. They were surrounded by grass and low shrubs, but no trees. They reminded Richard of the *blockhaus* at Dieppe, and they struck him as profoundly depressing. Kessler, guessing Richard's response, explained that the houses were beautiful inside.

"There are no trees in Iceland," he explained, "and so wood is expensive. They save it all for the insides of their houses. And they are elegant." In the distance, Richard could see large cranes, and buildings going up everywhere. It seemed the country was involved in some sort of building boom.

As they approached the centre of the town, the concrete pillboxes gave way to tall, white buildings with bright red, green and blue roofs. The harbour sparkled a brilliant blue, though the sun was still hidden. Just as they pulled up at the guest-house the clouds separated, and Richard stepped from the car into a stunning brilliance that made every building seem to give off light.

The woman who ran the guesthouse welcomed them and immediately brought them a thermos full of coffee. She warned them about the hot water. Apparently it came from a hot spring, and was near boiling. Richard turned on the tap in his room after she had left. The water came out steaming, but it smelled of sulfur.

A little later the inspector came by. He and Monsieur Delacroix were going to walk down to the harbour for supper. Did Richard wish to accompany them? Richard was suddenly unsure why he was here. His companions were solicitous and polite, but he could not imagine thinking of them as friends.

Across the street from the guesthouse was an enormous swimming pool, and beyond that the cathedral, a huge, concrete structure that did not seem to belong where it was. Its odd sweeping lines reminded Richard of the kinds of buildings that appear on the covers of science-fiction novels. From the hill on which they stood, they could see the sweep of the harbour. A couple of large ships and a dozen trawlers were moored along the piers.

They went along a narrow street that wound down to what appeared to be the main street of the city, a broad avenue that followed the contour of the bay. All along the street were expensive boutiques, and goldsmith and jewellery shops. Icelandic appeared to have very long words. The signs in the windows had single words as long as sentences.

Kessler led them from the main street past a row of fish-packaging plants. It was early evening, nearly seven o'clock, but nobody seemed to have quit work. The shops were all open, and there were many people in the streets. Through an open door, Richard could see a number of fishermen clustered around an enormous fish. A man with a huge knife slashed the stomach of the fish while two other men put a hook under its gills. Richard stopped to watch while they raised the fish with a block and tackle. When it was off the floor, it was taller than any of the men.

They ate in a little restaurant that overlooked the harbour. Most of the other guests were fishermen in woollen sweaters and rubber boots. Richard chose the daily special, a fish with a long and unpronounceable name. What he had chosen, Kessler told him, was monkfish.

"I have a particular fondness for monkfish," he went on. "The monkfish was spurned for a long time, because of its caul. I myself was born with a caul. It is considered a particular sign of luck." Richard tried to imagine Kessler as a child, his head encased in a sort of plastic helmet. The fish came in a tomato sauce, and tasted a little like lobster. After they had eaten, the waiter brought them a clear, powerful schnapps that tasted like licorice.

"Brennavin," Kessler told them. "The Icelanders call it Black Death. It's the national drink." The waiter left the bottle on the table. It had a simple black and white label with a picture of a skull and crossbones.

After they had been served coffee, Kessler offered a cigar to Richard and Hervé, both of whom refused. He clipped the end of the cigar with a small silver knife, and lit it.

"Druids," he began. "I suppose we should talk about Druids."

"Why not," Richard said. Monkfish. Druids. It seemed to fit.

"The body was found on a Druid shrine. Would you say it was in a sacrificial posture?"

"I'm not even sure now it was ever there," Richard answered.

"Well, assuming it was. We still haven't found it, by the way." He turned to Delacroix. "I told you some of the details of the case."

Delacroix nodded. "The Druids," he said, "have had a bad press. Mysterious human sacrifices. Strange blood rites. Almost all the information available about the Druids is wrong, nineteenth- and twentieth-century horror fantasies."

"They were a special priestly caste, weren't they?" Richard asked. "Julius Caesar wrote something about them." He turned to Kessler for confirmation.

"Yes," Kessler said. "But remember that for him they constituted the enemy. He was not likely to see their good points."

"It's always been thought that the Druids were a separate group," Delacroix said. "A kind of mystical order whose origin and even race was different from the people they apparently controlled. But it doesn't really make sense that way. How did they gain their power? How did they maintain it? It is much more likely that they were not different at all, but were in fact simply the ruling caste of the Celts, a theocratic power."

"You mean they're indigenous," Richard said. "Part of a sophisticated early European civilization."

"Exactly," Kessler agreed. "Only the Celts weren't supposed to be sophisticated enough to have such a civilization. They were supposed to be savages."

"The Greeks and the Romans," Delacroix said. "We are asked to believe that all civilization derives from them. But some of us prefer to find more native roots."

"You're a Druid?" Richard asked.

"Well, not exactly. But as you know, I have written on the subject. I think sometimes we look in the wrong places for our roots. We should look at home."

"I'm a Canadian." Richard reminded him. "If I look for roots at home, I'm going to find Indian roots. They won't do me much good."

"They might," Delacroix said. "They just might be more help than you think."

"At any rate," Kessler interrupted, "there's a definite tie. There are people who are a lot more serious than Hervé about the Druids. People who have begun an organization dedicated to reviving as much as can be learned about the religion and the area. Remember I mentioned the Hallstatt group? Some of the people who were in the photographs your wife took belong to that group."

"The couple on the motorcycle?"

"Yes."

"And the girl? The blonde girl?"

"Yes. I believe your compatriot, Monsieur Ferguson, told your wife something of this?"

"No. I've never even heard of him. Who is he?"

"He's from the Canadian Security Intelligence Service. He was there when the old woman had a heart attack at the Louvre. He gave your wife his card."

"She never mentioned it."

"He must have made an error. He thought he recognized her from her picture. At any rate, the woman died. It was all unexpected. But perfectly natural. She'd had a bad heart for some time."

"I know." Richard said. "I talked to the daughter. She's working as an *au pair* in Paris. But tell me about this Ferguson," he went on. "What's his involvement?"

"He's the Canadian representative in this. I met him once briefly. I thought he would have been in touch with you by now."

"No."

"Well, perhaps they're not taking it seriously. Or perhaps he has more important things to do."

Richard remained silent all the way back to the guesthouse. The others chattered in French about Monsieur Le Pen and his chances in the presidential race. Richard had not thought about the body for a long time. He had been too busy with his novel. Now he thought the body might have something to do with what he was writing, but he couldn't figure out what. He glanced at his watch. It was eleven o'clock but the sun was still high in the sky. A man stood on the roof of his house, repairing his chimney.

***

When Lois awoke the morning after Richard's departure, she was intensely aware of his absence. Richard always awoke first, had coffee made. He was cheerful in the mornings, whistling tunelessly or playing the radio softly so as not to awaken her. Now, the empty silence of the room seemed hostile, and it felt late, as if she had overslept.

Lois had told Richard that she loved to spend time alone, but she realized now that she had almost never had more than a day or so to herself. She remembered a sense of pleasurable solitude from her childhood, but she was not sure whether she was remembering the experience or the desire for it.

She decided to spend the day exactly as if Richard were still there. She went to the library and spent a couple of hours trying to puzzle out the subjunctive mood. She had expected French to come more easily, but she had begun to realize that, though she was becoming more comfortable surrounded by the language, it was not becoming clearer.

She walked down to the cathedral and looked at the clock. Small mechanical figures marched out of the wall on the hour. The central square was crowded with tourists, and Lois felt that her resentment of their presence helped establish a sense of her own place. She was pleased with this observation, but aware at the same time that it was artificial and pretentious. She was hardly more than a tourist herself. On the way back to the studio she stopped at a little shop and bought a white blouse she had been watching in the window for a couple of weeks. She was surprised that it fit her exactly.

At five thirty Lois set out for the Centre des Halles and the

Chamber of Commerce building. When she got there, she was informed that the classes for that week had been cancelled. Jules was out of town for the funeral of his grandmother. Friday was a holiday, and they had decided to *"faire un pont,"* or "make a bridge," so that everyone could have a week's holiday. There would be extra classes the following week and on Saturday to make up for it. Lois felt cheated, her vision of the progress of the week destroyed.

The only other student there was Fatima, the Turkish girl. She was dark and chubby, and seemed heavily laden with jewellery. She always wore two rings on each hand, and bright, extravagant scarves. Lois had found her coyness irritating at first, but now it seemed no more than a part of her style. The girl was pleased that the classes had been cancelled. They left the building together and Lois invited her to have a cup of coffee at a little cafe just across the street.

They said little until they were seated. Then the girl began to chatter in a heavily accented, but to Lois thoroughly comprehensible, French. She would go to Paris, she said. She had an uncle who lived in Paris, and who would be willing to put her up. This was her fourth French course in Strasbourg, and she had not yet been to Paris. After this course was completed she would go back to Turkey and teach French to children in a school. Had Lois been to Paris?

Lois was at first hesitant to answer, but found after a moment that the girl understood her without difficulty. It was an exultant moment, to be sitting at a sidewalk cafe, speaking to someone who spoke no English. She told the girl about the Louvre, about Notre Dame Cathedral, vendors selling postcards and paintings along the banks of the Seine. The girl listened intently. All her life she had wanted to go to Paris. But she was afraid. She would take the wrong train. She would be lost when she got to Paris. She would not find her uncle. Was Lois perhaps going to Paris? She would be more secure if she had a friend.

Lois told her that, no, she could not go, but even as she spoke she thought, I could go to Paris. There are no classes. Richard is in Iceland. I am a grown woman. She had a sudden image of herself walking along the Champs Elysée, looking at elegant clothing, catching a taxi back to the hotel. Richard would be upset, she was sure of that, but, she reasoned, there will be no difference whether I go to Paris or stay in Strasbourg. In either case, I am alone in a foreign country.

Perhaps, she told the girl, perhaps she would go to Paris after all. When did she want to go? The girl said Wednesday. But first she would have to phone her father for permission, and she would have to phone the uncle to see that he would be there to meet her. But it would be so much easier if she had a friend. The father could hardly refuse.

Lois told the girl she could not say for certain that she would go. She would decide tomorrow. She wrote down her telephone number, a little hesitant about whether Fatima would be as easy to understand on the phone as she was in person. The girl, however, was clearly delighted. She ordered them each another cup of coffee and talked of the Eiffel Tower. It would be so much easier to teach the children if she could tell them that she had seen the Eiffel Tower.

Lois walked home with mounting excitement. She could go to Paris. It was as simple as buying a ticket and climbing on the train. It struck her that she might phone Robert while she was there. She had a quick vision of herself in an elegant restaurant having dinner with Robert, but she pushed the idea from her mind. She would ask him only if there were any further news about the body.

By the next morning Lois had decided not to go. There were plenty of things she could do in Strasbourg. A trip to Paris would be expensive and unnecessary. She felt both disappointed and relieved by her decision. She went to the library to work in the morning, but she couldn't concentrate, and after an hour she returned home. She turned on the television and watched a cartoon about a car named BouBou and a young boy who was apparently a friend of the car. When it was over, the credits showed that it was a Japanese production. All the names were Japanese, and Lois wondered why none of the people in the cartoon had looked Japanese.

The ringing of the telephone startled her. She turned off the television and answered it. Fatima began with a rush of language,

168

and Lois had to tell her to slow down. She had spoken with both her father and her uncle. She was to be permitted to go to Paris, but only because Lois, who was the wife of a professor, would go with her. The uncle would meet them at the station. The excitement in Fatima's voice made it difficult to understand her.

Lois began to explain slowly that she had changed her plans and would not be going to Paris after all. At first the girl did not comprehend, but as soon as she did she started to weep. Lois searched for the language to console her, and found herself saying that, yes, after all, she would go to Paris. When she hung up the phone, she was amazed at herself. She had even arranged to get a taxi and pick Fatima up at eleven o'clock the next day.

The taxi driver chatted away on the way to the railway station, commenting on the other drivers and the traffic in Strasbourg, unaware that neither of his passengers could make out what he was saying. Lois and Fatima bought their tickets separately, but both discovered, as they were about to board the train, that there was, again, a supplementary fee. This was a luxury train, an experiment the railway was trying out. There was no way to avoid paying the extra one hundred francs.

The train climbed through the low mountains just outside Strasbourg and stopped briefly at Nancy. Fatima tried to speak English for a while, but Lois found it easier to understand her French. Fatima's family was wealthy. She had gone to school by helicopter. Her father wanted her to marry, but she had decided never to marry. She would be a school teacher instead. She loved American films, especially films about surfing. She would like to go to America some day and surf.

Lois tried to explain the difference between Canada and the United States, but the girl didn't seem to understand that they were separate countries, and Lois found it hard to make any real distinction other than the weather. Fatima was dressed in an expensive, flowered-print dress that made her look even heftier than usual, but she seemed to believe it was beautiful, and several furtive dark men who walked by seemed to agree with her. One even spoke a few words to her in a language that Lois guessed was Turkish, but the girl did not reply. Instead, she looked directly at Lois and spoke to her until the man went away. That, she explained, was why she was not permitted to travel alone.

For a while, Lois tried to sleep. As they approached Paris, she began to feel a sharp tension. What if there were no hotel rooms available? There had been no trouble before, but that had been the off-season. Now the city would be full of tourists.

They were almost at the station before Lois realized from Fatima's questions that the girl expected to be taken back to Strasbourg as well. It seemed an even larger imposition than getting her to Paris, and Lois tried to be vague about her answer. Richard would be back Sunday night. She would have to go back before then. The girl wrote down her uncle's phone number. She would be ready to go back whenever Lois chose.

Lois had already decided to go back early Saturday. She had left a note for Richard in case something should go wrong and he returned before her. She was pretty certain that wouldn't happen, but she wanted to be sure. Only now did it strike her that he might telephone and become worried if she didn't answer. She didn't tell the girl her plans, however. She merely said that she would phone.

The uncle met them at the platform of the Gare de l'Est. He said his name, but it was incomprehensible to Lois. He was a large man, swarthy, with a fierce black moustache. All he was missing, Lois thought, was a scimitar. He invited Lois to stay with his family. He had plenty of room, he insisted. When Lois refused, he offered to drive her to her hotel. Lois didn't want to tell him that she had not reserved a room, so she refused as graciously as she could, and slipped away.

At the tourism office, the line was long. It was nearly an hour before she was served, and then she was told that it was impossible, there were no rooms available. In desperation she asked them to phone the Hotel Maricourt. They did, and the young man who was serving Lois was astonished to discover that they had a room. It was only for one night, however, he informed her. After that she would have to find someplace else to stay.

Relieved, Lois clutched the confirmation slip, and went out to try to find a bus. From the map on the wall, she concluded that she needed a number twenty-three bus. People were waiting at each of the bus-stands just outside the station, but she was the only one waiting for number twenty-three. Well, here I am, she thought to herself, alone in Paris.

When she arrived at the Hotel Maricourt, she had a sense of coming home. The clerk recognized her and welcomed her back. Though she had never stayed in that room before, it, too, seemed familiar. The odd combination bathroom-sauna, which was advertised on the card on the table, was identical to the ones in the other rooms she and Richard had stayed in.

She wondered what Richard was doing at that moment. It would be earlier in Iceland. It was halfway to North America. He would be fishing in a stream. She tried to imagine Iceland, but could not. She thought of shining white mountains and snow, but that couldn't be right. They were fishing, so there couldn't be snow.

She thought she should do something about the fact that she had no place to stay the next night, but she knew it was not an emergency. She could stay with Fatima's uncle in an emergency, or she could get on a train and go back to Strasbourg. Still, she went down to talk to the clerk, who told her that she should check first thing in the morning. Almost always there were cancellations.

She wondered whether she should phone Robert. What could she ask him? She thought he might ask her to have dinner with him, and then she would have someone to talk to. Almost immediately, she felt guilty. She would not phone.

Instead, she would walk along the banks of the Seine all the way down to Notre Dame Cathedral. Maybe the bird woman would be there again. She had almost forgotten the bird woman and the old man with the cat. She was pleased to realize that now her trip to Paris had a purpose. She took out her sketchbook, but it was a new book with only a few drawings of a mime in front of the Strasbourg Cathedral. If she worked hard, she could make all the sketches she would need for her book. She might even discover some other characters she could add to her story.

The bird woman was nowhere to be seen. It was either too late or too early. She found the old man with the cat, but when she walked right up beside him, she could smell the rank odour of sweat and urine. He had a couple of bottles of wine in a paper bag hidden in a hedge at the end of a bed of flowers. Suddenly, she felt sorry for the cat on the end of its leash. Somebody dropped a coin into the old man's hat, and he leaped to his feet, bowing and crying, "Merci, merci, merci."

Lois felt cheated by her encounter. She crossed the street and tried to sketch the man. He noticed her and shouted and shook his fist. A little later, she ordered a pizza at a sidewalk cafe, and examined the drawing. It was incomplete, but it was clear that the man she had drawn was evil. His posture was cringing and aggressive at the same time. To try to change her mood, she made a sketch of the beautiful people from Seville getting into a car. She worked with quick, fluid strokes, but when she was done, the thin, elegant figures looked skeletal and hollow. She preferred the old man. At least his evil had a human dimension.

When the pizza arrived, it had, surprisingly, a fried egg in the middle. The orange yolk in its circle of white turned Lois's stomach, and she was able to eat only a couple of mouthfuls. That night, back at the hotel, she had vague, threatening dreams in which the old man and his cat figured in a way that she could not remember when she awoke.

In the morning, the woman at the desk informed her that there would be a free room for that night, though she could not guarantee another day. Again, Lois would have to check early to find out if there had been a cancellation. She decided to walk to the Champs Elysée. It was much farther than it looked on the map she had brought, and, by the time she had found the famous shops she had come to see, she was tired and wanted to sit down.

For some reason, Lois had expected the day to be sunny, and the steady rain was a source of disappointment. The street was broad, and there were a great number of expensive cars. Most of the people she saw looked like business people who knew where they were going and were in a hurry. She saw a couple of women, tall and thin, who she thought might be models, but nothing, other than the great expense of some of the clothes, made this street different from other shopping streets in large cities.

By early afternoon, Lois was exhausted. She had bought nothing, and the sheer effort of looking at so many things felt like a heavy weight. She couldn't bear the idea of walking all the way back in the rain, so she hailed a taxi. The driver made no attempt to speak to her until he stopped unexpectedly and asked for the fare. He had come from the wrong direction and let her off on the other side of the street, so for a moment Lois did not know where she was.

Back in the room, Lois showered and washed her hair. She would have liked to soak in a tub, but the base of the shower, which was evidently intended to serve also as a bathtub, was too small. On an impulse, she set the dial on the wall to Sauna, and in a moment the room was filled with steam. This is a mistake, she thought, but she waited a few moments then showered again. When she climbed into the bed she felt that every muscle in her body was relaxed.

She expected to fall asleep almost immediately, but sleep did not come. Instead, she began to wonder what would happen if she were to phone Robert. Nothing, she decided. He would tell her there was no further information, and that would be all. On an impulse, she got out of bed and found the card with the phone number in her purse. She sat naked on the leather chair beside the telephone, feeling the air as cold now. For a long time she looked at the number, then at last she dialed. She could hear the telephone ringing at the end of the line. It seemed a long distance away.

***

The road north from Rekjavik was gently rolling. To the left, low flats and river deltas stretched gently to the sea, which was the brightest blue Richard had ever seen. The sea was calm, and a distant boat seemed to hover above the line of the horizon. To the right, cliffs rose sharply to high mountain peaks, and, every few miles, spectacular waterfalls tumbled down the treeless banks.

They had left the paved highway not far from Rekjavik, and the gravel road was dusty whenever they met other vehicles. For a while, they seemed to move further inland, and Richard could

173

not see the ocean. The rivers they crossed were clear and fast-moving. They had been travelling for a couple of hours when Helgi, the driver, pointed out a road that led to the left.

"There is where Prince Charles of England fishes," he told them. "He comes every year and always to the same place." In some of the streams now they could see fishermen casting. The farms they passed were so brilliantly green that it appeared they were growing moss instead of hay.

At last, the driver pulled off on a side road and headed in the direction of the sea. A few minutes later, he pulled up at a white stone house with a brilliant red roof. They were welcomed by a young man who looked so much like Helgi that he might have been a brother. They put their luggage in their rooms and came down to a lunch served by a pretty blonde girl who looked, again, as if she might be a sister of the men.

The inspector explained that salmon fishing in Iceland was tightly controlled. All the fishing rights along the salmon rivers were owned, either by fishing clubs or by individuals, and it was illegal to fish without the permission of the owner. The government was also concerned about introducing foreign fish and bacteria into the streams, and for that reason people were discouraged from bringing their own fishing equipment. A little later, the young man led them to an equipment shed where they chose long, bamboo rods. The young man recommended a silver spoon, and the inspector and Delacroix went along with his recommendation. Richard wanted to try fly-fishing. The young man said that the trout were biting particularly well now, and he would be better off with a spoon, but Richard stuck to his choice. He remembered the rhythm of fly-fishing from his youth, and he wanted the feel of fishing more than he wanted fish.

His luck held. He had cast only a half-dozen times when a salmon rose to the bait and he hooked it. He played it carefully, but the fish did not put up much fight. It was a small fish, large enough to keep, but not much larger. He eased it off his hook and let it go. For the next three hours, he caught nothing. He worked his way down the stream, which was about sixteen inches deep, though Helgi warned that there were pools to be watched for.

The water ran very fast, and Richard could see small trout swim by within inches of his waders.

Still, though he had caught nothing, he was happy. Everything here seemed pristine and pure. He thought about Lois, and imagined her at the table in the little studio, meticulously writing out her verbs in her neat hand. This place was not like Europe, and it was not like North America. It was someplace in between.

A shout from the bank brought him back to attention. He waded in to find that the others had each had better luck than him. The inspector had three salmon and a trout. Delacroix had only two salmon, but one of them was large. The young man had appeared, riding on a thick, heavy-set pony, leading another. He gathered up the fish and the equipment, loaded everything onto the second pony, and disappeared around a rocky ledge.

Helgi asked the men to follow him, and he led them back upstream to a place where the river was much deeper and narrower. They crossed a small bridge and looked down into a deep pool, so clear that the hundreds of coins at the bottom glistened silver and gold. Richard guessed that the pool must be thirty feet deep, and he marvelled at its clarity.

"This is a lucky pool," Helgi told them. "If you throw a coin in here, you will have good fortune. Some of the coins you see at the bottom have been there for a thousand years." He pulled up a rope attached to a cage at the bottom of the pool and removed a bottle of Brennavin. He poured them each a drink in a small glass. They drank them in a single swallow, and Helgi filled each glass again.

On a whim, Richard found a Canadian dime in his wallet, and threw it into the pool. It sank slowly to the bottom, sliding downstream with the current, and settling where the coins were sparse.

"Isn't anybody tempted to gather the coins?" Richard asked.

"Nobody would do that," Helgi told him. "They would gather all the bad luck that these coins are holding here." He excused himself, saying that he would be back in a half-hour. He lowered the bottle to keep it cold, but told the men that if they wanted more, they should help themselves.

"Just beware of Nökkur," he added as he turned to go.

"Nökkur?" Richard asked.

"He lives on that mountain there," Helgi said, indicating the mountain before them. "He's the most beautiful pony in the world, and he will want you to ride him. But if you do, he will take you up to a lake at the top of the mountain and jump in and drown you. But don't worry. You will know him, because his hooves are on backwards." And he turned and left without looking back.

Each day was like the next. They would rise early and fish. The young woman would cook the salmon for them. They would sleep or walk in the afternoon, then they would fish again in the early evening. For the first few days, Richard enjoyed the fishing. The quiet rhythm of rising, fishing and sleeping was relaxing. They talked, sometimes in French, but usually in English, because when the conversation became complicated Richard was lost.

"He had the most beautiful voice I have ever heard," Delacroix said one day. They were talking about Heidegger. "When he spoke, you were compelled to listen. It was like something elemental, a river or a mountain avalanche. He would have been at home here, where everything is elemental." He gestured to the mountain that rose sharply before them.

"A deep, radio-announcer's voice?" Richard asked.

"No, no. Nothing like that. It was actually quite high-pitched. But it was always under control."

They had decided that day to take a picnic lunch and some wine and walk along the banks of the river as far as they could in the direction of the mountain. Their walk had not taken long, and the inspector had gone off to explore the area, leaving Richard and Delacroix together. Now they were beside a pool at the base of a waterfall about ten metres high. The rock behind the waterfall was hollowed out. When they had arrived, Richard had slipped behind the sheet of water, and it had struck him that this was an ideal place for romantic lovers to make love. Now, he listened to the sound of the waterfall and tried to imagine the philosopher's voice.

"I am too young to have known him in his prime," Delacroix went on. "But there are wonderful stories of bonfires in the Black Forest, speeches that drove audiences wild with excitement. He must have seemed very radical back in the twenties. Here was the rising star of philosophy, a professor who dressed like a peasant, who dismissed the greatest thinkers of history as mistaken, and who had nothing but contempt for his own colleagues. When I knew him, he was quieter, more reflective, but there was still magic in his voice."

"But his writing," Richard said, "is so complex. He says the same thing over and over again in slightly different ways."

"As you would if you were speaking. The best way to understand Heidegger is to read him aloud. But of course it must be in German."

"But German is not your first language," Richard said. "How do you understand him?"

"It is my mother tongue," Delacroix answered. "My mother was German, from Freiburg. I spoke German until I went to school. This is not unusual for an Alsatian."

"But how do you account for his relationship with the Nazis? Isn't everything at the core of his thinking suspect if it brings you to a profoundly inhumane position?"

"You have to separate the thinker from the citizen," Delacroix said. "Like many Germans, he believed in authority, and if you see his speech to the professors and students when he was made rector at Freiburg as simply an expression of his concern at a kind of growing nihilism and selfish anarchy, it is not remarkable for the head of a German university. It is only remarkable that it was made by Heidegger. And even then not so remarkable. Remember that, for him, truly authentic being came not out of action but out of the contemplation of your own mortality. That is not the sort of thinking that prescribes action of any sort."

Richard had found his conversations with Delacroix frustrating. Where he felt he understood Heidegger's message, Delacroix agreed with him. Where he felt he did not understand, Delacroix explained that only someone who was a native speaker of German could ever understand. Richard confessed that he had given up his study of Heidegger, and had decided to write a novel instead.

"Precisely what Heidegger would have advised you to do," Delacroix told him. "There are many paths in the forest, and the seeker after truth chooses his own. There is not one true path, though. Finally, only art matters."

At that moment, the inspector arrived. He announced that he had discovered a hot spring a short distance away. They clambered over rocks until they came to a stream, about a foot wide. It was so small that in places it was completely covered by the grass that bent over it. Richard tested it with his hand. It was warm, but not unbearably so. In winter it would probably not hold its heat for long.

Overhead, gulls circled. Richard had become accustomed to their cries the way you can get used to the sounds of traffic. This far north, the sun never dipped entirely below the horizon, and the gulls cried at all hours. Every day, just at noon, clouds scudded in, and there was a brief shower. Then it would clear again and the temperature would rise. Back at the house, the Icelandic girl tanned every moment she could. She lay naked on a cot on the south side of the house, and it did not seem to bother her who walked by. Richard thought of his own embarrassment at the beach in Portugal. He had assumed that Icelanders would be even more reticent, but that didn't seem to be the case.

Saturday was to be the last full day of their trip to Iceland. Richard had tried to phone Lois a couple of times, but there had been no answer. He was starting to become anxious, and had lost interest in fishing. He stuck deliberately to fly-fishing, though some days he caught nothing at all. He thought of Lois alone in Strasbourg. He felt his anxiety as a tension, a tightness in his breathing, but when he imagined Lois, he imagined her secure in the studio, at the table, or taking a long bath.

Saturday morning, Richard awoke with a hangover. The evening before, he had talked for hours with the inspector and the Icelanders about the First World War. The Icelanders told him that Iceland had supported both sides. The country had been in a severe depression, and then there was a huge demand for fish and mutton. They had referred to it as the blessed war, because it had made everybody in the country rich. Richard had tried to explain his idea that the war was what had created the idea of nationhood in Canada. It was the first time that people across the country were united in a single enterprise. They were drinking vodka and Coke, which seemed to be the Icelanders' favourite drink.

At some time during the night, Delacroix had disappeared. Richard had assumed he had simply gone to bed, but the next morning he was still missing. He had gone back to France, the inspector told him.

"Something to do with his father's estate. He was urgently required."

Richard didn't want to fish that morning. The inspector offered to go back to Rekjavik early, but Richard refused. It was clear that the inspector did not want to miss the last day. They had breakfast together, and Richard watched Helgi and the inspector disappear down the trail that led to the river.

The morning passed slowly. Richard hiked up the trail to the main highway, but he had become accustomed to the roughness of the landscape, and he found nothing that interested him much. When he got back, the girl was sunbathing again, stretched out on her stomach on the cot, her long blonde hair falling nearly to the ground. Richard watched her for a moment. Her body was as near to perfect as he could imagine, but there was nothing erotic about her pose. She seemed as natural as the rocks and mountain flowers.

Inside the house, Richard found a field guide to the birds. It was written in Danish, but he decided that, if he could identify birds by their Latin names, he could check them up later. He went down the path to the river, but continued downstream in the direction of the sea until he came to a spot where the river opened into a broad marshy area. There were ducks everywhere, flying, or swimming in rafts out on the water, but without binoculars he could not get close enough to make any identification. Richard had never paid much attention to birds, had found the notion of bird-watching slightly comic and trivial. Now he wished he could name things. It struck him then how foreign he was in this place. Around him were thousands of birds and grasses and flowers of every kind, but he didn't know the name of a single thing.

He wondered about the novel he was trying to write. He tried to re-imagine Dieppe, and found that he could remember the details of buildings and the look of the people, but he didn't know the names of the trees or of the birds. He remembered that there had been gulls, drifting in from the grey, foggy sea, but were there many different sorts of gulls? And did it matter? Would anyone care about the details?

Later, as they drove back along the winding road to Rekjavik, Richard tried to explain his concerns to the inspector, who was full of sympathy. It took him to the heart of his own craft, he told Richard.

"You can only see things you can name," Kessler explained. "You have to think of the world as a text, as something you read. It has its own nouns and verbs, its own grammar. If you wish to solve crimes, you must be familiar with the conventions of the criminal, the types of the criminal. You must know which actions are appropriate for a criminal and which are not."

"That actually sounds easier than I thought," Richard said. "Do criminals really fall into such patterns?"

"It's largely a matter of clichés," the inspector said. "Criminals have only the history of their own sort of crime to guide their conduct. Murderers all face the same problems. What weapon is appropriate, how shall the body be disposed of, what alibi must be set in place? In fact," and here he became confidential, "in the vast majority of cases the police know who committed the murder. The problem is not one of discovery, but one of putting together sufficient evidence to guarantee a conviction."

"But in the case of our own particular murder, you do not know the murderer?"

"No," the inspector said. "But it is not an ordinary murder, if it is a murder at all. We have not yet ruled out that you might for your own purposes have invented the entire story." The road was flatter now, and they were approaching the outskirts of Rekjavik.

"And why might we have done that?"

"For any of a number of reasons. You are, for instance, writing a novel, and might have chosen this as a method of research, a way of putting the machinery of French justice into motion so that you might observe it."

"And do you believe that?" Richard asked.

"No," the inspector answered. "But I don't think you came on a murder. There is too much the element of the spectacle, the thing staged. The structure is very dramatic."

180

Richard tried to get more direct information from the inspector, but if he had any, he did not reveal it. He wanted, instead, information from Richard. He asked dozens of questions about Richard's parents, about his schooling, about the philosophy department. By the time they boarded the airplane at Keflavik, Richard felt he had confessed more to the inspector than he ever had to Lois. He thought that psychoanalysis must be something like this.

The day had been grey, with an unfulfilled promise of rain, but, as the plane took off, the sun came from behind the clouds, and they left Iceland glowing like a jewel in the dark North Atlantic. They landed in Luxembourg in darkness, and during the train trip back to Strasbourg they hardly spoke. The inspector dropped Richard off at the studio, and spun the tires of his silver Mercedes as he left.

Richard rang the bell at the gate, but there was no answer, so he fumbled for his keys. The stairway was dark, and he walked carefully so as not to disturb the landlord. It was nearly three o'clock in the morning. He knocked on the door to waken Lois, then used both keys in the double lock. When he turned on the light he could see that the sofa had not been made up as a bed.

"Lois?" he called, but there was no answer.

***

The door of the restaurant led into a long hallway. Off to the left, people were dining at sturdy, wooden tables with red legs. The tablecloths had red and white checks that reminded Lois of Portugal. At the far end was what appeared to be an entirely different restaurant. Here the tablecloths were heavy, white linen, and the knives and forks were pure silver. Each table was lit by its own candle and the waiters flitted by in partial darkness.

The head waiter who led them to their table was elaborately formal, an attitude Lois associated with expensive food. He appeared to recognize Robert and treated him with deference. When Lois asked Robert whether he came here often, he laughed and said that the waiter was merely good at his job. He recognized everybody.

The menus were large. Lois solved the problem of deciphering hers by asking Robert to order for her. She looked around the room while he consulted with the waiter. The two restaurants might have been divided by the physical types of their patrons and not merely by decor. The customers at the red-checked tables were heavier, the men in shirts with open collars, the women in bold-coloured dresses. Here, in the white-linen section, everyone was thin and elegant. At the next table a slender woman with a small face and large, dark eyes whispered to her companion in what sounded like Italian. Lois thought she had never seen so many beautiful people in all her life.

"Lois," Robert said after the waiter had left. "It's a beautiful name."

"No, it's not," Lois told him. "I hate it. Everybody named Lois hates the name. There's a society of Loises in Minneapolis. The Lois club. They get together every month to commiserate with each other. They even have an education committee to try to get mothers not to name their children Lois. Their aim is to wipe out the name entirely."

Robert laughed. "Is that true?"

"I think it's true. Somebody told me about it once. If it isn't, it should be."

"Well, I like the name anyway," Robert told her. "I once decided that if I ever had a daughter I would name her Lois. Or else Glynnis."

"Glynnis is even worse," Lois said. "Name her Susan or Mary. Or Anne. Everybody named Anne is successful. They never have to go on diets or exercise, and they get all the best jobs." Lois was surprised at herself. She thought of herself as a listener, not a talker, yet here she was doing most of the talking. The waiter arrived with the wine, and there was a moment of silence as Robert tasted it and pronounced it acceptable. As soon as the waiter was gone, Lois continued. "Do you have any daughters?" She realized that she knew almost nothing about Robert.

"No," he said. "I have two sons. They're with their mother in Vancouver. I haven't seen them for five years."

"That's terrible," Lois said.

"Not really. They don't want to see me. The last time I saw them, I took them to a hockey game, and they both ran away between periods. I had to go back to my ex-wife and tell her I'd lost two teenagers. They blame me for the break-up of the marriage, even though it was my wife who left. I suppose we'll have a reconciliation some day, but right now I send them money on their birthdays and at Christmas, and they avoid all communication."

Lois remembered the break-up of her first marriage. She had been married five years. One day her husband had come home and announced that he was in love with someone else. He had packed his clothes and left, and she had not seen him again for months. She remembered feeling dried out and helpless and manipulated as he arranged the divorce. She had got nothing, but then she hadn't wanted anything. She had even given him all the photographs so that she would have no record of ever having been married. Later, when she had started with Richard, her ex-husband had phoned and threatened her a couple of times, but now she didn't even know where he lived.

The thought of Richard brought her back with sharp guilt, and she looked around the room. He was in Iceland, and would never know that she had gone out for dinner with Robert. She wondered what he would do if he found out. He could leave her, but she thought he wouldn't. He would be angry, but he wouldn't go.

Robert was smiling at her now, across the table. He looks like a nice man, she thought. His wide, freckled face seemed open and guileless.

"You know, when I first saw the photo of you in the file, I thought you were one of the most beautiful woman I had ever seen," he said.

"Don't," Lois told him. "Don't say things like that or I'll have to leave." She twisted her napkin, and suddenly felt vulnerable.

"Okay," he said. "I'm sorry." There didn't seem much to say then and, after a moment of silence, their food arrived. Robert had ordered them identical plates of salmon in a yellow sauce. The portions of vegetables were tiny, but they were elegantly arranged so that the meal looked like an illustration out of a magazine. Lois hesitated to eat hers, because she didn't want to ruin the composition on her plate.

"I didn't bring you out entirely on false pretences," Robert said. "There is some news. I've been talking with Kessler. He apparently thinks that there is some connection between your body at Mont Ste. Odile and a Middle East arms deal. Iraq or Lybia. And there's a Canadian connection. Some men who raise money to see that things get from one place to another. Canadians don't sell many arms, but we're apparently very good at financing deals. In this case, they're somehow tied in with a group associated with some strange practices. Druids, he said. I'll find out more from him the next time I see him."

"Richard was reading a book about Druids."

"Did he tell you about them?"

"He said there wasn't much to tell. Nobody actually knows much. A lot of the stuff he found out was about England. Richard doesn't like England," she added, unsure whether that bit of information was helpful or not.

"Well," Robert went on, "I don't want to alarm you, but it is possible you may be in some danger. If Kessler is right and this does involve Iraq or Lybia, then the Israeli secret police are also involved. It gets very complex. Your photographs and your descriptions of the people at Mont Ste. Odile are the main links we have to the group Kessler was talking about. Oh, and the girl. We've definitely established a relationship between her and Mann, the missing soldier, and presumably the body."

"Richard likes the girl," Lois said. "He wants to protect her." She realized that she had not made that connection before. "He went to see her the last time we were in Paris. Or he phoned her. I'm not sure which."

"Well, he'd best avoid her if he doesn't want to get in trouble. Do you know where she is? We can't find her."

"She's an *au pair*, somewhere in Paris."

"Yes, we know that much. But she's not where she's supposed to be."

"You'll have to ask Richard," Lois said. "He'll be back from Iceland on Sunday. Or better still, phone Kessler and he can ask Richard."

"Thanks. Is that sufficient business?"

"Yes."

"Now can I tell you that you're beautiful?

"Yes," she said. "Tell me."

"You're beautiful."

"How do you get to be a spy?' she asked.

"I'm not a spy," he answered. "I'm actually a bureaucrat. Mine is usually a dull job. I get to sit around in Ottawa and shift files. I'm here to assist in an international criminal investigation. It's unusual."

"You're not a Mountie?"

"No. I was once a Mountie. For eight years, actually. I was stationed in northern Alberta and northern Saskatchewan and in the end in Winnipeg." Lois felt somehow more secure at this news. If Robert had lived in Winnipeg, they had a connection she had not expected.

"What part of Winnipeg?"

"Westwood."

"Oh," Lois said, disappointed. "We live in St. Vital."

"I liked Winnipeg."

"But how did you get from being a Mountie to being a spy?"

"I'm not a spy. But anyway, I went back to university and took a degree in criminology. Then I worked in security for a couple of large corporations. After my marriage broke up, I went to Ottawa just when they were starting the CSIS, and I applied for a job and I got it."

When they left the restaurant, Robert turned to the left, and Lois was sure he was going in the wrong direction.

"Isn't it that way?" she asked.

"What?"

"My hotel."

Richard smiled. "Yes it is. But I thought we might take the scenic way back. Banks of the Seine. All that."

"I don't know," Lois said, but she joined him. For a while they walked in silence down a dark street, and Lois reflected that she would not want to walk here alone. Robert was heavy-set, not as tall as Richard but more muscular. He looked powerful.

"Aren't you afraid of dark streets?" she asked him.

"Depends where they are," he said. "Not here. But in almost any city in the United States."

They reached the Seine and turned right towards Notre Dame. Lois found herself terribly excited. This felt like dating when she was a teenager. She wondered whether Robert would try to come up to her room, and what she should do. She prepared the words in her mind. Thank you, it's very flattering, but I am a married woman.

As they neared Notre Dame, there were more lights and more people. Everywhere, lovers were locked in embraces or strolled holding each other so tightly that they moved in awkward shifts. They stopped at a break in the little stands along the shore to look at the moonlight on the water. A brilliantly lit boat full of people drifted down the river. Lois leaned over as far as she could to see the pathway just below, where people were walking. When she straightened up, Robert pulled her into his arms and kissed her.

She kissed him back, a long slow kiss. She could feel his tongue in her mouth and she pushed her own tongue back against his. Her whole body felt weak. Robert's hand was on the back of her neck, and he felt strong but very gentle. When he released her, she slipped out of his arms.

"No," she said, slowly and deliberately. "No more." She looked at Robert. He was smiling, sure of himself. He reached for her again, but she spun around, out of his reach.

"I'm sorry," she said. "That was nice, but I am not getting into anything more. I want to go back to the hotel."

"Of course," Robert told her. "Whatever you want."

After that they walked in silence for a long time. Robert led her through a bright area filled with restaurants and street vendors. On one corner, a rock band had set up its operation, and a crowd of people stood around listening. The music was not loud, and it was hard to say whether the band was good or bad. They emerged on the rue Ste. Germaine, and Lois realized where they were. She turned right without prompting and led the way towards the hotel.

They were just about to the hotel when Robert took her in his arms and kissed her again. This time she did not respond. She let herself be kissed, but she held her body stiff and unresponsive. After a couple of seconds Robert let her go.

"You were serious," he said.

"Yes," she answered. They had reached the hotel, and Robert accompanied Lois into the lobby.

"I'll give you a call tomorrow," he told her. "Just to see that everything's okay."

"I'm going home tomorrow," Lois told him. "To Strasbourg. On the first train in the morning."

"Well, give me a call from the station, then. I'll feel better." Lois had already decided that she would not call, but she told him she would.

Robert took her hand in his. "No hard feelings?"

Lois considered the speech she had prepared, but she realized it would sound ridiculous.

"No," she said. "Of course not." When she reached the landing she looked back, but all she could see were Robert's feet. He hadn't moved. She stood perfectly still for a minute until she saw him move. Then she climbed the stairs to her room.

The hallway in front of her room was dark. Usually there was a light burning so that you could find your key. Lois fumbled in her bag and found the key, identifying it by the triangular tag attached to it. She slid it slowly into the lock, and turned.

As she pushed the door open, she realized that she must have forgotten to turn off the lamp on the table. It glowed yellow, and she remembered clearly the act of shutting it off. For a second her body went stiff with panic, then she jumped backwards, slamming the door shut, but not before she caught a glimpse of a blond young man, his face bland and brutal. She could sense the beginnings of movement as he lunged at the door. She heard the heavy thud as his body hit it, but she was already running, spinning down the staircase as fast as she could.

She spun into the brilliance of the lobby. Robert stood there, chatting with the clerk. They both froze in gestures of surprise at her entrance. Lois didn't know how to say what she had to.

"A man," she gasped. "There's a man in my room."

Robert headed for the staircase but she caught him by the arm.

"No," she said. "Don't leave me here alone."

"Easy," he told her. "Take it easy. You'll be safe here in the lobby. Just don't go anywhere." He continued up the stairs. The clerk spoke to Lois in French, words of condolence, whispered in a blur of language, but she realized that he was also afraid. He led her behind the desk, and he took a wooden club out from under a pile of boxes. He moved to the front of the desk, prepared to defend her, and Lois noticed that he wasn't any larger than she was. The blond man would take the club from him in a second.

Robert was gone for what seemed like a long time. When he came down, he seemed troubled.

"There was no one there," he said. "The windows are all locked from the inside. Nothing seemed disturbed. What did the man actually look like?"

"He was big," Lois said. "And blond. He had a face with no expression on it." And then it came to her. "He looked just like the man on the motorcycle at Mont Ste. Odile. Except he wasn't in his motorcycle costume."

Robert consulted with the clerk. He took out the register, and went through it name by name. In each case the clerk repeated, "Non, non. C'est pas possible."

"There's nobody by that description registered here," Robert told Lois. "Let's go up to your room and see what's disturbed."

Robert led the way and Lois followed. She did not want to enter the room, but she did. Everything was exactly as she had left it, but she opened her suitcase to be sure. She saw immediately what was missing.

"The photographs," she said. She checked the little secret compartment of the suitcase. "But all the traveller's cheques are fine."

"Which photographs?'

"All of them. Every picture we've taken since we came. Including Spain and Portugal. They're all gone."

"Why did you have them with you?"

"I don't know," she said. "I just did."

"Well," Robert said. "What now?"

"I don't know," Lois answered. "You're the expert on this sort of thing. But I'm not staying here. I'm going to have nightmares about that face for a long time."

"Do you have anywhere to go?"

"No," Lois answered. "Take me to the Gare de l'Est. I'll wait there until there's a train to Strasbourg."

"Come to my place." Robert said. "I'll take you to the train in the morning."

"I don't know."

"You'll be fine. I'm not a monster. I have an extra bed."

"Okay," Lois said. And she felt much better. "But I've got to catch the train in the morning."

"First thing."

Robert carried her suitcase out to the car. It was a low, sleek, grey car, but she couldn't figure out what kind it was. It was parked almost directly across from the hotel, half on the street and half on the sidewalk. She had not expected Robert to have a car. She had thought he must have come by taxi or on the Metro. She thought again of the lost photographs. She could remember them clearly, but would they stay in her memory? Already she was unsure which of her memories of the beach in Portugal were real and which were memories of photographs.

They parked the car in an underground garage whose door opened when Robert pushed a button on the dash of the car. The door to the building and the door to Robert's suite both opened when he inserted what looked like a credit card and punched in a numbered code.

As soon as they were in the apartment, Robert offered her a drink, but she refused.

"I think I'd just better get some sleep," she said. The apartment was cramped. A narrow hallway led to a bathroom at the end of its length, and all the rooms were to the left of the hallway, a bedroom, a living room crowded with furniture, and a kitchen just big enough to turn around in.

Robert showed her the bedroom. "You sleep here," he said. "I'll sleep on the sofa."

"I don't want to put you out," Lois told him. "I can sleep on the sofa."

"No," he said. "It's no problem. I insist." He put her suitcase on the bed, and as he left, he pulled the door closed. "Sweet dreams," he said.

Lois undressed slowly. She didn't feel tired. She put on her white nightgown, and sat on the edge of the bed. The closet door was open and she could see Robert's suits hanging there. On the dresser was a pile of shirts, neatly folded with paper strips wrapped around them and a laundry bill stapled to the strip on the top shirt.

Lois felt tense and excited. She tried to go over the incidents of the evening in order, but she couldn't concentrate. She thought about Robert's kiss, but put it out of her mind and replaced it with the face of the blond man. She expected to feel the same fear she had felt when she had first glimpsed him in her room, but she did not. His face seemed merely neutral, devoid of meaning. For a long time she lay there, trying to sleep. She breathed deeply, counting her breaths, but even that didn't help.

A while later she heard Robert in the hallway. She heard the click of the bathroom door. She got out of bed and opened the door as quietly as she could. She could see a bar of yellow light at the base of the door. She took a couple of quick steps down the hallway. I will wait, she thought, and when he is finished I will go to the bathroom.

She heard the doorknob turn, and light flooded the hallway. Instinctively she slipped out of the light and into the living room. Then the light went out, and the room was in total darkness. She could feel Robert's presence as he neared her. Just as he turned into the living room, she slipped into his arms and kissed him, intensely, as he had kissed her before.

"My God," he said, and he kissed her back, hard. Then he picked her up and carried her to the bedroom. This is my doing, Lois thought to herself, as he lowered her to the bed. I have done this entirely on my own.

Robert's lovemaking was intense and hurried. Lois ran her hands along his muscular body, and heard herself moan. His skin seemed very smooth. She curled her body to meet his, then stiffened. Immediately Robert cried out, then collapsed on her, his full weight pressing against her. They lay like that for several moments, then Robert rolled off.

"I'm sorry," he said. "I haven't had a woman for so long I'd forgotten what it was like. It'll be better next time, I promise."

"No," Lois said. "No next time. This was just something that happened and it was wonderful, but that's the end."

There was a next time, though. At dawn Robert began slowly to caress her. She resisted at first, but then she let him continue. She had slept soundly, but had woken to a sharp feeling of guilt. Richard's face appeared to her, mournful and hurt. Robert's body felt foreign and wrong, and even though he was gentle and thorough, she could not respond. He stayed in her for a long time, but finally he finished in a way that was rough and painful, and she was glad that it was over.

Robert seemed hurt and disappointed, and that made her even more guilty. She apologized, and then felt that she had no need for apology. She dressed and walked into the other room. Robert remained naked all the while he made them coffee, as if his nakedness established a claim on her. She tried not to look at his body.

Robert was in a better mood as he drove her to the railway station. He joked with her, and teased her that he had hired the blond man in her room to get her to his apartment. His assuredness and good humour made her more apprehensive.

"I'm going to make a trip to Strasbourg," he told her. "I have to see Kessler. And I want to see you again."

"No, don't," she answered. "This is over. I won't see you again."

He didn't reply, but he kissed her on the cheek as he passed her her luggage. They were just across the street from the station. A family of Turks disappeared into the building, and Lois thought guiltily of Fatima. She would have to try to phone the uncle.

Robert waited in his car for Lois to cross the street, but she stood on the sidewalk until finally he drove off and disappeared into the traffic.

I have a whole day, she thought to herself, to get prepared for Richard. To find out how not to tell him about this. She stepped out into the street and felt herself hurled into the air. The sky seemed remarkably blue. She felt no pain, but the world closed down until it was a pinprick of light. And then that, too, disappeared.

***

The note on the table was in Lois's neat hand. It said simply, "Gone to Paris with Fatima for a couple of days. In case you get home early, don't worry. I'll be back by Saturday at the latest. You'll probably never see this. Love, Lois."

It was Sunday night, or rather, three o'clock Monday morning. Richard felt his stomach sink in a way he had never felt before. He felt panic and anger combined. She should never have gone. It was a stupid thing to do. Not coming back on time was incomprehensible. He carried the note in his hand, into the kitchen, back through the studio, into the bathroom. He knew he had to do something, but his mind could not get around the enormity of Lois's absence. He imagined her dead, lying in a coffin. Then he imagined her dancing in the door, smiling and apologizing at the same time, and he felt his knees go weak with anger and fear again.

Who could he talk to at this hour? He considered calling the police, but he knew they would dismiss it. A wife was late coming home from Paris, perhaps she had more shopping to do, perhaps she had a lover? Again Richard felt himself go numb. But, no, she knew nobody in Paris. It was unthinkable. The inspector? It would be impossible to get him at this moment, and what could he say?

Richard sat in the big armchair and put his head in his hands. He looked at the note again. Who was Fatima? The fat girl from the French class. The Turkish one. That had to be it. But how could he find her phone number?

Lois's books were piled neatly on the bookshelf. Richard started to look through them in case Lois had written the number in them. He looked through the pages of neatly copied verbs until, on the last page, he found a phone number. There was no name, just the number. Richard went to the telephone. The phone was sitting on the telephone book, and when he lifted it, he saw the same number. He dialed.

The phone rang many times, and, just as Richard was about to put it down, a sleepy woman's voice answered, "Allo?"

"Is Fatima there?" he asked.

"Allo?"

"Est-ce que Fatima est là?"

"Oui. Un moment." For a long time no one came to the phone. Richard could hear a discussion in the distance. At last another voice said, "Allo."

"Fatima?"

"Oui."

Richard explained who he was. He apologized for calling at this late hour, and asked if she knew how he could reach Lois. There was silence, then the first voice returned. Fatima had difficulty understanding French on the telephone. Could she help?

Richard explained once more. He listened to the background discussion but couldn't make it out.

"She has gone to Paris," the voice said. She was supposed to bring Fatima back on Friday or Saturday, but she had not arrived. The voice took on a note of accusation. Lois had not called, so Fatima's uncle had had to drive her all the way to Strasbourg, because there were classes on Monday. Richard asked for the uncle's phone number in Paris, and after a further wait, it was given to him.

The uncle could tell Richard nothing. Lois had refused the invitation to stay with him. She was staying in a hotel. No, he did not know which hotel. It was all very difficult. Fatima had been allowed to come to Paris because she was travelling with the professor's wife, but the professor's wife had not telephoned, and it had been necessary to drive all the way to Strasbourg. Richard thanked him and hung up the telephone. He phoned the inspector, but there was no answer.

The possibility that Lois had been abducted struck Richard for the first time. Suddenly, the body at the Pagan Wall took on a seriousness that Richard had ceased to give it. The strange group that the inspector had described had seemed like comic opera, but now it might be real. He imagined Lois bound, stuffed in a closet. Waiting for what?

He thought about Lois in Paris and what she might do. She would go to art galleries, she would go shopping. Where would she stay? The only hotels whose names she knew were the Savoy and the Maricourt. On an impulse, Richard called the operator and got the number of the Maricourt. He dialed and got no answer. He knew there was a night clerk, so a few minutes later, he dialed again. This time a man answered.

Richard asked if he could be connected to Lois Jensen. He did not know the room number. The clerk hesitated a moment, then reported that she had checked out Friday night. Richard, desperate, explained that he was her husband, that it was necessary to get in touch with her immediately. Did she say where she was going?

The clerk apologized. There had been a robbery. It was very unusual. She had gone with the American policeman. There were never robberies at the Hotel Maricourt.

Richard asked about the American policeman. The clerk knew nothing. He had acted like a policeman. He had asked questions. He had said not to call the gendarmes. Lois had gone freely. She was not under arrest, he didn't think. She was quite uninjured, though naturally she had been upset at finding the man in her room. She had not been charged for the room. The hotel had a reputation to take care of, and this was highly unusual.

Richard thanked the clerk, and hung up the phone. He went to the bathroom and took two aspirins. Then he phoned the inspector again. He let the phone ring for several minutes, but there was still no answer. After a while, he phoned the railway station. The first train to Paris would leave at seven o'clock.

Richard poured himself a large glass of scotch, and drank it in a single gulp. Then he poured another, mixed it with water and drank more slowly. He set the alarm on his wrist watch for six o'clock, and lay on the sofa, knowing he would not sleep. But he did. He fell asleep almost instantly, and when the alarm sounded, it seemed to be far away.

As the train pulled out of Strasbourg in the early morning light, Richard realized that he was doing exactly the wrong thing. He should wait in the studio, phone the inspector, phone the police, phone the Canadian Embassy. Perhaps Lois was on her way home now, in another train that would pass his on the way. And yet he was certain that he would find Lois in Paris, and that if he did not find her she would not be found.

The trip seemed infinitely long, much longer than he remembered. There were few other passengers in the first-class carriage, and they all looked bored and sleepy. The countryside itself seemed frozen. Fields stretched to the horizon in either direction with no sign of anyone working them. From time to time the train travelled parallel to roads, but the roads, too, were empty. No one walked on the streets of the little towns it passed.

When the train stopped, Richard awoke, surprised to find he had fallen asleep again. He had no plan. He was in Paris, but he had no idea where he would go. The last he had heard of Lois, she had been at the Hotel Maricourt. Well, he would go there.

He waited for a moment at the queue for taxis, then took the bus instead. He would first phone the Canadian Embassy, then the police. Then he would phone every hospital in Paris until he found her. He began to think of Lois as injured, as lying somewhere hurt. By the time he reached the hotel, his panic of the previous night had returned.

The clerk could tell him no more. He had not been on duty. The one Richard had spoken to had been on duty, but there was no more to say. Lois had left with a man, perhaps a policeman. She had not been charged for the room. Richard asked if he could register in the same room. The woman was doubtful, but Richard was insistent, and after she crossed out and rewrote a number of names, she gave him the key.

Richard searched the room carefully, looking for any signs of Lois. There were none. He did not know what to look for, but he even took the mattress off the bed in his search. He remembered, then, the inspector's words in Iceland. The Canadian representative in this matter. What was his name? Ferguson?

There was no telephone book in the room. Richard went down to the lobby and looked up the number of the Canadian Embassy. Then he phoned and asked for Ferguson.

"One moment," the female voice said, and he heard the phone ring several times. After a moment the woman came back on the line and told Richard that Mr. Ferguson did not respond. Was there a message?

"No," Richard said. "No message." He hung up, but then he called back and left his name and the message that he could be reached at the Hotel Maricourt. He went back to the lobby and found the book that had the names of hospitals in it. He decided, arbitrarily, to begin in the middle of the list. He did not ask whether Lois was there. In each case he asked in which room she could be found. Each phone call took several minutes, because they had to check records, and the clerk always sounded disappointed to have to say she was not there.

Richard had ceased to imagine a world without Lois. He took it for granted, as she did, that he would die first. Now, her absence forced him to think about it, and he began to realize how alone he was, and how powerless.

After about an hour, Richard was becoming discouraged. He had hardly begun his list. Then, to his surprise, he was informed, without hesitation, that she was in section A-five, bed twenty-six. An automobile accident, but she was in excellent condition. Richard wrote down the address. He was filled with a sense of triumph. He had solved the problem on his own, without intervention.

He caught a taxi on the rue Ste. Germaine. The hospital was closer than Richard expected, a grey monolithic building that from the outside looked like an old office building. The windows were grimy and unwashed. The streets of the district were narrow and dirty, and the people on the sidewalks seemed poor.

Inside, however, the hospital was neat and modern. He looked for some indication of where he might find section A-five, but there was none. Reluctantly, he approached the receptionist. She looked up Lois's name on a list, then asked Richard to go into an office and wait.

After a moment, an older woman came in. She slipped into a crisp English as soon as she heard Richard's accent. They had been trying to locate Richard for two days. The Canadian Embassy had been informed. Lois had been hit by a car, a hit-and-run accident. Nobody had actually seen it happen, but Lois was okay. She had no broken bones, only some scrapes and bruises. There had been a slight concussion, and they were watching her. She should stay another day for observation.

"No," Richard said. He would take her out now.

The woman did not resist. She asked Richard to sign some forms and she gave him a bill. It was much more than Richard expected, but he found the traveller's cheques he kept in his wallet for emergencies, and he paid. The woman gave him a form to take to the nurse on duty and told him to follow the red broken line painted on the floor.

Richard followed the line through swinging oak doors and down a narrow hallway. At one point he was confused when it appeared to run two ways, but he chose the left, and it led him to section A-five. Several nurses were clustered around a desk. Richard showed them the form, and they pointed to a door at the end of the hallway. They told him to call them as soon as Lois was ready to leave.

Richard walked slowly down the hallway, wanting to surprise Lois, but not certain why. The room was small. It had two beds. In the first one was a hefty woman reading a pocketbook. Lois lay on her back in the second bed, her eyes closed. Richard walked around the bed and stood watching her for a moment.

"Lois?" he whispered. She opened her eyes.

"Richard," she cried, pulling him into her arms.

"You're okay," Richard said. "You're fine."

"I'm sorry," she told him, beginning to weep. "God, I'm sorry."

"There's nothing to be sorry about," he said. "You can do what you want."

"You don't understand."

"I don't have to understand," he said. "Now they're going to let you out of here. As soon as you feel able, we'll go get a hotel room. Then we'll go home."

Lois continued to weep for several moments. Then she went to the washroom, and when she returned, she seemed composed and almost happy. She dressed with slow precision, as if her clothes were new and she had not worn them before. It took a few minutes for the nurses to find her suitcase, but in almost no time they were out on the street. Lois began to explain, but Richard told her no, to wait until they were settled.

They waited a few minutes for a taxi, and when finally they found one, Richard asked the driver to take them to a hotel near the Gare de l'Est. It didn't have to be fancy, he said. As long as it was within walking distance of the station. A few minutes later, they were let off at a hotel whose lobby was so narrow it was little more than a hallway. Lois was still weak, and Richard had to help her up to the room.

She began her story slowly, as if she didn't want to miss any details. She told Richard of the man who had slipped her a card at the Louvre, and how she had forgotten it until that time in Paris. She said that she hadn't told Richard about that meeting because he already knew the information. She told Richard about Fatima and the trip to Paris, about the dinner and the story Robert had told her about the neo-Nazis, and about the man in her room. She told Richard that she had spent the night at Robert's and that the following morning he had dropped her off at the Gare de l'Est.

"And that," she said, "was it. I stepped off the sidewalk and I felt myself spun around. I must have walked right into the side of a car. I'm just incredibly lucky that I wasn't killed."

She's frightened, Richard thought to himself. Lois was flushed and seemed to be trembling as she finished the story. He couldn't tell whether she was frightened by her brush with death or by the situation that led her there. He decided he wouldn't ask her anything more for a while.

She seemed tired, and she said she wanted to sleep. Richard told her he was going to go out for a little while. He asked her to keep the door locked, and he made her promise that she wouldn't leave the room until he returned. He waited until she fell asleep, then he went out to the street and took a taxi to the Hotel Maricourt.

The clerk told him there was a message, and gave him a piece of paper with a telephone number scrawled on it. Richard went up to the room and phoned. A man's voice answered and Richard said, "Ferguson?"

"Yes. And you must be Richard."

"Right. What's going on?"

"It's complicated. Can I talk to you in person?"

"Okay," Richard said. "Where?"

"Wait there. I'll be right over."

Richard waited down in the lobby. The clerk was nowhere to be seen, and nobody else came in. After about fifteen minutes, a man entered, walked directly to him and said, "Richard?"

Richard disliked him on sight. He looked like the kind of man who played rugby and drank beer and made loud jokes. He was wearing a short-sleeved shirt, and the pale hair on his freckled arms was thick and bushy.

"Yes," Richard said.

"Is Lois here?" Robert asked.

"No," Richard said. "She's not."

"We just got word at the Embassy that she was in an automobile accident. She's in hospital. I can drive you right over there now."

"No," Richard said. "She's fine. She's okay. Thanks anyway."

"I'd like to talk to her. It must have happened just after I dropped her off at the station. She was pretty distraught about the guy who was in her room."

"No, she's fine," Richard said. "I think you'd better talk to me instead. What's your involvement in this business? And why were you talking to Lois? Why didn't you talk to me?"

"It was just circumstances," Robert explained. "I just happened to encounter Lois, so I talked to her."

"Well, now you can talk to me," Richard said. "And in the future, if anything comes up, I'll handle it." Richard could see the resentment in Robert's eyes, and he was pleased. Robert opened his wallet and took out a card and gave it to Richard.

"Here," he said. "The number where you can actually reach me. I'm Robert Ferguson. I'm with the Canadian Security Intelligence Service. Do you mind if I sit down?" He sat down in one of the chairs in the lobby without waiting for a reply, and Richard sat in another across from him.

"Yes," Richard said, after Robert had taken his seat. "The inspector told me about you. What's your role in all this?"

"Well, essentially I'm a bureaucrat. I fill out forms, keep track of Canadians in France, try to help them out when they get into trouble. Or at least that's what my job appears to be. I've only been here for a few weeks, so I'm not sure quite what the job description entails. In your case, I'm supposed to try to keep track of you. You and Lois are apparently witnesses to a crime. A murder without a body to be sure, but the French and the Germans are taking it seriously. Now, from my point of view, the easiest thing would be if you and Lois were to cut your holiday short and go back to Canada. Then there'd be nothing to worry about."

"It's not a holiday," Richard pointed out. "I am on a sabbatical leave. I'm here to do research. And I intend to stay."

"Yes," Robert answered, "that's what I thought. The second-best course, then, is for you to do your research and keep your nose clean."

"What is that supposed to mean?"

"Well, basically, don't play detective. Keep away from anyone involved with this thing."

"Who, for instance?

"The German girl. Alexandra? That's her name?"

"Yes."

"Where is she now? The Paris police don't seem to know where to find her, but apparently you do." Robert twisted the watch on his wrist so that the face pointed downward, then he twisted it up again. Richard said nothing.

"Lois told me you talked with her the last time you were in Paris," Robert continued. He waited this time for Richard to reply.

"Yes," Richard said. "I talked to her. She was upset about her mother's death. I got the address from the woman at the bureau. If I could find it, it can't be hard to find."

"And what was the address?"

Richard hesitated. "I don't know. I wrote it down on a piece of paper, but I lost it. I think it must have gone through the wash."

"Try to remember," Robert told him. "It's important."

For a moment Richard was tempted to tell him and go back to Strasbourg and try to forget the whole business. He pondered for a moment, then said, "No, I'm afraid it's slipped my mind."

"This is not funny," Robert informed him, looking intensely into Richard's eyes. "You are a bit player in a drama you don't understand, but if you fool around, you could easily end up dead. This is not an innocent *au pair* girl. She was Mann's lover. She drew him into connections with some dangerous people. Mann was doing something that he shouldn't have been, and now he's almost certainly dead. Now try to remember the address."

Richard could feel the anger in himself rising. "Forget it," he said. "Even if I knew it, I wouldn't tell you. And besides, it wouldn't do you any good. She's not there any more."

"Where is she?"

"Look," Richard said, "even I know that the Canadian spy service is the laughingstock of the whole world. Why don't you just forget the girl and go out and burn a barn or investigate the Voice of Women for subversives? Isn't that more your speed, the kind of thing you're trained for?"

Robert didn't reply. He sat silently for a moment, and then Richard went on. "Now I'm going. And I sincerely hope that I'll never see you again."

"I'll be in Strasbourg in a couple of weeks," Robert answered. "In the meantime, you'd better reconsider your position."

"Don't bother to call," Richard said, rising from the chair and walking to the door. "I'm afraid I'll be too busy for guests." He left without looking back, and walked around the corner to the rue Ste. Germaine. There was a taxi parked in front of an ice-cream store, and Richard got in and asked the driver to take him to the Gare de l'Est.

On the way to the station, Richard considered Robert's remarks. It was almost impossible to believe the girl could have been Mann's lover. She seemed so quiet and tentative that Richard imagined her as lacking in volition, unable to make a decision. And she had certainly been an *au pair* girl. He had phoned and arranged to meet her. She had suggested a park, and when Richard had arrived she was there with two small children. She could only stay for a moment, because the mistress would be upset.

Richard remembered most clearly that she had been wearing a bright-blue sweater, and that her eyes had seemed intensely blue. And she had spoken to him in English. Her English had been hesitant and formal, but it was better than her French. It hadn't surprised him at the time, but now he remembered that she had seemed not to speak it at all when he had first met her at the Louvre. When she told him that she was going back to Kehl, Richard had given her his telephone number at the university, but she hadn't called. Now, he wished he had asked for her address.

When the taxi stopped at the station, Richard entered and watched through the glass doors to see if Robert had followed him. The traffic was heavy in the street, and after a minute Richard was embarrassed at his own game of cops and robbers, and he walked out onto the sidewalk. He was about to cross the street when a black motorcycle with two figures in black helmets and the same harlequin outfits he remembered from Mont Ste. Odile stopped at the light. Richard walked up to them and touched the front figure on the arm. "Pardonnez-moi," he said, not sure how he was going to continue, but the light changed and the motorcycle spun away from him before he could say anything else.

All at once, the world seemed dangerous. He thought of Lois waiting for him in the hotel room, alone. He imagined her as she had looked in the hospital, a stranger, helpless and vulnerable. And then he was certain that something terrible must have happened to her while he was gone. He was certain that when he got to the hotel room, she would be dead. He started to run, and the people on the sidewalk looked at him, startled. The afternoon sun was brilliant, and the street was bright and hot.

**

Lois woke from a dream of flying. She was soaring high over a valley that stretched to white mountains in the distance. Below her, a thin, silver river snaked to the horizon, but the cliff of the mountain she had just left loomed out of sight behind her. The freedom was ecstatic, delirious, and she tried to refuse waking, tried to recapture the dream, but it slipped away, and she was unsure of where she was. She remembered the blank white ceiling of the hospital room, the walls that closed in on her, the moment the car had struck her and she had known she would die.

She moaned and turned in the bed and felt Richard's comforting mass beside her. She opened her eyes and saw the leaded squares of glass of the studio window, like empty photographs. The morning light was grey and uncommitted. It was too early to know what the weather would be. She thought of Robert, remembering his freckled face. His eyelashes are blond, she thought, and it struck her that he looked like a farmer. She tried to imagine him in overalls with a straw hat, but she couldn't hold the image in her mind.

Beside her, Richard shifted position with a suddenness that made her think he must be awake, but she listened to his breathing and it was deep and regular. It amazed her that she did not feel guilty. She had expected that guilt would come as a pressure in her chest and that she would feel compelled to confess, or that she would feel her nerves tense and on edge. And that first moment when Richard had woken her in the hospital, it seemed that he was lost to her and she had felt deep regret. But now, she found that she could think about the night with Robert without feeling any remorse. In fact, she felt a little proud that she had done it, and she wondered, Am I lacking in some fundamental moral sense that other people have?

She still loved Richard, she was sure of that, even though he seemed even more distant than ever. He hadn't said anything, hadn't asked about the night she spent at Robert's, but he seemed even more anxious any time she was away. On the way back from Paris he had told her of his meeting with Robert, and the anger and contempt with which he spoke of him made her wonder whether Robert had said or hinted something. Still, she was sure he hadn't. Richard would have reacted more strongly if he had. He had warned her, though, that if Robert called, he did not want her to talk with him. He would do the talking.

They had been back in Strasbourg for a month now. The rain had stopped, and now the days were warmer, as if summer had been delayed. Everything was dark green, and there were flowers everywhere.

Richard seemed obsessed with the novel. Sometimes in the evenings he would try to explain to her that it had taken on a life of its own in his mind, but she couldn't imagine what he meant. They were going to have to go to Vimy Ridge, he told her. It had to do with being Canadian. Something had happened in Dieppe, but he wasn't sure what it was. He was certain he would understand if he could actually walk around the battlefield at Vimy.

In some ways, he seemed to her an invalid, someone who was sick and needed to be cured. She found herself buying special treats for him, and talking to him as if he were a child. Every day, he spent hours in the office writing, but he would phone several times a day to make sure she was home, and if he couldn't get her, he would be upset and worried when he came home. Sometimes he would stare at her, and she felt herself trapped in his gaze.

One day she told him that he would have to stop worrying about her. He confessed that he worried continually that she was going to die. He told her of his panic when he had feared that she would not be in the hotel room. He laughed and said he suffered from separation anxiety, and for a few days he did not phone. Then he went back to calling several times a day.

A new set of French classes had begun. Lois was moved up to the advanced course, but she found that most of the same people had moved with her. Fatima had been distant and hurt when Lois first talked with her, but when she heard about the accident, she was full of sympathy. The class had begun with a new teacher, a tiny woman with wire-rimmed glasses named Claudine, who spoke with a clear, bird-like voice. Lois found that she could understand every word the teacher said. Claudine invited the entire class for a glass of wine, and from then on they all went to a little bar not far from the cathedral after every class.

Fatima was in love. She was going to marry after all. Her uncle in Paris had introduced her to a friend of his who was a pharmacist in Istanbul, an old classmate of his. The wife of the pharmacist had died a couple of years ago. He was fifty years old, Fatima said, but he was very handsome and very gallant. He had promised her that they would visit Hollywood. Fatima insisted on getting Lois's address in Winnipeg. Perhaps they would come from Hollywood to visit her. But they would not be married for a year. Fatima had insisted that she must have a year to teach school. She showed Lois a diamond that looked expensive.

Lois had begun sketching every day. She had started doing the illustrations for the children's book. She did a series of finished drawings of the bird woman and the old man with the cat. When she showed them to Richard he said that they would never get published. The figures had become so monstrous that they would frighten children. It would be like a children's book by Käthe Kollwitz or that Norwegian who did the drawing of the scream. Edvard Munch, she told him. He seemed really disturbed by the drawings, and suggested that maybe she should go to the zoo and draw something a bit healthier. An animal that a child could love, not a series of street degenerates.

For a couple of days Lois was disappointed by Richard's response. She tried to make the bird woman more comic, but she lost interest in the drawing and couldn't finish it. Then she did a drawing of a beggar at the door of the cathedral. He smiled a false smile through a set of rotten teeth, but his eyes were full of hate. She was pleased with the drawing, but she didn't show it to Richard. Maybe, she thought, there is something evil in me that I have to draw. She liked that idea.

A few days later, the inspector was talking with Richard in the studio when Lois came back from her class. He and Richard had started meeting a couple of times a week, but they had never come to the studio. Lois had asked what they talked about, and Richard had laughed and said murder.

Lois was later than usual. The Iranian woman, whose name was Jeanne this week, had asked her to wait until the others had finished their glasses of wine and left. Then she had asked Lois whether she and Richard would sponsor her and her daughter to emigrate to Canada. She hinted that terrible things would happen if she had to return to Iran. Lois did not know how to reply, but she had promised she would phone the Canadian Embassy and find out what the woman should do. Robert had not come to Strasbourg as he had said he would, and he had not phoned. Now she had a reason to phone him. She was excited at the prospect of talking to Robert, but convinced that she did not want to see him.

Or even that wasn't true. She wanted to see him, to talk with him. It would be nice, she thought, to have him as a friend without any romantic connection. She thought that Robert would probably agree to that, but she was sure that Richard wouldn't.

On her way home, just at the corner where the rue de la Forêt Noire met the rue Schweighaeuser, Lois had seen an accident. A woman stepped from the curb and was hit by a car. She was thrown onto the sidewalk where she lay crumpled and motionless. The car had been going fast, and it had not even started to brake until after it had hit the victim. Still, in only a few seconds she was surrounded by people. Lois couldn't imagine where they had come from. Someone covered the woman with a blanket. Lois crossed at the far corner, so that she would not have to pass by the woman. She was certain that she was dead.

Lois was trembling by the time she reached the top of the second flight of stairs. She was intensely aware of how close she had come to death in Paris, and she imagined herself broken and dead on the street. I must have looked like that to the passers-by in Paris, she thought. She wondered whether a crowd had gathered around her, and she felt vulnerable and exposed. She took out her key to open the door, and was grateful for the solid dull gleam of the brass lock. It made her aware she was alive.

As soon as she entered the room, Richard and the inspector started singing "Happy Birthday." They were both out of tune, Richard a little worse than Kessler. Richard held a beautiful cake, elegantly iced, with a single tall white candle burning in the centre. They looked so comical, standing in the studio singing out of tune, with a candle nearly a foot high in the cake, that Lois burst into laughter. She couldn't stop laughing, and after a few seconds, the men joined her in the uncertain forced laughter of people caught by someone who laughs without control.

Lois's whole body seemed to relax. All the tension of the accident she had witnessed left her, and she felt the tears coursing down her cheeks. She threw her arms around Richard and kissed him passionately. He had to juggle the cake in order to prevent it from being crushed. Then she kissed the inspector, and collapsed into the armchair.

"Wow," Richard said. "I think I'm going to hold a birthday party for you every day." The room seemed full of flowers. There were a dozen red roses on the table and a spray of white and purple daisies on the window sill. Both Richard and Kessler beamed like small boys who have been unexpectedly praised.

"It's wonderful," Lois told them. "I didn't expect it at all. I didn't even remember it was my birthday."

"Thank the inspector," Richard confessed. "I'd forgotten, myself."

"You'll have to thank a computer," Kessler said. "It's a new police program. It's supposed to help you solve crimes by putting together evidence in unexpected ways. Today it discovered that you have the same birthday as the commissionaire at Mont Ste. Odile. You will remember the old man you talked to when you were waiting for the police?"

"I remember," Lois said. "He was quite elegantly polite."

Richard proposed a toast. He poured a glass of wine for Lois and the inspector, but he mixed himself a large glass of scotch. They all drank to Lois's health, and then Richard poured himself another.

"That's the end of the ice cubes," he said. "I can't believe that there's a city in which no place at all sells ice cubes."

"I'm sure there is someplace," Kessler answered. "Only I can't remember where."

Richard had taken down three plates and a knife. He set the cake on the table to cut it and moved Lois's sketchbooks, setting them in the bookcase.

"I hope you don't mind," he said. "I showed these to the inspector." Lois felt a thrill of anger. She wished Richard had not done that. It seemed an invasion of her privacy, a betrayal.

"They are wonderful," Kessler said. "You are a fine artist."

Lois had never thought of herself as an artist. The word seemed strange to her. It seemed presumptuous.

"Illustrator," she said. "Nothing so grand as an artist."

"I don't think there's a real distinction," Kessler answered, "but if there is, I'm certain you'd come down on the side of the artist."

Lois felt uncomfortable with the discussion, but the inspector went on. Lois thought he might have noticed the evil in the characters she had drawn, but he talked about the elegance of the line in her drawings, the play of light and dark.

The inspector did not stay long. After he was gone, Richard apologized for having shown the drawings, but Lois knew the apology was not sincere. In fact, Richard seemed as pleased at the inspector's approval as if he had done the drawings himself.

"You don't even like them," Lois said. "Why did you show them to him?"

"I like them as drawings," he said. "I just don't like them as illustrations for children's books."

Lois tried not to think about the inspector's words, but she turned the notion of artist around in her mind. I like the sound of it, she thought. A couple of days later a man with a delicate accent phoned her. He ran the exhibitions of art on the boat the *Bagatelle*. His friend had told him about Lois's work. Could she bring down some drawings and they might talk about an exhibition?

No, of course not, she thought. It is impossible. Still, she agreed to meet the man at two o'clock the next day, though she was equally certain that she would cancel the meeting. She spent every moment that evening going through the sketchbooks, alternating between being pleased at the invitation and despairing at how far the sketches failed to satisfy her. When she did arrive at the boat, she was as nervous as she had ever been in her life.

The man who greeted her looked preposterously young. He wore a blue and white striped tee shirt and jeans. Lois could hardly imagine that he was a friend of the inspector, but he seemed to be. His name was Charles, and he had only been back for a few months after spending five years in New York. His English was completely American. It was difficult to imagine that he was French at all.

"Terrific," was the first thing he said when he saw the sketches, and he said it at almost every page. Lois had removed all the early sketches. She had shown him only the ones she thought of as evil, but now she wondered how he might have responded to the others.

"In three weeks," he said. "Tuesday. Is that possible? We've had a cancellation of a travelling show by a Norwegian water colourist. It's only for two weeks, but these would be perfect."

"That would be fine," Lois told him, as if she held exhibitions every day. As if what was happening were not impossible.

"Do you have any more? I mean there's enough here, but it might be nice to select."

"I have some more," Lois said. "I could bring them by in a couple of weeks. They're not quite finished yet." Not quite started, she thought. She was certain she could do a lot more before the show.

"That'll be fine," he said. "Give us a week to get the show set up." He chattered on about the arrangements for the opening, a small wine-and-cheese party, some of the usual customers, but Lois scarcely heard a word he said. This can't be happening she told herself, but it clearly was. He gave her a handful of invitations. She was to fill in her name and the date. He was sorry, but there was not enough time to print special invitations. He hoped she would understand.

Outside, Lois caught a glimpse of herself in the window of a store. She saw a frail figure, almost too thin, bending awkwardly. She was startled to think that someone so awkward might be her. The reflection in the window was blue and grey, and for a second it disappeared in the blue-grey sheen of the glass. "I am no colour," she said to herself, "but I can do something about that," and she walked into the door of the shop.

***

Richard had begun to feel comfortable in the office at the university. At first, he had been amazed that he almost never saw a professor. The secretaries told him that most of the professors only came in to teach their classes, and that they interviewed their students at home. Richard found a lounge for the professors, but he never encountered anyone in it except for the cleaning staff. It made Richard think of the *Mary Celeste,* a vessel mysteriously abandoned as if the crew and passengers had simply vanished. There was a fridge, a small hot plate, cups and glasses, even a jar of instant coffee so old that it no longer had any odour, but it was clear that whoever had been there had gone away forever.

At first, the coldness of the place had depressed him, accustomed as he was to his Canadian university, where the professors spent all their time in their offices with the door open and shouted questions at each other down hallways full of students. Then, after a while, he realized that the place had a secret life. Notices appeared on the bulletin boards announcing meetings that inevitably took place somewhere else, and Richard found himself trying to decipher cryptic messages that appeared in his mailbox but seemed destined for some former boxholder.

Even Delacroix was apparently back. He left Richard a note apologizing for his hasty retreat from Iceland and inviting Richard to join him for lunch at some unassigned future date. Kessler, however, appeared every few days, always at five o'clock, and he and Richard would walk to a bar on the edge of one of the canals and drink wine for an hour.

"The myth of the great Canadian fighting man," he told the inspector one day, "is a newspaper myth." Richard had nearly finished reading a biography of Lord Beaverbrook that he had found in his office. "By the time the First World War started, Beaverbrook already owned half the newspapers in England. He wanted to join the Canadian army, and the government didn't know what to do with him. So they made him chief publicity officer. Beaverbrook sent out correspondents to the Canadian battles, and he published stories about the Canadian army in all his newspapers. The only news you could get in the First World War was about Canadians, and what great fighters they were. And the worst thing about it was the Canadian soldiers started to believe it and went out and got themselves killed when they didn't need to, and the British officers believed it and sent them into the most hopeless situations."

"This novel you are writing," the inspector replied, "just what is it about?"

"I don't know," Richard said. "I have no idea. It takes place during two world wars. It's about stupidity and brutality, I suppose. And it's also about Canadians and who they are." The words sounded pretentious to Richard. Every time he tried to explain anything about the novel to anyone, he felt he was a fraud. "Canadians worry about things like that," he went on.

"Do you have enough information? Have you ever been in a battle?"

"No, of course not. There were no battles for me to be in." Richard felt a little awkward and embarrassed. "There was the Vietnam war, but it belonged to the Americans. You know, for years they showed piles of dead Viet Cong on television, but the horror of the war didn't strike me until they started to show dead Americans. That was near the end. Dead young blond guys who looked like the kid next door. Then the stupidity and the waste struck me. How's that for racism?"

"It's about average," Kessler told him. "We always see things through our own experience."

"Yes. And of course I have no experience of war. The closest I've come is a body that might not even be dead. I know nothing of the experience."

"What do you mean, you don't know?" Kessler asked. "You've read dozens of novels about war. You've read history books, survivors' accounts, poems. You've seen movies and documentaries.

You probably know more about it than somebody who has been there but has only his own narrow, private experience."

"You mean it's a text?" Richard asked. "War is a literary experience? That's all?"

"Everything is a literary experience," Kessler told him. "Do you think that the few fragmentary images of a war that a ninety-year-old man can conjure out of his failing memory have any more reality than your text?"

"I don't know." Richard said. "I have nothing but fragmentary evidence. I have no idea where things are going until all of a sudden they start to click together."

"Precisely," the inspector said. "Your war is exactly like a crime."

"It is a crime," Richard interrupted.

"Yes," the inspector agreed. "A series of crimes without any solution. But once a crime has occurred, it is no longer an event. It is a story, a narrative with pieces missing. As a detective, I am in the position of the artist. It is my job to make sense of things."

"What if things don't make sense?" Richard asked. "What if it is just a stupid random happening, a murder done on a whim, or a mistake, the wrong person mugged?"

"It may not make sense in its own terms," the inspector said. "But there is always a larger narrative that will accommodate it. It's simply a question of imagining on a large enough scale." The waiter brought the inspector another glass of wine, apparently on his own initiative.

"But what about truth, then?" Richard asked. "It's not enough for things to make sense, to fit into some formal pattern of logic. They also have to be true."

"Whose truth in particular were you thinking of?" Kessler asked him. "Because, make no mistake, truth is always in somebody's possession. That's what power is. The ability to decide what is true. And of course that's the power of the artist."

"I don't know," Richard said. "I'm not sure I can give up truth that easily. I have this desperate fear that I'm concocting a giant lie. I think about the novel continually, no matter what else I'm doing. And yet I have no idea what is going to happen next. I haven't even given my main character a name."

He had begun to feel that he would have to go back to Canada to complete the book. He had to go to Vimy Ridge, but after that, there was nothing in Europe for him, and he was certain that he would no longer have anything to write. Lois would be terribly disappointed if they did go back early, he realized.

"Lois has a show," he went on. "The people from the *Bagatelle* talked to her. It's going to happen in a couple of weeks."

"Wonderful," the inspector said. "She is a fine artist."

Richard had at first found it difficult to think of Lois as an artist. It somehow threatened him. She was very happy but very nervous, and it was like having a stranger living in Lois's body.

"Look," Richard said, "did you have anything to do with this?"

"I told them how much I admired her work. The rest is their doing?" His voice rose at the end of the sentence as if he didn't quite believe it himself.

"I don't want her humiliated," Richard said. "This isn't some police trick, some little scenario you've invented to draw criminals out of the bush?"

"Of course not," the inspector said. "Even if I wanted to, I don't have that kind of power."

Richard suspected that Kessler did have exactly that kind of power, but he seemed sincere, and there wasn't much that could be done at any rate. They got up to leave, and Richard realized that he had left the Beaverbrook biography in his office. He decided to go back to get it. At the corner, the inspector went into a wine shop, and Richard headed back to the university.

The book was where he had left it, beside the typewriter. The department had loaned Richard a huge old portable typewriter with a French keyboard, and so his manuscript was filled with typos. It bothered him more than it should have. He was an excellent typist, though he had learned late, taking a typing course in the evenings during graduate school with a bunch of housewives whose children had left home and who were hoping to get jobs as secretaries. He had been the fastest typist in the group. Now his speed was a disadvantage.

Richard was struck by the sudden fear that something might happen to his manuscript, that it might be burned in a fire, and all his work lost. He had already written a hundred and fifty pages, even more if you considered that the French paper was larger than the typewriter paper at home. He had written the beginning and a section that would come near the end. The middle was missing. It was too late to make a xerox copy. The department did not allow professors to use the machine themselves. During office hours, an old man made the copies and charged you for them.

Richard put the manuscript into the plastic bag in which he carried it. He tried to remember if there was any scotch back at the studio. A *super marché* near the university had the lowest prices in the city, and it was only a block out of his way. He decided he would get some anyway. He locked both locks on the office door, wondering why such precautions were necessary.

He checked his mail on the way out. A lone secretary was working late, and when Richard knocked on the door she let him in. Surprisingly, his mailbox was nearly full. He took the mail into his office to read it. The studio was so small that there was no room for any additional mess.

Most of the notices were general notices to faculty about deadlines for examinations and the dates of committee meetings, but one was from Delacroix, written in his flowing and surprisingly feminine hand. He had been invited to the University of Trier to deliver a lecture on Heidegger. Unfortunately, he was unable to go. Complications with his father's estate. He had suggested to them that they invite Richard to give a paper called "Heidegger, a Canadian Perspective." They would be in contact with Richard soon. He hoped he had not been presumptuous in making the suggestion. Richard scribbled him a note of thanks and gave it to the secretary, who was just starting to lock up.

He thought he should probably call Lois and tell her he would be late. It was twenty to six. She would probably have already left for her class. His hand was on the receiver when the phone rang, and the sudden noise startled him. His answer was abrupt, and he realized he had spoken much too loudly. There was no response, so he spoke again, this time more quietly. "Allo."

"Hello," the voice said. It was female, low and hesitant.

"Yes," Richard answered. "Richard Angantyr here. Can I help you?"

"Richard?"

"Yes?"

"It is Alexandra." Richard felt his body go tense. He waited for her to go on, but she didn't seem to want to say any more.

"Alexandra. Where are you?"

"I am here, in Strasbourg."

"Is everything all right?"

"Yes, everything is fine." She paused. "I am no longer working in Paris. I am home now in Kehl."

"Where are you now? Can I see you? I'd like to talk to you."

She paused again for what seemed like a long time, but Richard decided to wait until she went on. He could hear voices in the background, a low hum of argument. After a while she said, "I can pick you up at the university. Wait for me in front of the bookstore. Across the street." She hung up without saying good-bye, and Richard was left holding the silent telephone.

He locked the door and hurried across the street. There were two bookstores a few metres apart, and he decided to wait halfway between them. The traffic was heavy on the street, and he was not sure what he was waiting for, but in a couple of minutes a white Mercedes-Benz two-seater pulled up beside him. Richard bent to look into the car to be sure it was Alexandra before he clambered inside.

"Hello," he said. She was dressed in leather, a brown so deep it was almost black. Her pants were so tight they seemed like her own skin. The jacket looked very soft, filled with folds and seams. She had on a frilly white blouse and bright-blue earrings. Richard felt he could hardly draw a breath. She had always seemed frail and vulnerable to him before, but she did not seem that way now.

"Hello," she said. "Where would you like to go?"

Richard felt shy. He could think of nothing to say. He thought he had never seen any woman so beautiful, even in a movie. Finally he told her, "I don't know. Let's get a drink. Do you know a place near here?"

"Yes," she said. "Yes I do. Quite near."

She slipped the car into gear and swung around a corner so fast that Richard was forced almost into her lap. He had to put his hand on her leg to catch his balance, and for several seconds his hand retained the soft, smooth feel of the leather. She drove with a wild recklessness that silenced Richard. In a few minutes they were out of the city and heading south on a road that Richard recognized as the highway south to Colmar. She drove at breakneck speed, passing cars even when it seemed there was no way of passing without having a head-on collision. Finally Richard spoke.

"Could you go a little slower? This is a bit more excitement than I can take."

"Of course," she answered, but if she slowed down, it was imperceptible to Richard. A few minutes later she pulled off the main road and followed a curving side road to a village dominated by an enormous hotel painted pink, and decorated with white balconies and awnings. At the front of the hotel was a long, wooden deck with tables and pink and white umbrellas. The sign on it said Hotel des Vosges.

Alexandra braked heavily, and the car ground to a halt in front of the hotel. There was a parking lot off to the right with a number of cars in it, but Alexandra paid no attention to it. She parked in front of a sign that forbade parking, and she was out of the car almost before it had stopped.

"This way," she said, as Richard struggled to get his large frame out of the small car. She led the way to a table on the deck, and Richard followed. The girl wore open-toed shoes with high heels, which gave her a stilted but deliberate gait. Richard, following behind her, felt like a voyeur. She sat down at a table, and Richard sat across from her. She fumbled in her handbag, found a package of cigarettes and lit one. She crossed her legs, and blew a cloud of blue smoke across the table at Richard.

"Well," she said. "Here we are."

"Yes," Richard answered. "Here we are. But perhaps you could explain why we are here?" The waiter arrived at that moment, and the girl ordered a glass of wine. Richard ordered a glass of scotch, which they did not have, and so he, too, settled for wine.

"There are some people I would like you to meet," she said. "They would like to meet you."

"Who are they?" Richard asked. He was suddenly threatened.

"Just some friends," she said. "It is not important. Come or not as you like."

"Where do they want to meet?"

The wine arrived. The waiter was contemptuously polite, placing the wine before them. His hair was tied back in a bun, and he looked as if he belonged in an ad for cigarettes.

"Just outside of Freiburg," Alexandra told him. "It's a place in the mountains."

"When?"

"Now."

"Now?"

"Yes. As soon as you finish your wine."

Richard thought of Lois. By now she would be in class. "How long is this going to take?" he asked.

"That will depend on you." She leaned towards him, and he caught a whiff of perfume.

For a moment he hesitated at the thought of Lois arriving home and finding him absent. Still, to go home now would be a loss. He could feel desire as a physical weight.

"All right," he said, draining his wine. "Let's go." The girl had hardly tasted hers, but she left it on the table. The waiter was nowhere to be seen, and Alexandra was already on her way down the stairs to the parking lot. Richard hesitated, then left a fifty-franc note on the table. She had already started the car by the time he got there.

She drove with the same recklessness as she had on the trip to the hotel. They wound their way through tiny villages, then crossed the Rhine over a series of locks with long, low cargo boats moored in them. When she reached the autobahn, she pulled into the passing lane, and Richard was sure she just stepped the gas pedal to the floor. When they came up on a Fiat trying to pass a line of trucks, she flashed her lights, and the Fiat slipped in between the trucks. The car seemed to move effortlessly and without noise at that speed, as if it had been designed precisely for her sort of driving.

She pulled off the autobahn at Freiburg, but skirted the city, and soon they were in the countryside again, beginning a long climb up a steep hill. She had turned on a tape, and the Guess Who serenaded them in the early German dusk. "American Woman" and then a song about running back to Saskatoon. Richard liked the guitar-playing, but the lyrics seemed even more empty here than at home. He could see a long, dusky valley stretching to his right, and unexpectedly a cable car whisked across the road above them.

"Where are we going?" Richard asked. The quiet of the ride, which at first had been a sedative, was beginning to bother him. The girl looked even more beautiful in the fading light.

"We're just about there," she said, and didn't seem to want to say any more. They crested the hill and began to descend. After a few minutes they turned left at a sign that said Todtnauberg.

"Todtnauberg," Richard said. "That's where Heidegger had his hut in the forest."

"Yes."

"Is that where we're going?"

"Yes."

"What does it mean? Todtnauberg?"

"It means dead district mountain. But I don't know why."

They had reached a village with roads that bent back on themselves in hairpin turns. She drove through the village and turned onto a narrow gravel trail. They followed the trail for a few hundred yards, then she stopped the car, above the village, but not near any house. It was already dark, and lights had come on in most of the houses.

The girl got out of the car and stretched deliberately. She moves like a cat, Richard thought, and was aware of the cliché. She took off her shoes and put them in the car so that she stood there barefoot.

"It's a good climb," she explained.

Richard looked up the side of the hill. He could see the rising sparks of a fire, and, silhouetted against the light, the edge of a low building. They climbed across a pasture that was amazingly steep, and which, from the smell of it, seemed to have been recently fertilized with manure.

After a few minutes, Richard realized that he was climbing alone. The girl had disappeared into the darkness above. He was out of breath, and his knee had begun to give him pain.

"Alexandra," he called.

There was no answer. Richard sat down in the grass and waited. In a couple of minutes she was back.

"Are you all right?" she asked.

"Yes. It's just that I have a bad knee, and I have to be careful if I'm ever going to get back down."

"Here," she said. "Let me help you." She took his hand, and he stood up. She slipped his arm around her shoulder, and put her own arm around his waist. "You can lean on me."

Richard caught a whiff of the perfume of her hair, and felt the surprising strength of her body. He felt a sudden, powerful rush of desire, and he pulled the girl to him and kissed her.

"No," she said. "Not now," and she pulled away from him. She continued to help him up the slope, and Richard felt like a fraud. He could climb easily by himself if he went slowly enough, but he liked the feel of her body against his. They stopped several times to rest, and each time she moved away from him. At last, they reached the level yard in front of the hut. The back of the building was buried in the hillside up to the line of the roof. The building itself was covered with shingles, though Richard could not make out what colour they were. When they rounded the corner, he could see further up the hillside, beyond a line of trees and a fence, a bonfire and a number of people. Their voices came to him as an indistinct murmur, but a shower of sparks lit the scene as someone put another log on the fire.

"Who are these people?" Richard asked. No one knows where I am, he thought. Everything now is dangerous.

The girl didn't answer. Instead, she slipped into his arms and kissed him slowly, pushing her tongue deep into his mouth. Richard held her like that for a long time. Slowly she disengaged herself from him and stepped back, taking a deep breath. Richard reached for her again, but she moved away.

"Come on," she said, and she started climbing the path towards the fire.

"Wait," Richard called after her, but it was clear that this time she was not going to come back. Richard hesitated a second, then followed her.

**

It was already dark when Lois and Fatima joined the class at the little sidewalk cafe. They had stayed for a moment to chat, up on the third floor where the classes were conducted. Lois had bought herself a new dress, bright red, a colour she had never worn before. Fatima was enchanted. She wanted to know where Lois had found it. She wanted to buy the identical one for herself. She would save it until after her wedding.

Lois ordered a glass of white wine, and realized with a start that she was happy. She had never thought of herself that way before, but the teacher had complimented her on her accent, and everyone had remarked on her dress. She was seated at a table in front of a cafe in France where the coloured lights from signs reflected in the wine glasses on the table. Elegant people in formal dress walked by on their way to the theatre.

The teacher had received an invitation to Lois's show, and she had xeroxed the invitation and passed it out to everyone in the class. They all insisted in solidarity that they would attend, and the teacher had offered to cancel the class for the occasion. Lois felt that she would remember this exact moment forever.

When she got back to the studio, Richard was not there. She looked for signs that he had returned from the university, but there were none. She poured herself a rum and Coke and took out her portfolio. She had drawn three additional portraits since they had offered her the show, but she was unsure of them all. Two were of the same *clochard* lying on the sidewalk with a bag of clothing and two bottles of wine. In one of the portraits, his eyes were closed, and he looked passive and hopeless. In the other, his eyes were open, and they glinted with dark malevolence. The third drawing was the face of the man they had found dead on the stone altar, except in the drawing he was alive and laughing.

Lois picked up her drawing pad and decided she would try one more drawing. She had promised she would take them to the gallery tomorrow, and if she worked late, she might finish. She began by outlining a street, with buildings and cars. She sketched a body, sprawled half on the sidewalk, a woman, the woman she had seen hit just the other day. She worked furiously, making the body twisted, the skirt hoisted up, showing the pathetic vulnerability of the woman, exposed. Behind the woman she drew in the glare of shop windows, the reflections of traffic. There was nobody on the sidewalk. There were no figures in the cars. The woman was utterly alone.

The phone rang, and Lois realized she hadn't thought of Richard since she had started drawing. She glanced at her watch. It was eleven o'clock.

"Hello," she answered, hearing a ring of false cheeriness in her own voice.

"Hi," a voice answered. "How are you feeling?" Robert.

"Fine," she said. "Just fine." She paused a moment, drawing a sharp breath, but when he didn't speak she went on. "Are you in Strasbourg?"

"No, I'm in Paris. But I'm going to be in Strasbourg in about a week. Can I see you then?"

"No," she said. "I don't think so. I don't think it would be good for anybody."

"Did you tell your husband?"

"No. That wouldn't be a nice thing to do."

"Some people do," he said. "Some relationships are like that."

"Not mine."

"Well." He paused. "You're sure we can't just meet for coffee?"

"No," she said. "I don't know. What are you doing in Strasbourg?"

"I'm going to meet with a couple of Canadian accountants who live there. Hutcheon and Fawcett. Do you happen to know them?"

"No."

"They're pretty nasty pieces of work. They buy and sell guns in the Middle East on a fairly large scale. They may even have something to do with your business."

"I can't meet you," she told him. "I'm having a show of my drawings, and I have to get ready for it."

"I know," Robert answered. "At the *Bagatelle*. The inspector told me. You won't mind if I drop by the opening?"

"No, of course not," she said. "It's a public event. Anyone can come."

"I won't come unless you invite me personally."

"All right. You're invited. Please come to the opening."

"Thanks," he said. "See you then." She heard a soft click, but she held the telephone, listening to white noise for several seconds. Then she put it down slowly. She walked to the window and looked out. She could see figures on the half-lit street, but none of them was Richard.

She went back to the drawing, picked up her pen, and began to sketch. This is a self-portrait, she thought. This is a drawing of me. She began to draw, paying meticulous attention to the body. I have to look nice, she thought, for when they take me to the hospital. I have to have clean underwear.

* * *

When Richard entered the glow of the fire, he was greeted by a young man, who thrust his hand forward.

"Helmut Dieter," the man said, "and this is my girlfriend, Lise Klaus. Alexandra has told us about how kind you were to her in Paris. We are very pleased to meet you." A pretty young woman tucked herself under his arm and nodded agreement. "So very pleased." The man was tall, at least as tall as Richard himself, and he was well-built. Both he and his girlfriend wore white tee shirts and jeans. The man's tee shirt read University of Chicago. Richard noted the flat, even beauty of their faces, and wondered whether they were the pair he had seen on the motorcycle.

"Can I get you a beer?" The man smiled broadly, and it was clear that Richard was mistaken.

"Yes, that would be nice."

Helmut picked up a beer out of a case that was almost at their feet, opened it, and passed it to Richard. At that moment, Alexandra arrived with a heavy-set older man. Richard recognized him as the man he had first seen her with at Mont Ste. Odile.

"This is my uncle," she said. "Hans Rausch."

"Pleased to meet you," he said. "And I must give you my thanks for your kindness to Alexandra in Paris." His voice was heavily accented. He said something in German to Alexandra and when she replied he went on, "You are welcome here." He took a small leather case from his vest pocket and handed Richard a card heavily embossed in silver. He smiled broadly, and Richard, unsure how to respond, put the card in his own wallet and smiled back.

Helmut led Richard around the group that circled the bonfire, introducing him to people whose names Richard immediately forgot. It seemed an oddly mixed group. There were several young people, though the group, about thirty people in all, was mostly older. Helmut explained that the gathering was somewhere between a meeting and a party. They were a local historical society, he said, the Hallstatt group, interested in early Celtic and Druid cultures of the area. They collected money to refurbish ancient sites and to mark them. Richard remembered his discussion in Iceland with Delacroix and the inspector. The group certainly didn't look dangerous. He asked about Mont Ste. Odile.

"It is of course one of the most important sites in the area," Helmut told him. "The Pagan Wall is ancient. And as you know, the Druid shrine is a very important ancient site." Richard watched him carefully, but Helmut gave no indication that the shrine was anything more than an historical spot.

"It is still an important site," he went on, "for certain ceremonies. Christianity has of course destroyed most of the major sites of temples and places of worship, but at the same time they did great service in helping us to find them."

"How is that?" Richard asked.

"Well, in their efforts to stamp out other religions, the Christians built their churches on the sites of pagan temples. So it is only necessary to find ancient churches to find pagan sites." Richard noticed that Alexandra had seated herself on a log that was just back from the glow of the fire. She was talking to a couple of young women whose faces he could not make out in the dim light, though he guessed that one of them was Helmut's girlfriend.

"Remember that hill you crossed on the way here?" Helmut went on.

"Yes. With the cable car?"

"That one. If you stand at the highest point of the Grand Ballon in Alsace at the summer or winter, what is the word? Solstice?"

"Solstice," Richard agreed.

"If you watch at the day of the solstice, the sun will rise precisely over the highest point of this hill. We call them calendar hills."

"But that's simply accident," Richard said. "Nobody actually made them like the Indian temples in the States that define the seasons."

"You are right," Helmut agreed. "But they noticed them. They used them. If you were to draw an exact line from the Grand Ballon to this hill at the time of the solstice, the line would pass through seven Christian churches. And the seven Celtic sites beneath them."

Alexandra came over and touched Richard's elbow. "They are going to start in a minute," she said. "Come, let's find a seat."

"I will talk to you later," Helmut said, and he wandered into the semi-darkness to find his girlfriend. Alexandra led Richard higher up the hillside, so that they were completely out of the orange glow of the bonfire.

"What is going to happen?" Richard asked.

"There is a speaker tonight, a man from the university," Alexandra told him. "He is a famous speaker in these parts."

"What is he going to talk about?" Richard asked.

"How to live a good life. How to honour your ancestors. It is what he always talks about."

"Is this a religious thing?" Richard asked.

"No," she said. "Not religious. Not exactly, anyway."

Just then, a tiny man walked into the centre of the group around the bonfire. Richard had not seen him before. He was accompanied by another man, who looked a lot like Delacroix. The other man said a few words in a quiet voice, then sat down with a group of older people who were sitting on a fallen log. The small man began to speak in a voice that was high-pitched, but had remarkable carrying power. He seemed very old, but he moved with agility, and circled constantly as he spoke. Richard could not understand a word of his German, but the voice was somehow soothing. It reminded him of a Gregorian chant, a rhythmic droning that was peaceful. Alexandra paid close attention.

"What is he saying?" Richard asked.

"He is saying that poetry is more important than philosophy," she said. "He is saying that it is more important to understand than to take action."

Richard watched the people who were gathered around the fire. They seemed entranced. Their white faces glowed out of the black background, and the orange light flickered. Richard thought about bonfires he had been to back home, but they had been profoundly different from this. He felt an intensity that was palpable. The thin, reedy voice went on. Far below them, the lights of the village glowed.

Richard put his arm around Alexandra, who had nestled against him. For several minutes they said nothing, then she whispered, "Come," to him, and she stood. Richard followed, and she led him by the hand up a path that led into the forest. After a minute, he could no longer see the bonfire below. There were no stars, but there seemed to be enough light so that they could make their way along the trail.

"Where are we going?" Richard asked.

"Nowhere," the girl answered. "The path just leads to where the woodcutter is working. It doesn't go anywhere." They reached a spot where the path intersected with another trail. The forest opened into a grassy area just beyond, and the girl stopped there. Richard took her into his arms, and they kissed long and hard. They stepped apart briefly, and Richard looked into the girl's eyes. He remembered that they were bright blue, but in the darkness he could see only the silhouette of her face, the curve of her cheekbones.

Richard unbuttoned the top button of her blouse. The girl stood perfectly still until he had undone all the buttons, then she shrugged out of her jacket and blouse and unclasped her brassiere. Then they kissed again, and Richard held her breasts in his hands. They were smaller than he had supposed they would be, and very smooth. Richard felt his desire rise, but he also felt afraid. The girl slipped off her pants, and came naked into his arms. He held her like that for a long time, until she started to unbutton his shirt. Then Richard took off all his clothes. When he reached for the girl again, she slipped to her knees and took him in her mouth. Richard reached down and stroked her hair.

In a short while, Richard felt he would not be able to restrain himself, so he drew the girl up, then laid her on the grass. She thrust her hips up to meet him, and when he entered her she cried, a cry so loud that Richard was certain they would hear below. She thrust herself at him and moaned, calling out in German, words he could not understand. Richard whispered to her, telling her, "Easy, easy," but she struggled as if she wanted to throw him off. Finally her cries became so intense that Richard put his hand over her mouth to silence her. She bit him, quite hard, but her body trembled and she lay still. Richard realized as much as felt that he, too, had come.

They lay there together for a moment until the girl pushed on his chest and told him that he was too heavy. Richard didn't want to leave her, didn't want the act to end. He raised himself on his arms, but she shifted and he rolled off. The air seemed to have grown cold. He pulled the girl to him, and they lay together on the grass. She found his shirt on the grass nearby, and covered them with it like a blanket.

"That was wonderful," she said. "You are a good lover."

"You're a tough girl," he told her.

"Yes," she said. "I like that. I am a tough girl."

"Shouldn't we be getting back?" he asked. "Won't they miss us?"

"It will go on for some time longer," she answered. "And what if they did miss us? What if they knew exactly what we are doing? What would that matter?"

Richard was sure that it would matter, but he couldn't think of any way of telling the girl. Instead, he asked her about the people at the gathering. Helmut was a lecturer at the university, she said. He was not yet a professor. He had met Lise at the University of Chicago, even though they had both grown up in Freiburg and never met. The uncle owned a trucking company. It was his car she was driving. Now that her mother was dead, she lived with her uncle. Her uncle had never married, and had no children. The others were people she had known most of her life.

Richard thought of Lois waiting for him at home, and was filled with guilt. He wondered what time it was, and then with a stab of panic realized that his novel was lying in the front seat of the Mercedes convertible. Anyone passing by could pick it up, and he knew he could never write it again.

"Shouldn't we go?" he asked.

"In a minute," she answered, and her hands began to explore his body. In a few minutes he felt himself erect again. He couldn't remember the last time he had made love twice in a row. He tried to roll over onto Alexandra, but she said no and slipped from beneath him. She crouched on her hands and knees, and said, "Like this." Richard mounted her from the rear, thinking, This is like an animal in the dark of the forest. In a few sharp thrusts, he was through. The girl did not make a sound until it was all over.

They dressed in silence. The girl was ready first. She took Richard's hand and led him back down the trail.

"That was better, I think," she said. "I was quiet and I didn't embarrass you."

"No," he said, "you were fine the first time. I was only afraid that someone would hear."

"But they didn't," she said. "Nobody heard."

"No," Richard agreed. "If nobody hears it, there is no noise." Below, they could again see the campfire. The little man seemed to have gone, and the people were standing around in groups chatting and drinking beer. Most of the older people had gone, and the group looked more like the kind of people Richard expected to see at a campfire.

Their arrival occasioned no comment. The uncle had gone with all the older people, and Richard was grateful for that. Alexandra said her good-byes, and Helmut clapped Richard on the back as if they were old friends and told him that they would surely meet again soon.

The trip down the hillside seemed much faster and easier than the trip up. When they got to the car, Richard checked for his manuscript. It was there in a brown paper bag, exactly as he had left it. Alexandra put on her shoes before she started the car. She drove back in the direction of Strasbourg somewhat more slowly than she had driven before, but still fast enough to make Richard uncomfortable.

"What time is it?" he asked. Richard hated wearing his watch, but now he wished he had worn it.

The girl pointed to the clock on the dashboard of the car. "Ten after one."

Richard didn't answer.

"You are late?"

"Yes," Richard said, "I am late."

"Will this be difficult for you?"

"No," he answered, "I don't think so."

They drove in silence for a while. Richard hesitated, then said, "I have to go to Trier for a few days. To give a paper. Would you like to come?"

"With you to Trier?"

"Yes."

"What will your wife say about that?"

Richard thought about Lois, waiting for him at the studio. "She will not know about it," he said.

"People find out these things," Alexandra answered.

"But you will come?"

"Yes. I can drive. When do we go?"

"Next Thursday. After my wife's art show. Quite early in the morning."

"Your wife is a good artist?"

"Yes."

"I will pick you up where I found you today. Nine o'clock."

They drove the rest of the way in silence. The girl did not drive the way they had come, but stayed on the autobahn the whole way, and Richard was surprised at how soon they arrived in Strasbourg. On the bright city streets he could see the girl's face clearly, and he was surprised once more at how beautiful she was. He was again filled with desire.

The girl stopped the car in front of his building. Richard wanted to kiss her good-bye, but it seemed wrong in that place.

"Good night," the girl said, and she drove away, her tires squealing in the night.

Richard unlocked the door quietly, as if he might escape from explaining by not awakening Lois.

"Richard?" she called, as if it might have been someone else.

"Yes." She was sitting at the table. She had turned over the sketch she was working on. "Where have you been?"

Richard poured out his story. He told her of the ride, the bonfire, the strange little man, he even told her of Alexandra's beauty, but he did not tell her of the events in the forest.

"That was dangerous," Lois told him. "You shouldn't have gone." Her voice sounded exhausted.

"I wanted to find out what was going on."

"And did you?"

"No," he admitted. "But I have a slightly better idea." Lois began to make the bed, and got into it. Richard mixed himself a glass of scotch and water and told Lois he wanted to think about things for a while. He wouldn't be able to sleep anyway. Lois turned off the light, and in moments she was asleep. Richard mixed a second scotch, and watched the traffic through the window. Finally, he got up to go to bed. On the way he turned over the sketch and saw the drawing of Lois lying on the street. It seemed to him the most hopeless and despairing picture he had ever seen. He would not go to Trier, he decided. He would not see Alexandra again. In bed, he put his arms around Lois, but she didn't move.

***

The opening at the *Bagatelle* was to begin at two o'clock, but Charles, the young man who was arranging everything, had asked Lois to come a few minutes early. She had asked him once whether Charles was his first name or his surname, and he had said it was both and neither. He was elegant, and though his English sounded New York his French was apparently impeccable. Lois was grateful to him. He had handled all the details, made the final selection of works and arranged for the framing.

The prices he was asking were far higher than Lois would ever have dared ask. The cheapest drawing in the show was five thousand francs. Lois had argued that no one would buy a single piece at that price. He answered that they would buy them or not depending on whether they liked them. The price was irrelevant. The sort of people who made their decisions on the basis of a few francs would not be at the opening. Lois was secretly glad. Though she would have liked to sell something just to prove to herself that she really was an artist, she didn't want to part with any of the drawings. She was beginning to think of them as a sort of diary.

When they arrived, three of the paintings had little red dots on them. A private collector, Charles told them. He had dropped by the night before and bought them. He wished to remain anonymous. He had bought the drawing of the woman lying in the street, the *clochard* at the cathedral, and the first quick sketch of the old bird woman. Lois calculated. Even after the gallery took its share, she would still have over three thousand Canadian dollars, an impossible figure. Richard pointed out that she would have to pay income tax, so it wasn't quite that, but he did seem impressed.

The German consul and his wife were the first to arrive. Lois greeted them and introduced Richard. She made her introductions in French, but they both spoke in English, he in a rich Oxford accent, she in a delicate American accent. Lois flushed. Though they had been in the same class since they had started, the woman had never spoken to her in anything but a French that was worse than Lois's own. The woman confessed that she loathed speaking French, and was certain that she would never learn it adequately.

Other people came soon after that. Lois had thought there might be a sort of reception line, like at a wedding, but there wasn't. She moved around the gallery, looking at the pictures, and chatting with people. Charles kept a stream of people coming up to her. He introduced them, chatted for a minute or two and went out to find others. All the people from the class arrived, and they congratulated her enthusiastically in French, but they were the only ones who spoke French to her. Everyone else spoke English.

The inspector arrived with Delacroix. They were elaborately complimentary, and the inspector immediately bought the drawing of the missing man.

"This is wonderful," he told Lois. "It is so rare that murder is successfully transformed into art. I will treasure this for many years." Lois was giddy with excitement.

"Is anything happening?" she asked him. "Are you near a solution?"

"A solution is imminent," the inspector answered. "I expect any moment that the thing may be solved. But then I am an optimist. I am always hopeful."

Lois didn't know whether to take him seriously or not.

"Did Richard tell you about the bonfire?" she asked.

"No," he said. "What bonfire?"

"Richard went out with them one night. The people from the Pagan Wall. The German girl. They sat around a fire and listened to a philosopher and talked about destiny and things like that."

"Well," the inspector said. "I shall have to chat with Richard. So he has taken to going to bonfires out of idle curiosity?"

Lois was struck with a momentary pang of guilt. Richard would not be happy that she had told the inspector. But, then, Richard's explanation of what had happened didn't seem complete. She was sure he had found out something he wasn't going to tell her. She looked for Richard and saw him outside, on the deck of the ship, talking to a woman. She went to the door and looked out into the glare. The gallery was softly lit to show off the paintings, but outside the sun was brilliant.

Lois was about to go over to talk to him when she realized that he was talking to Alexandra. The girl had her back to the river and was leaning on the guard rail. She was dressed in a grey tweed suit and wore a large-brimmed, black and white hat. She looked exactly like something out of a high-fashion ad. A yellow silk scarf was the only colour in her outfit, but it was enough. Richard was talking intently to her, gesturing with his hands. The girl looked at Lois without expression, as if she had never seen her before.

When Lois returned to the gallery, she realized she was trembling. Richard's conversation with the girl was not the conversation of strangers. He appeared to have been arguing with her, and it did not seem like an intellectual argument. Lois got a glass of wine from the table in the middle of the room and popped a grape into her mouth. The wife of the German consul came by and said that they had bought a drawing, the old man and the cat. Her husband wanted to hang it in the consulate, but she wanted to keep it at home. Lois tried to express her gratitude, but she found it hard to concentrate.

Charles came by and told her that the opening had been a grand success. Twelve of the eighteen drawings were already sold, and he was sure the rest would go inside a week. When she had more drawings, she must bring them to him. Perhaps something could be arranged in Paris next spring?

Lois looked around the room at her drawings with an acute sense of loss. She would never see them again. Whatever had moved her to make these drawings was lost forever. She was sure she would never be able to do another. Sitting down to do a drawing now seemed like an enormous effort, something far beyond her.

Someone touched her shoulder, and she turned around with a start. Robert stood there, smiling. The dark suit he wore seemed wrong for him. He looked as if he belonged in something athletic.

"Very impressive," he said. "I expected you would be good, but not this good."

"I'm not sure that's a compliment," she answered.

"It's my style. Always good intentions, but always a little clumsy. It keeps me humble."

"It's your most endearing quality, your humility," she said. The inspector had cornered Richard and the girl, and was talking intently to them. Richard had caught sight of Robert, and he nodded towards Lois. His look was hostile.

"Look," Robert said. "I'm sorry about everything that happened in Paris. I wanted to apologize, but you got yourself run over, and by the time I found out where you were your husband had spirited you away."

"It's okay," Lois told him. "No apologies needed."

"He's pretty hostile," Robert said, indicating Richard with a flick of his head.

"Just to you." Lois told him. "There's something about you he doesn't trust."

"Why?"

"Well, do you think he ought to?"

"No, I guess not. Anyway, things are starting to close down. I'm going to meet with some people, including the inspector, over the next few days, then it's back to Paris."

"Is there anything you can tell me? I mean, I don't know whether this is dangerous or not. We keep running into odd things. These may be accidents, but there just seem too many."

"This is not a good place," he told her. "I can't really tell you a lot here. Why don't you meet me for dinner, or a drink or a cup of coffee, and we can talk?"

"No," Lois said. "I don't think I want to do that. Or I could bring Richard. Would you like that?"

"No, I think I'll take a rain check if Richard is coming along."

"Well, maybe the inspector will tell me. He likes to be mysterious, though, and I'm never sure quite what he does mean."

"Yes," Robert said. "I've noticed that. I think he reads too much."

Charles arrived with a large man and an even larger woman in tow. They were the owners of the gallery. The man was dressed in a yachting costume, and looked out of place in the crowd. His wife wore a large, shapeless dress. They complimented her on the exhibit, and said how honoured they were to have the opportunity to show her work. Robert drifted away and Lois found herself trying to hold a conversation in French. It was going better than usual, when Richard arrived. She introduced him to the couple and he chatted with them for a few minutes.

When they left, he told her, "I'm going to have to go to Trier for a few days. The lecture on Heidegger."

"I thought you said that you weren't going to go. You said you were too busy to prepare."

"Well, Delacroix is really putting on pressure. If I don't go, then he has to change all his plans and go. I did tell him that I would, and my backing out now really screws things up for him."

"Shall I come?" she asked.

"What about your class?"

"Of course. I couldn't miss my class."

"What's wrong? If you want to come, you can come. You've got this grand success, you're making money hand over fist, why so edgy?"

"I'm sorry."

"Is it the creepy Canadian? The spy that looks like a janitor? I saw you talking to him."

"Of course not. I'm just a little tense. You go to Trier. I'll stay here and learn French."

"It's just Thursday and Friday. I'll be back Saturday by about noon. It's going to be incredibly boring."

"No, go ahead. It's fine." Lois noticed a young blond couple talking with Alexandra. They looked familiar.

Richard picked up the direction of her gaze and said, "They were at the bonfire. I thought at first that they looked like the couple on the motorcycle. At Mont Ste. Odile. Then I wasn't sure. What do you think?"

"I don't know. It's hard to tell without the costumes. What did the inspector tell you?"

"He warned me to be careful where I go. I'm not supposed to go to any more bonfires without telling him in advance."

"Maybe you could also tell me in advance?"

"Lois," he began, but she caught him before he could continue.

"No, I'm sorry. No more. You've already explained that you didn't know where you were going."

"How long does this last?" Richard asked.

"I don't know. It must be just about over. I'll check with Charles." She found him in the little office at the end of the gallery. Robert was with him, and he seemed embarrassed when she entered. Charles said that she could leave whenever she wanted, that most of the people who wanted to meet her had already come and gone. But could she drop by tomorrow or the next day and they could make arrangements about the finances?

Lois looked for Richard. He would be pleased that they could leave. He would want to go home and have a glass of scotch. Lois felt that they should celebrate. They would have more money now. Maybe she could take him to an expensive restaurant. She found him again in deep conversation with Alexandra. She hesitated at the door. Robert came up behind her.

"Well, congratulations," he told her. "It's a terrific show."

"Thursday," she said. "Call me about dinner on Thursday."

Robert's eyes widened, but he didn't say a word. He nodded, then climbed the gangplank to the street without turning around. Richard left Alexandra looking over the river at the guard rail.

"Christ, I'm tired," he told Lois. "When can we go?"

"Now," she said. "Right now."

***

The Mercedes pulled up at nine o'clock, and Richard got in, stuffing his overnight bag behind the seat. It was raining, a steady drizzle from clouds that hung low over the city. The light was grey, an early morning light that washed colour out of everything. It had been raining for days, and Richard, who had arrived early and waited under the awning of the bookstore, felt chilled to the bone.

Now the rain made dull sounds on the soft roof. Alexandra was dressed in leather again, this time a deep navy blue. She had done her hair so that it hung in thin curled strands. She looked as if she had just come out of the shower, but Richard realized that the effect was created through a great deal of work, and probably a great deal of expense.

Richard leaned over towards her, and she looked at him as if he had something to say. Then she realized what he wanted and gave him a short kiss on the mouth, a quick peck that was absent of passion.

"Well," Richard said, "time for adventures."

She didn't answer, but spun the car into the traffic. Richard had expected her to take a route that would pass the studio, and he half-expected to see Lois, but Alexandra turned left instead of right, and headed in what seemed to Richard the wrong direction.

"You know the way?" he asked.

"I looked it up on a map," she told him. "Here." She passed him the map.

Richard hated reading maps. He could never follow the lines, and it was worse when he tried to translate them into the real world.

Roads and towns appeared where no road or town should be. He would follow what he was certain was the correct route, and then find himself driving down country roads behind rambling hay racks and herds of animals. He glanced at the map and decided to trust Alexandra's reading.

All week he and Lois had circled each other cautiously. The atmosphere in the studio was so tense that Richard would not have been surprised to hear the air crackle. Neither of them seemed willing to breach the tension. Richard knew he couldn't. He was going to Trier with Alexandra, filled with misgivings, but determined to go anyway. Lois had never been able to open any discussion. She always waited for Richard to make the first move, and now that he was unable to, she seemed bewildered and confused.

Richard had spent as much time away from the studio as he could. He stayed in his office at the university, trying to write his novel, but he could think of nothing but Alexandra. He had made a xerox of the pages he had written, and he kept one copy in the office and the other at home. He had reached an impasse. He wanted a battle scene in the First World War. He had read detailed descriptions of such scenes, but he found he couldn't even begin to write one. From the first sentence, he felt he was writing parody. Faint echoes of other fictions.

He decided that he would have to see an actual battlefield, something other than the beaches of Normandy, which had failed him. Last night he had broached the idea to Lois. He would rent a car from the fellow who had the private fleet of old vehicles, the guy they had rented the green van from, and they would drive to Arras and visit Vimy Ridge. Lois was excited by the idea, and for a little while the tension eased. They drank a bottle of wine and talked about the plans. Then Richard asked Lois about the drawings. They were all gone, she said, every one of them sold, and she burst into tears.

Richard tried to console her, but he was awkward and clumsy. When he held her, he thought of Alexandra, and he seemed to lose the feeling in his hands. Lois said that she would never draw again. She wanted her drawings back. After a while, he gave up trying to make her happy, and mixed himself a scotch and water and sat by the window watching the cars go by. He packed his bags and shuffled through his notes on Heidegger once more. When he left in the morning, Lois stayed in bed. He kissed her gently, then slipped out, making as little noise as he could.

The Mercedes moved through suburbs with long, low manufacturing plants and warehouses, onto a perfect highway, three lanes in each direction. Alexandra drove fast, staying in the third lane, and passing everybody.

"Is there no speed limit?" Richard asked.

"Yes," she said. "In France there is a speed limit, but it is never obeyed."

"What is it?"

"I don't know. A hundred and twenty, a hundred and thirty, something like that."

"What if they stop you?" Alexandra appeared to be travelling at about a hundred and eighty kilometres, though it was hard to read the speedometer from Richard's angle.

"Nothing," she said. "They don't stop you." She slowed the car and moved into a nearer lane. "There, is that better?" The car, suddenly slowed, seemed to be crawling.

"Yes," Richard said. "That's better."

"Let's take the slower route then," she said after a few minutes, and she drove down an exit that took them through a small village. After that, they drove through low mountains and followed a canal for a short distance. A traffic jam held them for about a half-hour. A road crew had narrowed the traffic to one lane, but they were soon through and following the signs to the university.

They found it high on a hillside just outside of town. Alexandra said something to the gatekeeper and he allowed them to park in a parking lot near a tall building. The gatekeeper left the gate and came over to talk to them, giving elaborate directions to Alexandra. He was a young man, and seemed to wish to keep talking to Alexandra as long as he could.

Inside, the building was pure confusion. It didn't look like a European university. It looked much more like an American university. Students were everywhere, casually dressed, gathering petitions at tables, swirling by in enthusiastic conversation. Many of them wore tee shirts with writing in English on them, but the sound everywhere was German. Alexandra asked directions from a tall girl with a long, single braid of yellow hair. The fifth floor, she told them, not the philosophy department, but the Institute for Linguistic Research.

Richard was confused. He was sure he was supposed to go to the philosophy department, but there, on the wall beside the elevator, was a poster advertising his talk at the Institute. He checked his wallet for the slip of paper on which he had written the name of the man who was to be his host. Dr. Bernard Traxler, Institute of Linguistics, it said. The poster had been made by computer. There was a small picture at the top, but it was hard to say whether the likeness was supposed to be of him or Heidegger. Heidegger, Richard supposed.

A sign by the elevator directed them to the fifth floor. Two men were in heated discussion outside the office of the Institute for Linguistic Research. The taller of the two, a slim, elegant man with bright-blue eyes, introduced himself as Traxler. Richard guessed that he would be about his own age. Traxler in turn introduced the other man, who was short and balding, but, when he turned to face them, very young. His name was Jefferies, and he spoke in an accent that Richard immediately identified as Oxford. Richard disliked him immediately.

Jefferies was in a flurry. The talk was to start immediately. Richard was sure it was supposed to have been at two o'clock, but Jefferies said, no, twelve, it was on all the posters, as if that settled the question. They would go out sightseeing and then for supper this evening. And his wife? She would join them?

"Well actually," Richard said, "she isn't my wife. She's . . ."

"I'm his assistant," Alexandra said. "During his stay at Strasbourg."

"Of course," Jefferies said. "However, we have arranged for only one room at the hotel."

"Don't worry," Richard said. "We'll take care of it."

"It is a trifle embarrassing," Traxler went on. "If we had known, arrangements could have been made."

"I will stay with a friend," Alexandra said. "It is all arranged. There will be no trouble."

Jefferies hurried them to the elevator, though Traxler seemed inclined to dally and chat. He asked details about the trip, about the weather in Strasbourg. The road repairs that had delayed them were nothing new. It was nearly a year now since the authorities had begun them.

The lecture hall was a large, square space with windows just below the ceiling on all sides. Richard could see technicians wheeling about television cameras that seemed to be pointed at him at the front of the room. Behind him was a gigantic screen. It flickered as he took his seat, and he suddenly appeared on the screen, gazing back at himself. The image made him look heavier than he was, and bad-tempered. He smiled nervously, and the image smiled nervously back at him.

The room was crowded. Richard estimated there were fifty or sixty students there. Traxler introduced him with elaborate formality, describing his career in more detail than Richard thought it deserved. When Richard got up to speak, he felt a moment of panic. They would all know far more than he did, and he would reveal himself as a fraud.

His paper was going to trace the influence of Heidegger on modern French philosophy, and in particular examine Derrida's quarrel with Heidegger. He began by asking a few questions to gauge his audience. It rapidly became apparent that they didn't know even the most elementary aspects of Heidegger's thought. His paper would not make sense to a single person in the room. He was tempted to read it anyway, to make it as difficult as he could, then escape. Instead, he began to teach as he would to a first-year class at home.

After about fifteen minutes, he paused for questions. At first there were none. Then a young man with a fierce moustache asked whether Heidegger's thought didn't lead directly to Naziism. Richard found himself now defending Heidegger against the very same thing of which he had accused him. The students were hostile, not to Richard, but to Heidegger. Richard tried to argue that even if it were true that Heidegger was a Nazi, total ignorance of his thought was not the proper place to begin an argument about it.

Richard tried to go on explaining, clarifying the basic notions, but the topic continually returned to Naziism, and Richard sensed that his argument had been refused by the group, that they had closed ranks and rejected everything he had to say. Finally, in exasperation, he said, "If you want to avoid Naziism, then you have to understand it and its history."

"The only people who understand Naziism are Nazis," a girl dressed in what looked like a military outfit told him. She was dark, pretty in a way that reminded him of flappers from the twenties. She had no breasts.

"That's clever, but it's just too glib," Richard told her. "Ignorance is never a virtue."

By the time the session was over, Richard was nearly in a rage. The students seemed to him to be smug in their rejection of evil and their conviction that, by rejecting Heidegger, they had evaded it. After the lecture, though, several students came up to talk to him, and they seemed friendly. They apologized for knowing so little, and they hoped he would come back again and tell them more. Richard was bewildered. He didn't know how to read the response. Maybe what looked like hostility of the class is just part of a pattern, he thought, the way classes are conducted here.

Traxler seemed more amused than concerned at Richard's reaction to the class. "Would it be any different at home?" he asked.

"No." Richard answered. "It would be worse. They wouldn't even know who Heidegger was. They wouldn't care. It would make no difference to them whether he was a Nazi or not. They might even find that attractive."

"We made them wait too long," Jefferies said. "Students get upset when they have to wait, and then they react badly." Behind him, Traxler grinned and shrugged his shoulders as if to disown his colleague.

They left Jefferies arguing with a student in the hallway. "He is British," Traxler explained. "He finds us rude and undisciplined, nearly as bad as North Americans."

They followed Traxler to the hotel, a place right near the central square and not far from the McDonald's. He drove even faster than Alexandra, and they had difficulty keeping up. In the parking lot, he explained that the class was not usually like that. Normally they were passive, but this was a difficult subject. And not many people defended Heidegger as strongly as Richard had.

"No," Richard said. "It's my fault. I should know enough not to take philosophy seriously. Even Heidegger said that."

Richard left Traxler and Alexandra in the parking lot, and went in to register. He signed in and took both Alexandra's and his own bags to the room. He told the clerk, who, from his attitude, seemed also to be the owner, that they would share the room, and he would pay the extra amount. The clerk referred to Alexandra as Frau Angantyr, and Richard informed him defiantly that she was not his wife.

"Very good," the clerk told him without expression. "There will be breakfast for two."

When Richard rejoined Traxler and Alexandra, they had already found a cafe just behind the hotel and were sitting at a table looking at a map of the city. They were each drinking a beer, and when Richard arrived Traxler motioned to the waiter to bring another. They had been laughing when Richard arrived, and they continued to speak in German for a minute as if their conversation would lose its humour if it were translated.

Traxler had laid out an itinerary that looked exhausting to Richard. They would visit Karl Marx's house. Then the cathedral, the museum and the Roman baths. They would end up at the Porta Nigra, the gates to the ancient Roman city.

"Don't worry," he told them. "This is Jefferies's itinerary. He believes that everybody should be educated. If you don't want to do this, we can sit here and drink beer all day."

Richard was tempted to do just that, but Alexandra seemed eager to explore. Traxler turned out to be an expert guide. He seemed to know everything about the history of the city, and for a while they were followed by an American couple who thought he was some sort of official. He was pleased by their mistake, and explained that though he himself was from the north, he had made it his hobby to learn the history of Trier when he had arrived there ten years ago.

He led them through the cathedral, which was actually two cathedrals stuck together, and then on to an ancient red brick Roman temple, now a Lutheran church. After the richness of the cathedral, the stark, unadorned walls seemed cold and bare, the Protestant spirit at its meanest and most self-denying. Alexandra followed Traxler's descriptions with the rapt attention of a dutiful schoolgirl. Richard was keenly aware of the way she became the

240

centre of attention wherever they went. Whenever she moved away from Richard and Traxler, men would come up to her and talk.

After a couple of hours, Richard had seen all the ruins he ever wanted to see. At Marx's house, an elaborate building that suggested a good deal of wealth on the part of Marx senior, they became giddy. Traxler took a picture of Alexandra with her arm around a bust of Marx. A delegation of Chinese visitors appeared around the corner, and frowned in disapproval. Traxler translated a love poem that the young Marx had written, and which was now displayed under glass. The poem was sentimental, Traxler said, and he read it aloud in German in a deep syrupy voice, and they laughed again.

Then Traxler led them down a winding street, and they came, without warning, on an amphitheatre. It was well-kept, the grass green and newly cut. It didn't seem like something ancient. It seemed domestic, useable. Richard could imagine families coming with picnics to sit on the gentle slopes and watch a soccer game. He asked Traxler if it was still used, but Traxler said, no, it was just a tourist attraction now. He led them through a park-like area to the museum.

Traxler suggested that they skip the museum, but Richard perversely insisted on seeing it. The weight of so much history tired him, but it did not move him. The Roman artifacts, the glass, the coins, the urns and the statues all seemed recent, part of a seamless history that was not ancient at all, but so near that they were still useable. He thought of Canada and the Indian burial mounds he had seen in the Whiteshell area. They seemed immensely older than anything here. He had spent a month one summer working on a geological survey in northern Manitoba. His crew, four students and a geologist, had been dropped off by an airplane on a remote lake, where they had encountered no one, not even an Indian, for the entire month. He had felt the age of the place then. The geologist explained the ages of the rocks, hundreds of millions of years. The Canadian Shield was the oldest geological formation on earth. Richard had found himself afraid of death, his span so minute against the age of rocks and waterfalls.

Richard moved away from Traxler. He didn't want to hear any more explanations. Traxler didn't mind. He was much more interested in talking to Alexandra. He offered to find Richard a place to rest, and suddenly Richard felt beefy and aging alongside Traxler's slim elegance. He saw himself as cranky and unattractive.

Richard drifted through rooms, being careful not to read any of the descriptions of the exhibits, which were all in four languages. He found himself alone in a room with a life-sized boat carved out of rock, complete with crew. He was drawn to one face at the back of the boat. The stone sailor who stared at him was bearded with curly hair, and the expression on his face was pure drunkenness. At first glance, the face looked happy, but looked at more closely it seemed filled with something between panic and deep malice. It looked familiar, and Richard realized with a start that, except for the beard, it was the face of the body he and Lois had discovered.

Richard felt a sharp sense of dismay and unease. He moved to another room, but the image of the face wouldn't leave him, and he returned to look at it again. This time, he had the odd sensation that it recognized him. It seemed to say to him that it knew all about weakness and betrayal, that it shared with Richard his emptiness. He left again but looked back from the doorway. At a distance, the figure appeared to be laughing.

There were postcards for sale at the desk, and Richard found one with the face. He thought he would take it home and show it to Lois, see if she saw the resemblance to the body. Surely she would.

"Let me see it," Alexandra said. She and Traxler had come up to him just as he was paying for the postcard, and her voice startled him.

Traxler glanced over her shoulder. "The drunken mariner," he said. "One of our most famous citizens."

"He looks a little like you," Alexandra said to Richard. "Except for the beard." She held up the picture so she could see both it and Richard. "Yes, it looks just like you."

Richard said nothing. At supper, haunted by the face, he hardly spoke. Traxler talked about the French airbase and what the French meant to the town.

"It gives us a certain cosmopolitan touch," he said, "but there is a great deal of hostility. It goes right back to the Romans. The

Franks and the Alemani, a couple of northern tribes, one controlled by the Romans. And Trier was the northern capital of the Roman Empire in the district of the Franks. This was where things happened." Traxler seemed relaxed and willing to talk, but he noticed Richard's silence and cut the meal short, calling for the bill and insisting on paying.

Then he walked them back to the hotel, and offered to show Alexandra over to her friend's place. In the hesitation that followed he was suddenly aware of where things stood. Alexandra moved closer to Richard and put her hand on his arm as if to confirm his suspicions. Traxler simply nodded and slipped away, informing them that he would meet them for breakfast at nine the next morning. Richard wasn't sure whether the nod was conspiratorial or disappointed.

In the room, Richard kissed Alexandra. She kissed him back with an eagerness that surprised him. Then Richard took the postcard out of his pocket and showed it to Alexandra again. She looked at him blankly.

"It looks like the body. The airman. Mann, it looks like him."

"No," Alexandra said, "it looks like you."

"Was he your lover?" Richard asked.

"Yes."

"Tell me about him. What was he like?"

"He never said much. He wasn't an ordinary soldier. He travelled a lot. He went to strange places a lot. I don't know."

"Why was he killed?"

"Was he killed? I don't think so. I think he just went away."

"I saw him. He was dead."

"Then he is dead."

"Do you miss him?"

"No. I was frightened of him. He was very powerful. I don't mean he was strong, but he did what he wanted."

"How did you come to be his lover?"

"He came to the bonfire. Somebody brought him."

"And you fell in love with him?"

"No. I didn't love him."

"But he was your lover?"

"He took what he wanted. He wanted me."

"And you didn't resist?"

"It is hard to resist people who know what they want. I had never been with a man before. I was curious."

"And why are you here with me?"

"I don't know," she said. "I have no idea. I am simply here."

"What was he doing? What was he mixed up in?"

"I don't want to talk any more," she said. "I want to make love." She disappeared into the bathroom, and Richard took off his clothes and got into the bed. When Alexandra came out she was wearing an elaborate garter belt and her high boots. She looked like a prostitute in a movie.

"Not in the bed," she said. "Here beside the window, standing up." She was doubled in the reflected light.

Richard moved to turn the light out, but she said, "No, leave the light on."

Richard took her in his arms, and held her gently, but she suddenly bit him sharply on the neck, and he found himself in a wrestling match. He tried to make her stop, but she seemed intent on biting him again. He struggled with her until he got her arms pinned and her head pushed back against the wall. He found himself angry, ready to hurt.

"Now," she said. "Now make love to me."

When it was over, Richard felt exhausted, drained, as if something had happened to him that was far beyond his control. Alexandra lay beside him, silent, and for a long time he didn't say anything.

"Did you learn that from Mann?" he asked finally.

"Don't," she said. "Please don't be cruel."

"I don't want to be cruel," he told her. "I'm just surprised."

"I have my own ideas," she said. "I don't want to be made love to. I want to be in charge of myself."

Richard didn't answer. Some time later, he woke to find her weeping, and they made love again. This time, she was passive and silent. She hardly moved.

At breakfast, with Traxler, Richard wondered whether he was falling in love, and he thought guiltily of Lois. He imagined her in the studio in Strasbourg, memorizing her verbs, and then he thought of her sketching. The drawings she had been making now seemed to him full of anxiety. They hinted at something horrible to come. He had never thought of them that way before.

"You mustn't think of the students' reaction to Heidegger as a reaction to your talk," Traxler was saying. "A Nazi past is not easy to bear. Some of them have not forgiven their elders. And of course there is always the danger that something like it will re-appear."

Richard thought of the bonfire and the people there. On an impulse, he told Traxler about the bonfire and the speech, the small man with the hypnotic voice. Alexandra was uncomfortable as he talked, but when he was finished she said, "They are not Nazis. They hate the Nazis. But they are interested in nature and the natural world. They talk about history, about the Celts and the Druids."

Traxler smiled, and Richard saw that Alexandra was hurt by the smile. "There are forces," she said defiantly, "there is something of the spirit that is rooted in old places. You can feel it when you go there. Or at least I can feel it," she said to Richard. "Maybe you can't because they are not your ancestors. Maybe you will have to go home to feel it."

It was the longest statement Richard had ever heard Alexandra make, and he was surprised by her intensity. "At home," he said, "all the ancestors would belong to the Indians."

Traxler shifted the conversation to Indians, and Richard was grateful to him. One of Traxler's colleagues was writing a book about Indians. He was comparing Indian religions with the early Norse religions. He was particularly interested in the trickster figure.

Traxler offered to show them more sights, but his offer was without enthusiasm. Richard said that, unfortunately, they had to get back, so they would be leaving immediately. Traxler expressed his regrets without asking any further questions, and he left them there at the hotel.

"Why are we going back?" Alexandra asked. "I thought we were staying for two days."

"We don't have to go back," Richard said. "I just don't want to see any more sights. And neither does Traxler. Though I would like to go back to the museum and see the drunken mariner once more."

At the museum, the statue had lost all its power. It was only a carved rock, and the eyes now seemed blank, as if it were a representation of a blind man.

"It does look like you," Alexandra told him, "though not as much as the photograph. It looks like you if you would grow a beard."

"I always want too much," Richard told her. "I ruin things by never knowing when to stop."

Richard didn't want to stay in Trier with its weight of history. Alexandra suggested that they should drive along the Mosel until it met the Rhine, then follow the Rhine back to Strasbourg. They drove slowly, stopping at vineyards along the way. They visited an old, ruined castle, and explored it hand-in-hand, as if they were newly married. They spent the night in a town called Oberwesel. They went for a long walk in lightly drifting rain, and they slept in a big, old four-poster bed with a filmy curtain around it.

The next day, Alexandra dropped Richard off at the university in the early afternoon. Richard had explained about the trip to Vimy Ridge.

"I'll be back in about four or five days," he told her. "I'm not certain how long it will take. When can I see you again?"

"That will depend on you," she said.

"How will I find you?" he asked.

"You'll find me," she said. "If you want me." She slipped the car into gear and left with a squeal of tires. Richard realized with a start that if she did not call him, he might never see her again.

***

Rain had fallen all day, but by evening it had cleared, and the low, golden sunlight on the wet buildings made them seem shiny and new. Lois was early. Robert had phoned, and she had agreed to meet him for dinner at a restaurant called Amphitryon. The name sounded Greek to Lois, but Robert had told her it was run by Swedes. An Amphitryon, he had said, was a perfect host.

Someone who considered all his guests' desires. It was the favourite place for people who worked at the Palais de l'Europe.

Lois chose to walk along the canal and cross by the cathedral. She passed the *Bagatelle* and noticed that the poster advertising her show was still up. It was strange to come upon her own name, exposed and vulnerable. Another poster advertising a new show had covered everything but her name, which now seemed to have no reason for being there.

"It's odd," she told Robert, "to come on your own name like that. It's as if there was some other you, quite separate and distinct, that went on having its own life without you." It was dark in the room, the table lit by two candles. The restaurant was nearly empty. People at another table were speaking in Spanish, and a large man who looked like a Russian was dining alone.

"My life is like that most of the time," Robert said. "Often I have to operate under another name. I have a complete set of identification, including passport and credit cards."

"Who are you in this other life?" Lois asked. "What is your other name?"

"Now, it wouldn't be much of a secret if I told people about it, would it? I have sworn not to tell anyone, not even you."

"Was that part of the oath, not telling me?"

"Not exactly. They didn't actually mention you by name, but it was implied."

The waiter arrived with their food. Robert had ordered, and Lois wasn't sure what he had chosen. She found herself facing a plate of veal and sculptured vegetables.

"It doesn't look very Swedish," Lois said, after the waiter was gone. "It doesn't even look like food. It looks like something you should hang on a wall. Those little turnips are all carved to look like walnuts with seven sides."

"I said it was run by Swedes. I didn't say they served Swedish foods. Actually the chef is quite famous. They write articles about him in food magazines." Robert gestured, and Lois noticed that he had long hairs on the back of his hands.

"Richard has gone to Trier," she said. "To deliver a lecture on Heidegger. I think he took the girl with him."

"Alexandra? The *au pair*?"

"Yes."

"Why do you think so?"

"The way he talked to her at the show. The way he's been acting for the last week or so. Something's on his mind. He hardly spends any time at home."

"Maybe it's his novel. Isn't he writing a novel?"

"Yes, but that's a different kind of obsession. Richard's a kind of obsessive personality, as you may have noticed. But he's a bad liar, and I think he's been telling me lies."

"You think he's sleeping with her?"

"Yes." Lois had never actually formulated the thought clearly to herself. Now, having said it aloud, she was convinced that she was right. "The girl is very beautiful. She'd be pretty hard to resist."

"Is that the sort of thing Richard does?"

"He's not good at delayed gratification. He doesn't resist temptation very well. What do you think? Would you sleep with her if she asked you to?"

"A different question entirely. I'm not married to you. But yes, she is attractive."

"She's not attractive. She's stunning. And I'm pretty sure she's screwing my husband. So what do I do about it?" She felt herself angry, and hoped it wasn't evident in her voice. She wanted to sound wry and ironic.

"Actually, I hope you're wrong," Robert said. "It could be a pretty dangerous thing for him to do. Remember the accountants I told you I was going to meet? Hutcheon and Fawcett?"

Lois nodded.

"Well, I did meet with them. They specialize in arranging financing for arms deals, though they prefer to call it international trade. And they're afraid."

"What are they afraid of?"

"I don't know yet. I'm meeting with the inspector tomorrow. Maybe he knows. But Mann, the missing body you saw, either was or still is a courier. He carried money from one place to another. Very large sums of money. It's about the most dangerous job in the world."

"And this is somehow connected to the girl?"

248

"Mann was her lover. Her uncle is probably involved somehow too. We're dealing here with a world where people get killed for making other people nervous. If Richard is involved with the girl, he'd better hope that Mann really is dead."

"He's dead," Lois said. "I saw him. He was very, very dead."

"Well, I think you'd both be safer if you went back to Canada. My official advice is to go home."

"When? Now?"

"Tomorrow if you can. As soon as possible. Things are going to get very nasty, very soon."

"We're going to Vimy Ridge next week. Richard wants to do some research for his novel."

"Don't. Just get on an airplane and go home."

"I can't. Richard will never agree."

"Tell him it's better than ending up dead. Or I'll tell him. Do you mind if I come to your place and tell him?"

"No," Lois said. "You tell him. But I don't think he'll listen. Like I said, he doesn't like you much."

"Well, I'll take the chance. But if you do go, make sure you don't tell anyone that you're going. I think the inspector is setting a trap, and you might just be the bait."

"Would he do something like that? Take chances with other people's lives?"

"That's his business."

"I don't think I'm hungry any more," Lois said. The veal was delicious, but she had hardly eaten any of it.

"I don't mean to scare you. Or, yes, I do mean to scare you, or at least to warn you. I really don't want anything to happen to you." The cafe was starting to fill up with people. A group of black men speaking some indecipherable language was seated near them.

"Do you think some of the odd things, the man in my hotel room, the shot in Seville, even the car that hit me, do you think those things might all be connected?" Lois had discussed this possibility with Richard, but he had said no. That was the way paranoia worked, he told her. If you get a big enough explanation, then all the facts will fit into it.

"Maybe." Robert moved his food around on his plate with his

fork. "Probably not all of them, but it wouldn't surprise me if a few incidents were set up to frighten you away. You see, you really don't have much information. You aren't much of a threat. All you did was discover the body. But if Richard is now connected to the girl it's a whole new ball game."

Lois realized for the first time that she did not want to go home. Already the trees would have lost their leaves. It would probably have snowed, not a snow that stays, but enough to depress her anyway. She didn't want to buy food wrapped in plastic. If they went back now, she would have nothing to do.

"Maybe we'll go somewhere else," she said. "Maybe we'll go to Spain or Greece and rent a villa, and not leave any forwarding address."

"Canada," Robert said. "You'd stick out like a sore thumb anywhere in Europe. It's not easy to hide in a foreign country."

"Paraguay," she said. "Maybe we'll go to Paraguay and hide out with all the famous criminals."

"Canada," Robert said. "Home."

"I don't want to go back," she admitted. "I won't have anything to do."

"Draw. Become a famous Canadian artist. Maybe they'll let you into the Group of Seven."

"The Group of Seven is all dead," she said. "That was in the thirties."

"Are you sure? I think there's one still hanging on. The one nobody can remember. Carmichael, I think."

"No. Anyway, it doesn't matter. I can't draw any more. Those drawings for the exhibition used up everything I had in me. And I certainly couldn't draw in Canada. I never could." She thought of the stylized drawings she had done for the children's books, and it seemed as if they had been done a long, long time ago by somebody else. "I think it was a mistake to sell them," she went on. "Now I can't start anything. I used to look at the portfolio, then I could draw another one. It was like making yogurt. You need a little bit of the last batch to start a new one."

"Or sourdough," Robert said. "Sourdough is the same."

"Yes."

"How would you like to come up to my room and look at my etchings," Robert teased. "Maybe they'd give you some inspiration. Something to help you get started again."

"What do you mean?"

"I have some terrific drawings I purchased recently. I have one of a little old lady and some birds, another of a mean beggar, and a third of a woman who appears to have fainted in the street."

"It was you? You're the secret buyer?" Lois wasn't sure whether she was pleased or disappointed.

"An investment. I expect to make a great deal of money from these."

"And you've got them here? In Strasbourg?"

"Of course."

"Can I see them? I want to see them." Lois was suddenly sure that if she saw the drawings she would be able to work again. It would make all the difference.

"That's what I was suggesting. We can go over to my room, drink a glass of fine old brandy and contemplate their artistic merits. It's the way it's done in all the best old silent movies."

"No," Lois said. "Not that. I don't want any more involvement. But I do want to see them. Will you let me?" She heard herself pleading, and was angry. Robert seemed to sense her anger and he became serious.

"Of course," he said. "Now, if you wish, but if it makes you more comfortable I could bring them to your place tomorrow."

"Now will be fine," Lois said. "Is it far from here?"

"Nothing is far away in Strasbourg. It's about a fifteen-minute walk."

Robert's place turned out to be near the university. It was on the sixth floor of a block of flats that was one of several identical buildings. What Robert had called his room turned out to be a two-bedroom apartment which did not look like a place that was used temporarily. It looked like a place where somebody lived. There were a lot of books and magazines, and the place smelled faintly of pipe tobacco. Robert explained that a young bank clerk lived in the place when it was not used by the Canadian government. When anybody came, which wasn't all that often, he went to live with his mother. Lois looked at a picture of a dark, heavy-set girl framed in a silver frame, which was standing on a small table.

Robert offered her a glass of brandy, and she accepted. She didn't see her drawings anywhere, and while he was finding the drinks she walked out on the balcony. In the distance, she could see the spire of the cathedral, brightly lit, and the twin lower spires of some other church. Nearer, she could see the buildings of the university. Most of the lights were on in the rooms, and she could see dim figures moving around. If Richard phones, she thought, he will want to know where I was. And if he asks, I will tell him. Exactly and in detail. And he will have to tell me about the girl and what he intends to do.

The notion that their relationship might be at a critical point made Lois excited. If Richard left her, she would have a completely different life. And even if he stayed, she would insist that their lives must change. She had no idea what changes she would ask for. Robert joined her on the balcony, and passed her a glass of brandy. The evening had become chilly, and a breeze raised goosebumps on her arm.

"Cheers," Robert said, and they clinked glasses. The sound was sharply festive in the still night.

"You haven't hung them on the wall," Lois said.

"No. I don't expect to be here long."

"When will you go back?"

"Two weeks at most. Probably sooner."

"And then?"

"And then something else. Mostly routine things. I don't get to travel much. The drawings are in my bedroom. I'll get them out."

He turned to leave the room, but she said, "There's no great rush." She wasn't sure now that she did want to see them. Maybe I don't want to draw like that any more, she thought. They stood in silence for several moments, leaning over the balcony. In the distance the lights of a boat on the canal twinkled. Lois realized that it was too cold to stay on the balcony, but she stayed anyway for a few more minutes. When she turned to enter the room,

Robert followed. Lois thought he might try to kiss her, and she wondered what she would do. He didn't, though. He followed her into the room without touching her.

"I'll get the drawings now," he said. Lois thought she should stop him, but he had already vanished into the bedroom before she could decide whether to look at them or not. He lined them up on the sofa in the order they were drawn. The old bird woman was hardly a drawing. A few quick lines, a hint at the birds in the trees and in the air, a suggestion of part of a church behind her. Lois had not wanted to show it, but Charles had insisted that it was one of his favourite pieces, and so she had relented. The *clochard* still looked evil. His torn clothes and dissipated face seemed to have more to do with moral poverty than with economics.

She stood for a long time looking at the picture of the woman in the street. Her body seemed broken, irrecoverable. She stirred, remembering the pain of her accident.

"What's it like to contemplate your own death in such graphic terms?" Robert asked. "When I was a kid, I always thought that when I died I'd be somewhere near, looking at my own body and hearing what other people said. Was it like that?"

"Yes," Lois said. "It was just like that. I don't think you can imagine your own death in any other way. But when I did the drawing, I was intensely aware of how alive I was there at that very moment. Death seemed the opposite, an annihilation of everything."

"You're not religious?"

"United Church. Does that count? I joined the Church when I was fifteen, but mostly religion seemed to be about being nice to other people and not being a burden on them. How about you?"

"Lapsed Catholic. I was actually taught by nuns, and for a while I was a choirboy. I can still do Latin prayers. Want to hear some?"

"No. I had a boyfriend once who used to do them. I think he meant them."

"I don't actually mean them. But it is a comfort to be able to say them."

"Richard can recite the entire works of Robert Frost. He can do both *Hamlet* and *Macbeth* from beginning to end. He can do entire paragraphs from Nietzsche."

"That must be useful."

"It actually is. To a teacher. At least that's what Richard says. He uses the stuff all the time."

"And Richard's in Trier now, with the girl?"

"Yes. Or at least I think so. How can you be sure about these things?"

"Do you care?"

"Yes," Lois said. "I do care. It hurts my pride. And it makes everything uncertain."

"Why don't you stay here tonight. Sleep with me."

"As revenge? To get even with Richard?"

"No. Only if you want to. It mustn't have anything to do with Richard."

"Okay," she said. "Why not. But I won't stay the whole night. I want to go back home tonight."

"Fine," he said, "I can drive you."

"But first another brandy," she said, passing him her glass. Lois wondered why she had agreed to stay. She had certainly not intended to. And she was sure it was not a question of revenge. Desire, she told herself. I am staying purely out of desire. Robert found a tape in a drawer and played it on the little stereo set in the corner. It was in French, and she couldn't recognize the voice or understand the lyrics.

They sat in silence until the tape was over. They were both a little awkward about going into the bedroom, but Lois led the way and took off her clothes and got into bed as if they had been married for years.

"Just a minute," Robert said. "Would you like a backrub first?"

"Sure."

"Roll over." Lois felt her back suddenly cold. "Just a little baby oil."

Robert began slowly to massage the back of her neck. He worked methodically, rubbing her back, her buttocks, her feet, even massaging her toes. Lois felt lazy and languid.

"Did you train as a professional masseur?" she asked, but he didn't answer. She could feel that he was aroused as he pressed against her, but he was slow and patient. Finally, when she was nearly asleep, he entered her, gently and slowly. In what seemed a few seconds she felt her whole body respond. It seemed completely out of control, and when it was over she felt almost embarrassed at her response.

"There," Robert said. "That should make up for last time."

* * *

The train out of Paris chugged northward through ancient factories that looked more like ruins than like places of work. The sun, which had appeared intermittently through the morning, had disappeared, and the rain had settled in to stay. Richard had brought a notepad with him, and he held it now with a pen in his hand as he looked out the window. He had written nothing. There seemed nothing to say. Canadian soldiers had taken trains down these very tracks, had watched these very same hills and factories and scrapyards, but their seeing had not registered on the landscape. There was nothing of them there.

He had wanted to rent a car in Strasbourg and come down from the north through Belgium, but the fellow who rented cheap old cars had none that he would permit out of the country. Lois had suggested the train to Paris and then Amiens. They could rent a car in Amiens, she had said, and take their time looking at battlefields. In the long run, it would even be cheaper. She would drive so that he would have nothing to do but absorb the landscape.

The other passengers in the coach looked like farmers and their wives, people who had just gone into town for a couple of days of shopping and were now returning with parcels and shopping bags. Nobody seemed the least threatening. Ferguson's insistence that they return to Canada seemed melodramatic. His talk of arms deals and spies bore no relationship to these faces, these shopping bags. Ferguson had come to the door, and Richard had not wanted to let him in, though Lois had insisted that he should.

After he had gone, Lois defended him. It was his job, she said, to see that Canadians didn't get mixed up in trouble in other

255

countries. They had argued sharply, and Richard had been afraid that Lois would ask him about the girl. She hadn't, though, and he was grateful. He didn't think he would have been able to lie. He had agreed that after the trip to Vimy, they would discuss going back to Canada. It would solve the problem of what to do about Alexandra, but the prospect of departing left him feeling empty. He remembered Winnipeg in winter, the snow deep, and the weather bitter cold. Huddled inside through the long, dark nights, you aged sooner.

The factories gave way to rolling hills and farmyards. Richard looked for landmarks, a certain tree, the curl of a river that he might be able to use in his novel. He wanted his characters to confront history out of the details of places. He was certain that if he could get the details right, then the story would follow. He had brought a copy of Harrison's *Generals Die in Bed* with him, and Lois was reading it now.

"This is incredibly brutal," she said.

"Yes, I know," he answered. "But it's exactly as war has to be. I want to write something that is just like that book, but which puts things in a larger perspective."

"This is where these things happened?" Lois gestured out at the passing countryside.

"Not exactly, but close. Have you got to the part about Arras yet? Where they loot the town?"

"No."

"It's right near the end. We're going to stay overnight in Arras. It's right beside Vimy Ridge. I want to walk down the same streets and look in the same windows that the soldiers broke open to steal caviar and cognac."

"But will they be there? It's a novel isn't it? Didn't he make up most of the stuff?"

Richard was certain that the book was historically accurate. He had read it so many times that it had begun to feel like private experience, something he himself had gone through.

"I think it's pretty accurate," he said. "But we'll see."

The train pulled into Amiens at noon. Richard left Lois at the restaurant in the station while he walked over to rent a car from a place just across the street. The price was much higher than he had expected, and for a moment he felt perversely that he would go back to Strasbourg without seeing the battlefields rather than be so cheated. In the end, though, he paid the price, and the man told him to come back in a half-hour and the car would be ready.

Lois had ordered them each a beer and a *croque monsieur*. She was nearly finished the novel.

"Now the Canadians are shooting innocent children who are trying to surrender. Did the Canadians really commit war atrocities?" she asked.

"I don't see why not," Richard answered. "They were no different from anyone else."

"Well, I'm looking forward to Arras, anyway. Will there be any signs of the war left?"

"I don't know. I doubt it. There'll probably be a plaque in the main square."

The car came with a map of Amiens, and Richard had a larger map of the area that he had bought back in Strasbourg. Amiens didn't seem to correspond to the official map. Roads and streets weren't where they were supposed to be. Lois made U-turns and doubled back several times as Richard tried to navigate them out of the city. Finally, they found a road that took them out into the countryside, and a sign that said Arras convinced Richard that he had found the correct route.

"I want to stop in Albert," he told her, just as an arrow leading to the right said Albert 45 kilometres. Another sign about a minute later indicated that Beaumont-Hamel was ahead. Richard consulted his map again and realized that they were on the wrong road. They would get to Arras, but they would not pass through Albert.

"We'll go to Beaumont-Hamel then. Maybe we can go to Albert on the way back."

"What's at Beaumont-Hamel?" Lois asked.

"It's where the Newfoundlanders were killed at the battle of the Somme. July 1, 1916. The poor bastards were all keen to go to war. Almost every kid from every outpost signed up. They didn't have any rifles and so they had to practise with sticks of wood. They didn't even have uniforms until they met a Canadian ship in the middle of the Atlantic, and the Canadians gave them puttees to wrap around their legs. They were called the blue-puttee boys."

"And what happened to them?"

"They were wiped out. I think six hundred and eighty-five died in a few minutes. Only twenty-five survived. Or twenty-six."

"I thought you wanted to see Canadian battlefields. The Newfoundlanders weren't Canadians then."

"They are now. They'll do." Ahead of them a hillside was white, as if it were covered with snow. As they got closer, Richard realized that the white was a sweep of gravestones that reached to the horizon.

"Christ," he said. Within a few minutes they passed two more enormous cemeteries, and then so many smaller ones that Richard gave up trying to count. "I wasn't expecting this," he told Lois. "I somehow thought the graveyards would be hidden, away from the road, and, I don't know, enclosed with fences and hedges and things."

"They're scary," Lois said. "They're everywhere. There must be hundreds of thousands of markers."

"A lot of people died right here." They passed a low sign with an arrow that read Beaumont-Hamel. Lois was past the turn before Richard could tell her. She backed up and they drove off to the right on a gravel road that led through a farmyard and between a house and a barn. The road made a gentle curve, then straightened out and led to a grove of trees about a mile further on.

They found a parking lot and a gate marked Beaumont-Hamel. A low, stone fence led to a path through the trees. Lois drew in her breath sharply and called to Richard. She pointed to the fence. The stones were arranged so that they looked like bones and human skulls.

"That's not real is it?" Lois asked. Her voice seemed close to terror.

"No," Richard answered. "It couldn't be. But it sure is gruesome." They followed the path past a low memorial, which contained a list of the names of the men who had died there, and a visitor's book. Nobody had signed the book for over a month.

As they were looking at the book, three workmen filed by silently. One of them carried a lunch pail, and the other two carried tools that looked medieval, like the prototypes from which rakes and shovels have evolved. The men were bent, as if they had

258

suffered all their lives from too much work. The rain was not heavy, but it was insistent. It was already after four o'clock. Soon it would be dark.

Richard was stunned by what he saw as they emerged from the pathway into the open field beyond. The mounds and craters remained as they must have been just after the battle in 1916. The trenches were still full of red mud, and the grass on the mounds and shell holes was sparse and yellow. The place seemed full of pain. If there are ghosts anywhere, Richard thought, they will be here.

To their left, out of a pile of rocks, the statue of an elk lunged skyward. The statue ought to have been ridiculous, but it wasn't. There, in the grey rain, it seemed a pure embodiment of pain. A low deck ran around the base of the statue, and Richard followed it, reading the names of the dead. He wiped the rain from his eyes and found to his surprise that he had wiped away hot tears. For several minutes he stood behind the statue, where Lois could not see him. He was afraid that if he spoke he would sob, and he would not be able to control himself. When he came around the deck to where Lois was, he saw that she was weeping too. She turned away from him and walked a little distance back to the pathway. He did not stop her.

This would have been the Newfoundland position. The field covered about forty acres, and not a square yard had escaped the bombardment. The Germans would have been at the far end of the field, dug into deep trenches. They would have waited for the end of the bombardment, then brought their machine guns up and mowed down the hapless Newfoundlanders. To the right and about halfway to the end of the field was a small cemetery. Richard started towards it and found a path made out of red mud that stuck to his shoes. Lois followed a moment later. About halfway, they came on the blasted stump of a tree. The tree had been embedded in concrete and a brass plaque beside it read The Danger Tree.

The rain was lighter now, feathery and cold. Richard pulled the collar of his raincoat up around his neck. The workmen must have been tending the graveyard, though it was difficult to see what they might have been doing. Richard moved down the row of graves. A Soldier of the Great War, they said, Known to God. Sometimes there were names and ages. Eighteen. Nineteen. Twenty-three. The graveyard was full of children.

Richard continued down the row of graves, following the geometry of the place until he met Lois coming the other way. He embraced Lois clumsily, but there was no consolation in the embrace. She stood still a moment as he held her, and then she moved on in her own direction.

He had never felt the presence of death as strongly as he did then. Every single cross represented spectacular, pain-filled death. He tried to imagine the moment, the confused roar of shells, the drifting smoke, the screams of dying men. It was hopeless. His mind refused to concentrate. He thought instead of the widening circles of pain in distant outpost villages in Newfoundland, where all the men who should have been the future were dead.

Lois came up to him and he asked her, "What does it make you think of, all this?"

"It makes me think of women weeping," she said.

"The poor bastards," he said. "They knew nothing. They thought it was all a game. And the guy who ran it all was Sir Douglas Haig. There's no better example of criminal stupidity in history."

The rain was still gentle, but the clouds had lowered, and it was nearly dark. Richard took Lois's hand, and together they walked back past The Danger Tree, a skeleton in the centre of the field, and on to the monument.

"Why an elk?" Lois asked. "What made them think of that?"

"I don't know," he answered, "but it works. Maybe they couldn't find any way of representing all the human pain, and so they had to show animal pain."

As Lois pulled the car back onto the main highway, Richard realized that he had left the cemetery without ever looking back.

"Christ," he said, "I wasn't expecting that. I can't believe the power of that place."

"I know," Lois answered. "Is it going to be useful? Can any of that work in your novel?"

"I don't know. I don't think so. It makes anything I could write seem trivial and artificial. How can you compete with tragedy that's written in mud and stone?"

They drove in silence into Arras. They passed the Hotel de Ville, and Richard was struck with a sense of recognition.

"This is it," he told Lois. "This is the place where Harrison describes the mutiny. Those shop windows, those are the ones they broke, and right here, they got up on top of the buildings and fired at the British MPs. Stop the car."

Lois pulled to the side of the road, and Richard got out, crossed over and walked up the other side of the block to the next intersection. Lois followed slowly, driving along the curb. Inside the windows, it was just as he had imagined. He saw bottles of wine and cognac richly displayed in one window, cans of truffles and pâté in another. Women's clothes in muted fall colours were draped or hung from mannequins in elegant tableaux. Then a shop filled with pipes and tobacco. Further on, a chocolatier displayed a zoo full of chocolate animals. Mice, and bears, and elephants.

Richard was in high excitement when he got back into the car at the corner. "It's unbelievable," he said. "It's almost exactly as Harrison describes it." They wound around a corner and found themselves moving out of the business district into an area of large elegant houses.

"They commandeered these houses," Richard said. "They got drunk and shot holes in the windows."

"What are we going to do?" Lois asked. "Are we going to find some place to stay?"

"Head back towards the centre of town. I don't want to stay on the outskirts."

Lois turned left, then left again. The road seemed to be parallel to the one they had followed, but you could never tell, in France. A few minutes later she turned down a side street and almost immediately pulled into a parking space. A sign read Hotel de l'Univers.

"The hotel of the universe," Richard said. "Perfect. Exactly where we want to be."

The hotel was ancient, but elegant. A large dog lay sprawled across the doorway. Richard was a bit leery of entering, but the dog remained motionless as they went in. The clerk, a pretty young woman, handed them the key to a room without asking for any information at all. It was an old skeleton key, so large that it seemed a parody.

The room itself it was equally ancient and elegant. The wallpaper was delicately flowered, and so was the rug. Beside the bed stood a scrolled oak writing desk, and French doors led to a balcony that overlooked the street. A corner of the room had been sectioned off as a bathroom, and the shower was behind a curved sheet of glass embossed with flowers.

"They were in here," Richard said. "I'm absolutely sure of it. If they took over the town, they would surely have taken over the best hotel in town. Right here. This very room, they would have got drunk and stood on the balcony shouting to their buddies."

Lois walked slowly around the room, examining every detail. "It's beautiful," she said. "It's perfect in a way that I've never actually seen before, not even in a magazine. But there's a kind of story that happens in rooms like this. You read about it in novels."

They ate supper in the hotel's dining room, a dimly lit space that was furnished in heavy oak. Richard felt obscurely happy, as if he had accomplished something important. He thought about Alexandra to see if that would diminish his joy, but she seemed distant and unthreatening, like a figure out of a dream. After the meal, he ordered cognac, and it arrived in enormous goblets, amber and rich. He felt himself giddy. He couldn't stop talking. He told Lois about the war and about the life in the trenches as if he had been there himself. Lois didn't say much, and it was hard for him to tell whether she was listening or not.

The next day they drove to Vimy early, through a spurt of rush-hour traffic. Richard was surprised at how close the site was to the town. The red and white Canadian flag they passed as they entered the gate seemed anomalous. The area was deserted, except for a couple who had parked a Jaguar near the graveyard, and were walking a pair of tall, thin dogs with long hair.

The road passed a series of trenches and deep craters, circled by the graveyard and opened onto the monument, a monolith of white marble that seemed to reach high into the sky. Richard had seen pictures of it before, but he had not expected it to be so large. The washed-out sky was a perfect background for it, so much the colour of the marble that Richard had to focus his eyes intently so that monument and background did not become one. They drove in a complete circle around it, past the gun emplacements, which must have been preserved through the careful landscaping.

They parked the car near the office where guests were supposed to register, but which was now closed for the season. The monument had been intended to awe, and it did that, but it had nothing of the power of the Newfoundlanders' elk. It argued acceptance and reconciliation. Lois and Richard climbed the stairs to the base of the monument where statues of enormous draped figures leaned or bent in gestures of resignation and loss. Richard felt dwarfed by the heavy stone and the monumental sculptures.

All around the base of the monument were the names of the men who had died there. Richard started at the beginning of the alphabet looking for his own name, as if finding it might be a sign. There was no Angantyr at all, but Lois called to him, and when he went to see what she had discovered, she pointed at a name carved in the granite. David Mann.

"It can't be the same one, of course, but it's a weird coincidence, isn't it?" she said.

Richard traced the indentations of the name with his finger. "Our missing soldier," he said. "Killed in action over sixty years ago. No wonder they couldn't find the body."

"Don't say things like that," Lois told him.

"Why not? You're not superstitious are you? Remember, I found him in Trier. On the postcard."

"It looked a little like him," Lois conceded. "But if one of his incarnations was as a Roman soldier, he's been around for a long time."

"That's the thing about ghosts," Richard said. "You never know where they're going to turn up."

They left the car where it was parked and walked back around to the graveyard. The people with the Jaguar and the dogs were gone, but a jogger with a scarf tied around his head, as if he had been wounded and bandaged, ran by them without glancing at them. They walked up and down the rows of the cemetery, looking for Mann's name, but they did not find it there. The graves here were carefully tended and manicured. Richard tried to recapture the sense of loss that he had felt the day before but nothing happened.

"It's not the same," he said to Lois. "There are no ghosts here. I don't know what it is, but there is nothing present."

"I know," she said. "It's too beautiful. This is a park. All the disorder is gone. The monument isn't about dead Canadians, it's in competition with the pyramids."

They left the graveyard and walked over to the trenches. Richard was amazed at how close they were to each other.

"They could have thrown stones at each other," Richard told Lois.

"You certainly wouldn't want to put your head up. Somebody would be certain to shoot it off. Just a second," she went on. "Let's try something."

She ran over to the German trench and disappeared. A moment later she called, "Richard, can you hear me?"

"Perfectly."

"I'm speaking in an ordinary voice. Can you still hear me?"

"Just as if you were in the same trench."

"It must have been awful," she said. "They had to listen to everything the other side said."

"This must be a special case," Richard said. "It couldn't have been like this in most places." The trench was lined with bricks and perfectly preserved. Richard followed it until it came to an end. A door led underground, but it was locked. There were several deep craters just beyond the trenches. One of them was named The Winnipeg Crater. Lois asked Richard to go and stand in the bottom of it. She wanted to take his picture.

Richard clambered down to the bottom. The sides were slippery from the rain, and he nearly fell. The bottom of the crater was muddy, but Richard found a dry spot and stood there while Lois snapped his picture. He heard the sound of a motorcycle roaring by, but he could not see anything from the bottom of the pit. He found a small, white stone and put it in his pocket.

"Look at this," he told Lois when he showed it to her at the top of the crater. "It's got a hole in the centre. When I was a kid we used to find these on the beach and put string through the holes and wear them around our necks. We called them lucky stones."

The sky, which had been blank and neutral before, had lowered and threatened rain. A fog had stolen in from somewhere, and the pathway seemed to lead into nothingness. On both sides of the path were warnings not to stray onto the grass among the trees because of unexploded shells. When they got up to the car, the fog was even thicker. The top of the monument vanished into the blank sky. The little Renault 5 looked like a sanctuary.

***

Lois nosed the car into the traffic on the main highway. The fog was still thick, even though it was already noon. Richard had been sure it would burn off in a couple of hours, but, if anything, it was worse than it had been. His sudden decision to go back to Strasbourg pleased her. He had originally wanted to go to Passchendaele and Béthune, but had unexpectedly announced that he had what he needed. He was afraid he would ruin everything if he visited any more battlefields. If they went straight to Amiens, they could return the car, catch the train to Paris and be home by evening.

"Well," he said as soon as Lois had made the turn. "Do you feel any more Canadian after seeing the battlefields?"

Cars loomed suddenly out of the fog, and Lois kept her eyes on the side of the road to gauge her whereabouts. The question surprised her.

"Yes," she answered. "I think I do. At any rate, the question seems more important here than it does at home. I don't think much about being a Canadian most of the time."

"All those young guys," Richard went on. "Away from home for the first time. Farmers and fishermen and bank clerks. And then they're tossed into a trench with a bunch of other guys they don't know, and all they have in common is that they're Canadian."

"And that very soon they're going to be dead."

"They didn't all die. Actually most of them lived. Can you imagine what it must have been like for them to come home after this, and find a country that wanted them to go back to doing exactly what they were doing before they went to war?"

"Is that what your novel is about?" Lois asked.

"Partly. But it's also about thinking about death. In a war you have to do a lot of that. Do you want to read it? What I've done so far?"

Lois paused. "I don't know. I don't think so. I'd sooner wait until you're finished. I hate starting things and not knowing how they're going to end. But I'll read it if you want me to."

"No. In fact, I'm a little superstitious about that. It seems like if I let anyone read it, then I won't be able to change a word. It will be fixed there in somebody else's mind, and I won't control it any more." Richard reached around and took his notebook out of his bag in the back seat. He started to write in it.

"I thought you always got sick when you tried to read or write in a car," Lois said.

"Not when it's going this slow," he answered. The fog seemed to have lifted a bit, and Lois accelerated, but they crested a hill, and when they moved into the valley, the fog was thicker again. Lois wished there were a radio in the car, but it was the cheapest model, and it didn't seem to have any luxuries. The spot where a radio would go was open, and Lois could see a couple of wires. She wondered if someone had stolen the radio, but decided that they had probably just taken it out to prevent robberies.

Something flickered at the corner of her eye, and Lois looked out her window to see a black motorcycle driving right beside her. The two figures on the motorcycle were dressed identically in black. Lois wished they'd pass. It was dangerous enough in the fog, and they might meet another car at any moment. The rear figure turned and looked at Lois, a smooth, even, woman's face framed in the black helmet. She reached out her arm, as if she were trying to touch the window, and Lois realized with a shock that the woman held a gun in her black, gloved hand. She slammed on the brakes just as the window beside her shattered. The car careened, fish-tailing down the road, and, at the moment she was sure she had lost control and they would go off the road, she saw, at an angle, a gravel side road. She accelerated suddenly, and the car steadied.

"Keep driving," Richard said in a flat monotone. "As fast as you can."

She turned to him. His face was ashen and his eyes were wide open. She sped up, and, as if to help her, the fog lightened.

"Are you all right?" she asked.

"Yes," he said. "You?"

"I'm okay."

"We've got to keep driving. Turn right as soon as you can. I think it will take them a few minutes to figure out that you turned down this side road."

"I didn't turn. It was just a fluke. The car went off the road, but there was this other road there." Lois felt light, almost happy. She was alive.

"She had a gun," Lois said. "A woman with a gun fired from the motorcycle."

"I know," Richard said. "I looked up, and there she was. I thought at first she was a woman I met at the bonfire."

"But she's not . . . ?"

"No, I don't think so. I'm not sure. I couldn't see her hair."

Another road appeared, and Lois turned right.

"We better get the police," she said.

"We better get to the police without being killed," Richard answered. "They meant business." They approached a stop sign, and arrows that indicated Arras to the right, Amiens to the left.

"Which way?" Lois asked.

"Left. It doesn't make much difference. We've just got to take a chance whatever we do."

It was chilly in the car with the open window. Every piece of glass had shattered, and the window looked as if it had been rolled down. Lois realized that she had fragments of glass in her lap.

"How could she miss?" she said. "She was only inches away."

"She waited too long. You braked and she was thrown off." They met another motorcycle, but there was only one rider, and he passed them without slowing.

"I'm scared, Richard," Lois said. "This is not fun. I think maybe we should go back to Canada. Those people wanted to kill us."

Richard didn't speak for a minute. He put his head in his hands as if he were thinking too deeply to be distracted by sight.

"I don't know," he said. "I suppose we should. But it seems like madness. Why are we involved in this? It has nothing to do with us. I'd like to talk to the inspector before we do anything."

The fog began to clear, so that Lois could see buildings by the sides of roads. She could see the lights of cars at a distance. They no longer loomed out of the whiteness right before her. She realized that she was driving fast, too fast for the conditions, and she slowed.

"No sense killing ourselves in a traffic accident and saving them the trouble," she said.

"They've lost us," Richard answered. "I think we're okay now." They were moving into the outskirts of Amiens, and Lois recognized the intersection at which they had turned towards Arras the day before.

"I don't think they're likely to try anything where there's a lot of people around," Richard went on. "I think we're okay at least until Strasbourg. Then I think the inspector is going to have to find some way to protect us."

"Let's not go back to Strasbourg. Let's go to Paris and catch an airplane. We can send for our stuff."

"We won't be any safer in Canada. If this is as big an organization as the inspector thinks, then we won't be any safer in Canada than we are here. And besides, I've got to get my novel. I'm not taking any chances on anyone sending that."

They came up the main street of the town, and Lois could see the railway station ahead. Richard motioned her to turn right into a narrow access road, and she did. A moment later, they were at the car-rental office.

"Shouldn't we go to the police first?" Lois asked.

"We don't know where the police are. This will be the fastest way of finding them."

The man at the rental agency seemed much more concerned at the damaged window and the question of insurance than he did about the police. He wanted Richard to sign things, and it was obvious that he did not believe that the window had been shot out. Something far more sinister must have happened, he implied.

The police did finally arrive and they wrote down Richard's story. They seemed to have no interest in Lois's version, though she had been the driver. After about a half-hour, they were free to go.

Richard bought tickets for Paris at the station, and discovered that the train was leaving at that very minute. They ran out to the platform, and caught the train just as it was starting to move. Lois was afraid that she would lose her step, and Richard was no help, pushing her onto the train so that she almost fell because of his help. Still, once they were settled in their seats, he seemed exultant.

"That was great," he said. "If anyone was following us, then they've missed the train, because we were certainly the last people on."

He thinks this is an adventure, Lois thought. He thinks he's playing a little boy's game of cops and robbers. "If they were following us and they missed the train, then there will be somebody waiting at the other end," she said. The other passengers seemed to be the same collection of farmers and their wives that had travelled out from Paris with them.

In Paris, they were equally lucky. They changed stations and caught the train to Strasbourg with only a couple of minutes' wait. Still, Lois was terrified during those few minutes. Everyone she saw looked suspicious. This must be what a paranoid feels all the time, she thought. This sense that everything is dangerous, that everybody is waiting for you.

The trip back was uneventful, except that a blonde girl, Swedish or Danish, Lois imagined, and dressed as a hippie, took a seat across from them. When the conductor came around, she made a slow, elaborate search of all of her pockets and her bag, then claimed that she had lost her ticket. Her accent was thick but unidentifiable. The conductor took her passport and disappeared, but Lois noticed that the girl had another passport in her bag. At Nancy, the girl left the train. When the conductor came back to look for her, she was gone, and Lois was glad. The girl had looked frightened and alone.

After Nancy, the train moved a little more slowly through the hills, and when it followed a canal into a dark tunnel, Lois knew they were almost back. It had not rained here. The low, golden sunset slanted light on the trees, so they seemed particularly rounded and full.

She did not want to leave the train when it stopped. This, she thought, will be the most dangerous time. Someone will walk up to Richard and shoot him quietly, then disappear into the crowd while I scream. She felt in no danger herself. Richard seemed certain of his invulnerability, and this made her even more worried. He will take no precautions, she thought. He, who thinks so often about death.

As Richard picked up their bags and started for the exit without even looking back to see if she was following, it struck her that things had changed substantially. When they first arrived from Canada, Richard had smothered her, trying to take care of every detail as if she were an invalid. Now, he seemed prepared to abandon her, here on the train.

Dusk had closed in just as they left the train, so that by the time they found a taxi, it was almost dark. Strasbourg seemed like home. The lights flickered on the canals, and the cathedral welcomed them back. Lois felt almost secure now. If something terrible were going to happen, it would have happened by now.

The street lights were inexplicably off when they reached the studio, and the night seemed blacker than Lois could remember in Strasbourg. Richard paid the cab driver and collected their bags. The outside gate was locked. They had been given a key for it, but she could not remember it ever being locked before. Richard fumbled in his pockets and found the key. When they entered the main door, he flicked the switch, and light flooded the hallway.

The stairway was so familiar that she found it a relief. It was still early. The others in the building were not likely to be asleep, but they climbed the stairs as quietly as they could anyway. Richard entered first, dropping the bags by the closet as went in. When he entered the main room, he jumped backwards with a start.

"Stop," he said. "Stay there. Don't come any closer. You don't want to see this."

It was too late. She had already seen. Delacroix's body lay sprawled in the armchair, a neat hole in the centre of his forehead, with a thin trickle of dried blood sliding down to his nose. His hand was open, and in it she could see a statue of a bull with three horns.

* * *

"Grendelbruch," the inspector explained as soon as Richard and Lois were settled in the car. "It's a little village in the mountains. You'll be as safe there as anywhere. And the villagers won't notice anything unusual. There are always foreigners visiting for a few days at a time. The chalet belongs to the head of the Music School, and he uses it for guests."

"What was that business with Delacroix all about?" Richard asked. "That was pretty horrible." He and Lois had spent hours with the police before anyone could get in touch with the inspector. Then they were taken to a hotel near the cathedral. Neither of them had slept until the inspector arrived after breakfast.

"It was horrible," Kessler agreed. "And for me a great loss. But do not worry, justice will be served."

"I'm less interested in justice than I am in figuring out what's going on," Richard told him. "He was your friend. You must know something."

"He was my friend," Kessler said. "And he was a great scholar. His new book on the Celts would have made him famous."

"He was working on the Druids, if I remember what he told me in Iceland."

"No, that's only part of the question. You know that Mont Ste. Odile was originally a hill fort, a sort of early walled town from about 1500 B.C.? It is one of the great Celtic sites, though not so well-known as Dürnberg in Austria, or Stonehenge, of course. He was trying to establish a direct historical line between those early Celts and the people who have always lived in this area."

"So, why was he murdered?" Lois asked. She was sitting in the back seat of the small car because Richard did not fit.

"It's complex, and I don't know the answer yet. But I will know soon. In his investigations he came upon the Hallstatt group."

"The people who hold bonfires."

"Yes. A couple of them were ex-students of Heidegger, and so that was another connection. Not students at the university, but outside the university. They, too, were interested in old Celtic sites. It was their plan to investigate and discover these sites and to find enough money to restore them. That was difficult, of course, because many of the sites have other important buildings on them. Especially churches. And churches do not wish to support what they think of as heathen ideas."

"That's what the fellow at the bonfire told me. Helmut."

"You think this group killed him?" Lois asked. "Is that what the three-horned bull was all about?"

"The three-horned bull is a great symbol of power in ancient Celtic mythology. But that might be only a red herring to send us on the wrong path. The Hallstatt group supported Delacroix. They provided money for his research when the university would not. They would sooner have him alive than dead. It is a great pity, a great waste."

"What about that bonfire I was at? It didn't seem much like the meeting of a charitable trust to decide on worthy scholarly projects."

"The Hallstatt group is also something like a religion of nature. They do not worship gods, and they have no creed. But they believe that certain places, because of their history, have special power, and that ceremonies held at those places can have meaning for those whose ancestors have died there."

Richard thought about the graves at Beaumont-Hamel. "I think I know what they mean," he said.

"It is a common experience to find such places. The figure of a ghost is such an idea."

"He had a tiny round hole in his head," Lois said. "He was terribly dead. It's the most horrible thing I've ever seen. What does his death have to do with us or the body we saw?" Richard reached his arm over the seat, and she took his hand.

"That is the question we have to answer. You have spoken with your countryman, Ferguson?"

"Yes," Lois said. "He said something about an arms deal and the Middle East. Iraq or Libya. It involved a couple of Canadian accountants. What were their names? Hutcheon and somebody?"

"Hutcheon and Fawcett," Kessler replied.

"Yes. And Mann, the guy whose body we found, was some sort of courier."

"When did you find this out?" Richard asked. "He didn't tell me anything about it. He just wanted us to go back to Canada."

"At the show. I talked to him while you were talking with Alexandra."

"Why didn't he tell me?"

"He tried to when he came to the studio. You wouldn't let him. You didn't give him much time, if you remember."

"Mann is the connection," Kessler went on. "He became connected with the Hallstatt group either through the girl or through her uncle. The uncle is wealthy. He owns a large trucking firm that does business all over Europe. He has been suspected of delivering arms, but nothing has come of the investigations."

"She met him at the group," Richard said. "She told me that was where she had first encountered him. Somebody else brought him, not her uncle."

"So, who killed Delacroix?" Lois asked.

"That I don't know," Kessler answered. "Maybe the people who were supposed to get the arms but have not yet received them. Maybe someone who does not want them to receive any arms. Maybe the Hallstatt group after all. Nothing is certain yet."

"But why in our studio?" Richard asked. "What was Delacroix doing there?"

"That's not where he was murdered," Kessler said. "He was killed in his car. He was delivered to you as a message."

They passed through a town where gargoyles on a cathedral peered down on them. For some time, nobody spoke. Soon the road climbed abruptly and followed a shallow, fast-flowing stream. The car nearly stopped at a bridge, then turned off into a village of about thirty houses. The inspector drove up a short driveway into what must once have been a barn attached to a house.

"Here we are," he said. "I think there is plenty of food for the time being. And if the nights are chilly, there is plenty of wood."

He waved his arm to indicate a huge supply of firewood, a pile of about ten cords, Richard calculated. They went into the chalet, which was large and well-equipped. A note on the wall listed the fifteen things a courteous guest would do, including bringing in as much wood from the pile as you had used, and replacing candles.

"Ferguson will be out to see you in a couple of days," Kessler said. "He will bring more food and will explain what is going on. We expect something will happen in a couple of days, a week at the latest, that will either resolve this problem or prove it unresolveable. Then you can go back to Canada."

"Wouldn't it have been easier just to drive us to Frankfurt and put us on an airplane?" Lois asked.

"Yes," Kessler answered. "A week ago it would have been. But today it would be immensely more difficult."

"Can't you please tell us a few more details?" Lois asked him. "Are we being set up as bait for some sort of trap?"

"No," Kessler told her. "But Richard's presence here puts a bit of pressure on certain people to act sooner than they might like."

"The accountants? Hutcheon and Fawcett?" Richard asked.

"And others."

"Because I went to the bonfire? Is that it?" He felt the situation was slipping beyond his grasp, that more was going to be said than he wanted to hear.

"Yes," the inspector answered. "You are now the wild card in the deck. What you know or don't know is an important issue."

"Well, I don't know much," Richard told him. "In fact I don't know anything at all."

"You know more than you realize, if you could put it together. But in the short run it's probably safest if you don't."

"Is there a phone?" Richard asked. "Can we get in touch with you?"

"There is a phone," Kessler said. "But use it only if you have to. You will not be able to get in touch with me. You can call Ferguson if there is an emergency. My advice is not to call unless it is absolutely necessary. The whole point of hiding you is to see that you stay hidden."

"Are we supposed to stay inside the chalet?" Lois asked.

"Come." Kessler led them into a large garden in the back. It opened onto a field where wild flowers still bloomed. Beyond, a pasture stretched upwards towards the top of the mountain. "You may walk in the garden, but I advise you not to walk into the village. Somebody sees you and tells somebody else, and before you know it you are discovered. And remember my friend Delacroix. These people are playing for keeps."

For two days they did not leave the chalet except to walk out into the garden. Lois found an old-fashioned garden swing, and she sat out in it, looking through the old French magazines she found in the cottage. Richard had a copy of his novel, the one that he had kept at home, but it was missing several pages where the xerox machine had failed, and his notes in the margins were so faint as to be illegible.

He tried to write, using a pencil, but it seemed hopeless. Every time he tried to describe the battlefields, he saw instead the grave-yards they had visited, and his writing felt flat and dead. At the same time, he could not get Alexandra out of his mind. He wanted desperately to see her, but he also feared seeing her. He wondered whether she were in any danger.

Later, on the third day, Lois went out into the garden behind the chalet with her sketch pad. Richard watched her, and waited until she had settled herself on the arm of a wooden chair and was drawing. Then he opened his wallet and took out the card that Alexandra's uncle had given him. He dialled the number on the card, but hung up before the phone had even rung. He walked to the window and saw Lois in exactly the same position. He went back to the phone and dialled again. A woman answered in German, and he gave her Alexandra's name.

There was no answer for a long time, but finally Alexandra came on the phone. Her voice sounded strained and distant.

"Who is this?" she asked.

"Richard."

There was a long pause. "Where are you? Are you okay?"

"I'm fine," he said. "I'm hidden away somewhere in the mountains by a beautiful stream. I'll be back in about a week. Can you meet me then?"

"No," she answered. "It is impossible. But I will phone you at your office. In one week. At four o'clock."

"I may not be there," he cautioned. "I'm probably going back to Canada pretty soon."

Alexandra answered him in German, something he did not understand at all, and then she hung up. The click seemed final. For the rest of the day he hovered near the telephone, knowing it would not ring, but hoping it might anyway.

Lois made a drawing of the elk at Beaumont-Hamel. Richard found it eerie and powerful, but she said it was no good, and she destroyed it. Richard had never seen her destroy a drawing before, and he was surprised. Later, she refused to show him the drawings she was working on, but she left her portfolio open when she went out to the swing, and Richard saw that she had drawn three pregnant women standing together in a street. He guessed from the buildings that it was in Spain.

The fourth day, Richard could not bear being locked up any more. He said that he was going for a walk down to the bridge and back. It was mid-afternoon. The day was sunny, but the air was cool. Lois didn't think it was a good idea, but when he left she did not try to stop him. Richard was glad. During the trip to Vimy Ridge, things had been as they used to be. Now, together in the chalet, the tension had started to build again.

Richard followed the clear, bright, stream as far as the bridge. The houses he passed seemed empty, and he saw no one on the street. He turned and headed back. The path was uphill, heavier going than before, and Richard started to jog lightly. He hadn't run for a couple of weeks, and he could feel the strain. He sensed rather than heard the car behind him, and moved over to the side of the road. A dark-blue Volvo station wagon pulled up beside him, and Richard saw with a start that the driver was Alexandra. She wore a brown sweater, and even from outside the car, he could see that she wore no make-up.

He opened the door and slid into the seat beside her. He reached for her and she slid wordlessly into his arms and kissed him. As she drew back she mouthed the word "careful," and at the same moment he felt something cold touch the back of his neck.

"Don't turn around," a voice said, but it was too late. Richard had already turned and found himself staring at a heavy, square pistol.

Behind it was the face of the body Lois had discovered on the Druid shrine.

"Mann," he said. "So you aren't dead after all?"

"Don't talk," the voice said. "Sit absolutely still, and don't say a word."

"Did you know about this all along?" Richard asked Alexandra. She didn't answer, but he could see that she was weeping. Richard felt both anger and deep fear. He had been a fool all along, and now death could reach over and touch him behind the ear. He thought of his novel, forever unfinished. The thought struck him as insane. The situation he was in seemed impossible.

"Don't speak," the voice said again. "I am very serious about this. If you wish to postpone your death, you will do exactly as I say."

Richard did not speak again. Alexandra drove at break-neck speed down the narrow mountain road, until the man in the back told her to slow down. His voice had a crisp ring of anger to it. She drove slowly and deliberately after that, and he did not speak again.

Richard did not recognize anything on the way. He had not even noticed the chalet in Grendelbruch as they passed it. Lois would already be worrying. He hoped she would phone Ferguson right away, rather than wait for him to come back, but he was certain she would not phone until he had been gone for several hours. They made a sharp turn at a lookout point, where he could see far out over a deep valley. They passed a garage with ancient, rusting equipment in front of the door, and a farm with a sign nailed to one of the buildings, advertising shoes. He found himself memorizing details, as if, like Hansel and Gretel, he might use this information to find his way home.

Richard looked at Alexandra. The brown sweater was old and worn. It did not look like anything she had worn before. Her jeans were faded, and one of the knees was torn. Her face was puffy, as if she had been crying, and he noticed for the first time a red welt on her neck.

"Just ahead," the voice behind them said, and Alexandra slowed the car. A hand reached from the back seat into the front and indicated a narrow dirt trail that led into impenetrable undergrowth. Alexandra swung the Volvo onto the trail, and branches swept over the window, blocking all sight for a moment. After that, it was clearer. The trail met another trail and widened. After a few moments it opened into a bright clearing, and Richard saw that they had arrived at the ruins of an old castle.

It was not a large castle. One tower still stood, but most of the rest of the building had crumbled into ruins. It was in the wrong place for a castle, at the bottom of a valley, surrounded on all sides by hills. Lumber was piled near it, as if someone were intent on restoring it. They left the car, Richard and Alexandra in the lead, and Mann following a short distance behind them. As they rounded the castle, Richard noticed a red building just off to the left, and he realized where they were. This was the castle they had seen from the lookout on the Pagan Wall, just before they had discovered the body. Or rather, not discovered the body.

When they had completely rounded the ruins, they came on a door in the stone wall. Mann took a key from his pocket and opened the door. For a moment he was off-guard, and Richard had the impulse to leap on him and fight him for the gun. The instant passed, however, before Richard could make any decision, and Mann waved him into the passageway.

They went down a flight of stone stairs into a narrow hallway. At the end of the hallway was a small room, and Mann motioned Richard into it. Richard entered, and Mann closed the door behind him. It was a heavy wooden door with a barred window in it, perhaps six inches square. There was also a barred window on the other side of the room. It opened into a well.

"Make yourself comfortable," Mann said. "This will be your home for a while." Robert could hear the echo of Mann's steps as he ascended the stairs.

The room was tiny, a couple of metres square, and the only light came from the outside window. It did not look as if it had been used for several hundred years. Richard tested the window, and it seemed to give a little. He thought he might be able to work it free, but when he craned his neck to see into the well, he could make out another barred opening about five metres higher. To escape from here would only extend his prison.

He waited for what seemed a long time. A couple of times he heard noises in the hallway, but when he shouted, there was no answer. It was dark and starting to get cold when at last the door opened and Mann appeared. He set down an open bottle of wine and a bag in which Richard supposed there was food. He turned to go without speaking but Richard got to his feet.

"What's this all about?" he asked. "Why are you holding me here?"

"Because you don't know when to leave well enough alone," Mann said quietly. "Because you don't know what's good for you."

"Look, I don't know what any of this is about," Richard told him.

"I sincerely hope not," Mann said. "But it probably won't matter one way or the other."

"You were very convincingly dead."

"Yes. And I wish I could have stayed that way. But you had to connect yourself with Alexandra. And that makes things dangerous for all of us."

"She hasn't told me anything."

"No. That's because she doesn't know anything. But people who know some things will make connections."

"What are you going to do?"

"Arrange an accident, probably. The Canadian professor fleeing with his lover falls off a cliff in Switzerland. It happens all the time."

"That's not funny."

"No. This is not a funny business. I should kill you right now, but our compatriots are nervous men. And with any luck, some-body else will kill you first." Mann turned to leave the room, and Richard moved to stop him. In a second the pistol appeared in Mann's hand.

"Don't die any sooner than you have to," Mann said, as he left the room. "I'm not an accountant. I don't see any point in leaving you alive."

***

Lois took out her sketch pad and started a sketch of the monument at Vimy. Within a few strokes, she knew that it was

279

not going to work. The lines were without energy. She couldn't think of anything that could focus the drawing. She sketched for a moment, turning the figures at the base of the monument into gargoyles, but it didn't help.

A couple of birds squabbled just outside the window, and Lois thought about the old bird woman in Paris. She could picture her exactly, but she was not moved to draw her again. Then she remembered the two little girls in Seville and their dead sparrow. They had tendered it to Richard as if it were an offering. She started to sketch, and felt a charge come over her that she hadn't felt since the show. She sketched the girls with a few strokes, the larger girl with her hands aloft holding the dead sparrow, the younger one holding back, eyes wide with wonder. Where in Seville there had been tables with diners Lois sketched a forest thick with heavy trees and prehistoric ferns. She made Richard much larger in proportion to the girls, so that he looked like a king or a god. She sketched a crown on his head and on an impulse seated him on a throne whose feet were carved in the form of a three-horned bull.

Yes, Richard will like this, she thought. There is nothing diabolic here. This is an illustration for a children's book. She realized at the same time that this was not true. Richard looked threatening and powerful. The little girls were using the bird to save themselves. She glanced at her watch. Richard had been gone for over an hour. She wasn't worried. He often jogged that long, and if he were walking, he might take even more time.

After another hour, she began to feel concerned. She walked out to the street, but she could not see him. He had said that he was going to the bridge, so she walked toward the centre of the town. It was nearly a half-hour before she reached the bridge, and she guessed that Richard must have decided at the last moment to go the other way. He would be back by now and worried about her. She ran for a short ways and then walked and ran again. When she got back to the chalet, she called his name, but he did not answer. She searched from room to room through the whole house, as if he might be hiding on her, but he was nowhere.

When she realized that he was not there, she had a moment of near panic. She sat in a chair and thought, if I phone Robert, something terrible will have happened, but if I just sit here for a few minutes, Richard will return. She imagined him slumped in a chair like Delacroix, a neat hole in his forehead. She couldn't bear to think about it.

After a few minutes she got up and went to the telephone. She dialed Robert's number, but the telephone rang several times and there was no answer. She hung up and immediately dialed again. She let the phone ring for a full minute, and at last Robert answered.

"Richard's gone," she said as calmly as she could. "He went out for a walk over two hours ago, and he hasn't come back."

"What do you think has happened?"

"I think somebody has found him. I think he's probably dead by now."

"Do you think he might have phoned the girl, Alexandra, and got her to come and pick him up?"

Lois had not considered this possibility, and it made her angry to consider it now.

"I don't know," she said. "I doubt it. Anyway, I can't stay here any more."

"Stay with the old woman next door. She won't mind. I can't get you right now. Something important is going to happen in a little while and I have to meet with the inspector."

"I'm not going to stay. I'm going to start walking back to Strasbourg. I don't want to be trapped in a house. If something horrible is going to happen to me, I want it to happen outside."

"Don't. That would be stupid."

"Then I'll be stupid. Good-bye"

"No. Wait. I'll pick you up in an hour at the chalet."

"At the bridge."

"Please stay in the chalet."

"No. I'll be at the bridge."

Lois left the chalet, because it seemed full of danger, and she turned away from it. She walked towards the centre of the town and the bridge. She saw no one, but imagined that behind the curtains the villagers were watching her. The air was absolutely still, and she realized that there was no sound, not even the trill of a distant bird.

When she reached the bridge, she stopped and looked down at the clear, bright water below. The stream was shallow, no deeper than a few inches, but it ran fast. If Richard were dead, she would have to identify him. She tried to conjure a vision of him dead, but she could only come up with a mental picture of Delacroix. "Don't let him be dead," she whispered to herself. "Don't let him be dead."

A car rumbled around the corner and over the bridge. She did not turn to look at it until it had passed, a bright orange car that she thought might be a Volkswagen. She had not looked at the time when she had started walking, so she did not know how long she had been waiting. In the next few minutes several cars came by, but no one paid any attention to her. Finally she decided she would not wait any longer. She started walking along the side of the road.

She had not walked far before she met the low, grey Mercedes she identified as the inspector's car. It stopped beside her, and she got into the back seat silently. The inspector was driving, and Robert was seated beside him.

"Now you are going to have to do everything we tell you," Robert said. "We are going to arrest some dangerous people, and you are going to have to keep out of the way. Do you understand?"

Lois nodded. "Yes."

"We are going to Mont Ste. Odile. You are going to stay at the main office with the commissionaire until we are through. It will take us several hours."

"Okay," she said. "I'll do exactly as I am told." She felt lighter, as if whatever had forced her out of the chalet had left her.

Robert relaxed at her acquiescence. He had seemed tense and stern, but now he smiled. The inspector was solicitous. He asked her how she was feeling, and she told him she was worried.

"Tell us exactly what happened with Richard," he said. "Are there any details you didn't mention to Mr. Ferguson?"

"No," Lois said. "He simply said he was going for a walk to the bridge and back. I started a drawing and I guess I lost track of time. When I checked, it seemed he had been gone a long time. Finally, I phoned."

"Did you see anything, any vehicles, any people you didn't recognize, anything out of the ordinary?"

"No. I didn't look out the window. I was drawing, and that's all I was thinking about."

"The fact that he's gone does not mean that he's dead," Robert said. "Did you look around to see if he left you any messages? He might have planned this on his own."

"No," Lois said. "I never thought of that."

"Or even if somebody has taken him, it does not mean that he is in great danger," the inspector added. "He may be held as a hostage, or simply to keep him out of the way for a while. For professionals, murder is always a last resort. It is messy, and it makes too many complications. It keeps the books open on a case for too long." By the time the car climbed up the long, winding road to Mont Ste. Odile, they had convinced Lois that Richard was probably still alive. Now she was apprehensive. She wondered where he might be.

"This arrest you are going to make," she said. "Might Richard be there? Do you think they might have brought him here?"

"No," Robert said. "This is not a place where anybody could be hidden."

"We are going to attend a ceremony," the inspector said. "You remember the Hallstatt group?"

"Yes."

"They are holding a special ceremony this evening at the Druid altar. We think that a certain amount of illegal money is going to change hands during the ceremony, and we intend to intercept it."

"The shrine? The place where we found the body?"

"Yes."

"Is this a religious ceremony? The Druid thing? Are they mixed up in this whole arms-sales plot?"

"We think so. At least some of them are. But this is a big operation, and we are only in on one part of it."

"We are not alone," Robert reassured Lois. "There are a great many police officers from Interpol involved. The woods around here are full of police."

They pulled up past the lower parking lot to a smaller lot right near the gate. There were quite a few cars there, but the inspector found a space in the middle of the lot. They got out and walked through the main gate. Lois was surprised to see that there was almost no one there. A couple of people came out of a building and headed towards the parking lot.

The inspector and Robert led her towards the cafeteria where she had waited the first time she was here, when she had discovered the body. The same commissionaire greeted her.

"Madame," he said in heavily accented English, "welcome. I hear we have the same birthday."

"You will stay here until we come back," Robert told Lois. "Don't even leave the building."

"Yes," Lois nodded. The two men left without saying anything else. The commissionaire offered Lois a glass of wine. She accepted, and when he returned with the glass, she asked him, "Is it dangerous?"

"Ah," he said, "trés, trés dangereux . . ."

***

Richard prowled around the narrow cell. At first he had been worried that Lois would not know where he was, that she would be anxious and worried. Now it struck him that she, too, might have been captured. He had been counting on her phoning Ferguson and getting the police, but if she were also captured, then no one would be looking for either of them.

He heard noises in the hallway again, but no one came when he called. After a few minutes, there was silence. He felt a pain in his chest, and his breathing was constricted. He rattled the window, and again it seemed loose. He started to work at it, shaking it back and forth. At first it seemed as if it would go only so far and no farther, but it gave suddenly, and came free in his hands. He reached his arm through the opening and found the latch, but he could not get it free. He realized that he could not get through the opening, and the broken bars were only evidence of his attempt.

In despair, he kicked the door several times, but it was solid. He gave up then, and settled into a corner of the cell. He tried to contemplate his own death. He would be shot. There would be one moment of fierce pain, and then nothing. He could imagine the pain, but he couldn't imagine his not being there. He remembered a text he had read somewhere that described death as "personal annihilation." The phrase had chilled him, but now, when it seemed certain he would die, it meant nothing to him.

When he strained to hear in the silence, he imagined he could hear rats moving around, and he thought of the rat that Lois had seen in Lisbon. Then he imagined he heard his name spoken in a low whisper. He stood absolutely motionless and listened. A moment later he heard it again.

"Alexandra?" he whispered back into the silence.

"Shhh." The voice seemed to come from the well, and he moved to the other window.

"Are you there?"

"Be quiet. I will open the door in a minute. Then you must follow me in absolute silence."

"All right," he answered, and moved to the door. He stood there for a long time. At last, he heard the latch lift, and the door creaked gently open. A hand reached out for his, and led him down the hallway, then up the stairs and outside. Moonlight made it much brighter than it had been in the cell. Alexandra led him around the corner of the castle and along a path that led into the forest. After a few moments they came to a clearing, where a large motorcycle was parked.

"Can you drive it?" she asked.

"No. Or maybe I could in daylight."

She climbed onto the motorcycle. "Get on," she said. "I can drive it."

"Wait a minute," he said. "What's going on?"

"If you don't get on we will both be dead in a few moments," she said. Richard got on the motorcycle behind her, and she started it with a roar. It was soon evident that she was no better at driving it than he would have been. The big machine skidded, and she almost lost control just as they started, but it righted itself, and in a few minutes they emerged from the forest onto the asphalt road. Alexandra continued up the sharp hill, and when they slowed to turn abruptly left, Richard realized that they were at the peak of the hill at Mont Ste. Odile.

"Stop," he said, indicating that she should pull into the parking lot.

"No," she answered. "It is too dangerous."

"Yes, stop," he said, and she pulled off the road and stopped the motorcycle as far from any of the parked cars as she could.

"Where's Lois?" he asked her.

"I don't know. I haven't seen her."

"Why did you help them capture me?"

"I had no choice. I would have been dead if I hadn't. I will be dead if they catch me now."

"Mann is alive."

"Yes. I hate him." She spat out the words in anger.

"What is going on?"

"I don't know. The group is meeting tonight at the Druid shrine. Something big is going to happen there. Mann made me come with him, but I slipped away when the speeches started, and I got you. He does not yet know that I am gone. Now we must go away."

"Where to?"

"Anywhere. Switzerland. We can hide for a few months and then it will all be over." She saw his hesitation and went on, "There will be no difficulty. I have money."

"I can't," he told her. "I have to find Lois."

"Do you love her?" Alexandra asked.

"I don't know," Richard said. "I think so. I have to know that she is safe."

"I could love you," Alexandra said. "If you give me the chance I could really love you. If you don't love her, then come with me."

He could see her perfect face in the moonlight. She was as beautiful as anyone he had ever seen, and yet as they spoke she seemed increasingly distant. He knew it would be impossible to go with her. Everything in his life made it impossible.

"I can't," he said. "It's too much pain. I can't go through that pain. And you don't know me. In a little while you would not want me any more."

"I am capable of great love," she told him. "If you choose not to come with me, you will regret it all your life."

Richard was certain that she was right, but he couldn't go with her.

"I have to find Lois," he said.

"You'll find her at the Druid altar," Alexandra said. "If they have not found her already. But if you go there, they will kill you."

"What is she doing there?" Richard asked, amazed.

"I don't know. But I saw her there before I left. Are you going to come with me?"

Richard did not hesitate. "No," he said, "I'm going to find Lois." He stepped away from the motorcycle. Alexandra started it with a roar.

"Good-bye," she said. Her words were swallowed in the sound of the engine.

"Good-bye," Richard answered. He watched as she swung the motorcycle back the way they had come and disappeared around a corner.

* * *

"Why are there so many cars in the parking lot?" Lois asked the commissionaire in halting French. She remembered how easy it had been to speak to him that other time, and she realized that she had almost given up trying to speak French lately.

A meeting, he explained, and she found she could still understand him. The Hallstatt group met at the Druid shrine twice a year, in the spring and the fall. A strange group, he told her, but they did good work. They contributed to the up-keep of the place. They published books of history, they encouraged scholars. But they did odd things too. Strange ceremonies, it was rumoured.

Lois was suddenly certain that Richard would be at the ceremony. She pictured him there, seated beside Alexandra. There would be a fire, and speeches would be made. She asked the commissionaire whether the inspector and Monsieur Ferguson would be at the ceremony, but he grew uncommunicative. He thought not. He thought that they were engaged in something completely different.

The commissionaire filled up her wine glass once more, and Lois found herself feeling a little giddy. The wine seemed powerful. The commissionaire was convinced that her French was fluent enough for him to tell her his life story, and he began to speak much faster. He had seven children, three girls and four boys. The language came in a blur now. The girls were born first, she thought he said, and they had all married and given him grandchildren. But none of his sons was married, and it was a great worry to him. He did not want his line to die out.

Lois excused herself. She had to go to the toilet. The commissionaire pointed the way and went to fill up their glasses again. When Lois returned, she saw that his back was to her and he was pouring wine. Just to her right was a door that led outside. Lois opened the door as quietly as she could, and stepped out into the near darkness. She could see a full moon already high in the sky in the gathering dusk, and she was pleased. It would be a bright night. She was still giddy from the wine. I will go to that ceremony, she thought, and no one will see me.

She hurried so the commissionaire would not find her and bring her back. She knew that the path along the Pagan Wall would be to her left just as she left the main gate, and she ran toward it, keeping in the shadows close to the buildings. Just as she started down the path, she noticed that it branched in three directions. One was marked with a yellow circle, the others with a red triangle and a blue square. She was trying to decide which to take when two men and a woman passed by her and followed the highest pathway, the one marked with the yellow circle. She waited a moment until they moved around a corner and out of sight, then she followed them.

As soon as she rounded the corner she saw a bright torch in the middle distance. When she got to it, she discovered that it was a gas torch in a bamboo holder that had been stuck into the ground. She could see another torch a little further on, though it disappeared for just a second as the others passed it. She hurried. She didn't want to get too close to them, but she thought that it might be safer. If anything happened, they could hear her.

The trail wound around the top of the hill, sometimes dropping slightly, but then climbing again. She stopped when she realized that the people in front of her had paused to rest just at the lookout where she and Richard had seen the castle. She was almost on top of them before she saw them, and she stepped off the trail into the shadow of a tree. It was completely dark now, and the moonlight did not make it as bright as she had hoped. She noticed that the woman was older than she had first thought. Her hair was silver in the light of the torch.

The effects of the wine had worn off, and Lois began to wonder whether she shouldn't have stayed with the commissionaire. Robert and the inspector would be angry if they found out. She looked back into the darkness, but it seemed more dangerous to return than to go on.

It was not a long way to the Druid shrine, she remembered, and it was downhill all the way. The others started, and Lois followed as close behind them as she dared. Once, she kicked a rock that tumbled down the slope making a great deal of noise, but the group didn't notice, and after pausing a few seconds, Lois continued.

Soon they arrived at the opening, where the Druid altar was located. Lois could hear the hum of voices before she could see anything. Then there were many torches and a large gathering. A little below the altar and in the clearing someone had set up metal folding chairs. In the opening to a path that led down and away from the altar, she could see the tractor and trailer that must have been used to bring the chairs. She hesitated for a second when the others walked out into the light of the torches, but when no one greeted them, she followed as if she were part of the same group, only a little slower. For a few minutes, she stood close to them, which they did not seem to notice. Then she moved to the far side of the seating area, and took a seat near an elderly couple.

She couldn't see Richard anywhere, and the fear that he was dead came back with a sudden chill. It was madness to have come here, but it was impossible now to go back. Robert and the inspector were going to make an arrest right here. They were probably watching from somewhere in the darkness. She felt her chest tighten so she could hardly breathe, and realized she had been holding her breath. She exhaled deliberately and looked around to see whether she had been noticed.

Many people were walking around, drinking beer and chatting with each other, but there seemed to be just as many either standing or sitting by themselves. She guessed that there might be sixty or seventy people there, and it seemed that they were unlikely to notice her.

Lois looked around carefully to see if she recognized anyone. She saw a tall, blond man and woman standing at the front right beside the altar, and she wondered whether they might be the couple from the motorcycle, but it was too far away to identify them, and she didn't dare go any closer. A heavy-set, grey-haired man seated by himself near the front might have been the girl's uncle, but again, it was impossible to be sure. There was no sign of Richard. She thought again of Robert and the inspector. She hoped they would turn up soon.

A few minutes later Alexandra appeared, her hand in the hand of a medium-sized man who moved with a cat's grace. They stopped for a minute to talk to the blond couple, and Lois realized that they must have come from the path below, must have walked right past her.

Lois watched them intently. After a few moments, the tall, blond man walked into the edge of the darkness, and brought back two small owlish-looking men with round glasses. He introduced them to Alexandra and the other couple, and they all shook hands. They spoke for a few of minutes, and one of the owlish men passed a leather bag to the man who was with Alexandra. This is it, Lois thought. This is the transfer of the money. She looked around for police to intercept them, but there was no one.

The man lifted the leather bag as if he were weighing it, then turned and peered out into the darkness at Lois. His face was clearly outlined by the glow from a torch. It was the face of the man whose body she had discovered on that very shrine, and Lois held her breath in a moment of rising panic.

After just a second he turned away and led Alexandra into the darkness at the edge of the clearing. Lois could see them, shadows moving in her direction, and she realized that they were not holding hands. The man had Alexandra's wrist tightly in his grasp. They paused a few metres away from Lois, and she could hear the sound of angry whispering. Then she heard a loud slap and the girl's sharp intake of breath. Alexandra ran past Lois, so near that Lois nearly put out an arm to stop her. Nobody else seemed to have noticed. Then a man at the front shouted directions. Everyone took a seat, and a tiny man appeared, standing on the altar above. He began to talk in a slow-paced, hypnotic voice.

***

Richard forced himself to walk slowly along the trail that followed the Pagan Wall. He stopped often to listen for any sound that might indicate someone else was there, but he heard only silence. Whenever he came to a torch, he circled just outside the range of its light, moving carefully so that he did not make noise.

At the lookout point, he thought he saw two figures outlined in a torch's light. He moved towards them, but they melted into the shadows before he got near, and he could not be sure he had seen anything. Still, he moved even more carefully. Where there were openings the full moon made it bright, but under the shadows of the trees was complete darkness.

Richard rounded a corner in the trail at a spot where the right side of the trail was a sheer cliff and the left dropped off into darkness. He had no choice but to walk through the light of a torch, and he did so as rapidly as he could. Beyond, he could hear voices and see the flicker of firelight. He searched for a trail that would lead from the main path, and found one that led to a mass of fallen rocks. A little farther on, he went down what seemed to be steps carved into the rock. The land became flatter, and the path widened into a broad trail that met another that continued back upwards, towards the lights. Below him in the distance he could hear the roar of a motorcycle.

Ahead, the end of the path was blocked by what proved to be a tractor and trailer. Beyond that was the gathering. Richard moved off the path into the trees and circled to the right, away from the tractor. He climbed a slope until he found a position from which he could watch. A crowd of people sat on metal folding chairs in an area lit by torches. Their gaze was concentrated on a man who stood on the Druid altar and spoke to the group first in French and then in German. He was a large man, but he spoke in a soft resonant voice, quite unlike the high sing-song of the little man Richard had heard at the bonfire. It looked much like the outdoor theatre he had attended years ago at the university.

The man ended to the applause of the crowd. People got up and began to move around. Someone was handing out bottles of beer, and a couple of men unfolded a table and set it up just to the side of the seats. A woman brought up a picnic basket and began to lay out sandwiches on paper plates. Richard tried to make out faces, but it was difficult in the flickering glare of the torches. Helmut and Lise were easy to make out, standing near the altar with two slight men with glasses, but Richard could not identify anyone else.

Alexandra had said that Lois was here, and Richard scanned the group for her. Finally, a heavy-set man and woman stood up in the far corner of the seating area and left behind a figure that could only be Lois. She, too, stood up, and Richard recognized her immediately. Instead of joining the others near the food, she stepped back into the semi-darkness at the other side of the gathering. A man walked up to her and offered her a bottle of beer. She took it with a nod, and he moved on.

Richard felt safe where he was, but had to get to Lois. If he could circle around and call her into the darkness, they might make their way down to one of the little villages that circled the hill. He could not imagine how she had got here. She seemed under no constraint, free to move around as she pleased.

Richard moved back the way he had come, in the direction of the tractor. He walked with immense care, making no sound. He could feel his heart beating, but the pain in his chest was gone. Three men passed just in front of him down the path behind the tractor, and he stood absolutely still until he could hear them no more. Then he crossed the path and made his way towards the edge of the seating. Many of the people had gone back to their seats, as if the intermission were over and another act due to begin. Lois had taken her seat once more, beside the heavy-set couple. She was within whispering distance of Richard, no more than a couple of metres away, but he didn't dare say anything for fear of attracting the attention of the other couple.

Richard felt sudden pain, and he dropped to his knees. He cried out. He was certain of that. His head throbbed and felt as if it would split open. The pain was unendurable. He felt himself picked up and dragged along. He wanted to protest, but he couldn't formulate words. After a moment he was hauled to his feet and shoved along the path. He tried to protest but a voice told him to shut up or he would die immediately. He recognized the flat Canadian vowels. Mann.

"Where is Alexandra?" the voice asked.

"I don't know. Gone. Italy or Greece. Someplace far away."

"You're a fool," Mann said. "Neither of you would have got away, but you're a fool not to have tried." Richard's head throbbed. The side of his face felt wet and sticky, and when he licked his lips he recognized the salt taste of blood. He tried to make out Mann's face in the moonlight, but his vision was blurred, and he saw only several shadowy forms.

"A slight change in plans," Mann said, and he signalled with a nod of his head. Richard felt himself seized from behind. A large hand held a wet cloth over his face. He recognized the sickening smell immediately. Chloroform. His head began to spin, and he fell into a great darkness. The last thing he remembered was that he was being stuffed into a sack, and he had a vision of a clock whose hands were spinning backwards.

* * *

Lois had begun to wonder how she was going to get away from the ceremony. Richard was not there, and it seemed unlikely that he would arrive now. If the inspector intended to arrest anyone, it was probably too late.

She didn't feel in much danger. For all the drama of the night-time torches, the people at the gathering seemed particularly ordinary. There were several old women there, though they must have been in good shape to have made the walk down the path from Mont Ste. Odile. In fact, most of the people here were middle-aged.

She had missed her chance to leave at the intermission. She could probably have just walked back to the cafeteria, apologized to the commissionaire, and waited for the inspector and Robert. Now she would have to sit through another series of speeches. She imagined that when it was over everybody would leave at once. She could just stay in the middle of the crowd and probably no one would notice her.

The woman who was sitting near her said something to Lois in French. Lois missed what she said, and answered, "Pardon," accenting it first as English, then as French.

"The pageant," the woman repeated in a flawless British voice. "In a moment the actors will be here. This is the most interesting part of the ceremony."

"Do you belong to the Hallstatt group?" Lois asked her.

"Oh, no," the woman answered. "We're just visiting. I teach for the University of Syracuse. We have a special program in Strasbourg. Some of us come out each year for the ceremony." The man beside her said something and she turned to listen to him.

Good, Lois thought. Then I am not out of the ordinary. Nobody will notice me here.

Just before the second half began, Lois imagined she heard a cry. She looked around and saw nothing but the darkness. No one else seemed to have noticed, and she thought it was probably an animal, or more likely, nothing at all. My nerves. Richard's absence.

She was called to attention by the sound of a gong. A figure appeared on the altar, dressed in a close-fitting helmet and carrying a shield. He wore a sword harness and skirt, and carried a long, flat sword. Other than that, he appeared to be naked. His body gleamed in the torchlight, as if he had just been oiled. The shield was large and decorated with three birds, one perched, one rising and one in flight. He held the shield in front of him and struck it three times with the sword. Lois watched in fascination.

As soon as the last reverberation of the shield died away, another figure appeared from the left and took his place to the side of the altar. He carried on a staff above him the figure of a sheep-horned snake. The snake's body dangled over his arm and onto the ground. The eyes of the snake he held aloft gleamed in the light of the torches. The man was dressed in leather armour, but his bare arms were oiled and gleaming.

As soon as he had taken his place, three women dressed in shapeless black shifts entered from the right and took their place beside the altar. They looked identical. Each had black hair, and Lois guessed that their faces had been blackened. They stood so close together that they appeared to be a single formless shape.

When they were in place, the man with the shield struck it three more times. Another figure appeared out of the darkness behind the altar. He, too, seemed nearly naked, though he wore a sort of leather skirt. His head was completely covered with a mask in the shape of a three-horned bull. It was half again the size of the man who bore it, but it did not seem heavy. Lois guessed that it was made from *papier maché*. The man carried an axe that seemed to be made from a single piece of metal, and a long, broad sword. He laid sword and axe on the altar.

He walked to the front of the altar. Two small girls walked up the central aisle between the folding chairs and approached the altar. They were both dressed in shapeless black shifts, just like the three women at the front. Each was carrying something she held tightly. The altar was high, and the girls had to stretch upward to pass the man their gifts.

The man reached down and took the offering from the first girl, then stood and flung it aloft. There was a whirr of wings, and a dove flew up into the darkness. The crowd murmured approvingly. Then he took the offering from the second girl, a large copper cup. He drank from it, then swung the cup, spraying the liquid across the altar.

Lois sat absolutely motionless in her chair. The girl offering a bird reminded her of her drawing and of the two little girls in Seville. Something about the ritual seemed familiar, but now she was filled with dread. She tried to remember what Richard had said about Druids when he was reading the book in Spain, but she couldn't remember. They bury people in bogs, she thought. They slit their throats.

The man stood motionless for a moment, then took a dagger out of his belt and held it, arms outstretched, in front of him. The dagger was large, and the hilt seemed to be made from a series of small wheels. He kissed the blade, then laid it down ritually between the sword and the axe.

Then he began to speak in a language that Lois knew was not German. It didn't sound like any language she had ever heard. It was filled with trilled vowels and slurred consonants, so that it sounded gentle and musical. At various points, he would pick up the dagger or the sword and hold it high in the air. After a few moments, Lois forgot that he was wearing a mask. The voice seemed to come from the mouth of the three-horned bull.

Then the figure dropped to his knees and began what was clearly a prayer. His voice took on a rhythmic monotone, and the crowd became even more silent. When he stopped speaking there was only the slight hum of a breeze through the trees.

Then the gong sounded three more times. The kneeling figure picked up the axe, and moved to one side of the altar. Two large men dressed as warriors in leather armour led in a man with a black hood pulled over his head and shoulders. The man was not dressed in costume. He wore a pair of jeans and running shoes, and he stumbled as they led him forward. His hands appeared to be tied behind his back.

It's Richard, Lois thought in horror. The man in the hood is Richard. She was frozen, unable to move.

The two warriors led the man in the hood to the front of the altar. They pushed him down to his knees, and made him put his head forward onto the rock. The crowd murmured in apprehension. The man in the bull-head mask stepped forward. He raised the axe high over his head.

"No," Lois screamed. She started to run towards the altar, and the entire crowd looked at her as if she were part of the ceremony. "No, don't," she called again.

The man with the axe stopped momentarily and turned towards her, the axe still held high above his head. Then there was a loud cracking noise, followed by two more cracks, and the bull-headed figure dropped silently to the ground. The mask tumbled from his shoulders and rolled down from the altar into the crowd.

The next moment there was pandemonium. Everyone in the crowd stood at once, and they all seemed to be talking at the same time. Then a voice came over a loudspeaker in French. It told everyone not to move, to stay exactly where they were, but it was completely ignored. People surged out of the area and down along the pathway, and they disappeared into the trees. In the distance, Lois heard the fading sound of a motorcycle.

Suddenly there were police officers everywhere, their guns drawn. Lois clambered onto the altar to the hooded figure, and tugged at the hood. It resisted a moment, then slipped off, and she saw Richard, his eyes glazed and the left side of his head dark with blood and matted hair. Spread-eagled on the altar beside him was the body of Mann. His naked chest was covered with blood, and there was a large hole in his neck. There was no doubt that this time he was very dead.

"Are you okay?" Robert asked, helping Richard to his feet. Lois wasn't sure whether the question was intended for Richard or for her.

"I think he's okay," she said. "But if you'd come a second later, he wouldn't have been." She indicated the body of Mann. "He was just about to murder Richard."

"Thanks," Robert answered. "Only that wasn't us. Come on. We'd better get him to a doctor." Richard moaned, but he followed

Robert, leaning heavily on him. Lois looked for the inspector and saw him at the far side of the opening. He appeared to be chatting pleasantly with several of the actors and the two small men with glasses.

"You're lucky you weren't both murdered," Robert said. "Why did you leave the cafeteria?"

"I wanted to find Richard," Lois said.

"Well you found him," Robert told her. "And messed up about a million dollars' worth of police work in the bargain."

* * *

The morning light, filtered through the blinds in the hotel breakfast-room window, was blue and grey, exactly the right light for the tablecloth, Richard decided. The bandage on the left side of his face did not cover his eye, but it prevented peripheral vision. He ran his hand along it, and it felt rough and grainy. The doctor had wanted him to stay overnight in the hospital in case he had a concussion, but Richard had refused. Lois would not go back to the studio. As a compromise they had stayed in the hotel.

The inspector broke a chunk from his baguette and coated it with strawberry jam. He and Ferguson had just arrived. Richard and Lois had already finished eating, but they had each ordered another cup of coffee.

"Where to begin," the inspector said. "That's always the question. And where shall I begin?"

"Eliot," Richard answered. " 'The Lovesong of J. Alfred Prufrock.' Begin with who killed Mann."

"That's probably the end of the story, and we don't have a good answer yet. We probably never will have."

"Alexandra," Robert said. "Almost certainly her. Everybody else is accounted for. It wasn't any of our men. And we had the ceremony under careful watch."

"Impossible," Richard said. "She would never do it. Besides, as I told you last night, I talked to her just before I went to the gathering. I left her on a motorcycle, which, by the way, she can barely drive, at the top of the hill. She said she was going away, to Switzerland, I think she said. There's no way she could have got back to the ceremony before I did. And she had no gun, I know that."

"She had ample reason," the inspector said. "Mann was very cruel to her. Especially after he returned from the grave. Some of the people in the group believe he beat her. And as you probably know, she was an impulsive young woman."

"Well, he's certainly dead now," Lois said. "I can hardly believe he wasn't dead the first time we saw him. But this time, I saw him close enough to know for sure."

"This time we have a body," the inspector agreed, "but we are not certain it is Mann. We have been unable to make a positive identification. There are no fingerprints on record. He is the man that the members of the Hallstatt group knew as David Mann, but your armed forces refuse to believe that this body is his."

"That's ridiculous," Richard told him. "He's the man whose body we saw on the altar. He matches the picture we took."

The inspector carefully lit his pipe. "Perhaps," he said. "You, of course, are the only people who saw the body, and the picture does not show a very good likeness of the man who died last night. We will not, at any rate, close that investigation for a while."

"What are you going to do about Alexandra?" Richard asked. He imagined her caught, locked in a prison. It would destroy her.

"We will ask her questions if we find her. But we will probably not find her for a while. And if she denies that she shot him, then we have no case against her."

"She'll deny it," Richard said. "Because she didn't do it."

"Perhaps not," Kessler answered. Perhaps it was the Iraqis or the Lybians or even the Israelis. It could even have been the Canadians themselves."

"Not the Canadians," Robert said. "Not our style."

"What about that grotesque ceremony?" Lois asked. "You guys were there hiding in the bush with half the police in France. Why did you let that go ahead? Richard might be dead right now if Alexandra or someone hadn't pulled the trigger at the last moment."

"It's not what you think," the inspector said. "It is not unusual. The Hallstatt group holds the same ceremony of mock sacrifice every fall. They re-enact ancient Celtic ceremonies as authentically as they can. But they do not kill anyone. I have attended the ceremony myself on several occasions with Delacroix. I doubt that Richard would have been killed in such a public way. It makes no sense. A murder in front of fifty witnesses? No, they would have been satisfied with frightening him."

"I don't think so," Richard said, rubbing the bandage along his head. "They meant business. But at least I can stop worrying about heart attacks. If that moment didn't get me, then nothing will."

"Well, the position held by Helmut is that you were an intruder, and that hauling you up on the platform was an unwise prank to teach you a lesson. A bad joke. It was Mann's idea. He doesn't know who actually grabbed you. They were strangers, friends of Mann's. He knows nothing of your captivity in the castle, and says he does not believe it happened."

"What about the tourists? What about Lois? Wasn't she an intruder? Why didn't they choose someone else?"

"You were the one skulking about in the woods."

"What about the time he and his girlfriend tried to kill us on the road outside Arras?" Lois asked.

"They have never been to Arras, they say. There are many witnesses who saw them at a wedding that very day."

"You don't believe that, do you?" Richard asked.

"What I believe doesn't matter. What a court will believe matters. And there is no evidence."

"The Canadian accountants. The arms deals," Lois said. "Surely you can get them on that?"

Robert shifted in his chair. "They were there all right. The two little guys in the glasses. Hutcheon and Fawcett. And they had a great deal of money with them. They gave the money to Mann just before the ceremony started."

"It was in a leather bag," Lois said, remembering. "They passed it to Mann."

"Yes," Robert went on. "And if you hadn't been sitting in the audience, we might have stopped them right then. But that made it too dangerous. And when we got there it was gone."

"Gone where?"

"Maybe somebody in the crowd slipped into the forest and got away with it. We couldn't stop everybody who was there. But the answer is probably simpler. Alexandra."

"He slapped her," Lois said. "Just after they got the money. I heard them as they passed me. They were arguing, and he slapped her, or else she slapped him. Then she disappeared and she didn't come back."

"Without the money, we have no case," Robert said. "They were simply tourists attending a local Druid ceremony for an evening's entertainment. We might charge them, but I doubt if there's enough evidence to convict. Now, if the two of you had stayed put, or better still, gone back to Canada when I suggested it, we might have broken up a major arms sale. Instead, we have another cryptic murder and no more evidence than we had for the first."

"We're going back to Canada all right," Richard told him. He looked to Lois. He wasn't sure she would still want to go. "But I need a story I can understand. Am I paranoid?" he appealed to the inspector. "Did none of this happen?"

"The body," the inspector said, "the first body, I mean, was probably intended for Alexandra and her uncle and mother, just to let them know they were involved in serious business. And of course Mann wanted people to think he was dead so that they would not be looking for him. Something went wrong, and you and Lois discovered the body instead. And that changed everybody's plans. Alexandra was sent to Paris as an *au pair* to get her away from Mann or whoever had killed him. Remember, they, too, thought he might be dead. It was pure chance that you were at the Louvre when Alexandra's mother had her heart attack. In the meanwhile, Mann had recruited Helmut and Lise, whose job it was to keep an eye on you. They may even have intended to get rid of you, though they don't seem to have been very good at that."

"Not yet," Robert said.

"So, now, if Alexandra is a presumed murderess who has run off with the cash, I don't imagine she's going to be safe," Richard said.

"She probably has another job as an *au pair*," the inspector said. "Soon she will come back to live with her uncle, and life will go on as usual. The uncle will be more careful of the cargo he carries. The Hallstatt group will go on doing good work. And everybody will live happily ever after."

301

"So what about our story?" Richard said. "It's as if nothing ever happened."

"The best story wins. Unless you have something else you want to say, we have to go with the best story we can get."

"No," Richard said. He stood up from the table. It was a signal that all of the others followed. "Well, thank you for everything." He shook hands with the inspector. "It's been nice knowing you."

"If you are ever back and wish to fish again," the inspector responded, "just let me know. You have my number."

"Do you mind if I talk to Lois privately for a minute?" Robert asked. Richard did not wish this to happen, but he couldn't think of a polite way of preventing it. He walked with the inspector to the door of the hotel and out into the street. Through the window, he could see that Robert was talking intensely to Lois, gesturing with his hands. The inspector was anxious to be gone, and Richard said good-bye to him again.

A few minutes later, Lois came out of the hotel. Robert was nowhere to be seen.

"What did he want?" Richard asked. "What secrets do you two have?"

"He's my buyer," Lois said. "My secret admirer."

"What?" Richard said, bewildered.

"My drawings. At the show. He was the one who bought the three drawings before the show began."

"Oh," Richard said. "I'd forgotten about that."

"It wasn't important," Lois told him. "It didn't mean anything."

*　*　*

Just as Richard and Lois walked through the skywalk that led from the hotel to the Frankfurt airport, the sun appeared in a blaze through the rolling black clouds. It was still raining heavily, big silver drops that glistened in the sunshine. Everybody they saw walked with crisp efficiency. A family of Americans, mother, father and three children, came by with a cart so loaded with suitcases that neither Lois nor Richard could believe it. They saw themselves reflected in the glaze of the skywalk windows, hovering above the ground, but not distorted.

They had breakfast in a restaurant in the airport, and were amazed at the price. Richard had to put it on his credit card. They didn't have enough deutschmarks between them to pay for it. Then they checked their baggage and picked up their boarding passes. Neither of them wanted to walk around the airport, so they went through security and found their gate. They were the first people there, although a girl behind the desk was filling out forms.

"There's going to be snow when we get back," Richard said.

Lois didn't answer for a moment. Then she said, "Well, I guess I'm not going to open a restaurant."

"Did you really want to?" Richard asked. "I'd forgotten about that."

"No. It was just an idea. I didn't know what else I would do in France."

"My book on Heidegger is not going to be written. Like ninety percent of the professors on sabbatical in Europe, I have not done what I came to do."

"You hate Heidegger. You didn't even like him when you taught him."

"I don't hate him. That's mostly a game. I just don't think I'll ever be able to understand him, because I'm not German. In the end, I think he's a mystic, like those crazy people and their Druids. The only way to live authentically," Heidegger says, "is to contemplate your own death. I've certainly had the opportunity for that in the last while."

"Well, you've got your novel. At least you got that out of your trip."

"It's not finished. It may never be finished. I may not be able to write in Canada."

"I don't know if I'll be able to draw. What will I do if it turns out that I can't draw in Canada?"

"We could go back. Some day we will go back, and I'll finish my novel and you'll draw pictures and become a famous artist."

A couple of men came into the room and took seats on the far side of the room. They were both smoking, and the blue smoke hung above them like a cloud. Richard and Lois sat silently for several minutes. A couple of times Lois took a deep breath, as if she were going to say something, but she lapsed into silence again. More people began to filter into the waiting room. Finally, she took Richard's hand so that he turned and looked at her.

"Are you in love with Alexandra?" she asked. She didn't want to look at him until after he had answered, so she turned away.

Richard didn't say anything for a long while. His breath came in catches, and Lois thought he might be crying.

"No," he answered. "I don't think so." Then as if he were surprised by his own answer he went on. "No, definitely not. Obsessed for a while, but not in love."

"But you slept with her?"

"Yes."

"She went to Trier with you?"

"Yes. Does that make a difference? Does it make things impossible?" Richard felt that, if Lois decided at that moment she was going to leave him, he would not be able to stand the pain. He felt it as a pressure on the top of his head. A voice came from a hidden speaker, giving its message in many languages. At last it told them in English that a flight was delayed. Not their flight.

"It makes a difference," Lois said, "but not an impossible difference. If you were in love, then it wouldn't be possible." She turned to look directly at Richard. He was looking at her as if he wanted to read something in her face, some message that could make him secure. We are all alone in our skins, she thought. All of us ordinary people. I can't tell him anything. And I don't know whether he is telling me the truth or not. He might still be in love. All we can do is make promises.

Richard looked so sad that Lois burst out laughing. Richard laughed too, as if her laugh had set him free. The announcement said that they could board the aircraft, and they found themselves caught in the swirl of passengers down the long entrance to the airplane. Their seats were halfway back, in the heart of the aircraft. They looked down together from the window of the plane, but Europe was hidden below a mass of clouds. Up where they flew, there was no weather at all.